THE LAST AMERICAN

NICHOLAS ROGNESS

ISBN: 978-1-7339517-0-8 (Paperback)

ISBN: 978-1-7339517-1-5 (eBook)

Library of Congress Control Number: 2020918571

Book cover illustration by Marie Weider.

Printed by Ingram Content Group in the United States of America.

First printing edition 2020.

Publius Publishing
1015 Riley St.
#1815
Folsom, CA 95630

www.thelastamerican.us

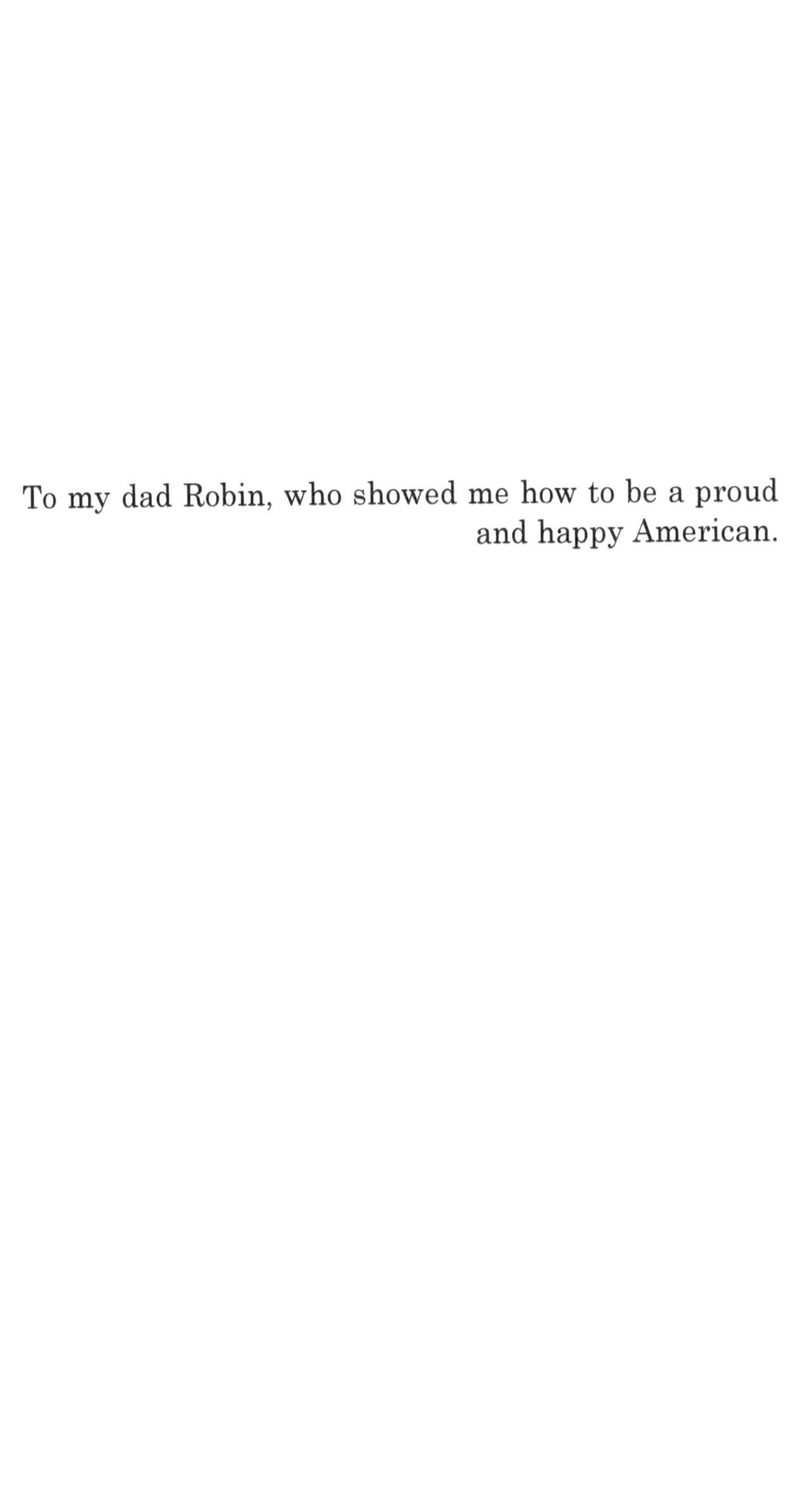

To my dad Robin, who showed me how to be a proud
and happy American.

PREFACE

Two months after graduating from my undergraduate program, I embarked on a typical right-of-passage trip for a young American—a backpacking trip across the major cities of the European continent, taking advantage of the benefits of their Eurail trains all along the way. Every three or four days, we'd fly away to a new city, delighting in the different culture, language, and history we discovered at every stop.

Early into our journey, we spent four days in Rome. On our first or second day (I can't remember exactly when at this point), we walked through the ancient ruins of the city—the Colosseum followed by the Forum. Towards the end of this experience, my friend and I crested a hill. It was hot—somewhere in the low 90s, or the low 30s for non-Americans—so we stopped at a nearby faucet, refilled our water bottles, and took a drink.

During this brief rest, I looked over the spectacle below me. The fragments of pillars reminded me of a project I had started undertaking in earnest on this extended trip. The aspiring writer in me thought aloud and shared with my friend the motivation for what became this book.

I told her that I had wondered some time ago what it would be like for some future version of the human race to look at the ruins of our American civilization many hundreds, or even thousands, of years from now.

It was experiences and thoughts like those surrounding the uncertain future of Western democracy that motivated *The Last American*. I suppose the kernel of my passion for this multi-year project began at a young age, with experiences as a lifelong Catholic and as a dedicated Scout. Later on, I can specifically place my desire for writing some kind of series addressing America's future in 2010, somewhere between age 15 and 16. I had just read George Orwell's *Animal Farm* in high school, and was dismayed at how the tenor of debate over Congress's efforts to reform health care had soured. The result was a brief stint of chapters I scribbled for a book titled *Woods of Liberty*. It was a little too on the nose for the times, with characters called Barack the black bear and Sarah the doe. But it was telling of my gnawing interest in the subgenre of political science fiction.

I never did finish that silly little book, despite my growing sense at the time that some permanent kind of dysfunction was sticking itself to the American political system. The reader would do well to research the political headlines from 2011, should you be unable to recall them readily. It was the first year the phrase "kicking the can down the road" became commonplace, as leaders in Congress suddenly decided that every single time a federal budget deadline loomed, having a political game of chicken was an acceptable way of running a government. Various factions tapped into the worse angels of our nature, willing to blow up the system if each of their fringe demands were not met. Congress asked for expert advice in the form of the Simpson-Bowles Commission to figure out how to finally deal with our national debt—then proceeded to ignore its recommendations. There was worry the federal government might default on its loans if our country couldn't get its crap together. The financial experts joined this nervous chorus, downgrading the U.S. government's credit rating. This from the country that rebuilt and transformed the global economy into its own image after World War II. At the time of writing, I still can't believe how the nation's finances have been managed so poorly.

A past version of myself also fretted, but then reassured myself that my youth was causing me to overreact. The country has seen more divided times, I thought. Then 2016 rolled around.

From that year there came the final push I needed to see the first part of this book through to its finish— almost like a calling. Some of the contents for my first chapters had floated around the internet over the past few years, but the passion was not there yet to collect my ideas together. I wanted this novel to be an autopsy of our beloved country from a future person's perspective. But I also knew that my perspective on politics was unique, that it didn't rely consistently on liberal nor conservative ideology for its basic assumptions. Before I finally found confidence in calling myself a political independent, I first registered to vote as a Democrat. Then 2016 happened and I re-registered as a Republican—mainly to resist the campus left, or the "being woke" ideology that was making appearances at most of my undergraduate political science classes.

The reader may know that the trendy figure on college campuses at the time was Bernie Sanders. Polls suggested that he garnered over 85% of the vote among Democrats aged 18-35. Among UC Davis political science students, I'm willing to bet the number must have been even higher. I grew frustrated with campus politics during my last academic quarter there. For all that California and its university system liked to pride itself on free speech and free thought, the "Bernie Bro" phenomenon seemingly encouraged students to give their guy votes not on the basis that he had actual, thoughtful solutions to the problems he'd pledged to tackle, but because he would solve all their personal problems and so what, capitalism's overrated anyway. (Please note—I don't mean to deride those voters that genuinely believed in his policies. Just those who followed him out of trendiness.) So, my disillusionment of both sides gave me the sense of purpose I needed to finally make *The Last American* possible. Now, at the time of writing, I find myself enthusiastically part of the political movement I hope will come soon to an election near you—a new movement that seeks to bring fair competition to our defunct two-party system in a spirit of democratic reform and renewal, with the country's needs raised above those of the political parties.

If you give this book a good read, I hope you'll find it offers resonant features for everyone. I ask the reader to seek this as a goal in reading *The Last American* because of a belief I have that states we have a civic duty to listen to each other's opinions in debate, however uncomfortable, while still repudiating all of our worst and malicious ideas. (Please also note as a disclaimer—my portrayal of gender identity as rigidly enforced in Bohem is not meant to assert silly things like being gay is a matter of personal choice.) After all, if you examine some of the personal relationships (and tremendous political differences) the Founding Fathers had with one another, you'll find that they managed to establish our representative democracy in such a way. Reflecting on this idea, I have gone so far as to outline a group strategy for broaching difficult topics such as those of a political nature in the accompanying Appendix A—a proposed list of principles for what I call "consensus culture."

What happens if we don't figure out how to get along with each other when it comes to the present trials our country faces? This book dares an answer as to what that dreaded scenario looks like. Think of it like what would happen in the last season of *Game of Thrones* if the Seven Kingdoms kept fighting one another instead of teaming up against the approaching Night King and his apocalyptic army of the dead.

To quote *Earth 2100*—a social problem film of the time (albeit with its own imperfect predictions): "To change the future, first you have to imagine it." Let history and the reader take note that this work is only one among many in this age that not only imagined what the future holds for our beloved country and the world, but sought to change it so that its joys may be continually passed down for generations to come.

PART I

THE REPUBLIC

PROLOGUE #1

The following is an excerpt from the nonfiction work The Decline and Fall of American Democracy, *written by Sam Usami in January 2035:*

Consider the future.

Consider all the things that people of all opinions worry about for the future: climate change, disease outbreak, government overreach, income inequality, corroding cultural values, or America losing its status as the world's military superpower. The list goes on in a certain order, depending on your preferred ideology.

These considerations were at the heart of America's game-changing presidential election nearly twenty years ago. In 2016, the situation was entirely unique: the people not only needed a leader that would address present threats, but a number of large, future ones as well—ones that had yet to have been fully realized.

America was at a crucial crossroads in 2016, the decisions made from which point in time could ensure the nation's survival or continue its trajectory toward anarchy and dissolution. The truth of this was reflected in the rhetoric of its nauseatingly polarized election season.

Yet, many Americans continued to be optimistic in the wake of the poisonous political discourse of that fateful year. After all, the country was more prosperous, tolerant, and internally stable than ever before. So many had become accustomed to an incredibly civilized, dignified form of politics. Some referred to this as "political correctness," but this definition was merely a haughtier, sanctimonious corruption of the modern concept of basic human respect.

As hyper-partisanship accelerated its arrival in the 2010s, decency and respect for the opposition further eroded. Indeed, this and other decades-long trends would ensure the culture of fear and war of ideologies continued, until they became permanent features of American politics. Social media and the unceasing news cycle helped the process by turning Americans into hypochondriacs over the smallest of social problems, while also giving a powerful new tool with which a plethora of new political movements organized, each pushing a one-sided agenda less profound and less nuanced than the last.

All this served as an immense disappointment to the growing masses of disillusioned "non-partisans." Unprecedented numbers of voting-eligible people simply refused participation in the political system, and thus the rise of the ideologues was completed. Without the votes of moderates, a group that politicians previously answered to, the two political parties' different versions of reality drifted further apart.

Now, with the decade of the 2030s well under-way, the future still seems as uncertain as it did nineteen years ago. Will the complacent people, whose democracy they are responsible for driving, take action and reverse the country's chaotic course? Will they finally start standing for a knowledgeable, yet values-based brand of politics? Or will the two intolerant versions of politics and culture on the Left and Right continue to drift until they are worlds apart, leaving those in the middle behind in the process?

Who will stand up again for the true purpose of politics, the one that rebirthed the notion of the Republic and spread its ideas across the world? Who will reawaken the pursuit of the common good?

1-1

At precisely 0600, citizen J-65216 was awoken by his alarm. He let out his usual low groan, wishing he could sleep in just a little longer and escape the relentless monotony of his carefully regimented schedule. J-65216 looked around his spartan quarters, which more often felt like a cell than his home. He lingered on the one decoration he had taped onto the dreary gray metal bulkheads in secondary school—a poster of the marbled gem, planet Earth, with the words in large font that read:

"HISTORY: Stay on the right side of it, because its losers only get to fail once."

J-65216 remembered the dream he had had that night. It was a dream unlike anything he had ever had before. Not the usual random reminisces of social embarrassment from his day, but a meaningful dream. Just thinking about it gave him a most unusual sensation, as if he felt . . .

"J-65216, get up. Your loitering time has exceeded that of the 90th percentile," blared his digital arm device, otherwise referred to as his SIM (Sensory

Individual Monitor). He saw his social credit score displayed in large block numerals on the small green monitor attached to his forearm: 660. Not great, but not horrifying.

He always hated it when anyone in Authority referred to him by his official designation. He preferred calling himself Josik, for short. So, Josik resigned himself to start his day on Bohem, the space station of millions of people that he pretended to call home.

Josik stood up and engaged in his normal regimen of stretches. He was always mildly impressed looking over the features of his young, athletic body: his trim figure and average stature, his light-brown olive complexion, his wide brown eyes, and straight, thick, short walnut-colored hair. For being twenty and in good physical shape, he should have been excited about the future. But Josik wasn't. He hated life on Bohem because of the loneliness and isolation he always felt there.

Josik proceeded to the next step of his daily routine: breakfast. Obviously, there was nothing notable about that, other than how the fruit ration had an orange hue as opposed to the neon red of yesterday. But such was the case with F days in the 10-day weekly cycle, or decod, according to the Bohemx calendar.

It was time for Josik to get to work. He took the elevator to receive his new assignment on the 12th Level.

Something immediately caught the attention of Josik as he stepped into the elevator. It was his old friend M-70995! But he knew him as Meset. He was—actually, they were, since Meset assumed no gender—somewhat shorter than Josik and quite stockier. Their complexions, however, were the same by design.

"Meset!" Josik cried. "How's it going? Do you remember me? It's been ages!"

Meset's stayed focused on the screen of the ocular projector in front of them. Their personal news feed seemed obviously more important. But this was typical anti-social behavior for a Bohemx.

Josik felt a twinge of embarrassment from this response; however, he still pressed on.

"We went to secondary school together! The one in sector Q?"

Meset sighed and gave a response, keeping their focus squarely on the virtual reality in front of them.

"Yes," they flatly stated. "I remember those days. However, I believe I have determined that my permanent assignment to the eugenics department makes our relationship incompatible."

"Eugenics department?" cried Josik, ignoring Meset's broader point. "With a permanent assignment there, that must be pretty neat! I'm sure they have big plans for you with the new population authorization. Did you hear about that news?"

Meset flashed a quick side glare to Josik, and their eyes immediately turned back to the screen.

"There's a word that the past used to describe what

you're doing right now. They called it 'small talk,' and I'm glad our society has progressed past it."

"We can't be friends, Josik, and there's a big reason why. In the years we've been apart, I realized something. You act like a person of the past, with all of its micro-aggressive, patriarchal ways. There's a reason I've progressed upwards and you haven't, Josik. I have accepted progress and refused to accept gender and other harmful social constructs."

The screen was momentarily switched off, but Meset still struggled to make proper eye contact. "I'm saying this as a concerned fellow humxn-being," they preached. "You are twenty years old and still haven't grown up and grown out of your gender. Almost everyone else your age has had their Liberation by now. At this rate, you're not going to have any friends if you keep acting like a man."

The elevator reached Meset's floor.

"Farewell, Josik," they added nonchalantly.

***

By the time Josik reached the 12th Level, he was close to tears. It made no sense. How could Meset suddenly break off their friendship so cruelly? Josik had had many trivial relationships, but Meset was one of his few meaningful friends back when Meset still identified as a young man.

In the time Josik had been lost in these thoughts, he finally arrived at his workstation to suit up for the vacuum of space. Today he was starting on building the new residential wing in preparation for the recently authorized increase of five million people.

As he donned all the necessary apparel, the memories of Meset still plagued his mind. They had been through so much together, even though that was nearly two years ago. All the lab experiments in biology, whispering behind their e-textbooks in lecture. They would even debate about which girls— they were of an age when there were those who still identified as girls—they considered most attractive in each category of hair color. Truly, he had never been close to anyone like Meset before, and he would very likely never be able to find such a friend again for the rest of his life. The Bohemx checked his SIM and his social credit score: down to 650, clearly a sign of Authority's disapproval of his handling of the preceding conversation.

At last, Josik stepped outside to start his work. The lack of gravity was not unfamiliar, considering he had been assigned to many "outside" jobs before.

It was the usual safety procedure for going out into space: close the airlock before opening the outer doors, secure the tether in case the jetpack failed. With these steps completed, Josik set out into space.

Even though the sensation of weightlessness was an old one to Josik, it still gave him some sense of euphoria; after all, his last "outside" job had been years ago. Swimming in the open air, he could see Earth below him—a reminder to Josik that all of Bohem depended on the planet for its orbit. He remembered learning about Earth's basic features sometime in primary school: an atmosphere of 78% nitrogen and 21% oxygen that once teemed with the conditions necessary for life before humanity irreversibly destroyed its balance. Still, Josik couldn't help fantasizing about a visit there every time he saw the beauty of the planet's colorful harmony of blue, green, and white elements. The thought of exploring Earth always made him feel reinvigorated, as if a feeling of childhood innocence had come back to him.

"J-65216!" bellowed the large foremxn below. They were graying in the black hair around their temples but still seemed to possess a youthful vigor. "Get down here at once! Or else I'll take 20 points off your credit score!"

Josik readily obeyed, without a word, almost how a child might obey a parent when he or she or they had been harshly scolded for some sort of innocent negligence, like forgetting to water the plants for a few days. Even though Josik had not meant to get distracted, he still felt incredibly embarrassed for doing so and receiving the public humiliation from the foremxn.

"It's a pretty simple process," said the foremxn to the baker's dozen of workers a small distance from them on the platform extending from Bohem. "You will lay these steel beams out from the hull," pointing to a floating platform tethered to the station on their right. "Then you will set the floor in place," pointing to some metal sheeting to his right. "Also use that for the first layer of walls. This bot," they added, pointing to the floating mechanical organism about half-a-meter tall, "has all the instructions you need. Should there be any deviancies, especially horseplay . . ."

The foremxn gave a quick glance over to Josik, and he felt a hot flash of embarrassment again.

"I will be informed, and I will come out and find the offender. And they will be punished!"

The foremxn left and the thirteen people set out on their work.

***

For Josik and everyone else, the hardest part of construction jobs (and pretty much all other jobs on Bohem) was not the actual grueling physical labor. To people in such physical condition as the foremxn (at least without their age-reduction enhancements), this might have been the case.

No, to Josik, the hardest part of the job was the sense of repetition. In the case of this job, you were supposed to *move, place, and weld* the beams. Then you would *move, place, and weld* the metal sheet. For the sheeting, the process would once again repeat itself. And so this three-part macro-cycle ran on for hours, only to be interrupted by an impeccably scheduled lunch break.

For this, Josik and the others stepped into the airlock as the pneumatic ports delivered their individual rations: 250 milliliters of vegetable paste, a 75 gram protein cube (today's flavor: turkey), five compacted flat noodle product (for carbohydrates), and 200 milliliters of chocolate pudding (sweetened with aspartame) for dessert.

With a substantial portion of their allotted daily intake of nutrients having been met, the thirteen set out to their work again after twenty-eight minutes, staying true to their schedule. And so, the cycle of cycles continued again ceaselessly, without need for stoppage due to thirst, a full bladder, or exhaustion. Everything needed for the workers was provided in their suits. They had everything they needed to be perfectly productive.

And yet, mistakes were still made. One of the welders, a red-haired individual who appeared to still be at least ten or fifteen years from middle age, apparently welded at least two or three of the flooring units at incorrect distances exceeding that of two standard deviations of the mean, as the bot had blared out the times such events had occurred.

Very likely, Josik thought, their attempt at making small talk was to blame. He normally would have participated, had it not been for Meset's rebuke earlier that day.

Unsurprisingly, when the red-headed person's third excessive deviancy occurred, the foremxn was alerted. After pulling them into the airlock, the two disappeared.

Josik and the remaining eleven stayed focused on their work, despite the fact that their minds were dwelling on what happened to the redhead all along. After several minutes, they finally emerged, trudging along with one hand covered on their crotch, another outstretched for balance.

Nobody dared say a word to the person except for Josik.

"Are you ok?" he asked with honest concern.

Hunched over with their hand still held on parts below, their grimaced facial expression only allowed them to utter a few words.

"No more deviancies." They showed their SIM, revealing a precipitous drop in social credit to 500. Josik remembered that a score below 550 meant indefinite confinement to quarters outside of assigned work.

No more deviancies. That's how the thirteen worked for the rest of the day.

***

The next day came and went; nothing notable at all changed in Josik's life (after all, the Authority on Bohem kept everyone on the same decodly meal plan). Pretty soon, the nearly unconscious repetition of routine over these next twenty-four hours rolled into several days of further repetition. Josik had already surrendered to this state of affairs since before he was even old enough to reason. At least his credit score remained unchanged. He could only hope that his next assignment would come by next month; yet, future work assignments from Authority were hardly ever predictable.

Finally, one day, something different happened.

"J-65216!" cried the foremxn. Josik obediently

approached him as usual, his magnetic boots clomping along the completed portions of metal corridor.

"I have a different task for you at the moment. It shouldn't take more than a few minutes, so I'm sending you alone." Josik heard and comprehended these words; however, he found the foremxn's unusually less-wrinkled face slightly distracting.

"One of the coolant pipes towards the south pole is leaking. Go out there and fix it. The bot has all the tools you need." Josik grabbed from the bot a small metal box with two latches that kept it closed. He started walking on the rounded portion of the Bohem dome towards the leak below him. Or was it above him, since he was walking upright towards it?

"Wait!" the foremxn growled. "You need to come off of your tether."

Even though he wasn't part of Authority, Josik had a surprising knowledge about Bohemish laws and enforcement, simply out of his interests from school. And he knew that Authoritarian policy required all "outside" workers to have two approved methods by which they remained attached to the station.

"Excuse me, sir," Josik responded. "But that would violate the Safety and Welfare Department's policy for workers in space found in Article IV, Section 2 of the Declaration of Workers' Rights."

The foremxn stared menacingly at Josik and let a moment of silence pass. The other dozen workers stopped their work to watch the spectacle.

Then, in an instant, the foremxn grabbed Josik's neck with a suffocating grip. They leaned in close to Josik's ear and whispered.

"You understand something, you teenaged, barely post-pubescent, male-gendered piece of shit. I don't care about whatever damn rules you happen to know. What I say is the law, because I am the law. Now," they adjusted their grip a little, "I'm going to let you go and you are going to do your job because I say so, got it?"

Josik's purpling face meekly nodded. The foremxn threw Josik down to the floor of the corridor and turned to address the dozen onlookers.

"Remember this, you dumbasses: I am in charge and you do everything I say without question! There is no Authority but me! I am Authority!" They briefly paused to glance back at Josik.

"What other authority is there?" they yelled, asking Bohem's most contrived question.

Even Josik responded with the other workers as clearly and in unison as he could: "There is no Authority but Authority and Power is its profit!"

"Now back to work!" they added with an air of conclusiveness.

1-2

Loneliness. Being alone. This was a feeling with whom Josik—along with most people on Bohem—was intimately acquainted. He had to wonder. Did anyone else feel bothered by this?

Did anyone here feel anything genuine? His thoughts were leading down his usual, useless chains of logic. Sure, people in Authority like the foremxn took no scruples to exhibit anger and even sheer rage. But did anyone like him—a lowly, expendable, transitional laboring youth—experience true emotion? Sure, everyone on Bohem experienced crying, induced by the official propaganda films, but did anyone know what it was like to hold back tears from the real fears he would relive in his dreams? Did they ever think back on all their friends that had vanished overnight throughout the years? The fear that many of them would one day die without any meaningful difference in this place, their social credit zeroed out forever? Josik took a deep breath and finally checked the adjustment the foremxn had made before sending him off: a score of 610. Worse, but still not horrifying. He'd have to conform much harder if he ever hoped to reach an elite score of 750 out of 800 and earn a round-trip shuttle to a destination of his choice.

He could think back to his first quadod—four decods, according to the calendar—of secondary school, just a few years before most of Josik's peers had their Liberation, when they all renounced their gender and sexual identity. In that year, Josik made another (though comparatively short-lived) friendship, aside from the one he started with Meset.

His name was Biwun. His skin, through some accident of the geneticists, had an extremely dark tone. This made him stand out from the rest of his peers, who were engineered to consist of a mixture of all the basic racial categories from the past human race. The only physical differences tolerated between individual Bohemx were hair color, height, and body type—with a few exceptions such as Biwun. Besides his darker complexion, Biwun was indistinguishable from everyone else in terms of physical and mental competency. Yet he was avoided by everyone in the classroom—everyone except for Josik, who seemed to be able to look past Biwun's appearance and appreciate him for his diverse, out-of-the-box ideas. When they would talk in the corridors after class, Biwun posed questions that were never asked: What were humans really like in the days before Authority existed? Had humanity's existence aboard space stations become its inevitable destiny, as the Authoritarian teachers so vigorously asserted in the classroom?

One day, he disappeared. No one in Josik's class (even Meset) talked about it, since vanishing people were a regular occurrence. Josik heard a rumor that he was exiled—like every other prisoner—to Earth, doomed to perish in its toxic atmosphere.

Josik glanced back at Earth for the umpteenth time. He focused on the white spirals spread throughout its globe. Could it really be the noxious cesspool he had learned to imagine? Perhaps if he ever earned that shuttle ride he'd choose Earth as the destination just to see if the claims were true.

At last, Josik had arrived at Bohem's south pole (or so his navigational unit claimed). Regardless, the stream of whitish coolant, spraying less than fifty feet away, presented his task at hand.

The last step in this task would normally take less than fifteen minutes to complete, given Josik's ability level. But this was not a normal day for Josik. He was unusually pensive. And like most people in moments of thought, his attention was inordinately drawn to the elusive sphere before him that brought him a strange sense of peace.

How odd, he thought, *that a planet can contrast in its colors so widely. What a strange place it must be where the blue and greenish-brown meet.*

Blue. Greenish brown. They were land and sea, as he remembered from Bohem's educational system. A moment of déjà vu made Josik feel as if he had been to their point of intersection, for which he did not know its name. But how was this possible?

That was when he finally remembered something from his dream last night. He was walking with a blue sky above, warm, yellowish particles beneath him, and the waves of the sea on his left. At one point, he made a 90-degree turn to his right. Less than twenty feet in front of him was a modest blue beach-house.

But Josik was interrupted from operating in this recall mode. He was sharply jerked by the space station beneath him, sending his face plummeting to the metal exterior and nearly twisting his right femur out of its socket.

The semi-decodly pole reversal was taking place. While Bohem's earthlike levels of gravity would be maintained as usual, Josik would be torn in half at some point along his legs.

But before that could happen, Josik disengaged his magnetic boots and set himself at the mercy of space.

He would have thirty minutes to live.

1-3

Within fifteen minutes, Josik had become slightly delusional. His suit was running minimal oxygen levels in an effort to extend his length of survival, but Josik realized that this measure would make little difference.

His mind became lost in pondering the stars before him. *How wondrous*, he thought. Until now, he had never considered how truly phenomenal the very existence of the universe was. He knew the presence of the stars had a rational explanation, the accumulation of various gaseous compounds over millions and billions of years.

This knowledge answered *how*. It still did not answer *why*.

Was there any meaning to it? Josik wondered. Was his speculation about existence purely the result of an extremely coincidental error? Did anyone else question this way?

His socialized Bohemx instincts quickly snapped him back to more concrete thoughts. His being would cease to exist, and he simply had to live with it. He shouldn't bother with such fantasies about Earth, because Authority would certainly find some way to make his experience miserable were he to be sent, even if their storytelling about its horrors weren't true. But this attempt at rational thinking offered no comfort in confronting humanity's most basic fear.

So, Josik simply despaired. He was alone in the universe—physically, mentally, and emotionally. In this sense, he was an alien amongst his own kind.

And there were ten minutes left. Ten minutes left, and Josik had no solace. He would die an outcast.

Then he felt a sensation that he had never experienced before in his young life. He was familiar with the lump in his throat and the shakiness in his limbs, certainly. He was familiar with his own emotional experiences, even up to the moistening of his eyes. This time, this episode of misery was different. For the first time, he would not stifle the sound of true tears.

He thought of the lonely, cold, metal, standardized world into which he had been born. The hardware that had been attached to him ever since he could remember. The thoughts he had kept tucked away in the deepest corners of his mind. The lectures and mantras that ignored the world that existed outside of Bohem. The games and pornography he utilized in his quarters every time he realized his life was meaningless.

He wondered why his SIM hadn't stopped his cascade of thoughts. Normally, it was programmed to neutralize feelings of despair with an effective dosage of dopamine.

He didn't care that he was out of Authority's control. For once—in his final moments—he was in control of himself.

He turned his tear-stained face toward Earth for what would be the last time. He tried to think of the word that would describe the joyous place of his dreams. But in Bohem, he never learned of any such word. Finally, the darkness seemed to find it for him in his moment of need.

Paradise.

Josik drifted into unconsciousness. Beneath him once more was the warm yellow sand; in front of him was the beach-house. He simply stood there, letting his toes wiggle into the soft ground. All he could do was simply observe the house, which was an unusual piece of old architecture. He got no joy or wonder from seeing it. He simply observed, kept waiting for something to happen. Nobody answered his call. It was his move, and he needed to take the first step.

But he never got the chance. It seemed that he had only remained in this state for a moment. He awoke, with the shivering and tears having departed him. He was lying on a plain cot in a brightly lighted, gray-tiled prison cell. Josik had been returned to Bohem in the futuristic equivalent of chains.

***

A few hours later, a blonde-haired person in their

early thirties walked into the prison corridor. Josik had assumed them to be a man, but he didn't want to risk questioning their denial of gender identity. Their syntho-leather uniform suggested that they were a ship captain, while their clacking shoes attested to their status in the Authoritarian upper-crust.

The guard closed the door behind them as they approached Josik's cell. Josik shot up into an upright sitting position on his cot, his wide brown eyes raised to his visitor.

"How are you feeling?" asked the captain.

"Just fine, Captain," responded Josik, with his usual air of unswerving politeness.

The captain turned to the guard. "Leave us for a moment, please."

The guard left. Apparently, trust was a precious commodity only Authoritarians could afford to exchange among themselves.

The captain stepped into Josik's cell, the prisoner blankly observing their every move. They keyed in a command on their SIM, sat beside Josik, and locked their gaze on him.

"How do you really feel?" the captain inquired.

"Sir?" This kind of question between an Authoritarian and a commoner was unprecedented.

"You can be honest with me, Josik. There is no one else here to eavesdrop, no cameras to monitor us."

Josik continued his uneasy gaze toward the captain.

"Do you trust me, Josik?"

Josik could see that the captain's expressions resembled something like genuine concern. But he wasn't entirely certain.

"I don't know," he said, directing his attention to the wall in front of him.

The captain grabbed his arm. "Josik, it's okay to have feelings. *True* feelings. I understand."

The captain even removed their hat, revealing a neat haircut Josik knew to mean that the person before him was one of the few grown adults on Bohem who identified as male-gendered.

The gestures were too much for Josik to comprehend. He locked eyes with the captain yet again for an instant, only to bury his moistening face in his hands.

Josik was not just crying, but sobbing. The captain gently patted Josik between the shoulder blades.

Minutes later, Josik raised his puffy eyes to the captain's concerned expression.

"I trust you."

The captain moved his hand to Josik's shoulder.

"That's good. Now how do you really feel?"

It took a moment for Josik to find the right words to describe how he had felt almost his whole life.

"Confused. Lost. Miserable. Like I don't belong anywhere."

The captain lowered his voice to just above a whisper.

"How can I help?"

26

1-4

Chris, the name with whom the captain introduced himself, explained the series of events that occurred between Josik's near-death and subsequent rescue and arrest. Chris estimated that Josik had been unconscious for about five minutes before being retrieved by the captain's star cruiser. Within thirty seconds of being brought aboard, the citizen was linked to oxygen and regained life. Unfortunately, due to heightened security measures at the present time, illegal abandonment charges had to be pressed against anyone who left the boundaries of Bohem unauthorized, no matter what the circumstances. Thus, Josik's case was no exception.

"Yet," furthered Chris, "out of the mercy and kindness of Authority, you cannot be legally punished without formally appearing before Judgment. You have a chance to defend yourself. And I am here to vouch for your innocence. But before we do this, you have to agree to appear to a hearing."

At this, he pulled a data pad from out of his jacket pocket.

Despite the trust Josik had in Chris, he still had some hesitation in affixing his thumbprint to the consent form. But what other defense against a life-condemning move to Earth did he have? Chris returned Josik's decision with an approving, uplifting grin. He grasped both of the citizen's hands.

"You're going to be all right, Josik. I guarantee it."

***

Two days later, Josik faced Judgment—the judicial arm of Authority. Like most other rooms in Bohem, the hearing room was circular and lined with walls of shining silver-colored metal, with the rivets from its comparatively ancient construction quite obvious. The floor was made of dark, dull steel. Unique to the hearing room was its incredible size, with an enormous black capital "A" on the wall. Seated in front of this were the Judgment officials, who spoke with a commanding echo while they were in session. Josik, like all other suspects before him, was seated in a small round chair located in the center of the room. Behind him, lined halfway around the circumference of the room, were curious observers. Chris, his apparent defender, stood to his left. The three Judgment officials sat in massive, impeccably shiny aluminum towers above both the captain and citizen. The one in the center raised their right hand in a call to order.

"Citizen J-65216-552-494," they bellowed, reading off of the screen located in front of him on his stand. "You have been summoned for Judgment in the name of the collective justice that Authority provides. As such, you face charges of illegal abandonment of

Bohem in one of its most desperate times of need. How does the defender respond?"

"Guilty as charged, your Excellency," said Chris, unflinching. Josik, horrified, turned to get his attention but to no avail. He was going to become a criminal in the eyes of his government, the official damnation from the rest of Bohemx society. Accepting a charge of this nature guaranteed his exile to Earth, ensuring that he could never walk the corridors of Bohem as a citizen ever again. Life as a Bohemx citizen was by no means pleasant, but it at least guaranteed a long life well into one's eighties or nineties. Perhaps what angered Josik most of all was Chris's success at emotional manipulation and coaxing of trust. Still, it was Josik who felt the fool for having expected true justice from the Authoritarian judicial system to begin with.

So, he was handled, while dripping with tears, back to his cell. Days passed. The gravitational field must have reversed its polarity at least seven—no, maybe eight—times as he did nothing but pace aimlessly in circles, yank neurotically at his growing mane and beard, and press his face against the windowpane in what passed for entertainment. As a typical Bohemx, Josik had little patience to silently wait for long periods of time. Approximately twelve hours in, he gave up on physical activity and instead resorted to sleeping for most hours of the day.

He was dispensed his prison rations twice a day. Thus, when he finally heard his cell door unlock with a sharp metallic thud, Josik shot upright, lowly whispering his estimate of 3.5 decods having passed.

At the doorway was Chris, accompanied with a pair of Authoritarian bodyguards. He rushed over to Josik and gave a warm embrace. The prisoner was in far too dazed a state to return the affection—as it was, his fury over the glaring injustice done to him was returning.

Chris caught onto this reaction after having broken off the softening attempt and gazed into Josik's intensely furrowed, bloodshot expression. In an instant, his mannerisms snapped into line with his Authoritarian companions. Why, Josik could have even sworn that Chris had shifted to addressing him with his nose slightly upturned.

"The pleasantries are over, Josik. Right now, you are thinking what all those who have become before you in your case have thought—that you've been disserved at our hands, that I've personally betrayed you. The reality is that there was little I could have done to help you. Yes, fabricated evidence and false testimony was given against you. Although it may seem hard for you to believe, your conviction is a service to our humxn race. You may recall, for instance, how your friend Biwun's sendoff along with a number of other convicts attracted a public rally."

Josik's facials contorted that much more. He of course was aware that no personal information, including friendships, was kept private to the individual. And yet, Josik felt Chris's use of knowledge of Biwun's true status deepened the emotional wound caused by a shattered sense of trust. Still, Chris continued, unyielding. But now, he returned to using direct eye contact.

"This should come as very little surprise to you, Josik. Humxnity has always needed an enemy, as much as we only discuss how peaceful and utopian our society was, is, and always shall be in our schools. The specter of the prisoner exile gives the people another way to break the monotony of work, education, pornography, gaming, and sleeping by letting them release their primeval rage, as evolution intended. Oddly enough, anger is one of the few emotions the SIM has few chemicals to regulate very well."

Josik's face remained frozen.

"You should consider yourself lucky for Authority's progressive spirit, Josik. In the past, we'd simply shoot the body into the vacuum of space. At one point, we even changed it so that the oxygen was slowly let out. We eventually reworked the whole thing, since it became a logistical problem once the population became too large to maintain a proper execution schedule."

Josik put up no last defense against this. His social credit score evaporated, ran down to zero. He was escorted to the prison exile shuttle launch bay the next day at 1000, where his name would be made known among his fellow citizens for the first and last time.

1-5

That next morning, Josik was presented before a jeering crowd of his fellow citizens. It wasn't his first time playing a part in the spectacle that was made of prisoner ejection. After all, it was hard to resist one of the few opportunities Authority allowed for almost purely unstructured entertainment. All insults and thrown objects (except those of the exclusively lethal kind) were fair game. In fact, Josik often saved up cubes of his vegetable paste to throw at passing convicts. How sorry he felt for those prisoners he dehumanized, now that he was in their shoes.

Of course, no one fully paid attention to the event, even if they had a few synthetic eggs or their own shoes to lob. Everyone's ocular screens allowed for an enhanced version of reality, if not a place to post pictures and recordings of the event for their friends to see. Being splattered with artificial comestibles was certainly demoralizing, but the insults more or less washed over Josik. The words "racist," "homophobe," and "misogynist" were so commonplace in Bohemish vocabulary that its power of negative connotation had been lost on Josik for years.

But the rest of Bohem, from what Josik could tell, did not think as he did. If the people were allowed, they would find a way to use one of these condemning words—from the Man-Male List, as it was called—in nearly every sentence. Fortunately, Authority kept the use of these tightly controlled, and only allowed items of the Man-Male List to be spoken or written in video, movies, by teachers, and in all other forms of authorized propaganda. But here in this auditorium, everything, including the Man-Male List, was fair game as Josik soberly realized.

Finally, a short bald individual wearing a black Authoritarian jumpsuit and tie gathered the attention of the crowd from a tall, gray podium located in the center of the space in front of the semicircle of seated spectators. Josik was directed to walk through the space between the audience and podium to the considerably shorter podium next to the speaker.

"Genderqueers and gentlefolx," they began. "Authority is proud to present a special case of prisoner today. J-65216-552-494, aged twenty, has admitted to treason against the state in attempting to escape Bohem."

The crowd interrupted with chants of "traitor." That charge was quite a rarity, Josik recalled.

The announcer waited for the uproar to die down. "Moreover, *his* choice to stubbornly maintain *his* identity as male-gendered is further proof of malicious and micro-aggressive intent. Therefore, it is my privilege to declare *him* a macro-aggressor to the people of Bohem!"

The crowd thundered even louder in a combination of cheers and boos.

"But before we watch him be sent to his eventual, slow, rightful death—let us sing The Intersectionale together," the announcer invoked.

It was then that everyone, in unison, repeated Bohem's official anthem as taught at its schools, its melody identical to its centuries-old predecessor—"The Internationale":

"Rise up, you victims of oppression!

Rise up, your vict'ry is at hand!

Now ends patriarchal aggression

We have stomped it out from the land!

Away with the old superstitions

Good folx, get woke, get woke!

Reject the Old Society's traditions

And sing these words that once were spoke:

So comrades, come rally, 'gainst the white man we deplore!

Let all constructs that divide us be made to exist no more!

Yes comrades, let's rally, 'gainst the enemy that we face

The Intersectionale unites the humxn race!"

Again, the crowd erupted into cheers. It continued all throughout Josik's loading into one of the prisoner pods. In the heat of moment, he finally questioned his gnawing curiosity about Earth. He certainly didn't look forward to seeing Earth in the cesspool state that he remembered his schooling had described so vividly. With all of the remaining pollution of the inherently exploitative capitalist system, they claimed, no one could expect to live past thirty-five.

An Authoritarian guard on hand strapped Josik in. Captain Chris, perfectly emotionless, was beside them with a large hypodermic spray-needle filled with a vial of fluorescent, bluish fluid. The captain injected Josik in his forearm, just above his SIM. The device deactivated; the screen turned completely black.

With the jeers of the crowd now turned to harmless muffle, his pod was ejected and hurtled towards the marbled planet below.

1-6

The trip was almost instantaneous. So much so that Josik had no time to appreciate his view of the stars, nor the mountains, ocean, and the clouds below him.

It made little difference in the end to Josik. He stepped out of his silver pod only to realize that he had been forced to trade one version of hell for another. For one, his lungs tightened within seconds, choked by the thick dark yellowish haze that surrounded him. He was barely able to see his hand in front of himself, let alone make out north from south.

Still, he had hoped there was some way out. *Surely,* he thought, *they wouldn't let me die this quickly.* Led by his arms in a feeble swimming motion, he made it out with just enough oxygen left in his brain to keep standing.

Evidently, his pod was slightly off-target—he had crashed in the once-wooded hills high above the settlement to which he had been banished. As it turned out, he ended up in the middle of the wake of a tall smokestack's toxic fumes. Despite being outside of town, he was surrounded by tall concrete walls on all sides which eventually lead to the main settlement.

As usual, Authority had figured out how to give him a choice by giving him no other choice—he went down to join the people down below, all too naively embracing his exile.

The town, when he stepped through it within a few minutes, could be described as dingy at best. All of the people wore roughly patched overalls, many without adequate shirts underneath to provide a barrier between the crude denim and bare skin. All were missing at least one or two teeth, and not one person could be found with shoes. The entire town rested on a giant patch of asphalt, now almost completely black from absorbing centuries worth of pollution. The buildings consisted of neat rows of shacks, an ugly combination of canvas, tree parts, and old pieces of lumber.

Every shack, however, was ornamented with the town's symbol of patriotic pride—a simple orange and gold-starred flag. He continued walking down what seemed to be the town's main street towards its town square. The square itself was an appalling contrast to the rest of the town's slums, as it was lined with flashy stores and restaurants with glass windows in the front and all matter of overdone electric lighting, its ground paved with cobblestones.

But the open space drew the most attention towards the town's lone monument, a single pile of stacked marble blocks less than twenty feet tall. It featured a strange orange clump of fur in a glass display case on its top. It was flanked by an even taller pole, with the orange town flag wavering at its top.

His attention was also drawn to the imposing black cube house to the west end of the square, behind the strange neon-orange fur monument, whose façade was gilded with golden steps and columns supporting a balcony. The house's exterior consisted of giant, black, tinted marbled windows, which roughly gave this residence the appearance of a giant, darkly tinted Rubik's cube.

From the steps, he spotted an older man wearing a tattered top hat and tie, flanked with two taller, younger men carrying shotguns and wearing straw hats. They still wore the overalls underneath, however. They approached Josik within minutes as he simply pondered their strange attire. He quickly realized that he had little basis to critique, however—the gray Authoritarian form-fitting elastic jumpsuit he was wearing wasn't much more of a fashionable choice.

The man in the top hat gazed up and down at Josik. "Wonderful," he finally sighed. "Welcome to our town. You would seem to be in the wrong place, though. The Reg office is back towards the factory plant."

Josik didn't respond but blankly stared back.

He gave a wheezy chuckle. "This prissy Bohemian still doesn't get it, does he?"

"We're actually referred to as the Bohemx," corrected Josik.

The comment fell on deaf ears. Instead, the man

aimlessly took out the pistol from his pocket to check its bullets.

"You've been banished here, son. But you're in luck, because as this town's maga, we've built an amazing town that you'll be proud to live in. You'll start working here and you'll love it, and it'll be a beautiful thing, I guarantee it."

Then, as if saluting, this maga, whom Josik assumed to be the town's ruler, stretched out his right arm in a thumbs-up along with a ridiculously approving facial expression. But Josik didn't know the proper response and stood dumbly still.

The Maga turned immediately into a full red-faced bout of rage, ordering his guards to pounce on the innocent new arrival. The guards moved swiftly, smashing Josik's cheekbone against the concrete, keeping their feet on his back and head. Josik peered up once he finally caught a breath, could see the Maga standing over him.

"You have a lot to learn, pussy. And rule number one in my town of Appatown—law and order always come first. Our government's not a joke, like yours is."

The Maga ordered Josik be dragged down to the Reg office, where he was given his set of overalls and directed to consult the desk for job openings, all while trying to ignore the swelling pain in his jaw.

"What kinda work you interested in?" asked the women behind the desk, whose hair seemed to have not been brushed in years.

"I can do anything with a college degree," Josik said hopefully.

"Aw, right. There's a lot of those that come from that tin station of yers. Haven't met one that's lasted more than a year."

Josik digressed for a moment. "I'm surprised you all speak Bohemish here," he observed.

The unkempt women stood up from her chair in outrage.

"Yer mistaken! What the hell be 'Bohemish'? We speak Wapese, passed down by generations of our big and great Wap ancestors."

Josik slowly inched out of the office, meekly and profusely offering apologies along the way.

When he came back minutes later, he settled on a job as a lumberjack. Workers in this industry were in high demand, since the wood he and his coworkers collected was burned, alongside any other fuel the town factory could get its hands on. These other fuels unfortunately no longer included coal, as the town's mines for it had been exhausted for several decades.

The first week turned out to be physically grueling but invigorating more than anything else. Despite the twelve-hour days he'd spend chopping with his axe, the fresh air allowed him to regain his strength quickly.

Even with his meager earnings, he was quickly able to buy enough pieces of refuse to make his own tiny shack. And while he wasn't able to afford enough food for three square meals, he at least was able to buy enough food to not go to bed hungry.

Perhaps, he reasoned, this town was not quite the hell he had made it out to be. Perhaps the town was a second chance for him after all.

Another few weeks passed. Fall turned into early winter, and that brought the first frost and snow flurries. In the wake of the colder temperatures, the factory was in need of more fuel. Josik's boss and his foreman started keeping him and his workers even longer past sundown, bringing the average workday to well over sixteen hours.

Josik's coworkers had their suspicions of where the large demand of wood was really coming from. The average poor resident of Appatown had no way of burning firewood, since doing so was illegal in the streets and hardly anyone could afford a chimney. They could pretty easily guess that the government officials and company elite—who were often one in the same anyway—were burning it for their own personal comfort.

One morning, as New Years' Day approached, a festival the people of Appatown celebrated, the company gathered all the lumberjacks with an urgent bit of news. In order to keep the factory and the town's economy alive, they would have to leave their measly huts and be kept under the close eye of the company at all hours of the day. They would all have to travel deep into the forest and sleep overnight in tents pitched in the snow when they weren't chopping, which was now becoming fewer than six hours a day.

Josik had overheard from a coworker that the company was struggling to find new trees to chop because those closer to town had been rapidly decimated in the name of Appatown's economy. But what difference did this plausible rumor make? The workers would never complain, much less rebel against their town, because even speaking out against the practices of any town leader was considered unpatriotic. Appatown believed the right things, did the right things, and the Maga did an amazing job doing it on the town's behalf. The Maga and the magas before him knew how to do a great job as they had done since its beginning over 800 years ago. The current maga would often put it best: "Every maga has done an even greater job at making Appatown even greater again, and I have made it even greater."

But all of Appatown's greatness could not save the lumberjacks forced to wander in the wilderness. Those that were separated from their work group succumbed to frostbite, with the company even forcing some of them to keep working even after having a hand or foot amputated. Those who survived the frostbite often finally fell victim to hypothermia, with more in the group dying in the middle of the night. Still, more lives were taken by those who tried to escape this traveling labor camp by felling trees on themselves, affording them a quick, yet gruesome death.

Finally, with less than a third of the original group left, the company brought the lumberjacks back to town. Rumor had it that all of the trees of the surrounding area had been consumed, the supply line of wood slowing down to a trickle as the company struggled to transport product from places outside of the town's surrounding valley.

Within a week, the factory had to shut down. Combined with the large layoffs of the lumber company, more than half the town was now without work and without a way to survive. Josik turned to begging near the few lavish buildings near the town square, often pestering the patrons of the stores where large-chested women were on display. Everyone else turned to looting and clashes with the police force. In fact, after a few days, Josik witnessed such disorder becoming commonplace, and it started to become a distraction to his alms collection. When the police fortified a barricade around the Maga's house, after the fifth day of rocks and sharpened stick spears pelting the exterior, Josik realized—he was witnessing a society on the verge of collapse.

That night, it seemed a truce had been struck with the rioters. The police had apparently found and arrested a group of saboteurs (everyone in Appatown referred to them as "sabotagers," as they preferred the more Wapese version of the word), whose black skin served as a definitive proof of guilt. The blacks, they explained, were historically a problem. And it had become their logic that it was far better to arrest any blacks—or any unusually colored people, for that matter—found near their town as a precaution so as to nip any chance for them to commit crime in the bud. It just so happened in this case that these blacks were found to have intentionally started their own shadow lumber operation in the area, with the full knowledge that they were causing the town to descend into chaos.

The four they convicted were hung publicly in the town square that night, in front of a backdrop of a burning wooden cross. The whole town turned out to become frenzied with the spectacle, but Josik stood towards the back of the congregation. His every instinct was simply unbelieving that these people were treated as the enemies of mankind.

He knew for certain that he didn't belong in this place. It was only a matter of time before he would be purged for his mixed appearance. Josik had to escape, and soon.

1-7

The next few days were spent scraping together whatever Josik could beg, borrow, or steal with the help of the measly alms he had saved up. Within forty-eight hours, he had just enough food for him to stretch out across several days of foot travel. It was certain that he would leave town before dawn. There would be hard times ahead, to be sure, but he could hardly contain his excitement. For once, he would have the opportunity to choose his own destiny, one that didn't guarantee death or oppression. The land outside of Appatown was an incredible wilderness, with possibilities at every turn. And the blacks brought before the town square made Josik start to wonder—were there people on this planet outside of the town after all? Was there a place for him in this universe that wouldn't force him between one or the other lesser two evil kinds of societies?

The optimism tamped down Josik's anticipation, and he fell asleep just after sunset. That was when he saw the blue house again in the distance, several hundred yards away. He walked forward, unsteadily, struggling to balance on the sandy terrain beneath.

He could wait no longer, so he ran, full-speed, ready to head deeper into this rabbit hole of a vision. But the sand got the better of him and he tripped on his own foot, landed face-first, taking in a mouthful of grit. He looked up at the beach-house, coughed up the sand, and tried to take in the view as much as time would allow.

This unfortunately wasn't much. He heard banging, but he was still far away from the door. The knocking couldn't have come from him.

He woke up back in his bed of stacked pieces of cardboard, his shack illuminated by light. There was a full moon out, but that alone didn't explain the situation. A throng of the townspeople had torn away the front of his shanty. Still gripped by sleep, Josik stood no chance against the crowd. They pulled him out of his bed, dragging him away to the town square. Few missed the opportunity to kick him in the face, torso, genitals, or other sensitive body parts, leaving a widening streak of blood behind him in the process.

Once he was taken to the town square, one of the straw-hatted guardsmen took over. He roughly strapped him to a metal chair facing the Maga's house. Josik was being charged for a crime he didn't commit, just like the blacks a few days before. And he was just one in a line of half a dozen other convicts. He identified two as other Bohemx, judging from their mixed skin tone. The others consisted of more blacks.

Now Josik waited, his adrenaline fully charged, feeling drowned amidst a crowd shouting "kill." Then the Maga waved both his hands deftly, motioning for the crowd to fall silent.

"Well, I gotta tell you folks. This is some pretty disgusting stuff right here. Absolutely horrible, absolutely disgusting, just awful. Those Bohemians—or as they call themselves, the Bohemx . . . by the way, what the hell is a Bohemx?" The crowd booed in response.

He repeated himself emphatically for dramatic effect. "What the *hell* is a Bohemx?" He was met with laughter, the crowd catching onto his peculiar sense of humor.

"Well, these Bohemx thought they'd trick us, they'd thought they got us by dumping their prisoners on us." The crowd booed again. The Maga continued.

"You know this outside world, they all send us prisoners, sabotagers, traitors. And some, I assume to be good people. But not anymore. We do not allow people to walk around the streets of this town illegally, and we will enforce law and order." There was cheering again.

Then the Maga removed his top hat, revealing a thin bit of wiry hair underneath whose color was not unlike the scalp on display in the middle of the town square.

"You know, I gotta tell you folks. Our town is having some rough times. But let's not forget who we are and what we fight for! This hat . . . this hat," he pointed to it for emphasis. "Has been passed down from maga to maga and originated from the Colored One himself, the torchbearer of the Wap people. He even left behind his own scalp." He looked and pointed toward the marble rock pillar. "Although his name has been lost to history—and this is important—he left it to remind us that his message is always with us, okay? He taught us that peace came through strength, to never apologize for doing the right. And, by God, he taught us that orange is the color of strength!"

The square filled again with raucous noise, the Maga having fully whisked them into a populist frenzy.

"And hear this, folks—we have a plan, an amazing plan, an incredible plan, and we will keep Appatown great, I guarantee it. How 'bout that?"

There were more cheers, but the Maga had to interrupt again. A task was at hand, and Josik saw the finger point towards him.

"But first, we have to remind our guests that we are a town of law and order. Guards, get 'em outta here!"

The crowd resumed their chants of "kill" as the straw-hatted men brought Josik and the other condemned deplorables up to the execution platforms. Josik almost couldn't believe it, but his death was at last at hand. As the noose was slipped around his neck, he instinctively stared up at the heavens.

He took comfort in thinking: *At least I didn't end my life up there.*

But his final thoughts were interrupted. Not by more of the Maga's bellowing, but by gunshots. A few dozen black men armed with pistols surged into the square, unleashing a salvo into the depths of the crowd and towards the Maga. Appatown's leader was taken down in a burst of blood quickly, as was the glass preserving the putrid scalp of the town's mysterious ancestor.

The guards instinctively rushed towards the Maga, leaving Josik the opportunity to duck for cover. He didn't know which way to run, certain that any direction would catch him in the crossfire.

He managed to push his way through the panicked crowd and finally decided on a dingy sausage shop. He nearly tripped on the broken glass in the entranceway but found his way to the unlit butchering room in the back. After coming across the cellar entrance as a dead end, he found the way out at a back door. Now he had only a few obscure rows of shacks to pass before making his way out of town.

He took one last look back to see that the town square was set ablaze before running for the hills. One quick look, and nothing more.

1-8

$\mathbf{P}$umped with adrenaline, he ran for the first several hundred yards away from Appatown, until the effort of hurdling through the deep snow finally caught up with him. Where was he to go?

East seemed the most logical direction, since the shorter side of the ring of mountains that surrounded the town lay that way. It was not long before he started scaling its densely wooded foothills. He worried for a moment about mounting the eleven-foot wall circling the town, but these worries were quickly put at rest. There were plenty of twelve-foot ladders to be found, left behind around the perimeter of the wall.

His troubles weren't finished once he scaled down the other side. Josik walked the whole night to keep himself warm. He tried to manage some level of sleep with short naps throughout the next day, but this was not nearly enough. Josik knew so little about wilderness survival, and he considered it a miracle that he had even survived that first day as he climbed into the first mountains.

Fortunately, clever instinct began to kick in that

second night. Although he still had no food or tools, he took shelter underneath the large lower branches of a pine tree. The weather was working in his favor, as it was the latter half of winter and the first thawing had begun. Yet, that still hadn't prevented Josik's legs from feeling chilled throughout the night, his tattered brown sleeping pants having gotten soaked from the snow melting beneath him from his body heat.

By morning, Josik was shivering uncontrollably. He struggled to continue his solo march, finally coming down the other side of the mountain and onto an outcropping overlooking a shallow valley. By now, he was completely without any calories to burn, his body in the first stages of hypothermia. His SIM offered no help. It offered none of the usual chemicals to keep him going anymore.

By the time he lowered himself into the valley, he was stumbling. It was the middle of the afternoon at this point, and Josik was certain he could not survive another day.

Then he heard some murmurs. Were these delusional voices in his head? No. He was just about to enter another clearing, the middle of which was occupied by a half-dozen group of men dressed head-to-toe in lightly colored wool. None of these were people from Appatown, nor were they Bohemx. By catching glimpses of their faces, Josik realized that they were all black. They were all warming themselves by a fire, apparently settling down for the day, leaving their crude wooden sleds filled with gear to the side.

Josik decided to risk a slow approach. Perhaps they

were far more forgiving and compassionate than the racist Appatown people. Besides, how else could he hope to survive?

His first minute of approach went well. He could tell that they spoke what he thought of as Bohemish, which he took as another good sign.

But Josik's luck was not to last. One of the black men stood up to go relieve his bladder, spotted Josik, and the rest of his circle sprang into action. Josik was instantly kicked down, his wind knocked out, and his body surrounded by loaded handguns from all sides.

A taller man with a thick parka and gray beanie spoke, his view being the clearest to Josik.

"What are you doing here, albino?"

Josik coughed up some snowflakes. "What?"

The tall man nodded to his counterparts. All six of the men fired a shot towards the trees, jolting Josik into terror.

The tall man leaned in closer to Josik, his gun pointed just a foot from his chest.

"You're a white man. You're not supposed to be this far out from that ghetto of yours."

"Wait!" said Josik with shocking realization. "You all speak Bohemish?"

"I don't know what the hell you're talking about, albino. Here we speak Liberan, the secret language our ancestors used to speak underneath the oppression of the white man. Hell, we probably would have never won freedom without being able to communicate through Liberan."

One of the stouter black men, wearing a wool hoodie, interjected.

"Boss, he's got a bit of olive in him. And his hair is pretty dark brown. He looks a bit too brown to be an albino."

The boss must have wanted to err on the side of caution.

"I'm not taking any chances. The village deserves to see him after the barbarism those bigoted murderers have done to us."

The black men quickly undid their camp, taking care to tie Josik to one of the sleighs next to their fur-trapping equipment.

They didn't have any animals to move their sleighs, so they didn't arrive in the black village until after sundown. The village had a rather simple layout, with one row of orderly lumber-framed shacks facing another, with about twenty-five feet separating the rows and a large bonfire in the city center that was lit every night. The group parked itself in front of one of the smaller box-shaped structures covered in canvas. The boss instructed his comrades to wait as he talked to the man inside.

The boss walked through the front flap in front to find the man he needed was kneeling on his rough wooden bench as usual, meditating before a simple three-foot tall cross perched above him on a table. The man, wearing his long black robes and white Roman collar, readily stood up, as he was often interrupted by people of the village in the midst of trouble.

"What is it, Deshawn?" the priest asked indifferently.

"Father Kris, I have found an albino."

The priest cut him off right there. "Deshawn, you know how I frown upon such hateful things. I doubt God has such patience for doing such horrible things against our enemies."

"I have not taken a life, Father, I promise you that. But this white man deserves justice."

"Then what are you consulting me for? Nobody cared about my objections to raiding the white town either."

"There's something about his appearance. He's not very white. He seems to be somewhere in between, but still looks mostly white."

"Then send him to the Ispanians. Their people are definitely that 'in between.'"

"And just let him go, after all his people are doing to us?"

"Deshawn, this village had almost no problem welcoming the first priests who came in and taught me their ways. They left me on my own so the village could look to me for guidance on leading a better life. The people have been doing a lot of wrong lately, and it makes me feel like a failure."

"Then why do you still bother with us?"

The priest returned an answer soberly without hesitation.

"Because someone has to stand up for what's right."

Deshawn, holding back some tears of guilt, left the priest, determined to perform an act of mercy. He had learned from Father Kris all about the New Testament and how much its message conflicted with the belief held by the villagers. They believed that the townspeople of Appatown deserved whatever revenge could be brought upon them at every turn. Appatown, after all, had the upper hand in everything: economics, well-being, even military power, at least relatively speaking. The two groups, for all they knew, were at war with each other and would always be at war with each other. And he would be giving up a golden opportunity to earn approval in the eyes of his people, as white people were almost never brought back to the village alive.

Despite all this, something about the inspirational words he had once heard spoken aloud from Father Kris from these so-called books of "Good News" was stirring up a reaction in his heart entirely different from hate in this moment. It was some need to put the words into action, fueled by an overwhelming sense of pity for the "in-between" stranger he had under his care.

Deshawn walked outside, but his underlings and Josik had disappeared from the sleds. He spotted a crowd forming at the edge of town and rushed over, terrified at what the village people might have done.

He managed to break through the cacophonous crowd, finding the youth and the other fur-trappers in the middle of it. They had stripped Josik of most of his clothes, and were stomping on and kicking every last part of his body. The snow near him had been melted by the blood that was let out in the process.

Deshawn pushed the men aside as he approached the unconscious victim, even kicking the wind out of some of them. He felt a pulse and hoisted the mangled body over his shoulder to a suddenly silent crowd. He said only one thing before leaving his own people.

"He's mine to take care of!" he reprimanded. "If you have a problem with it, you can try to kill me yourself."

No one took him up on the offer that night as Deshawn kept a vigil in patching up the boy's wounds. He had stopped the bleeding and brought back regular body temperature, but Josik did not regain consciousness in the morning.

Deshawn knew there was safer place for Josik, one where the foreigner could get the treatment and protection he needed. That morning, Deshawn loaded up his sled with his charge and made the daylong journey to the Ispanian village.

1-9

Josik found himself on the beach again. He was in front of the beach-house, but somehow it didn't carry any interest to him at the moment. He wanted to see the places to the north.

Josik went in that direction for several hundred yards, until he realized that the beach was narrowing. So, he approached the steep cliffs to his left, eager to continue the journey. But the crumbly sedimentary faces seemed indomitable, their tops over a hundred feet above the beaches. To attempt a climb risked a fall and certain death.

The cliffs disappeared in an instant. He woke up on a bed with linens made of crude, yet comfortable fabric. His arm lay immobilized in a white cast, covering up where his SIM used to be. His room was dimly lit, the walls consisting of neatly stacked 2x4s laid on their sides, but no floor was located underneath. The roof above him consisted of some corrugated metal, and an elongated wooden cross hung above an entryway. This still didn't help much to explain his situation.

Within a few minutes, a young woman entered

wearing light fabric greenish-blue scrubs, sandals, and a nurse's hat. She pulled aside the hide over the entryway and walked into the room. Josik couldn't help but notice her fit physique, her light brown skin, and the bun in which she kept the full length of her black locks under wraps.

She walked to the small window and pulled aside the curtains, brightening the room considerably.

"Buenos días," she said. "¿Cómo te sientes?"

Josik didn't know any bit of any other language outside of his native Bohemish (or Wapese, which seemed to him to be the same thing), so he simply gave the nurse a blank stare.

"Umm . . . I'm sorry. I don't speak . . . uh . . . whatever that is."

"That's okay," she responded impeccably. "I've known English almost my whole life. It's a necessity for all of the outreach we do to the local villages. Kind of the universal language around here, if you will."

"English?" replied a puzzled Josik. "I learned that language as Bohemish."

"Bohemish? Is there some vague legend behind that one too?" asked the nurse, eyebrows raised sarcastically.

"Yes," Josik responded almost robotically, preparing to sarcastically parrot Bohemx history. "After white cisgender capitalist society reaped its own ultimate plunder, Authority gathered the People to itself under one society, one language. We call this common language Bohemish."

"Yes, I get it. Congratulations, then, since you're one of the few Bohemx to know now that that isn't true. All of the factions here on the continent have different origin stories for the same basic language we all speak. Its name doesn't belong to any one of us. It was revealed to us very recently that it's all called English."

The nurse's eyes suddenly opened wide, looking up and down at Josik in sudden realization.

"Oh, yes. You belong to those space people."

"What's that supposed to mean?" scoffed Josik. "It'd be nice to know what the earth is actually going on."

The nurse gave an involuntary smirk.

"You seem quite upbeat for someone who was just unconscious for the last thirty-six hours."

Josik innately took this sarcasm as social condemnation for his subtle sass. He was only able to react as his Bohemx upbringing had taught so precisely.

"I'm sorry, ma'am," he stammered. "I mean lady. Person."

Josik applied palm to face in embarrassment. He needed to politically correct himself quickly.

"I'm so sorry. I should have asked you for your preferred pronouns. With which do you identify?"

"Hold on," she gestured with a look of amusement. "I don't know that much English."

This interaction made Josik think back to his secondary school history lessons. Ancient human civilization, he learned, resorted to incredibly primitive and anthropocentric understandings of the world around them. Even the people of the so-called "modern" civilizations, they explained, still sometimes chose to attribute events to supernatural causes, when in fact reason and science was enough to explain it all. This woman and her people had all the look of one of these "old-fashioned" civilizations, and yet she spoke not just one, but two languages flawlessly. How could a person who worked in such a basic structure as this makeshift hospital appear so learned?

The reflex Josik had developed on Bohem to this kind of confusion was one of arrogance. He had learned it was the only way to keep his nerve in these situations.

The nurse concentrated her look towards him with what Josik was starting to recognize as annoyance.

"¿Tú crees en Dios?" she asked, not expecting him to understand.

"What the earth does *that* mean?"

"It's part of a series of questions the people here ask themselves often. It's meant to be an exercise in self-reflection, a way of helping everyone to realize right and wrong. It's also one of the most basic questions of existence we answer from our faith."

Josik suddenly realized the acute soreness in his

body. He had regretted losing his patience, and had begun to wonder if whatever deity these strange people likely worshiped was responsible for his rising pain.

"Can you tell me what's going on with me?" he grunted. The nurse remained silent and watched him shift his pained body around on the bed for several moments.

Finally, she relented. "You lost a lot of blood as a result of your injuries. But you also managed to sustain just one fracture, in your forearm at the same spot where your strange device used to be before I removed it. All the rest of your body is only badly bruised, thanks to the work of your friend. You should be able to be on your feet within the next few days, as long as you don't move around much."

"Whoever brought me here isn't my friend," Josik snapped. "I don't even know who he was, because I wasn't conscious enough to see."

"Whether or not he was your friend doesn't matter to me," said the caregiver matter-of-factly.

She shifted back toward the entryway.

"In the meantime, you might find it best to be a bit more open to our culture. Even if you're interested in being sent back from whatever place you came from, you're probably going to be stuck with us Ispanians for a while."

She pulled the hide aside.

"Wait," Josik interrupted. The nurse acknowledged him with a side glance.

"I assume you're taking care of me. May I at least know your name?"

The nurse responded with a sigh, annoyed by the lack of apology.

"Maria," she said. "My name's Maria. Now I have other patients to get to."

1-10

Josik passed the next few days by speaking and moving little. Maria offered very little conversation, only speaking to tell him to turn over or some simple medically related command. Josik, significantly lacking social awareness as a result of his Bohemx upbringing, hadn't realized that Maria was still resentful for his ignorant comments upon his first waking.

Finally, on his third morning in the hospital, he was struck with the true guilt of the situation. For once, this guilt wasn't motivated by fear of social retribution. Unlike with what had happened on Bohem, his rudeness towards Maria couldn't be spread on social media across the ocular screens. Though he still had little concept of the difference between the two, he was simply acknowledging right from wrong.

Josik was in the midst of mulling over these thoughts when Maria entered the room.

"Hey, good morning," she said unenthusiastically. "I think it's time we get you moving again this morning. Why don't you go ahead and stand up?"

The request required an unusual amount of thought. He wanted to see if he could at least move his legs apart, which he accomplished with considerable stiffness. Next, he transitioned himself ninety degrees on the bed, allowing himself to sit upright. With his arms locked over the bed frame, Josik prepared to dangle the whole of his weight over the floor, his legs still largely absent of sensation.

Maria interjected. "Easy now, easy now," she said, while swooping underneath Josik's arms and pressing herself against his chest in the process. Fortunately, this gave him the additional support he needed to transfer his entire body weight to his feet.

"How are you doing?" she asked, still grasping him firmly, his head resting on her shoulder.

"Never better," he said peacefully, with a strange sense of warmth and calm that was coming over him. Despite all the videos he had watched about sensuality, Josik realized that this was the closest he had ever physically gotten to a woman.

He abruptly let go to head off the impending awkwardness, even though it required him to reach out his hand for the bed frame.

"You sure you're okay?" Maria asked with skepticism.

"Yeah, yeah, I'll be fine," assured Josik. "Thank you."

"Okay then. I have to get back to other patients, but you're welcome to leave whenever you're ready. You're our guest here, so there's no charge."

She turned to leave, closing Josik's window of opportunity quickly. Now was his last chance to try out a genuine apology, putting the oratory skills he learned in Bohemx school to at least some good use.

"Wait, Maria," he stammered. "I'm sorry."

"¿Qué?" she returned, unbelieving.

"It took me a while to realize it, but I'm sorry for the way I automatically looked down on your people. I haven't even met them yet, so it's unfair for me to make those assumptions. I suppose I said what I did because this planet is so unlike the space station where my people come from, and so far it hasn't been a good experience."

"Oh really? I couldn't tell at all looking at your injuries from head to toe."

Josik laughed heartily in response. He hadn't expected Maria to be full of such good, sarcastic humor.

"My point is, that doesn't make what I said or the way I've been acting okay. I want to learn more about the people here. I want to see its good side, the side that I've seen in you this morning."

"I accept your apology. But if we're going to start teaching you about the Ispanian people, you also have to apologize in our people's language."

"What language is that? I only know Bohemish."

"You mean English?"

"Oh right, they're pretty much one and the same."

"Right. Anyway, you'll have to learn a lot about our Spanish language. We have enough interactions with the other . . . would the term be 'English-speaking'? Sorry, this word 'English' is still new even to us. Anyway, having other English-speaking villages around here makes being bilingual a necessity, but that still makes knowing our language base's native half of primary importance."

"Okay, okay, I get it," chuckled Josik. "How do I apologize to someone in Spanish?"

"Lo siento," she said.

"Lo siento," he repeated in his neutral Bohemish accent.

"That was acceptable for a first time," she commented. "Next time, don't say it so flat. Our people's language is meant to be spoken more . . . colorfully. With passion and feeling to it. But without thinking too hard about it either."

Josik was all chuckles again. "Understood."

"Anyway, I should really be getting back to the other patients. But perhaps our paths will cross again. I'm here most of the time, but you're welcome to come find me if you're ever in need of anything. If you don't, I may just have to come find you and make sure you're still alive."

Josik chuckled again.

"You laugh, but I mean it," Maria said through a smile. "Taking care of all my patients even after they leave here is how God lets me sleep at night."

"Fair enough," responded Josik, choosing to ignore the religious reference. "So where does a foreigner like me go?"

"Oh," she exclaimed, suddenly remembering. "Our town priest, our pastor."

"A priest?" cried Josik, recalling all the negative connotations Authoritarian education attached to that word.

"Yes, our pastor has been asking me about your condition these past few days. He kept visiting after you'd fall asleep at night. He requested that I tell you to find him at the church as soon as you were on your feet again. He also said I should mention his name to you. Something about him being an old friend of yours."

"Well, what is it?" interrupted Josik, already knowing the answer but still incredulous.

"Father Biwun is his name. He was the one who made the discovery about the English language we all speak."

Josik limped away from his room, down the makeshift hospital's main corridor, and out onto the wide main path of the village. With his piecemeal knowledge of Spanish, he frantically asked locals for the location of the town church.

1-11

It seemed Biwun was waiting for Josik. He was standing outside the town's simple steepled wooden church, just in time to grab Josik's attention by waving his hand. Josik changed his direction towards the modest chapel and slowed his approach.

"I hadn't realized we could cross paths again," said Josik, between large breaths.

"Neither had I," replied Biwun. "Though I had hoped and prayed that the Creator might guide a fellow Bohemx to me before I pass on into the next life."

Why the earth would he be pondering death at his young age? Josik mused. One quick scan of Biwun's unusually pale complexion and peaky frame said it all: he was seriously ill. But it was Biwun himself who fully informed Josik's concern.

"It may seem fairly apparent to you at this point that I'm dying, Josik," he said with a weak, yet unapologetic grin.

Josik's warm feelings disappeared and his gaze took to the rough ground path. "I thought the medicine here would be able to cure you," he said with touches of pity and frustration.

"I'm afraid the Ispanians have never encountered an illness of my kind before. Before I was exiled from Bohem, the Authoritarian guards gave me and several other prisoners the strain of this disease while we were detained. They said something along the lines about how our sacrifice would be of great service to humanity, though I heard the same disease they gave us is also running rampant amongst the Authoritarians themselves. Given the drugs and tests they had been occasionally giving us since then, it is probably reasonable to assume that they were using us as test subjects in their quest for a cure."

"And that doesn't make you angry?" cried Josik.

Biwun returned the question with an intimate stare. He let a long moment of silence pass, as if preparing for some greater wisdom to show itself working through him.

"What use is there in being angry? A great thinker who once lived on this true home of ours wrote: 'Bless those who persecute you. Bless them and do not curse them.' For it is impossible on this planet for true justice ever to be achieved, given our limited nature. While we must be careful with who or what we judge as good and evil, our incredible ability to reason gives us some way to distinguish between the two. Once this has taken place, we must not 'be overcome by evil, but overcome evil with good.'"

Josik stared back with a blank face. He had no idea

what his good friend had said in the slightest.

"But you have not yet learned fully of the way of life to which I speak. I must also confess to you, Josik, that I feel little reason to complain now that you have come." Biwun added another friendly grin.

"Why do you say that?" quipped Josik.

"You are still regaining your strength, Josik. I will take you on the journey there when you are physically ready, someday soon," Biwun said.

***

Four days later, Biwun gently tapped Josik awake in his hospital bed at dawn. Initially Josik jerked upright, shocked by the unexpected visitor. But the priest gently helped his friend out of bed and invited to meet just outside the facility once Josik was dressed.

Josik emerged through the front a few minutes later, loudly yawning and stretching. He had gotten used to sleeping in at the hospital, a welcome break from the early-morning routine that was rigidly enforced on Bohem. Biwun pointed ahead of them to the east, grabbing Josik's attention.

"Come, follow me," the pastor said. "And I will show you where humanity lost its path."

Josik followed Biwun to the outskirts of the Ispanian town. They approached a riverbank that was heavily forested and almost devoid of human presence save for a few small, well-constructed huts. Biwun knocked on the door of the one closest to a single pier that extended out into the water with a few medium-sized fishing boats attached. A short-statured, long-haired typical mustachioed Ispanio answered the door.

The fisherman, like most inhabitants of the Ispanian village, instantly recognized the dark-skinned town figure from his robes and collar. "Padre Biwun," inaudibly gasped the man, doing a quick cross motion in front of himself with his hand that was entirely lost on Josik.

"There's no need to humble yourself, amigo," replied Biwun. "I have come to request one of your ships to cross the river. I will pay you well for your generosity."

With much expressed gratitude for Biwun's fairness, the man asked for his purpose in making such an unusual journey. For the Ispanians, the ships served few other purposes aside from bringing back large catches of fish from the sea to be found at the end of the river.

"I am taking him to the Follies," said Biwun solemnly. "He is to continue some of my work."

Josik's ears perked up at this. At Bohem, he had always been a generic laborer. How on earth was he now being expected to live up to the work of such a wise thinker that his friend had apparently become, especially when he had such little idea of what this work was?

Josik had waited until he and Biwun crossed the river to demand a better explanation for this expedition.

"You can get out of the boat now, Josik," said Biwun, attempting to coax him with an inviting arm motion.

"I still don't quite understand. That makes me uncomfortable. I can't be dragged out of town like this when I feel uncomfortable."

At this, Biwun gave a most unexpected reaction. He stepped back into the boat, sat next to Josik, and put his arm around his shoulder. And, of course, he gave another one of his characteristic grins.

"I used to feel the same way about these things when I first escaped the grasp of the Authority. On Bohem, we were raised with limitless technology and convenience. We were also taught to trust in reason alone. What I'm asking you to do has nothing to do with reason," he continued. "It makes little sense now, but I'm asking you to have faith in what I have to say because it speaks from the eternal wisdom of the ages."

"Eternal?" Josik muttered, never having heard the word.

Then Biwun clasped his hands together.

"Father, please guide our brother Josik on this journey we must continue. I pray he will have faith in what I have brought him to do, even though he has never had faith in anything else before."

Josik couldn't help but contrast this moment to the one he had with Authoritarian ship captain in the prison cell. There, his trust and faith in someone else had been broken. But in this moment, he felt urging from within, some force beyond his grasp that gave him the sense that Biwun was worthy of his faith and trust.

"I have faith in you," said Josik, hesitantly.

***

Half an hour later, the pair was still traversing a lone, winding dry path through a visually endless swamp, a geographic feature that had also been totally unfamiliar to Josik until today. Finally, they scaled a short grassy slope into a dense deciduous forest, with Biwun making a point to dodge every large green bush in its understory.

"Avoid these at all costs," he warned. "The locals call it poison ivy, and it itches terribly. Although the villagers are coming close to a cure."

After another fifteen minutes or so, the cleric stopped abruptly, turning back to address Josik.

"What is it?" inquired Josik.

"What do you remember of the teachings of pre-Authoritarian history?"

Of course, it had been months since he had been liberated from the regime's propaganda. But he was still able to recite the Authoritarian account of history that was summarized and printed on the first page of all instructional textbooks—not to mention sang as a kind of pledge of allegiance at events like Josik's exiling. This was of course Bohem's "The Intersectionale".

"Impressive," returned Biwun. "I'm going to tell you something that may still come as a surprise to you—

that account of history is false."

"Of course! I was skeptical of the Authoritarian history course from day one."

"Praise God!" cried Biwun, looking upward with arms outstretched. Having folded his hands together, he muttered, "He must be destined to deliver us after all."

Once again, Josik made his bewilderment visually obvious. He was expecting further explanation. Him, one apparently skeptical Bohemx resident, a chosen one? Still, the other part of him seemed to keep urging him onward.

Biwun gave another comforting grin. "Come, I have not much time left. I must show you where humanity went astray." He disappeared down the slope where the edge of the forest met an upcoming clearing. Josik followed suit after some moments of hesitation.

He met up with Biwun in one of the barren fields up ahead, next to one of the many piles of ancient refuse that were scattered throughout the surrounding area. The visual landscape up ahead left him awestruck— the magnificent Greek pillared buildings, the statue-topped off-white dome, the impressively tall obelisk. Josik only knew the former metropolis ahead of him to be a long-lost testimony to his species' true past.

"Welcome, Josik," Father Biwun said. "To the magnificent capital they once called Washington, DC."

1-12

The pair returned to the Ispanian settlement just after dusk. During their pilgrimage throughout the city ruins, Biwun offered few answers to Josik's constant questions. He'd occasionally give a generic response such as "all that is dark now will be revealed," or even "in due time." Most of the time, Biwun simply seemed to ignore his younger companion. Understandably, Josik was hot and impatient by the time they returned to the Ispanians.

Sensing this, Biwun chose to address him at long last just outside the church, priming the message with another weak grin.

"Sit, my friend." Josik obeyed by squatting on a nearby short stump, having been disturbed by the progressively worsening hoarseness in Biwun's voice. Still, this frail *amigo* of his pressed on.

"The sights you have seen today are much to take in. Think deeply on what you have seen and heard today, as they will carry you in the trials to come. What you witnessed were the remains of a great and noble country—perhaps the most interesting one humanity has ever known. Its legacy was established through the ages when it blazed a better path for humanity by professing one simple belief—that all people are created equal."

Created equal? thought Josik. This was among one of many questions that popped up in Josik's simple Bohemx mind at this moment. He tamped down his curiosity by asking just one question.

"Then how did this great country come to fall?"

"The answer is too much for one to hear in just one night. The American story can only be told through experience, especially through those who came to the country in search of its promise, often with little money and with little welcome."

"American?" whispered Josik.

"Yes, American. An American, a citizen of a once miraculous country. After I am gone, you will be met by another friend who will teach you about the great things that this nation was and what its people overcame. He will give you the experience of the American story, to tell you how it came into being and where we lost our way. Perhaps, God willing, America will one day breathe life again. Once I am gone, you will become the last American. Not immediately, but in due time."

Josik was terrified, yet overwhelmingly spellbound by this charge. Still, one more question lingered.

"When will I know that this has happened?"

A long pause passed.

"You will know it when you feel a sudden connection, a true and overwhelming feeling that you have joined the American story."

Josik had little patience for such vague responses, but it made no difference in this case. In an instant, Biwun waved a hand over the youth and the latter was overcome with a deep slumber.

When Josik awoke the next morning, it was approaching noon. Oddly, he had been moved off the side of the village's main path and behind some tall green shrubs. He found himself embracing a large chunk of marble as a pillow. Odder still, large pieces broke from it as soon as Josik relaxed his grip.

Putting this aside, he soon found his way back to the hospital, with Maria being his first instinct for confiding the details from the previous evening.

"What time is it?" he inquired, with groggy mannerisms.

"Aproximadamente a las once," she chimed through the task of operating a deep handwashing, using a foot-operated station.

Josik gave another one of his characteristic "I'm not bilingual" frowns.

"Oh. A little after 11am," she added, with a sniffle. Although she turned around, she kept her head locked down, tears dripping.

"Where is Father Biwun?"

Maria's tear-stained head finally rose and he learned the answer. Biwun had died that morning.

1-13

Biwun's had been a peaceful death by Ispanian standards. Of course, the whole of the village knew he had been suffering for months with what they called El Sida, or the Incurable Illness, despite their ability to cure nearly everything else using their tremendous knowledge of homeopathic remedies. Nobody knew the exact time of his passing—they simply found him early that morning tucked in his straw bed at the village church, seemingly enjoying his last slumber.

The whole of the town attended the funeral ceremony to pay final respects to their padre, a sight that throttled Josik with emotion. On Bohem, passionate emotions such as fury and sorrow were constantly propagandized and even physically stimulated. "To validate one's own emotions," he was taught, "is a humxn right. To interfere with such is micro-aggressive and deviant." Josik experienced true grief alongside a sense of despair regarding Biwun's charge. How was Josik to complete this quest without him? The Bohemx refugee had nowhere to go for an answer.

Nor did Josik have any of the old creature comforts

to distract him from his emotions. A few of the villagers took notice of his heavy consumption of the maize-brewed cervezas, even asking about his state in simple Bohemish in passing. Most of his time was spent slumped against a chair in the local cantina, confiding in no one his true feelings, and turning away from all the would-be friends save for his own grog. The barkeeper would have asked after Josik's troubles too (and even kicked him out, for that matter), except that he believed perhaps a bit too strongly in the Ispanian tradition of courtesy and politeness.

One morning, Josik woke up on the floor of the cantina. If he could have guessed the time, it was sometime in the late morning, based on the rods of light poking through the flap of leather at the entrance. Scarcely a few minutes had passed after he peeled himself off the dirt and lowered himself back into his booth when he was approached by Maria.

"Miguel, the barkeeper, told me you had spent the night here. He's not the type to confront people he's worried about."

Josik let his weak gaze at her wander off.

"I'm quite different. I'm not afraid to be direct, Josik. I know there's a special connection Biwun made with you, that he left you a special task. And I can understand how him being gone after all he did for you as a friend has left you feeling betrayed."

"How would you know?" accused Josik, through a clenched jaw. He tossed the last of the mug's dregs into his mouth.

"When you first arrived in our village, he told me about a vision he had had months ago while in the church. He couldn't explain much of it in terms that I could understand, but the message was clear: God was to send our people a stranger to learn our ways and to bring peace to all of the different towns in this wilderness. *Josik*—you were the one sent to us."

Josik's eyes screwed shut with tears. "No, no." he objected. "If I'm some savior, I wouldn't be letting myself go to waste. Tell me why I should believe anything of this story. Why didn't Biwun share any of these details to me? Why didn't your God come down himself and send some vision to me? I've been waiting and suffering long enough."

"It's how faith works, Josik. A lot of the time, God speaks to us in very indirect ways, and there are times when we must live with the pain. It's up to us to look at the pieces of events in our life and put the puzzle together. Faith does that for us."

"How is someone supposed to find this faith? If you have some textbook example on it's supposed to work, I can tell you that it's not working that way for me."

"You can only reason it out so much, Josik. At some point, you just feel it. That's the best way I can explain it."

Josik's eyes glazed over.

"You haven't been taught to treat feelings the way I have," he added, suddenly aware of his rising voice.

"Then learn differently. Everyone in this village is

here to support and love you."

He waved off the offer disdainfully. "Hmph. Love. That word was never made a part of my vocabulary, and I don't see any point in starting now."

Left anguished by this rejection, Maria marched out into the street. Josik, on the other hand, lowered himself back into his post-drunken slumber. When he awoke in a few hours, he was immediately shocked with his guilty conscience, the effects of a hangover pounding reminders of his self-neglect into his head with every heartbeat. But now he realized that the harm he was inflicting was not simply upon himself. His Bohemx upbringing had also failed to prepare him in thinking for the well-being of others, and his scorn towards Maria came to mind.

He now knew that alcohol was not enough to soothe his grief, nor his newfound sense of guilt. So, he treaded his way outside of the village and made his best guess towards the coast. A suitably sized cliff would do the job.

He found the right place after about half an hour. As he gazed down at the sandy depths below, a feeling of déjà vu passed over him. It was roughly the same landscape as he saw in the visions of the beach-house, sans the structure. Then again came the voices and urgings from within, the ones that had not moved him since before Biwun's death. They were telling him not to jump.

In an attempt to quell them, he thought back on his rather unremarkable life. Josik had to acknowledge his true self: a fully socialized Bohemx citizen from birth. He knew no other way until the Ispanians, and the Ispanian way offered few answers and many beliefs. Faith. Their God. Family. Most of all: love. But most questionable was the falsely uplifting quest he was charged with, with few instructions. As far he was concerned, these native people were just as manipulative as the Authoritarians.

He was determined not to have any of it. He would take matters into his own hands. But while his decision was final, his very soul felt on the verge of rebellion. He dared his left foot just over the edge, ready to take a leap of despair.

In an instant, the brightness of the afternoon maritime sun filled the sky. Josik, taken to blindness, was brought down to his knees. A familiar hand pulled him off the precipice and into her tight embrace.

"It's okay, Josik," Maria sobbed. "I'm here."

1-14

The sun had finally reverted to its original place in the heavens. Josik was once again with Biwun, during their tour of the Follies.

His mind was set on finding out about the peculiar events. But his body wasn't cooperating.

The two stopped in front of a set of tall marble steps. They led to a square platform on top with a tremendous amount of rubble. Only the bases of many of its formerly tall front pillars remained.

"This was the country's Supreme Court," informed Biwun. "It worked similarly to Judgment, except that it adhered to a set of rules they called the Constitution. Plus, it was full of nine people similar to you and I. Except they were all at least twice our age. Think of most of the Authoritarians without their age-reduction enhancements."

"Why does Judgment and the rest of Authority not follow a type of Constitution?" chimed his younger companion.

Crap, thought Josik. *That's exactly what I said*

before.

"In due time, you will learn," repeated the cleric.

The pair continued down the remains of the one of the streets in the eastern section of the former capital. None of the non-stone buildings had remained, now decomposed piles of wood and brick. They characterized the area with tiny undulations, most of which sported shrubs and small trees.

It was another four blocks until Biwun turned back to Josik.

"Quickly, find some cover!" he whispered, motioning to a large lot densely filled with Japanese maples. Josik followed as directed.

"Authoritarians." Biwun explained, as the two waited in the thick of the grove. Within a minute, at least two dozen of Bohem's elite could be seen strolling down the east-west cross street on stand-up hovercraft. A tour guide, sporting a neon orange hat and small flag rode backwards at the front of the group.

"If you look on your right, you'll see the remains of the White House in the distance. But first we have the building the Americans referred to as the U.S. Capitol. Its architectural style imitated that of the Greeks and Romans, perhaps as a nod to the way the country modeled its political system. And yet, for a supposedly democratic, elected legislature, the body was dominated by racist, cisgender, patriarchal males. Little wonder, then, that the United States met the same fate as their ancient counterparts. Let's move on to the Celebration of Sexuality Monument, shall we?"

At last the tour group was no longer within earshot. But Biwun was nowhere to be seen. Nor could the Authoritarians be spotted once Josik returned to the ruined streets. Where to go next?

The sun gave a sharp flash. After some thought, the answer was made clear. For whatever reason, he needed to find his way back to the place of the beach-house. At the very least, Josik figured that going there would perhaps show him a way out of this fantasy. He had gone down the rabbit hole far enough for today.

Whether the journey to the cliff beach took him hours or even minutes, he could not tell. For earth's sake, Josik couldn't even tell if he was just dreaming— or perhaps he was hallucinating or something worse than that. Regardless, he stood once again at the white wooden door, the sun nearly set now. He longed to test the very reality of the dream that was brought back to him: with a sharp inhalation, he firmly knocked on the door.

Moments later, a man perhaps twice Josik's age emerged. He bore a remarkable resemblance to the vagrant, save for his slightly shorter height, pale complexion, and heavily wrinkled brow and forehead. The man also sported jet-black hair, square-ish black-rimmed glasses, and a short beard flecked with its first bits of grey.

"A traveler, I assume?" sighed the man.

Josik looked back quizzically, his lips pursed in a small round shape.

"Yes," the traveler said, playing along. "You've been

expecting me?"

"In a manner of speaking—Lord only knows," exasperated the man, as if not directing the comment at Josik. "Please, come in."

The new guest cautiously shifted into the entryway, the host closing the door behind them. Josik looked around, still curious how much of this was real. The house boasted a rather quaint indoor set-up—one side of the main room had a round wooden table with two chairs, a sliding glass door facing the ocean, and a cushioned gray armchair; the other side had a simple kitchen set-up, with a short row of dark wooden cabinets, stovetop, sink, tile counter, transistor radio, and a small window facing the ocean. Despite its small footprint, the space still fit most of the essential necessities of a modern-day dwelling. Still, there were no places for screens in this place—it simply would have distracted from the dining room's incredible vista of the Chesapeake Bay.

Opposite the cozy living room and kitchen of the building was a short hallway into Josik's new guest room. Its size was modest but its furnishings sufficient—fit with a dresser/mirror assembly, nightstand, full-sized bed, bedside lamp, and small shelf. On the east side of the room was a compact window which provided a glimpse of the beachfront.

"This should provide for all the basic necessities," added the host neutrally. "You're welcome to read some of my own writing in case you get bored." He pointed to a thin book on the nightstand. "There's also a Bible in the dresser drawer. Breakfast is at seven."

"Seven?" Josik questioned. "Don't you mean 0700?"

"No, seven," the host reasserted rather impatiently, but Josik still hadn't caught on. "A.M. You been living in the military your whole life?"

"No sir," Josik said quickly. "I understand now," he pretended with a short nod. He was more interested in stopping his latest benefactor before exiting the room.

"Excuse me, sir," Josik successfully interjected. "I was hoping you could tell me . . . well, I'm not sure how I got here and I was wondering if you knew anything about it."

The host had too little imagination to take Josik seriously. "Why are any of us here? Couldn't tell you, and I prayed eight years ago once trying to get the answer. God knows if any of us will ever find it. Your guess is as good as mine, kid. All I was told was to expect a visitor."

The host turned again to the door. Still, Josik pressed. "I'm sorry to ask, but could you answer just one more question of mine?"

The host unenthusiastically whipped back 180 degrees.

"What is your name?"

"Sam. You can call me Sam. I'll let you get settled in." With that, he finally escaped the room.

Josik's head ached with more questions. But he was too overwhelmed with a craving for rest, the room now dark from the sun having gone for the day. He settled

in his new bed for just a moment and fell into another
deep sleep.

1-15

His waking place was clearly back with the Ispanians. But his senses were not at full strength, namely his sight.

As a matter of fact, he was blind. The cloth he felt wrapped around the middle of his face was the definite confirmation.

Then he began to notice the quiet sibilants on his right side. Josik squirmed a bit so he could try to hear better. That's when his side rubbed against the hands on top of his bed.

But what were they doing? Josik clamped his own on top of them. They were much slimmer and softer to the touch than his.

"Maria," he croaked.

"Josik," she weakly returned.

He laid back down on his flat pillow in relief.

"I was just saying some prayers for you," she whispered.

Without any rational reason, Josik's emotion flooded out. He felt the guilt of his decision, the weight of the past brought upon him, the pain of his tormentors. And he felt all the tears for all despair in his life, each trickle rolling off his face and absorbed into his protective bandage.

Maria had no words. She could only offer a gentle touch. Determined, she scooped him up, pressing her cheek into his and grasping both his shoulder blades.

From Josik's perspective, they might have stayed in that position for over an hour. Maria's affection had the effect of wringing out the emotion of the situation; she eventually had to change her patient's covering at one point as a result.

Finally, as his sobbing died down, she laid him back on the crude medical linens.

"Shh," she coaxed him. "You'll start to dehydrate yourself."

Fortunately, he was much too exhausted for the sadness to well up again. Then he felt it dribble down his throat. Water.

"Sorry," confessed Maria. "I should have warned you."

Josik let out a steady sigh, a sign of his resignation. "How bad is it?" he spoke. "My condition?"

"You're alive, most importantly."

Josik took a guilty swallow.

"You should also know that you won't be blind permanently. Your cornea will eventually heal, but I can't say when. I'll be keeping you here for some time while we keep you monitored on various things. My coworkers also volunteered to take over some of my other patients for a while so I can keep you under close watch."

"How did you figure all that?" Josik inquired.

Maria sneaked in a bit of sarcasm. "Hmph. We're not that technologically backwards, you know."

She turned Josik on his side. Since she also pressed a spread hand across the right side of his face, the patient had assumed that was the caregiver's stranger attempts at intimacy. That is, until he could sense an immaterial thing slithering through his head.

"What are you doing?"

"We call it a seeker glove," she answered. "Uses something you might know as X-rays so we can take a look inside."

"Hm. Interesting." Josik gave it away that he was easily impressed.

"You'll notice a common feature of our technology as you continue being a part of the village. We don't use much of it, but we keep it as small and practical as much as possible."

Josik offered only additional affirmation. "Ah. Hm."

An awkward silence took hold. A few minutes ago, Josik would have been content to sleep. But now he felt electrified by Maria's presence, an aura he felt that she was begging to speak with him further.

"There was once a tool our ancestors used to try to ease uncomfortable situations such as these," she abruptly lectured. "I believe they called it 'small talk.'"

Josik thought back to Meset. "I know what it is, but I can't say I've heard good things about it."

"Why am I not surprised?" Maria shot back. Josik let out a more generous chuckle.

Maria continued. "Tell me something about you that I don't know, Josik."

He merged his hands together in a casual fit of thought. "There's a lot about me you don't know. Just the introduction could take hours."

"Heh," she reacted. "I've got time. I'm not leaving you much during daylight hours anytime soon."

Josik indulged her in the more extended version of his life story. But he could only tell the sanitized version of his origins and life aboard Bohem, per the social conditioning with which he was indoctrinated. Maria was patient to hear out his account, but it took just one question from her to try to get him to break through to his real story.

"So why did they send you to Earth?"

"For uh . . . well . . . uh. Discipline. Punishment. I did something I wasn't supposed to."

"Then it must have been something pretty serious."

Josik nervously rubbed the back of his neck. "Umm . . . yeah. Yeah, I guess."

"You don't have to explain if it makes you uncomfortable."

"No, it's . . . it . . ." Josik was on the verge of panic.

Maria gave his shoulder a gentle squeeze. "It's okay, Josik. Don't worry about it."

Josik found himself growing steady again now with each deep breath. For the first time, he needed to speak his true mind on the matter.

"You know, it's all bullshit. It wasn't anything serious that I did. They were made-up charges, all of them. The whole lifestyle there was made-up, an enforced utopia. I didn't know I was doing anything wrong because they never said what was right and wrong. It was all what everyone thought was right. Except that what everyone thought was right was actually what we were told was right."

Maria hung on every word of his. So, he continued.

"And they tortured me for all that thinking. I don't know how they found it out, but I suffered for it when they found a way to turn me into a criminal. But with hardly any beatings or violence. Somehow . . . somehow they turned the torture into a science. And everything else. My life has been one careful calculation."

Maria appeared breathless too. "What kind of futuristic place would do this?" she begged rhetorically.

Josik answered her anyway. "Some place your

ancestors didn't know that they'd one day create."

"I don't understand."

"I don't quite understand, either."

A sudden surge of fatigue tipped him off. Yes, the method to Biwun's madness just became a bit clearer.

He let out a large yawn. "But that's what I'm being called to find out."

Strangely, he felt his excitement building even as his consciousness was slipping. Maria, meanwhile, was still troubled.

"Josik!" she cried. "Josik!"

But it had no effect. Josik dove in a deep slumber and thus the next leg of his journey, back to America's past.

1-16

Josik had been returned to the exact point where his boarding with Sam was taking place, tucked comfortably in the linens of the modest twin-sized bed.

The impulse was set towards finding Sam. He was instead sidetracked by the thin hardcover book on his nightstand. Its title, printed in modestly sized, golden capital letters, ran thus:

THE DECLINE AND FALL OF AMERICAN DEMOCRACY

He skipped over the foreword and went straight to Chapter 1.

"America and Human Civilization: An Inevitable Endpoint?

For nearly 240,000 years, the Homo sapiens species as we've come to know ourselves, lived a rather quiet, simple existence. Food was simply hunted or gathered and the relatively few humans who populated the earth congregated in tightly knit villages, never to struggle over modern concepts of total warfare, religious persecution, or human rights.

Then, with the dawn of the Agricultural Revolution, the destiny of the human race was changed forever. Human society settled down and became sedentary out of necessity. More complex systems of rule needed to be put in place as a result. It is here that such concepts as civilization, empire, government, and conquest were born. A small number of historians still debate the pros and cons of civilized living. In many regards, however, its triumph can be considered a double-edged sword. On one hand, the specialization of labor it demanded created new arbitrary and largely unjustified social hierarchies. On another, it allowed the individual at least some leeway into focusing on one's true "calling", or most enjoyed work in life. Irrespective of the trade-offs considered, every human civilization throughout history always failed to avert an inevitable endpoint; that is, a point at which the civilization's source of social, cultural, and economic cohesion simply collapsed due to a combination of poor governance and the undermining of its natural resources. It is unclear, however, which of these factors most strongly determines the collapse of any given civilization. History itself would seem to suggest that the relative magnitude of either one of these factors depends on a case-by-case basis.

As the environmental toll of the new, 21st century American lifestyle became increasingly apparent, it was also realized by scientists, politicians, and other experts that the United States of America was by no means immune from the possibility of traumatic collapse like the dozens of impressive civilizations before it. In fact, by 2010, an overwhelming abundance of scientific evidence pointed toward a need for a radical reduction in the average American's consumption of natural resources. And yet, the public largely chose to ignore the calls for relevant political action. Additionally, the political elites of the American government took little to no leadership of their own accord on the issue, many instead choosing to diminish or even flatly deny the facts at hand.

But the debate over the very environmental sustainability of the so-called "American experiment" was just another crack that was forming in the foundation of American political culture—a foundation that now seems in the process of being cleaved apart. In social scientific terms, this phenomenon takes on the term of political polarization. And its consequences began to draw everyday people into debates over the most controversial of topics—gay marriage, abortion, racial tension, and other multicultural issues—that were decided as the best topics to be brought onto the national stage. This phenomenum overlooked the possibility that such social issues could be better addressed by state and local authorities, as opposed to imposing universal policies over the entirety of the country. Such coercive federalism, as it was called, went against the spirit of the federal system of government, diminished the importance of state and local politics in the eye of the public as a result, and was uniquely a negative practice for the United States, considering how relatively large and socioeconomically diverse the country had always been and was becoming.

The system once boasted virtues that allowed the country to make unparalleled accomplishments. The old American way of politics, at least at the federal level, had once mastered the concept of cooperation and compromise; indeed, they were practically the country's invention as attested by the results of the 1787 Constitutional Convention. Moreover, the history of the United States is ripe with examples of leaders with tremendous vision, intellect, humility, and, to an arguable degree, ethics and morality. Perhaps most crucial to America's political successes was the country's pioneering of the then-nascent worldview of Liberalism, with its commitment towards defending individual freedoms and personal property. While many have come to criticize these originally American values on account of the country's hypocrisy in promoting them in its early days, history demonstrates a truer commitment to these values panning out in subsequent centuries—namely, in the eventual extension of universal suffrage and other civil rights and liberties.

Yet, of these three key virtues of American democracy—compromise, leadership, and liberty—the first two became largely extinct by the end of the first quarter of the 21st century (or, at the very least, the supposed illusions of them had been shattered by popular belief). The three-part American way had successfully steered the country through its early dysfunction, the abolition of its slave trade, held it together through its Civil War, led the defense of democracy worldwide through two world wars, and emerged as a world superpower against the menace of communist regimes throughout the rest of the globe, while harboring thousands of terrorized refugees and promoting the opportunity that allowed its people to achieve the impossible.

Thus, this begs the question—what has happened to us now that we have come to show contempt and repulsion at our own people, those we regard as "the other side of the aisle" or, even worse, "that other America"? How have we come to lose sight of the values that made America a source of democratic inspiration for the rest of the world? To answer these questions, or at least providing some much-needed insight for discussion, is this book's aim . . ."

Josik let the book slip onto his bed. Someone had stepped into the room.

"Ah," bragged Sam, with a subtle air of swagger in his step. "I see you've taken a look at some of my work. It was published just earlier this year."

Sam's sudden enthusiasm allowed Josik to quickly recompose himself. Well, mostly.

"Yes," Josik started uncertainly. He cleared his throat. "You seem very proud of your topic. Your writing has a very . . . optimistic, idealistic kind of tone."

The bubbliness in Sam's mannerisms abruptly dissipated, his gaze now fixed on the wall.

"I'm not sure proud would be the right word to use. There's not a whole lot this country has to be proud about these days."

Josik tightened a curious gaze on Sam.

"I'm afraid I wouldn't know."

"That's alright." Sam eased himself against the

wall he had eyed. "A lot of the people in this country don't even know either. Or, at the very least, they know about the problems but chose to ignore them or say that it's the other guy's fault. And that's what the politicians have to answer to. But I guess that's democracy, eh?"

"Eh?" sounded Josik awkwardly.

"Don't tell me you don't know what democracy is."

"I do, but uh . . . the people where I come from don't have much good to say about it."

It was true. The democratic process Josik learned about on Bohem was painted as the handmaiden of the exploitative, patriarchal, and classist pre-Authoritarian capitalist societies. Or at least those were the adjectives Josik could recall.

"Where do you come from?"

Josik scrambled for a moment in his mind for an answer. Sam seemed friendly and likeable, and Josik was too hungry and groggy to think straight—the traveler didn't want to confuse him right now with the outlandish truth. He thought of the praiseworthy places he remembered learning about in pre-Authoritarian history, hoped he'd be able to play it off.

"Cuba," Josik responded with as neutral an expression as he could muster. "You heard of it?"

"I have, but I've never met someone from there. I'm surprised you don't have more of an accent—fascinating! You'll have to tell me more about your experiences there."

Josik added nothing else in reply, nervously chuckling at the thought of his fake origins.

"Well, we have much to discuss, my friend," Sam exhaled, crossing his arms awkwardly, "But I'm also hungry, and I've had breakfast prepared for a while now. And you seem at least vaguely interested in this American government you've just started learning about, which I happen to know quite a bit about. So—

Yes, thought Josik, realizing for the first time in his life that he felt a sense of purpose in what he was doing. *I've come to the right place.*

"I'd love to learn more about it," Josik interrupted with a confident smile.

Sam seemed to brighten again. "Sure. Let me tell you all about it over breakfast."

They moved down the hall to the scenic nook at a round table, with some coffee and pastries ready to be consumed. Josik looked around quickly, noticing the blue-colored walls. On one side of the room there hung a wall clock and calendar. The calendar had several days of the month meticulously crossed off. The wall clock, with two hands and no numbers, ticked rather loudly. Near to both a wooden guitar with a dull sheen sat in its corner. Sam sighed in relief as Josik noticed these objects and the two of them both sat.

"Ah, where do I begin?"

Sam must have gushed on about democracy,

with all the rich history and political theory behind it—not to mention American politics, history, and government—for more than three hours. Josik simply sat, occasionally questioned, but primarily just absorbed.

By the time they were finished with this lecture, Josik sensed a need for a nap.

1-17

Josik, rather unusually, shot upright when he woke up in the hospital. The first thing he would have spotted was Maria at the foot of his bed, crouched over her elbows and knees in prayer. But of course, he was still blind in this dimension, so he could only detect her from her whispers and the unusual amount of weight on his bed. Still, Josik felt no embarrassment in asking, "What are you doing?"

"Oh, um . . . just the usual. Making some extra observations, that's all." She added a sheepish chuckle, totally unconvincing.

There was something about feeling her close presence, in calling her out on her obvious fib that was starting to make Josik wonder if he had been poisoned with some noxious gas. He started to feel every rapid heartbeat, the quivering in his lungs, and the burning sense of euphoria that went with it.

Maria was still looking to divert. She grasped his upper arm.

"For instance," she emphasized while introducing

him to his own appendage. "Do all of your people have such poorly-toned biceps?"

Josik only managed to shrug his shoulders. He was becoming infatuated for the first time, after all, and suddenly had lost his well-educated way with words. But alas, despite all the classroom lectures and propaganda regarding sexuality, life in Boehm offered no lessons in the act of courting. His current symptoms all pointed to nervousness, so he yanked his arm from Maria's clutch. She backed off and began walking toward the far side of the hut.

He needed to change to another subject, and quickly.

"So you're not at all curious about my last dream?"

"What did you think I was praying about?" she retorted.

"I'm sorry?"

"It took me a few hours after you fell asleep for me to remember the importance of dreams. Most don't mean much of anything, and some can help remind us of who we are deep down, our real desires and our real fears. Science has always questioned it, but some people who dream experience true visions in their sleep by forces outside of them. Biwun even told me about his, and then I realized that you were probably called to the same thing. We have a word for it here: the gift of sueña."

"And it's just him and I, the two who have received this. . . gift?" Josik thought the word "gift" was an overly generous description.

"Throughout history, people of our faith have been blessed with it. In fact, it even was responsible for saving our religion's founder once."

The word "religion" instinctively sounded alarm bells in Josik's head, a consequence of his upbringing. Still, he managed to restrain himself from speaking out of impulse. Maria, meanwhile, continued to rummage.

Moments later, he felt a heap of rough fabric tossed in his lap.

"What's this?" he asked.

"Some clothes. Put them on. We're gonna go for a walk."

Josik followed along and started feeling rather refreshed, despite his complete dependence on Maria. It was nice enough that he could change out of the plain white one-piece hospital gown for once. They weren't out for very long, but he could sense some of his strength returning. Bohem knew of no such concept as "going out," or even "fresh air" for that matter.

Yet his walking through the village square was a sorrowful reminder of his near-suicidal decision. For now, at least, he could not appreciate the appearance of the bustling, yet simple village market. He merely had to settle for its sounds and smells.

Maria was very attentive to his need for rest, so she changed the linens for Josik when they returned to the medical hut and directed him to bed. Despite his lingering conversations with her, he was asleep again within an hour.

When he awoke, Josik found himself at Sam's beach-house again. This time, he approached Sam by finding him at the dining table, as expected, with a breakfast layout of toast and fried eggs.

"I'm ready to begin my lessons," said Josik knowingly.

Sam rose from his seat rather majestically. He was wearing a plain short-sleeved shirt and jeans, which he took care to straighten.

"Then you are prepared to hear the truth of the so-called American experiment? Every brutal detail of it?"

Josik wasn't sure how brutal a single country's history could be, especially one that only lasted less than 300 years. Surely any of the atrocities lectured about in Bohem regarding the previous world orders were either highly exaggerated or entirely fabricated. So, he accepted the disclaimer.

"Yes. I'm ready to learn the truth."

"Very well. Have a seat. And eat up. We won't stop with lecture until we break for lunch a few hours in."

Josik rather disliked the constant sitting, but Sam's animated teaching style certainly kept him interested. Their first stop: American history, and to such detail that Sam would have likely taken several volumes if he ever chose to publish his own textbook about the subject.

Josik continued this back and forth journeying across dimensions for several days, never growing tired of his rhythm—for once, he was excited about his life. Breakfast and lecturing with Sam, learning more about Maria and Ispanian culture while being treated in the hospital, and the two people continued to come and go.

As the weeks went on, Josik noticed both Sam and Maria providing a greater range of activities. For Sam, they had begun taking long walks on the beach, with Josik taking care to appreciate every soft step he felt on the sand. Maria, however, was constrained by his handicap and started bringing him all forms of Ispanian food from her family's home, including the enchiladas and tostadas he particularly enjoyed.

Still, one thing about Sam nagged Josik. It was on one particularly well-rested morning of his that he resolved to ask.

First, they started walking to the north immediately after breakfast. He let the thought of the how to deliver the question roll around in his mind for a while before asking. Josik was seldom one to pry, but he finally resolved that there was no shame in asking.

"Sam?"

Sam kept his gaze forward.

"Why are you here by yourself?"

Sam simply kept walking, pretending that the steady coastal breeze had suddenly made conversation impossible.

Josik stopped for a moment. Nope, he thought.

There would be no figuring out this Sam for a while, or whatever fantasy place this was for that matter.

1-18

One day, when Josik awoke in Sam's realm, they discussed the American electoral system. At this point, Sam treated their lessons as more of a discussion rather than a lecture, He welcomed Josik's newfound sense of constant questioning. Josik rather enjoyed it too and had started to think himself a budding philosopher.

As usual, Sam had his whiteboard marker in hand, never failing to scribble notes and incredibly poor-quality diagrams on the board hanging behind him on the dining room wall.

He wrote and underlined the words *Electoral College* on the board. "As you will recall from our lecture on democracy, we learned that its basic principle rests on the idea that decisions in the country for its people are best made by its people."

"Yes," his pupil returned.

"But we also discussed how a pure democracy cannot work in practice because decision-making becomes impossible if everyone has to vote on every decision the government is planning to make. For this reason, all countries that are considered democratic also have a republican form of government, whereby leaders are elected by the people to make decisions on behalf of the people."

"Yes, I recall."

"And we've also briefly discussed the importance of elections in American history, and I've also briefly mentioned the Electoral College. We're going to spend today talking about American elections at the federal level."

"Okay. Proceed." Josik stored his note-taking pen on top of his ear.

"There are two kinds of elected office at the federal level, if you'll recall."

"Yes."

"Repeat them, please."

"For Congress and for the presidency."

"Very good. And how often is an election held for each office?"

"Every two years for the House, six for the Senate, and four for the Presidency."

"Good boy." Sam tossed Josik a Tootsie Roll, which Josik didn't care for much anyway.

"Now the House holds elections for its members by individual Congressional districts, whereas the

Senate has elections on a statewide level. The rule for winning in the general election is simple—whichever candidate gets the greatest number of votes wins. But the rules for electing the President are a lot more complicated and are just barely constitutional, or are at least a gross corruption of the original design."

"Okay."

"According to the Constitution, a body called the Electoral College is supposed to elect the President. This was actually one of the smaller compromises made at the Convention between those who desired a directly-elected President and others who thought he should be chosen by Congress or some other branch of government."

"Interesting."

"It's hardly even the interesting part, if you want to give it that compliment. Originally, the electors in the Electoral College would be voted into office by the public. The Electoral College would in turn be the only ones to cast ballots for the various presidential candidates. So, the people, according to the original design of the government, only indirectly elected the President."

"Okay. So, what's the point?"

"Getting to it." Sam quickly wiped his brow out of his nervous teaching habit. He added two bullet points, the first reading *original design* and the second pointing towards three boxes—the first one representing the *electorate* pointed to the *Electoral College* box on its right, and this second box pointed to yet another box on the right reading *President.*

Sam continued. "Since the original creation of America's constitutional government, the procedure of the Electoral College, and thus the presidential election process, has changed quite a bit, and arguably for the worse. With the Electoral College system, each state elects a number of electors equal to the number of members they have in the House of Representatives, in addition to their two senators. Over time, these electors came to agree on giving up their independence in voting for whichever presidential candidate they thought of best according to personal discretion. Instead, they agreed that each state's entire delegation of electors would throw all of their votes to the candidate receiving the greatest number of votes in their respective state."

"Wait, what? I thought the presidential election wasn't supposed to have everyday people voting in it."

"Well, yes, but technically it doesn't. As the American political system evolved to work as a more 'democratic process,' a popular vote was included. What so few Americans understood, however, is that the average citizen is not actually voting for his/her desired candidate when checking the box next to a name: they are actually voting for the set of electors pre-selected by the corresponding candidate's political party."

"That sounds quite complicated."

"That's one way to put it."

"So, what makes it such an awful system?"

"Aha!" he projected, nearly launching his whiteboard marker across the room with a finger pointed upward. "The problem is threefold. The first is that the current system goes against the Electoral College's intended design as agreed upon by the framers of the Constitution. Which is bad if you agreed with the average framer's worry that too much direct democracy subjected the system to too much of the changing whims of the people. Another part of it is the 'winner take all' concept that all but a few states follow. A candidate could win a bare plurality of actual votes, but still win all of the state's electoral votes. It makes the 'losing' voters within a state feel utterly unimportant in a presidential election. But the biggest part of the problem with the current arrangement creates far more obvious dysfunction—it places all of the importance on so-called 'battleground states' whose leanings towards one major candidate or the other are uncertain and their number of electoral votes are significant. So, the candidates end up spending most of their time and energy campaigning and crafting a message towards those states' needs, and the rest of the country is largely ignored because many other states are considered to be in the pocket of one candidate or the other. Most of all, it actually makes it possible to win the electoral vote but not the popular vote, which has happened in several elections throughout history."

"You keep mentioning this 'one or the other' thing. Are there only two candidates in these elections?"

"Technically the answer is no. But the American system has a funny way of making people consolidate into the fewest number of factions as possible. You see it throughout our history—Federalists versus Anti-Federalists, North versus South, Democrats and Republicans. More or less the same kinds of factions, just with different names."

Josik needed some time to let the information sink in again. He was getting better at the retention, certainly, but still needed to take a thoughtful pause every once in a while. Josik thought he noticed Sam leaning slightly toward him, eager to hear his next thought.

"So, if the Electoral College is so awful, why is it still around? Why hasn't it been changed?"

Sam took an unusual moment to ruminate on his answer.

"The Electoral College could only be reformed by changing the Constitution. There's a very high level of consensus required to change the Constitution, and I think that's fair. Heck, even simple changes to public policy through legislation seems impossible these days. But I'd also point out that the country has been able to make good decisions in the past, even under the system's inherently conservative design. There are also ways that the individual states can and have reformed in the past, paving the way for national consensus. There's a silver lining in that at least. At the end of the day, even a good system can still be doomed to fail if the people in it don't get along. Our current two-party system is special in that it's helped to create a society where division and disagreement are encouraged as part of everyday political life."

"Then why not do what it takes to change it?"

"I don't have much of an answer to that question. I think that gets to the very heart of the problem. Special interests, especially business groups and activist millionaires, spend a lot of resources to maintain the status quo when it comes to policy. But as it is, Americans don't seem interested in driving the change they want because it requires them to get along, especially when part of the country is convinced that they're right because God told them so—another part is convinced that reason and science has all the answers."

Sam continued, was so riled up now that he rushed into his next thought.

"And you may have started wondering what become of these elections," he half-shouted through a frustrated cherry-red complexion. "I honestly don't know what's become of them, and the majority of people have lost faith in the system. Most strain to remember a time when there were such strictly-set rules to the game, the demands of political correctness. It was even the stuff of parody. And now, for the last twenty years, we asininely put ourselves through a self-inflicted ordeal of picking between the less obvious of two evils."

Josik could feel his face warm. The gravity of this moment in history he was not just learning, but of which he was being physically immersed, was beginning to sink in.

"How do your people rationalize this?" he dared to ask.

"Most just don't bother to vote. Some of the few who do these days just want their side to win at all costs. And the rest want a different option, but are still convinced that the alternative can't win and that they'll risk wasting their vote. It doesn't help that the third-party candidates have incredibly unworkable ideas too. Once it's Election Day, we pick the candidate who's the least bad example of leadership and everyone holds their breath for the future of the country. The side that wins gets their turn at imposing their ideological agenda on the whole country instead of leaving those decisions to the local people. Then we stop caring through the midterm Congressional elections until the four years are up—and the whole cycle starts up again."

Josik waited for his instructor to take in some calming breaths. He rather disliked this pessimism. For if America was as awful and dysfunctional as Sam just described, how was the Bohemx version of history he had learned not justified?

Josik could see it now in Sam—he was wallowing in despair, as demonstrated by his removed spectacles and slumping against a vase table.

"It certainly can't be that bad," said Josik. "There has to be some kind of hopeful point to all of this."

Sam stubbornly shook his head.

"Listen, if a negative person like yourself can even admit that this place was once some great nation, then what will it take to make it great again?"

Sam let out a modest chuckle in response.

"There was someone who claimed he had the answer to that question many years ago, back when the big part of this current mess started. You might even say that he started the beginning of the end."

"I'm just trying to be optimistic," Josik retorted. "There has to be a better answer than that. I refuse to believe otherwise."

And that's when Sam broke, his frustration becoming unchained.

"There is nothing to be optimistic about!" he shouted. "You've read my first chapter—every country has its end, and America is no different. Just look at Rome, Greece, the Venetian Republic! They were all democracies in some way, and the people just squandered those freedoms. Hell, it's a miracle America didn't do the same years ago."

Josik returned with a shocked stare.

"What reason do I have to be optimistic? There is none. I become more and more convinced with each passing headline I hear over the radio. There's no one who can be looked up to for a way out. First, the public failed in its democratic duty. They fell asleep at the wheel and let the experts do all the driving for them for decades. Then the leaders failed in response; all they care about is getting reelected. And the media failed by playing along with the game for the sake of ratings. This country is at its end, Josik."

"Is that why you're here now, away from everyone?" Josik said accusingly. "To wait it out, not even try to change it?"

Sam's hand went over his face. "Get out."

Josik let some silence pass, shocked. The ticking from the wall clock filled the void, building up his discomfort.

"I couldn't hear you. What?"

"Get . . . out. Now."

Josik wasn't sure whether to feel guilty or resentful. Regardless, he promptly walked out the door and threw himself underneath a nearby palm tree, determined to get away from this place.

1-19

Josik woke up again to a black canvas, but something was different this time. He couldn't hear, nor sense Maria in the room.

Just great, he thought. *She probably hates me too.*

Fortunately, she had simply gone away from his bed to get some more clean linens. Although he found it odd that she'd only acknowledge him with a simple "hey."

"Don't tell me you hate me now, too," accidentally speaking his mind.

"Lo siento?" she queried. "Ah, I'm sorry?"

"Yeah, I'm sure you are."

"No, I mean I'm sorry as in 'I didn't hear you the first time.' "

"I'm sure you know what I'm referring to."

"Josik, you don't have to play these silly games with me. I really have no idea what you're talking about."

Josik would have rolled his eyes if he wasn't still blind. He sighed instead.

"I don't have time for this," she exasperated, moseying for the exit.

But Josik stopped her in her tracks.

"Maria, wait."

She acknowledged Josik with a huff. "What?" she declared.

"I'm . . . sorry," he confessed awkwardly, realizing that this was his second lifetime attempt at an apology. "Again. I've been acting like a selfish jerk these past couple days. And an idiotic, selfish jerk at that."

"Josik, I've been a nurse for a little over four years. If anyone's patient enough to deal with your self-centered Bohemx upbringing, it's people of my kind."

"Guess it's gonna be a while until I learn not to be so selfish."

Maria sat on the bed and gently massaged Josik's scalp. "Give yourself some credit. Nobody can be blamed for feeling a bit spiteful for losing their sight."

"Maybe that's just the way it's supposed to be. Maybe I'm supposed to learn that I'm better off without it."

"Now don't say that. God should give you back your sight any day now. At least that's what my medical readings have suggested."

But Josik felt surprisingly indifferent to gaining his

sight back. After all, without it, he would never have to see the kinds of horrors that he had witnessed ever again.

"Come on, let's go out for a walk," she urged.

Josik followed, his other heightened senses taking in the calming bustle of the village square again as they wandered for what seemed like hours. Based on the sun's gentle heat he felt when they walked in the streets, he figured winter was over. According to Maria's explanation of the changing seasons of the year during one of the many conversations they had had in the hospital, it was spring. Still, despite his senses being engaged, Josik found his mind distracted from the task. He thought back to the bad terms on which he had left Sam.

He gave Maria's arm a subtle tug to the side. They both stopped.

"Yes?" she asked.

"What's the word you use to describe when people disagree?"

"You mean a disagreement?" she replied sarcastically.

"No, it was something more complicated than that. The type where people get really angry."

"Oh. You mean an argument."

"Right. That's the word I was trying to remember."

"Why were you trying to remember it?"

Josik could start to feel a hot wave of embarrassment wash over. "I think I might have had one in these dreams—well, I guess they're more like visions—I've been having."

"And you're asking me what to do?"

"Yeah, pretty much."

Maria prefaced her response with an affectionate touch of her hand to the side of his face.

"Just do what you've been practicing these past few weeks, Josik. Have some humility, don't think of an apology as a sign of weakness, and just be honest. It's just about how any relationship works. That doesn't mean constantly giving your ground, but it does take some effort to keep your personal desires in check."

"You think I've been acting humble lately?" said Josik sarcastically.

"Well . . . you're getting there. I've been impressed with your progress; I'll leave it at that."

Josik laughed modestly in response. Causing a humorous reaction seemed to be Maria's forte.

Though Josik hadn't perceived it, they had arrived at a small restaurant. He heard something slide across the table towards him after he sat, the delicious aroma filling his nostrils.

"Go on, take a bite," Maria urged.

"Take a bite of what?" Josik said. "Where are we?"

"It's called a restaurante," she responded. "It's where people go to eat food that's better than anything they're capable of cooking at home."

This certainly sounded more pleasant than what was offered at the hospital, which usually consisted of nothing more than bread or tortillas, some meat and cheese, and tomatoes or other local vegetable. He wasn't complaining though—nearly any type of Earth fare beat the highly processed, synthesized edibles to be found on Bohem.

Josik placed his hand down on the table, worked it over to what Maria called carne asada tacos. Feeling the corn tortillas and its meaty complements made him realize he was eating a dish unlike anything he had previously experienced.

"How the earth am I supposed to eat this?" he said aloud.

Maria sighed in good jest. "Here," she said while reaching over to his plate.

"Now what do I do?"

"Take a bite, carefully, and don't chomp off my fingers."

His heightened sense of taste afforded from his blindness made the first bite of the meal even more incredible than Josik could have expected. The combined taste of grain, pork, and bitter herbs was all the education Josik needed to understand the logic of Ispanian cuisine.

"Now you try handling it." She transferred the small taco over to his right hand.

He quickly learned that the trick to preserving the taco's diverse tastes lay in keeping its flavorful package within the protection of the relatively small tortilla. Still, that didn't stop him from feeling a strange viscous liquid run down his forearm.

Maria quickly took notice, as she could be heard giggling at Josik's every step.

"You may want to let that go on the plate," she advised.

"What is it, exactly?"

"It's called 'grease' in English. Us locals call it 'grasa'. I'm guessing Bohemian food doesn't have that either?"

"Nope. I wouldn't exactly call our stuff 'food', though. Actually, we don't use the adjective 'Bohemian'. We refer to anything that is "'of Bohem' as Bohemx."

"That's weird. Why is that?"

"Using the prefix '-ian' has connotations to the word 'man,' which carries a lot of negative meaning in our society. So, we replace it with the gender-neutral prefix of '-x.' "

Maria leaned in closer, putting her own dish aside. "Josik, I know you still speak about your life on that space station a lot. I've seen how much of your identity it's formed. But I can also see how everything it's taught you doesn't fit with who you are. Bohem isn't your home. There's a reason that you found our people, and we want you to be a part of us. If you're willing, we will teach you more about our simple life. We use just one word to describe it: *agape*. Our people have been practicing it for generations and it has bound us together in love and happiness."

Josik scoffed, recalling his broken relationship with Meset.

"You don't think I'm too white-skinned and lighter-haired to be a part of your village?" he retorted.

"No," she said. "Every one of us here is an equal before God. We Ispanians judge each other by our deeds and how we care for one another, not by our origins or our past."

"Josik," Maria continued. "Your own people banished you. It seems like they don't want you to be a part of them. I'm saying you should let that go and choose a people who are willing to accept you."

Josik's unseeing eyes watered. At least they were good for something at this time. He was touched.

"Thank you," he said with a sniffle. "How do I start?"

"You already have," declared Maria confidently. "Next you will learn more about our people's faith. It's not strictly required, but we want you to be a part of our church."

Despite all his education on the vices of religion, this was a price Josik was willing to take.

"I accept," he stated.

Maria responded to the good news with a warm hug, although Josik was unsure how to respond (especially with his greasy fingers). Such physical gestures were still foreign to him.

With some *cervezas* to complement their meal, the two enjoyed some mindless chatter until after sundown. Afterwards, they returned to the hospital for sleep, with Josik determined to make things right in the other dimension.

1-20

Josik woke up in the past at precisely the spot he had forced himself to sleep, underneath a palm tree in the sand. It had seemed he was only asleep for a few hours according to this version of the world. The day had not yet ended and it was just before sunset.

This time he had been awoken by the dark cloudy skies and strong wind. A storm was coming, and Josik would have been wise to seek shelter. Within a few minutes, he was back at the beach-house, and the last bit of sunlight had left the sky.

Josik knocked. No answer. He jiggled the doorknob to discover it was left unlocked. He walked inside and found all the windows covered in plywood. He finally encountered Sam walking out of his bedroom with a few fully weighted boxes in hand.

"Listen, Sam, I wanted to say I'm sorry," started Josik.

Sam cut him off. "There's no time to talk. A hurricane is passing through within a few hours. Grab a box and let's get going."

The two were out the door within minutes, with Josik managing to grab the two books from his bedroom. Sam had a small shelter built into one of the nearby cliffs, as hurricanes, he explained, were a common annual occurrence. It wasn't much, with its size approximating a prison cell. Fortunately, Sam had enough experience to make sure a separate closet-size bathroom was included this time, even if it was just a simple, deep hole in the ground.

"It was pretty bad the first time a storm rolled through here after I moved in," he noted while zipping up the front entrance. "I had to resort to a re-closable plastic bag and no toilet paper for about two days. Let's just say things got pretty uncomfortable."

Josik chuckled. Thanks to Maria, he was an acute sufferer of a sense of humor.

"And I do accept your apology. Truth be told, I really deserve the blame. You're my guest and my student, and you don't deserve to be spoken to like that."

"I accept your apology," said Josik hesitantly. He hadn't expected to be on the receiving end.

Sam had the foresight to prepare some pasta before leaving the house, so the two took a moment to eat in silence. They were too troubled to talk, watching the larger waves forming outside the makeshift window sewn into the thick canvas, protecting the front of the shelter.

Finally, it was Sam who sought to ease the fear in the room with conversation.

"There are two big hazards with a hurricane. The first are the intense winds, which can sweep up deadly debris through the streets. But the larger one that applies to us is something called storm surge. The winds can push large waves on shore that have the potential to flood whole cities. In our case, just a few feet of storm surge could sweep away the entire house."

"How has it managed to survive so many storms?"

"No hurricane has ever come close enough to cause enough damage. I just hope and pray really hard every time, and somehow, miraculously, it always seems to work out."

"That's incredible," Josik commented.

Sam put his plastic container back in a box, still half-full of food. He wasn't very hungry, after all. Josik, in the meantime, felt it was time to change the subject.

"Is there anything else I should learn about American politics?"

"That's for sure," scoffed Sam. "It has a pretty screwed-up history in many regards."

"How do you mean?"

"Hmm . . . where do I begin? The Declaration of Independence declaring that 'all men are created equal' when many of the Founding Fathers condoned the practice of slavery, and even owned slaves? The numbers of Native American tribes driven off their lands in the name of the apparently divinely determined 'Manifest Destiny'? The war we provoked Mexico to start so we could take the northern half of its land? The war we provoked Spain to start so we could take its land? The African Americans we discriminated against, the Chinese we exploited to build our railroads, and the gays we scientifically designated as feeble-minded? It's downright hypocrisy, is what it is."

"But it's also your past," Josik objected, trying to find something defensible against the Bohemx version of history. "I don't doubt what you're saying is true, but didn't you eventually learn that that was wrong?"

"Well, yes," Sam responded after a deep sigh. "That's true."

"I'm not trying to argue that your country is perfect," Josik explained. "If you just consider where I come from, America seems an earth-uva lot better. Your people seem to keep learning and move past the injustices."

Josik marveled at his own words for a moment, realizing that he was unconsciously referring to his Bohemx citizenship in a manner that Sam hadn't detected. He remembered that Sam still thought he was from the place called Cuba.

"And I would agree. For the most part. So many more of our people once had a spirit of improvement. There was engagement in their communities, whether that'd be in a church, service club, or some other local organization. As a result, state and local politics were considered so much more important. The faraway Feds were only supposed to interfere when absolutely necessary."

They were back to the meaty political science-type lectures again. Josik was engaged.

"Then, in the 1960s, a Pandora's box opened. Federal government intervention in the areas of education, poverty, and anti-discrimination were needed. Yet it wasn't long before its reach proliferated. The drinking age, standardized testing, healthcare—the federal government developed standards in these areas and more and found ways to impose them on the individual states. It took away responsibility for social problems away from the state and local governments, and thus made those local authorities less important. Voter turnout in local elections have plummeted over the decades as a result, and somehow the people of this country thought it was better to start debating all issues at a national level ever since."

"I thought you said that the people were to blame, not the government."

"It's both who are to blame, I've concluded. That's the part a lot of commentators these days choose to forget. In a representative democracy like America's, what the government does is a reflection of the people. Certainly, there are politicians and groups that have been pointing out for years now whenever it seems a bureaucracy is going against the wishes of the people. But there are some times that these fears are overblown and used to partisan advantage. A newly-elected president may have an enterprising new political solution based on decades of personal career-work in a policy area, but the opposition can so easily use today's technology and tools to almost instantly whip up skepticism and opposition from the masses, regardless of the solution's merits. While elections are inherently democratic and majoritarian, the policymaking system still remains disconnected from public opinion because it primarily caters to business and special interests, the only actors who have the resources necessary to capture constant attention. But again, none of this behavior would be considered okay if the people didn't allow it. Populists rarely talk about real solutions and make their message about taking down their enemy. The election almost twenty years ago was the very starting point where this erratic populism became an established force in the system. In fact, it now has its own political parties."

"You keep bringing up this election from nearly twenty years ago. In 2016?"

"Yes."

"Why was that so important? What were its results?"

"The explanation is far too complicated to explain it all today."

"I've got time," Josik said through a smirk.

"You have to trust me on this one, Josik. I know you say that your faith in this country hasn't been shaken, but telling you the story of the 2016 election will certainly do that. It's how—" he cut himself off. "Anyway. I will explain it to you some other day."

"Okay." It was all Josik was willing to say in response. He was deeply curious, but didn't want to risk starting up another argument.

"I'm sorry to do that to you."

Josik stood up and laid his hand on Sam's shoulder.

"It's okay. I trust you."

Sam responded with a weak smile, the first such one Josik had ever seen. And Josik responded with his own friendly smile in turn. Josik could feel his heart lift in the moment, his spirit coming to life as never before. He had spread some good will.

But the happy moment did not last for long. His body, instantaneously aching for slumber, dropped to its knees and fell over in sleep.

1-21

Josik woke up again from where he had left off. But there was an important difference. He could see again.

He failed to contain his joy, running up and down the main corridor of the hospital indefatigably, his body once again able to navigate. Maria arrived within a minute or two from her compact sleeping quarters within the building, and Josik charged her with a hug at full speed. She didn't mind in the slightest, the intense happiness of the moment spreading to her infectiously.

"¡Gracias a Dios!" she cried after pulling him outside of the hospital shack, hopping excitedly in tandem with Josik. "¡Gracias a Dios!"

"What does that mean?" Josik shouted.

"I'm thanking God!" she proclaimed. "He's given you your sight back!"

Josik could have chosen to air his usual Bohemx-taught skepticism. Instead, he chose to accept the inexplicably boundless joy of the moment.

"Yes!" he spoke back up to the impeccably azure sky above him. "Thank you, God!"

***

Josik spent the rest of the day moving out of the hospital. He once again had no further need to be medically monitored or treated, and he was determined to start a new life. Josik quickly realized that Maria would be indispensable in helping him start over, and he was determined to hear her every word to him. She still lived with her immediate family in a large brick house just a few hundred yards away from the hospital. Her parents graciously allowed Josik to set up sleeping quarters in their guest room. This didn't consist of much more than an eight-foot by eight-foot space, a wooden bed frame, a small opening in the brick to the outside for light, and an animal hide for a door, but the generosity it represented was well-appreciated.

Josik laid out the linens given to him from Maria's mother, then took a moment to sit up on the mattress. Like his quarters on Bohem, his new bedroom was a tight space. Yet there was so much more warmth he felt in this place, a true sense of belonging with these welcoming people. He was becoming part of a family in his new life as an Ispanian, even though his life on Bohem knew of no such concept. Josik's single parent was a geneticist working 9-5 in a laboratory, his siblings the thousands of ovaries fertilized by the same sperm donor.

Maria eventually found Josik and directed him to her family's *salón*, where her parents were seated on a coarsely upholstered couch, waiting intently.

"Um . . . hola," Josik said hesitantly.

Both of Maria's parents—with their dark hair, eyes, and complexions and patterned ponchos—glanced at each other, apparently unimpressed.

After a few seconds of this, they burst out laughing.

"You're alright, Josik," Maria's father, Manuel, said as he stood with a grin and his spectacled half-head of hair peppered with gray, giving Josik a generous pat on the back. "You don't have to worry at all about our English."

"I don't believe I properly introduced myself earlier. I'm Clarita, Maria's mother." She offered her outstretched arms, which took an awkward pause for Josik to give proper response. Like her husband, she was somewhat wrinkled and was not afraid for others to notice the various gray threads in her long, otherwise jet-black hair. He still found the female tradition of hugging in this village nerve-wracking, although it did carry a soothing after-effect. The Ispanians were not ones to give cheap hugs.

"You'll have to forgive us for our little act," Manuel added. "We've made it standard practice when it comes to meeting any of Maria's new novios."

"Papa!" interjected Maria. "It's not like that. At least for now."

Maria stopped herself, flashed a panicked look towards Josik.

"Never mind what I said."

Fortunately, Josik had not yet come across romance-related terminology in the Spanish language. Maria's embarrassment was entirely lost on him, so he said nothing and grinned awkwardly.

Dinner was also ready to be served, and here, Josik met Maria's two sisters and three brothers, all of whom were more than five years younger than her. Thus, the table maintained two separate conversation circles according to age level. Josik resorted to keeping silent, as mealtime conversation was still a new custom to him, as was the thought of containing such a large number of genetically similar people all under the same roof. He took delight in hearing Clarita reminisce about the more embarrassing aspects of Maria's childhood, many of which revolved around her unfortunate first attempts at "surgery" on her siblings, and usually involved details about some loose rags and a pair of kitchen shears on early Saturday mornings before her parents had stirred. Besides, Josik was also fixated on the delicious meal of *pollo enchiladas,* black beans, and tomatoes laid before him. Ispanian life certainly wasn't rich in amenities by Bohemx standards, but they definitely knew how to eat well. As a consequence of their culture, Josik jokingly justified in his mind, Maria's parents learned just the basics about him—he used to be one of the strange space people who lived on Bohem, he was sent to "experience" Earth just a few months ago, and his travels left him sustaining some substantial injuries. And that's just how he hoped to keep it, considering how gory and depraved many of the other details were.

" 'Sent' and 'experience' is stretching it a bit," Maria objected. "And your injuries were a bit more than substantial."

"Nothing I couldn't endure in the end," Josik said, meaning to counter sarcastically. But a bit of his Bohemx self-centeredness affected his inflection, and Maria rolled her eyes in annoyed response.

But the good humor at the table soon returned, with Manuel continuing the story of Maria's discovered passion for nursing from his perspective.

"I hadn't thought education was much of a thing around here," Josik interrupted at one point in the story, his growing fatigue and full belly turning him more sociable.

"Well, yes," replied Manuel. "The religious people of the church have been pushing it for as long as we can remember. Having a well-educated pool from which they find people with callings to the religious life is in their interest, among other things."

Around 9:00pm (which Josik now knew converted to 2100 in his traditional Bohemx time), Maria's siblings were sent to bed. The conversation between the remaining four must have last only a little more than an hour more, as it evolved into a casual Spanish lesson for Josik.

Then the rest of the table adjourned, with Josik nearly stumbling back to his room to get some sleep. His adventures in the American dimension were far from his mind as he fell asleep. And yet, they didn't continue that night. Josik woke up late the next morning, well-rested from his first dreamless sleep in a long time.

He stepped out of his room into an empty house. The children were away at school and the three adults of the family at work. He quickly ate a flour tortilla he dripped with honey, then headed over to the hospital, where he had arranged to meet Maria for lunch. The two went out for lunch again, with Josik ordering the same pair of tacos. He thought it was only right to give its experience to all five of his senses this time.

Afterwards, Maria went back to work and Josik to the house. But Maria had a bit of news before they parted ways again.

"Meet me at the bar tonight at seven," she said.

"¿Por qué?" he responded, attempting to show off his emerging bilingualism.

"It's a surprise. There's only one way our town spends los jueves, and that's to celebrate it. And make sure to dress up."

Josik showed up at the appointed place and time, finding his way through a crowd of townspeople dressed in their finest. He wasn't sure how the Ispanians defined "dressing up," so his plain, blue collared shirt and baggy black pants stood in contrast to everyone else there. The rest of the group wore a mix of brightly colored dresses, dress shirts, and vests. Some other sported bright blue jeans and tall boots. An ambitious few of the men boasted bowties.

Everyone was also wearing a pair of closed-toe

shoes, which was unusual by Ispanian standards. Josik knew these people generally enjoyed keeping their feet exposed to the elements. After all, it was also why so few of the village buildings were built with any flooring.

Josik and Maria found each other quickly, as the latter of the two was wearing a simple sleeveless red dress. Extending just above her knees, Josik found it hard not to notice how the garment curved around her rounded hips, a thin V-shaped opening pointing out a small length of her sturdy back. Her long black hair flowed freely instead of being up in its usual bun; her smile was wide and radiant.

"Wow," was all he could manage. "You look great."

"You're not too bad either. Ready to dance?"

Such a word didn't exist in Bohemish vocabulary.

"I have no clue what that is," he answered with a chuckle.

"C'mon, I'll show you. Just follow my lead."

The crowd was gathered under a large awning-type structure, topped with a sturdy roof of corrugated metal that was supported by many large pine trunks all around the sides of its eaves. On its underside was a large circular electric lamp—one of the few in the village, as a matter of fact. This was used to ensure the townspeople could enjoy their Thursday night well into the first parts of the Friday to come.

Within a few minutes, the town's band set up

in a corner next to the bar, armed with fiddles and dressed smartly in dress shirts, pants, and bolo ties. As much as Josik would have liked to have taken in his first experience of live music from them, he had other priorities this evening. These mainly consisted of minimizing his step on Maria's feet, as well as his constant bumping into other dance couples as she walked him through various kinds of line and square dance.

Maria finally allowed Josik a five-minute break outside of the crowd once they were finished.

"Holy crap!" he shouted, slightly deafened from the country music. "This dancing thing must be considered some kind of intense sport around here."

"Surprisingly not, actually," she said. "Most of us used to think of it more as a kind of delicate, touchy art form. Fortunately, most of the people put away their aversion to dance once we started organizing these regularly. That idea is courtesy of yours truly."

Their return to the dance floor gave some opportunities for Josik to be more casual, as the band announced that they would play the Ispanian version of the "classics"—namely, what twenty-first century society would call "popular music." Josik tried to look to the other people in the crowd for social cues on how to move to the genre, but his observations were in vain. Unlike the previous part of the evening, it seemed everyone had their own style to try out, some moving better in tempo with the music than others. Josik, unfortunately, was on the lower end of this spectrum, as he simply and awkwardly shifted his body from side to side.

Maria offered no criticism after all of the line dancing she had just put him through. She could tell he was gradually enjoying and feeling the beat better as the night wore on.

The bar band eventually transitioned to some slower jazz music as the evening drew to a close, trading their instruments for saxophones, other brass instruments, and one even taking to a drum. The crowd followed with the changing mood of night. Josik found himself, along with the rest of the room, gently swaying with his partner in a close embrace. The atmosphere was quiet enough to carry a normal conversation again.

Josik peered around aimlessly at one point.

"How'd you do that?" he asked.

"Do what?" Maria replied with a grin.

"The room. It feels so calm and peaceful all of a sudden."

"A philosopher once said that life without music would be a mistake. It might surprise you how much good it can do for the world. Practically a gift from above."

Something else tangentially related came to Josik's mind.

"I've been thinking a bit lately about how you mentioned the whole religion thing to me the other day. I'm not sure how I feel about it. I'm not sure I believe it all."

Maria reacted with an intense focus on Josik.

"There's nothing wrong with that, Josik. Your faith starts with you and God. No one else can change that for you. But we are here to support you when you're ready to learn more. In fact, this whole village is here to support you."

"Thank you," he said through a smile.

"You're welcome." She grasped Josik's left hand, interweaving the fingers on her right hand between his.

Josik smiled even wider. Maria stared at him and smiled widely back.

For once, in that moment, Josik didn't struggle to look a person in the eyes. In fact, it was all he wanted to do.

Their sway was now a complete afterthought, replaced with idle stepping back and forth.

"Have you been wondering—" he started, but then his thought was interrupted.

The sounds of gunshots instantly broke apart the sereneness of the moment. A band of white, blonde-haired men rushed through the dance floor within seconds. Josik didn't hear any more shots, although his senses were overwhelmed by the sounds of the crowds running and screaming in blood-curdling panic.

He found his way out of the awning and could hear more gunshots. He kept reaching his hand back, hoping to feel Maria at the other end. But she was not even seen or heard as Josik navigated the mob.

Josik escaped into a grove of nearby trees. Within moments, it was apparent what had happened to Maria. As he rushed back to her family's house, he spotted the horse-drawn carriages galloping through at a distance. He could hear the shrieking women, as the men in rough overalls tied and gagged them.

He snatched the lantern left outside of the house's entryway, rushed into Manuel and Clarita's master bedroom. Both of them shot awake upright, sharply inhaling in the process.

"Josik," Manuel said, giving himself a moment for his grogginess to wear off. "Where's Maria?"

"She's been taken," he said, in between shallow breaths and a racing pulse. "Kidnapped. But I know exactly where to."

END OF PART 1

PART II

BLUE WALL

PROLOGUE #2

From Chapter 2 of Usami's The Decline and Fall of American Democracy, *titled "Tear Down the (Blue) Wall: The Implications of the 2016 Election"*:

They called it the Blue Wall: the white, poor to middle-class, working class voters of the formerly industrial Midwest and Appalachia. For decades, their interests were considered in line with that of the liberal Democratic Party, on account of economic policy and the political faction's alignment with trade unions.

However, in 2016, expectations that this Blue Wall would hold were shattered and torn down, just as the Wall itself was torn down. Analysts claimed, and protected classes of voters agreed, that the populist presidential candidate of that fateful year could never hope to win their votes with his obtuse, zero-sum, and divisive rhetoric. Yet the populist nationalist won, and a new political movement suddenly gained credibility overnight.

This parallels the event of the Blue Wall's collapse to that of another wall torn down not too long ago:

the Berlin Wall of 1989. Like America's Blue Wall, the collapse of Berlin's Wall had been building up for decades through a combination of social and economic dynamics poorly handled by a dysfunctional regime. But the tale of the two walls also represent contrasting bookends of an optimistic, promising period of American history: at its beginning, the apparent triumph of democracy and Western institutions in the face of the collapse of totalitarian Communist regimes; at its end, a retreat from America's role as a promoter of freedom and international cooperation in the world, and a dismissal of democratic norms and institutions as weak and obstructive of progress.

In short, the collapse of the Blue Wall began a new historical period not anticipated by the educated elites, well-sheltered in their own bubbles by America's now-monstrous inequality. It was not the age of widespread democracy, or "end of history" as some experts had erroneously predicted in the post-Cold War period. Rather, it was the Age of Nationalist-Populism, which questioned modern democracy with the incorporation of rhetoric and practices more in line with authoritarian regimes.

America's political outlook in resisting Nationalist-Populism did not look very promising with the development of the millennial generation into full adulthood in the 2010s. Many of them, burdened by their poor economic circumstances, were persuaded by a left-wing variant of Nationalist-Populism: a new movement that emerged after 2016 known as the People's Party, clearly aligned with the socialist rhetoric that would have dissuaded them had the Cold

War still existed. But unlike previous generations, the millennials did not know of the existential threat to personal and economic freedoms that communist and socialist ideology presented. Nor did they understand and experience social discord and hardship as their parents had, at least for those millennials who grew up in households that were well-off. As such, the rise of right-wing Nationalist-Populism among the older, working-class whites and their victory in 2016 took millennials entirely by surprise.

The millennial generation after 2016 would form the plurality of America's electorate, which necessitates a new sense of social responsibility to them. A willingness to sacrifice and respect for the ways of America's past would need to be developed among them. This chapter explores how this did not happen (i.e. mainly due to inadequate voter participation), and its contribution to future "Blue Wall" events in American history.

2-1

One day, Bohem hosted a secret visitor, unbeknownst to its general public. A shuttle from Earth was discreetly docked in one of the station's ports in its northwest region around 0920.

An audience gathered shortly afterward between the three-person Authoritarian Consulate and one of Earth's most powerful leaders. It was the Big-League Maga of Averita, the American continent's largest faction.

The Maga met with the Consulate in one of the Authoritarian, fluorescently lit boardrooms. As was his style, he entered the room with a smug grim, removed his trademark top hat, and greeted the three each with a firm embrace of the right hand and lower forearm. Despite his thin, long, slicked-back hair, it was not hard to find the Maga influential, if not outright intimidating. Perhaps it was his pitch-black suit and tattered red tie, which contrasted with the unremarkable tight gray full-body robes worn by the Consulate.

Unfortunately, the Consulate was unmoved by the

Maga's attempts to influence through sheer force of personality. They simply settled into their three stiff steel chairs at the table, ultimately forcing the blond-haired one to take his on the other side as well. The grin was gone now, his expression overly dour. The Maga was all business and he was ready to cut a deal.

The dirty-blond haired Consul, seated at left, was the first to break the silence.

"You know why we requested you here today," they said snootily. "The North American continent is becoming unrulier and more unstable among the factions. And your latest military shenanigans don't help in the slightest."

The Big-League Maga eyed these words skeptically. He was in no mood to apologize for his recent political successes. After all, Averita was the largest empire to have been formed on Planet Earth since the early part of the second millennium.

"What you say are 'shenanigans.'" he mocked, "my people say is survival. These towns, in the Midwestern region—they've been living in hell. For decades, centuries, they've been in famine, poverty, attacked by outsiders. And then *I* said: 'No more.' From the lake cities to all the little mountain towns, we brought the people together."

The blonde Consul interjected, "Then how do you justify—"

"Let me finish!" the Big-League Maga boomed, bringing an upward-pointed finger down just above the table.

"As for the issue of violence against foreigners," he continued. "We're doing it because it's time we fought back against them. The people of Averita will be kicked around no longer!"

The Consulate tightened their stern body language at this point. The Maga, for once, felt that his words were in poor taste.

"Sorry, I realize I was getting a bit too much in-character just now. It's how the people keep liking me and I get to hold onto my power. I'm sure you understand?"

The three Consuls turned to one another and grinned.

"Yes," the brown-haired one said plainly. "That we understand."

The third Consul, with their longer black hair, made a point of directing the room back to the agenda at hand.

"Now there is still the matter of J-65216," they said, enunciating. "When your town of Appatown fell into chaos, our citizen escaped the town. You know that this has never happened in the history of our prisoner arrangement. Have you recovered him?"

"No, but he would have definitely been killed if he came across any of the other villages. Believe me."

The Consulate was not convinced. They almost never believed him.

The brown-haired Consul started again, with force.

"You must understand, Maga, that this prisoner must be stopped immediately if he is found to be alive. Along with your recent raid on the Ispanian village, him telling his story of oppression under us and under your people would be sure to draw retaliation. Our sociologists know just as well as you do that these circumstances could very well cause all the different villages to unite. Those lands have a history of successful rebellion. That history must not repeat itself."

"And if you don't," the dirty blonde Consul said ominously, "we won't defend you when you get overrun."

The ultimatum made the Maga uneasy, despite his best attempts to hide it. He let his eyes stay focused on the table, his hands pressed on it as he thought of what to say next.

"I understand," the Maga returned eventually. "But I know these villages won't unite for simply one reason—racial identity. As long as each of them know that they're fighting against the whites, then guess what? Every one of the races keeps to itself. Fighting for your identity becomes more important than the greater good. Oh yeah, we've seen it in the past. The other villages will even start fighting each other. Just you watch."

The Consuls eyed one another once again. They were in agreement.

"You'd better be right about this," the dirty blond responded.

The Maga leaned in about a foot forward toward the Consulate, curling out his lips into a rough "o" shape in the process.

"It'll happen," he emphasized. "Believe me."

Just this one time, the Consulate believed him.

2-2

It was hardly fifteen minutes into work and Josik had already spotted another blister. He knew both of his palms would eventually turn to callus, but the additional sharp pain, on top of his typical late morning hunger, was simply distracting on a day like this. After all, today was the Ispanians' *Miércoles de Ceniza*, which meant today would be Josik's first fasting experience. The scant food he consumed today was fortunately not too much of a stretch for a young man raised on hyper-consumerist convenience. The last ten months had been a period of spiritual conditioning for Josik, engaging in most of the religious nine yards. He went to Mass weekly, Eucharistic adoration once a month, and even scripture study every other Tuesday evening. Still, he was far from being a perfect Christian. He embraced the symbol but resisted the spirituality. He allowed himself to be moved by the ceremony, but not by the homily. Josik was still not convinced of salvation or eternity. But he acknowledged, for whatever reason, that still seemed elusive to him, that the prayer and meditation he practiced was the only thing that could help him keep things straight. The only thing that even brought him the tiniest solace about . . . Maria.

Josik couldn't stop his wandering mind from bringing her back to memory. Her absence had caused Josik to yearn for spiritual presence, if only to bring him the occasional return of catharsis.

And now, with the trigger of physical pain, the sorrow and emptiness returned. He put his face in his hands and his knees to the ground. He was reminded of his failures; his unsuccessful rescue mission to Appatown during the summer, only to be stopped by their newly militarized border wall; his vain plea to the village elders for diplomatic negotiations, only to find that the town's leaders had become overly fearful and indecisive. It seemed to him that God was responding to him in this moment of anguish, saying "My poor Josik, this is not your fault." But Josik started punishing himself, thinking, *I could still do more.*

Was he being overly self-critical? Perhaps. Still, as Josik got back on his feet after another attack of weeping, he still found good reason to scold himself. Over the winter, it seemed he had given up on Maria. He had settled.

Then, it was Christmas. Josik went to Mass with the Martezes—Maria's family. He heard for the first time the full biblical account of the baby Jesus and his predicted coming into the world. *Why were all these ordinary people from nearly three thousand years ago so happy about a helpless baby born in a feeding trough,* Josik wondered? He was struck by the story with an emotion he knew he had never felt before—hope. So, Josik was inspired with a thought during his usual pensive moments waiting in the Communion line later in Mass—maybe his sense of reason was too limiting. Maybe, in this crisis, it was telling him the wrong things. He prayed to let go of his overthinking mind for a moment, to let his emotions and his intuition tell him what felt right.

It told Josik that he needed to try again. That he could have a real shot at finding her if he prepared a plan.

This thought brought him to the farm at which he began to live and work on the outskirts of town. He found, lived, and trained with a father-son pair that didn't take kindly to Averitans—in fact, they spoke daily at dinner of how they hoped for a coming war and as they saw it, an opportunity for vengeance. Josik and his new comrades—Juan and Raul Colella—were a motley team. Juan, the father, was dark tan and sun-wrinkled with a head of full gray flat hair, despite being in his early seventies. Raul, nearly forty, looked heavier than his father and had short black hair and a mustache. Their matron, Claudia, had also been kidnapped during the Averitan attack last year.

The three steadfastly trained together in their spare time in scouting techniques, marksmanship, and even hand-to-hand combat. Between these exercises and the daily back-breaking labor, Josik felt himself becoming rather fit and alert. With each passing day, he was growing more prepared for the three to hatch their plot. Raul and Juan had been ready for months now, but Josik had not. They promised not to execute their plan until Josik made the call. This gave Josik more confidence, a sense of empowerment.

But today was a day to call to mind his faults. Josik felt himself having second thoughts, questioning his newfound confidence. He was focused on dropping tomatoes seeds into the ground, his eyes focused on every tiny particle of earth below him.

"Is this to be my future?" he growled to the soil. "Are my desires only to be quenched with a grave?"

But Josik's new spiritual defenses were quick to respond. He thought back to the words of the new church pastor, Father José, who had related the Native American Story of the two wolves during homily at Mass that day. He could remember the simple dialogue between the story's two characters clearly:

"There are two wolves fighting inside of you," said the old man. "One only wants to do good. The other wants to do evil: anger, envy, sorrow, regret, greed, self-pity, ego. This fight goes on in everyone."

"Which one will win?" the boy asked.

The old man let a long moment of silence pass.

"The one you feed."

No, the wolves of Josik's past—the ones that had nearly led him to take his own life almost a year ago—would not be fed. But turning away from his Authoritarian instincts towards comfort, luxury, and convenience was still not easy and had to be done quickly—rather like waxing skin with fly paper.

The decision was made. On this day of sacrifice and self-denial, Josik would finally prepare for the journey.

He gathered the Colella family and they decided to leave at dawn the next morning. He left a brief note on the kitchen counter for Maria's family before sunrise, and he headed west out of the town with the Colellas on the *Rastro de Esperanza*. It was mid-morning by the time they had overcome the weather-worn ridge that obscured the view of the Ispanian village, their light leather rucksacks in hand. Almost all of Josik's thoughts turned to the journey ahead and for Maria's rescue, save one: a voice he thought he heard during a quick prayer made outside of the church that morning.

As usual, it sounded like Josik impulsively talking to himself. But the voice uttered words that he had not expected:

"So it is time your teaching begins again."

And that night, while Josik slept soundly beneath his woolen blankets and treated leather tarp, it did. He found himself back at Sam's beach house, the resident scholar in waiting as usual with breakfast.

2-3

Without warning, and without foretelling, Josik found himself back in the realm of the historical past. He felt the familiar plushness of his old two-pillow time traveler's bed, settled for a moment back into the legendary luxury of its mattress. *Even if the past was also screwed up*, Josik mused, *at least its people knew how to sleep comfortably.*

Josik snapped to action. After a ten-month hiatus, he knew he was returning to a mission, whose objectives remained yet elusive. But the next task was clear: find Sam.

This was strangely more difficult than usual. A quick survey of the inside of the house yielded no results, but troubling observations. Dishes crammed the kitchen sink, used canned goods littered the whole floor, and all the furniture and living items were strewn throughout the room. The wall clock and calendar were carelessly left against the kitchen counter. Chairs were upturned and its table torn to pieces; even the instructional whiteboard was broken in half. A peek outside the master bedroom's north-side window told enough of the story: Sam was franticly sculpting in the sand. If

Josik had had a bad year, Sam's had apparently been even worse in his student's absence.

He looked outside and saw him. He was hardly recognizable from the beloved philosopher. From the back, as he approached, Josik spotted a long, uncombed mane and a tattered extra-large dress shirt. As he drew closer, Josik heard these words lowly sung:

"The other night, dear, as I lay sleeping

I dreamed I held you in my arms

But when I awoke, dear, I was mistaken

So I hung my head and I cried."

Sam, or whatever was left of him, noticed the unexpected company, brushed off his hands, pursed his lips shut, and stopped his work. He turned and stood to reveal a face that was worse for wear due to several weeks of self-neglect. His hair was much thinner and grayer, apparently compensated with a foot-long curly beard. Despite being outside on a rather sunny day, his complexion was ghostly pale. He looked over Josik's head to the ocean, tears beginning to drip down his face.

"Rachel? Is that you? Are you ready for me?"

He dropped to his knees. He looked up, with clenched fists outstretched.

"Oh!" Sam cried. "Rachel, are you ready? I've waited, I've waited for so long."

Josik intervened, determined to put an end to Sam's

delusion. He advanced to just inches from the man, taking up Sam's full view. Sam looked blankly back.

Josik lowered to his knees. He needed to comfort Sam, but how? Intimate friendships weren't included as a school subject on Bohem, so he thought back to the common Ispanian gestures he remembered. Josik settled on grasping Sam's hands in his.

"No, Sam, it's Josik," he spoke. "Your student."

He took a pause. Josik was determined to prove that he meant more to him than simply being his mentor.

He added a key phrase.

"Your friend."

With a gasp, Sam's face flashed to new life, his eyes finally finding the courage to meet Josik's. His hands seized, then settled around Josik's wrist.

"Josik," he gulped.

"My friend. I've missed you."

For a second, the two smiled to each other, hand-in-hand. Yet it didn't last. Sam fell unconscious on his side, the victim of his own lack of self-care.

2-4

The next few of Josik's days in the 2030s were spent attending to Sam's every need as the older man rested in bed. Meanwhile, Josik of the present continued to trek along toward the Appatown border, his mind fixated oddly on the past.

Yet this was for good reason. He made a point of listening to Sam's radio in the hopes of remaining in touch with the history that was taking place somewhere nearby. Many of the headlines, however, did not herald cause for relief.

"In a special session of the Association of Coastal Governments, legislatures from its twelve participating states voted overwhelmingly to withhold federal income taxes collected from their residents by the Internal Revenue Service. The president has strongly condemned the move, describing it as 'treasonous' and a 'slap in the face to all other states in this great Union.' She has promised retaliatory action."

"The governor of Florida declared a state of emergency today in the wake of widespread flooding caused by Hurricane Bartholomew. Included in the aftermath was the catastrophic failure of the Miami Seagate, which the Army Corps of Engineers has stated will cause the city to remain underwater indefinitely."

"Skirmishes continue along the disputed California-Jefferson border between National Guard troops and local militia. Conflict first broke two weeks ago over declarations of independence ratified by the governments of eight formerly Californian counties, citing a list of thirty shared grievances against the state government. Fifty-six fatalities and an additional 349 injuries have been attributed to the breakdown in relations thus far."

As the days and the miles to Appatown wore on, Josik grew accustomed to rolling around these many distress calls in his head. He kept the thoughts to himself, as his companions the Colellas were not the talkative type. He would also often lose track of the magnificent green trail scenery in the process, choosing instead to consider the connection between the America at the point in time he was witnessing and its apparent end. He knew from Sam that many of the country's figures had spent most of their lives' work dedicated to what many called the "American experiment," even in Sam's present day. So why, despite the good intentions of several zealous individuals throughout history, was this lucky, or seemingly blessed, country—with all its ideals, triumphs, people, and resources—on an ever-steeper road to collapse?

Josik didn't have an answer. But he could at least think back to a passage from Sam's book that gave some continuing food for thought on the subject:

Chapter 6

One Nation, Nonstop

"Why do you write like you're running out of time?
Writing at night like you're running out of time . . . "

From Hamilton: An American Musical

There is one particular song from the 2015 hit musical Hamilton *that fairly represents the passion and enthusiasm with which many of the Founders went about in the formative days of the country. The song's title—"Non-Stop"—while meant to solely focus on the figure of Alexander Hamilton, could also apply in describing the disposition of many of his counterparts of the time. In other words, these individuals, despite their tremendous differences in opinion, thought it worthwhile to make a career in what at least outwardly appeared to be public service to the American nation. Their efforts led to the establishment of America's failed confederate form of government, and, more importantly, its successful revision to the country's existing form of government under a new U.S. Constitution. Hamilton's own career as a statesman, as an example, represents the extent to which these men were willing to contribute to the continuity of American civilization, simply for what they would describe as a love of country and a love of others. This concept can be summarized in one word: patriotism.*

Some have argued contrarily, pointing to the high socioeconomic status of many of the Founding Fathers as evidence of an ulterior motive in forming stable

American government: protecting the status-quo concentration of wealth. But a glance at just some of these figures' life stories reveals some different desire, a larger desire, being pursued aside from mere self-interest.

Alexander Hamilton, of later musical notoriety, came to not only advance from his status as a poor orphan, but to author and publish fifty-one lengthy essays in pushing for the 1789 ratification of the U.S. Constitution. He would later serve, at President George Washington's request, as the country's first Secretary of Treasury, a position in which he persuaded the Continental Congress to assume the war debts of individual states, and boosting the United States' financial position in the global economy in the process.

Here is another example: Thomas Jefferson, first Secretary of State. For all the controversy surrounding his debunked opinions on the inherent inferiority in people of African descent, Jefferson also seems to have done his public work with the advancement of American ideals in mind. Consider the words he penned in the Declaration of Independence: "That all men are created equal, that they are endowed by their Creator with certain unalienable rights, that among these are life, liberty, and the pursuit of happiness." Even with the certain risk of being charged with treason against the British crown, Jefferson and the Declaration's other signers established and committed to defending the ideals that would come to liberate more and more of the country's citizens from oppression with each successive generation (even if none of these Founders realized it at the time). Such was their dedication to these values—proclaimed on July 4, 1776 for a worldwide audience—that these men pledged, in their own words, "[their] lives, [their] fortunes, and [their] sacred honors" to its cause.

Finally, there is the case of George Washington. After serving as commander-in-chief of the Continental Army in the War, he looked forward to a quiet retirement at his residence at Mount Vernon, Virginia. But he eventually let his plans be interrupted, answering instead a call to serve as president over the 1787 Constitutional Convention, and later as the nation's first president by unanimous vote of the Electoral College. Over his forty-five years of service, he was presented with many opportunities that would have allowed him to assume absolute power over the fragile country—after his victory as Revolutionary War general, his popularity would have very likely permitted it. Instead, he chose not to draw up such nefarious plans, intentionally limiting himself to two four-year presidential terms, and finally returning to retirement afterward.

In short, these individuals represent a small sample of the kinds of attitudes with which succeeding generations, as many patriotic American historians would attest, have made America great. They include such subjective values as self-sacrifice, humility, unrelenting hard work, and perseverance. As some would posit, present-day America is not too far from rediscovering these values. They—and admittedly, I— see no reason as to why a return to them is not possible. It is simply a matter of looking to the past and accepting and fixing its faults, while ensuring that the foundation of American democracy fundamentally remains the same in a spirit of constant self-improvement. It represents an attitude of constant, optimistic reform that aims, in the Constitution's own words, to form a "more perfect union."

The words managed to give Josik a most unusual sensation. It was a shiver, but it wasn't induced by the cold. He started feeling it from things much less concrete—from mere ideas, it would seem. Then another shiver came down his spine.

He, Juan, and Raul had stopped himself in his tracks. Just ahead within eyeshot was the Appatown border wall, thick with concrete and now painted a deep royal blue color. Since his last venture to the area, Josik thought it must have gotten ten feet taller.

2-5

The trio approached the impressive structure. Their plan was to scout out a potential point of entry, nothing more.

Although Josik's feet propelled him forward, his mind turned to the larger implications of what he was witnessing. Between this, Maria's kidnapping, and whispers of other raids he heard rumored through the Ispanian villagers, it was becoming apparent that perhaps the attacks were part of some new campaign coordinated by Appatown, not simply the rogue actions of a few disgruntled white laborers. The chaos and horrors he saw last year had apparently not been the end for Appatown—rather, its troubles were used as a rallying cry to build up its forces. Josik thought back to a memorable quote from his studies with Sam on the topic of the early twentieth century: these people still weren't speaking softly, but they sure were beginning to carry a big stick.

Moving past the trees, the three reached a fifty-foot buffer zone, removed of all vegetation. It was then that they could fully acknowledge the great, big, beautiful, blue-painted wall in front of him. Impressive orange painted stars dotted the top of the design every twenty-five feet, and there were two levels of enclosed corridors running up and down the entire perimeter, each with openings on both sides around eye-level.

None of them had detected the soldiers keeping guard on the inside. Josik had never developed much of a fighter's instinct, try as he had in his last few months with the Colellas. A sudden, spreading pain in his upper arm finally acted as a wake-up call. He had been hit with one of the more advanced 30-millimeter bullets. This was his warning shot.

With nothing but his injured self and his compact 9-millimeter pistol with which to respond, he trotted back hurriedly into the wood, his left hand held over the wound. He sat down next to a large elm tree, cursing under his breath about what he had done.

He looked around. Neither the father nor the son could be found. He looked down at the area where a small bit of flesh was now missing. *Since when did the Averitans carry such big sticks?* he thought. Josik opened up his leather rucksack and grabbed a bit of gauze from a first aid kit. In these frenzied moments, he was able to think back to Maria's bits of medical instruction she gave to help him pass the time all those months ago in the hospital. He took care to wrap the wound tightly from distal to proximal.

A thought popped in his mind that made Josik chuckle. He found it ironic that in his mission to rescue the nurse Maria, he was apparently putting himself in situations that were testing his own proficiency in medical treatment.

After a few minutes, several murmurs could be heard. A few figures emerged from the tree. They were men from the village of dark-skinned people, wearing their distinct fur parkas.

Josik instinctively panicked and clenched his back against the tree. His abuse at their hands last year was starting to fade from memory, but he didn't dare risk reminding them of his story by exposing himself.

Within moments, the black men noticed the wall and its formidable defenses. Each picked a tree to shield themselves from the view of any sentry standing watch. One of the men took his place on the opposite side of Josik's spot, leaving the stranger in a cold sweat.

The man removed his hood, his sounds almost as frantic as Josik's. Oddly, this put Josik at ease. Considering that the blood left in the snow would soon give him away, Josik was beginning to think it worth the risk to introduce himself with no intent of harm. So, he found himself cautiously peering around the circumference of the tree, focused on judging whether the man behind him was a potential friend or foe.

Upon Josik's first glance, he had his answer. The man was intimately familiar to him. It was the man who had rescued him from the taunting crowd that perilous winter night from last year, had taken him into the care of the Ispanians that next morning. But Josik did not know his name, and did not know of any way to greet him.

He stayed focused on his rescuer's face, spotted a

large, scoped pistol in his hand, and absentmindedly stood up.

"You!" Josik cried.

A volley of shots rang out from the wall. He caught the man's attention, but the reaction Josik got was one of anger and frustration. The man grabbed Josik's upper arm.

"What have you done? You've ruined our ambush! Run!"

Josik did as directed, still trying to do his best to stop the gash. As he followed behind, he realized that there were dozens more planning on the attack, as they broke off from their hidden positions to join the company's retreat. But where were they going? Back to the village? Josik found his attention drawn back to the Wall for a moment, as more sections of it seemed to be coming alive with machine gun fire.

A commander at the front directed the troops' movements. A fleet of sleek, rounded, silver helicopters whirled overhead at that moment.

The men stepped up their pace to an all-out sprint. The helicopters had turned tightly to follow behind them, ready to fire some kind of payload.

"Get down! Spread out!" bellowed his rescuer. Josik dove into a nearby snowdrift.

The trio of helicopters let out their first volley of Incinerates, all of them missing the group but hitting foliage just ahead of them. The projectiles burst into an instant bonfire, whipping up flames nearly fifty feet in diameter in all directions. Some of them who were still running found themselves continuing full speed into a supersonic inferno, unable to stop in time.

Many of those unlucky few were knocked to their feet by the force of the blast, which left them unconscious but cooled most of their third-degree burns. Some others made the unwise choice of standing immediately back upright, which exposed them to the roaring blaze of the burning trees.

The remaining group split off from that point, with the commander and Josik's group taking a more wooded route and the other in a more open clearing. They all let the adrenaline propel them forward as fast as it could, knowing that their muscles would fail them just as soon as they finally stopped, hopefully at least in safety.

Another few minutes passed and the helicopters had not noticed Deshawn and Josik's group. Josik had noticed that the attackers were firing on the unfortunate other half of the regiment, and franticly pondered the others' fate at the end of this skirmish.

Their group had finally reached the clearing where the entrance to the checkpoint was located. But the snow was inches deeper there, changing their mode of travel from a sprint-hop to more of a fast-stomp. The other half was fast approaching too, but they were immediately tailed by the helicopter trio, which had lowered to about twenty feet above the ground. The attackers were all waiting to take their last shot.

The commander eventually stopped at one of the snowbanks and motioned for everyone to slide down a nearby tunnel. Josik found himself the second to last in the group to get to safety, long enough to witness the fate of the other half. With less than fifty feet to go, they were fired on from their flank. All were consumed in the flames.

As for Josik, he was knocked off his feet from the blast waves. He got on all fours to notice that a few spots of his outer clothing had caught ablaze. Josik crawled over to the commander, gave him a quick shake. His face and outfit were completely charred. He was gone.

Still dazed from the last explosion, but still fighting for his life in the heat of the moment, Josik lifted himself into the narrow tunnel and slid headfirst to the entrance for Point Bravo.

Josik found himself back at Sam's, reasoning that he had either gone unconscious or randomly fell asleep. From his usual bed, the dampened sounds of shuffling plates, utensils, and food could be heard.

The traveler emerged from the bedroom to find Sam at last upright and active, his face clean shaven and his body casually in a plain t-shirt and jeans but at least fully clothed. He was preparing some fried eggs, French toast, and sausages, the kitchen transistor radio playing its usual habit of public radio.

"Good morning," Sam turned to say with a warm grin. "Glad to see you again."

He laid out the plates and utensils on the table. Josik looked back skeptically.

"You know, I've been wondering what happened that caused you not to see me for several months. Am I just here and asleep for the time I'm not here, or do I just show up whenever whatever force out there decides it's time for me to show up? Do you know?"

Sam transferred eggs from a frying pan to two small

ceramic plates. "I don't understand the question. What do you mean you just show up? I had assumed you left in the middle of the night months ago and were too embarrassed to tell me face-to-face." His face was expressionless as he slid some toast slices out.

Josik was silent a moment, his expression baffled. It took some time to recompose himself, the silence cut by Sam's absent-minded cooking.

"No. Sam, listen to me. I have to confess something to you."

Sam dropped his cookware down, peered his eyes towards Josik from behind the counter. "I've had worse secrets kept from me for too long. Go ahead, tell me."

"I never told you where I'm really from. I'm not from Cuba."

Sam put his hands on his hips, looked down, and bit his lip in suppressed frustration.

"Then where are you from, traveler?"

Josik looked down a moment, accepted what he was going to say.

"I don't know how to explain it or prove it to you. But I'm from the future."

Sam furrowed his brow and widened his eyes.

"How far into the future?" he asked matter-of-factly.

***

Hours later, the two hadn't found a full explanation

for Josik's distant travel. But they had at least enjoyed a full breakfast.

"I know neither of us know why we've been connected like this," Josik said. "Despite that, you are a gracious host. In case I've forgotten to say it before, thank you for welcoming me into your home."

"You're very welcome, Josik," Sam responded. "Come and go as you please. Or come and go as God pleases. If he's really out there. Or if he's benevolent as they say he is."

Josik picked up on the skepticism.

"I understand where you're coming from. In my future world, there's this girl I got to know pretty well who keeps finding these moments to lecture about her people's religion. I've tried my hand at some of it, but I still don't know how I feel about it yet."

"Yeah, I've never been a very religious guy myself. Which one is she trying to convert you to?"

"Christianity."

"Hm. That's considered one of the more generic categories in this era. Which denomination is she a part of?"

Josik reached for a seat, readying himself for the upcoming meal and inevitable classroom session on mid-twenty-first century American culture and politics.

"I'm sorry, denomination? I don't think the future has any of those."

"Interesting. If you look at our history books, that's more or less how Christianity was about 600 years ago before now. Of course, it had a whole set of different problems back then, too, but Church history is an entirely different topic altogether."

Josik remained silent so the two could get a few minutes of eating in. After a few days being away from the place, he took the opportunity to appreciate the seaside view.

He figured it was time to move things along after the brief reprieve.

"So, what did you want to talk to me about?" Josik inquired. "I'm eager to start our lessons again if you feel well enough."

Sam set down his fork, leaned back, and crossed his arms, apparently contemplating. He looked lazily back at Josik.

"Sure," he shrugged. "Where shall we pick things up?"

"I seem to remember you telling me last time about the 2016 election, and how important it was in understanding the current events of this time."

"Ah, yes. *I* seem to remember the shock and surprise that went around when the results of it finally trickled in on that long night. I must have stayed up until 2:00am, or 0200 in your time."

"So, what happened?"

Sam sighed, rubbed a hand on his nose.

"The names are irrelevant at this point, but the leaders, actions, and especially the trends of the time are important to understand. Do you remember the chapter from my book on America's role in twentieth century globalization?"

"Yes," Josik answered. He recalled from his limited knowledge of the topic that the technology of the era had grown advanced enough to ensure the cheap transport of goods from around the world to well-developed economies.

So, Josik surmised, "It doesn't seem that there's much to understand about it, it sounds like it did a lot of good to me. Unless there's something about it I don't know or understand."

Sam, the natural instructor that he was, fired back a response.

"Oh, I don't think you know the half of it. Globalization is unequivocally the most important factor explaining the socioeconomic and political turmoil of twenty-first century democracies."

"How so?"

"I'll explain. In the quest to provide cheap goods to people in the developed world, businesses turned to the parts of the world that could provide the materials for said goods cheaply—the so-called developing world, or what are sometimes called third-world countries. With few better opportunities for work, many of the native peoples in these third-world countries would undertake the work demanded by these businesses to supply to their international markets, even under poor working conditions. But here's the real kicker."

Sam took a sip of orange juice.

"Go on."

"Part of those poor workplace conditions included working at a pay grade significantly lower than what it cost to have people within the developed world to do the same thing. But many of the third-world people did the work because that amount was still significantly higher than what they could earn in other jobs around them. Which meant—"

Josik finished Sam's thought. "Which meant that some of these 'developed' people were out of a job."

"Exactly. And this happened in particular kinds of businesses and industries that used to form the bulk of what used to be something in America called its middle class. Between the workers who were displaced, and the United States' tendency to get involved in conflict all around the world—because of its role as a global leader for almost a century—a large part of the public turned against globalization."

"Turned against? So, they used to support it?"

"Remember what I taught you about American history in the mid-twentieth century? The event that established the United States as a world leader in defending freedom, especially through its role in starting the United Nations?"

"Oh right," drawing a blank for a moment, "that was the Second World War?"

"Yes. It was a war that engulfed almost all the countries located in what is known as the European continent. And it was so destructive that the much of it needed to be completely rebuilt. That's when the United States stepped in and spent billions on a project with such an aim, at the very least to prevent our rival at the time, the Soviet Union, from stepping in instead."

"And why was it so important to oppose this Soviet Union?"

"You remember the term 'ideology.' "

Josik nodded his head.

"Many of the chapters you'll find in my book make reference to it in the context of America's current affairs, as the widening gulf between democratic liberalism and democratic conservatism. But the difference in ideology we shared with the Soviet Union was on an even more distant, entirely different frame of conflict. Whereas most Americans believe in democratic capitalism as a good framework for public policy, those in the Soviet Union followed the ideology of communism, where the government controlled and tightly regulated most aspects of everyday life—from speech, to art, to religion, even the food supply — which was seized by the government to theoretically be evenly distributed amongst the people."

"Theoretically?" Josik said with raised eyebrows.

"Well, long story short—communism just doesn't work in principal and in practice. It's built on the principle of sharing things in common, much like the very first human societies, which didn't have the problem of inequality. But the problem of maintaining this harmonious state becomes more difficult as technology and innovation continue to progress. The improving technology tends to make it easier for less-skilled workers to produce goods and wealth to the benefit of the owner that hired them. Once fair labor standards were put on the books, and goods were able to be produced more cheaply, the problem seemed to level out for a time. This demonstrated that the right combination of a competitive economic setup and democratically-sanctioned regulation could work. Communism, by contrast, simply dictates everything under the assumption that government will cease to exist once all wealth has been evenly distributed. But this fails to account for the human temptation to greed and lust for power. Other ideologies at least take some of this into account."

"It sounds somewhat similar to my days developing on Bohem."

"I'll have to show you *The Communist Manifesto* sometime to further explain," Sam continued. "At one point, America's capitalist economy managed to keep its inequality under control, especially across the period of the 1940s to the 1970s. But this state of affairs relied on a combination of policy choices and the strength of the country's middle class, much of which was comprised of manufacturing workers. Then came the age of globalization and the age of the computer, which changed the equation again. New, complex global markets opened up tremendous opportunities for earning exorbitant amounts of untapped wealth, especially with the advent of products such as pocket-sized computers that everyone wanted. But production of such products went overseas, which, in combination with labor-saving technology, meant that those middle-class manufacturing jobs went to developing countries or disappeared altogether."

Josik thought for a second. "So, then those middle-class people. They didn't like globalization."

"Yes. And it wasn't much of a stretch for those people to vote for someone who not only promised to bring the good jobs back, but to resist all the other forms of so-called 'globalism.' Namely, this meant retreating on the U.S.'s precedent for global leadership, which carried all kinds of implications. But this went against the inevitable trends that were to continue throughout the 21ˢᵗ century—economics, technology, and common threats simply continued to push countries together and make the world smaller."

"So, globalization continued no matter what, but people didn't want it?"

"The *working class, white* voters didn't want it," Sam emphasized. "Actually, they turned against it rather dramatically in 2016, and it's what ultimately swung the election as surprisingly the way that it did. Sure, the results were also motivated in part by racism, and a call for immigration restrictions. But the voters who fell in those categories had always voted for the side they did in 2016. It was those particular white blue-collar worker types that were really only concerned with one issue—the fact that their communities, both in terms of culture and the local economy, had unraveled over the decades, underneath the rest of the country's radar."

"Sounds complicated."

"It is." Sam took a moment, then clapped his hands together in excitement. "Sounds like we have a study topic for the next couple weeks!"

In response, Josik politely excused himself, feeling a need for a nap.

Sure enough, his adventure with the soldiers resumed. He was startled awake, prone and underneath the gaze of the survivors of the Appatown ambush.

2-7

It was Juan and Raul Colella, alive. They reached down and set Josik upright. They looked grimy and shaky, anxious and unnerved.

Josik peered around his dark, earthen-colored surroundings, only interrupted in places with lanterns on the walls. Along with the other men, they were located at some kind of circular entryway, with a vaulted door on one end and a corridor on its opposite.

"Where are we?" he asked.

One of the tall black soldiers entertained the enquirer.

"Where do you think we are? You fell close enough to here to figure it out."

Josik had never seen anything of Earth's underground before.

"I don't know."

Deshawn approached from nearby with an answer. "This is our solution to the albinos and their damned

Blue Wall. If we can't go over it, can't go around it, and can't go through it, then we'll just keep going under it."

Josik was amazed, his mind lighting up in excitement at the revelation of this organized opposition. Like so many youngsters before him, he was falling under the romantic, intoxicating spell of unequivocal, idealistic resistance. Strength surged into him, and he stood taller. Josik felt ready to join the cause, to march into battle proudly. He remembered a motivating fact that furthered these urges—that behind these defensive lines his love could be found.

Deshawn could tell this as he paced around Josik for a few moments, all too familiar with the feeling of blind obedience to a cause. But Josik's torture at the black village a year ago had changed Deshawn, made him uncertain of his exclusive loyalty to his people. With the Bohemx before him again, Deshawn's ingrained hatred was wearing further away.

"Be careful, young man," he chided, realizing that Josik didn't look like more than ten years younger than himself. "I can see the passion in your eyes, but you must understand what it is we're doing and trying to accomplish first. We used to be known as the Diaspora Liberation Front, a reference to the forcible manner in which our people were first brought to this land over one thousand years ago. I was one of its field commanders but was recently promoted to one of its generals. Since then, I've been working to reform our group and its purpose. Now we are simply known as the New Homeland Resistance, at the service of our fellow Rican people."

"Resistance. Against the Appatown people," Josik said, with a tinge of lust for violence in his voice.

His rescuer grasped his shoulders, gave one of them a comforting clap.

"What did they do to you that brought you to the Wall? I sense a great deal of anger rising in you, not just crude idealism."

Josik paused, shocked at these accurate perceptions.

"They took her. A friend of mine from the Ispanian village, an amazing woman who was guiding me in this new world. They took her, just as I was developing these feelings that I never had before, and I can't stand to think about what they might be doing to her. I'm going to rescue her, or I'll die trying if I have to."

Josik felt weak, lowered himself to his knees, realizing that he had kept these thoughts locked away for so long.

He looked back up to Deshawn with wet eyes as he uttered.

"Forgive me, sir. I also owe my life to you. But she prevented me from almost taking my own, and showing me a new way. If I can't find her, there's not much else for me to live for. I'll fight no matter what, I'll keep fighting till my very end. I can't lose her."

Deshawn shook his head, as he coaxed Josik back on his feet.

"Josik, Josik," he scolded. "Your life and your purpose are so much more than that."

Josik looked at him with scorn. "How do you know?"

"I know, Josik. I know your story, about your connections with the past, with the priest named Biwun, everything. It was revealed to me in a dream."

Josik was resigned. *Sure*, he thought. *I'll believe it. Why not?*

Finally, he changed the subject back to logistical matters. He was done with the metaphysical matters for now and was ready to fight.

"So, what exactly are we up against?" he asked. "How did Appatown put together the resources for such a big wall?"

Deshawn sighed. There was an inconvenient truth he needed to reveal.

"It's not just Appatown anymore. After their maga was killed, it was thought that the town would descend into chaos. But that's not what happened. The hateful groups banded together, swallowing up all of the albino communities whether they wanted to join their new toxic ideology or not. They formed a new country, a vast territory bringing together dozens of tribes in the area. They call themselves Averita, headed by a Big-League Maga."

"I'm sorry," interrupted Josik. "Did you say, 'bigly?'"

"No, *Big League*." Deshawn emphasized, doing a decent impression that was lost on the rest of the group.

He continued. "I'm certain I know where your friend is. All prisoners are taken to the Averitan capital up north. The rest of our regiment and I will show you the way as far as we can until reinforcements arrive. Then you'll be on your own."

Josik nodded in consent, adrenaline now coursing through his system.

"Then let's get moving."

Looking to the Rican soldiers, Juan and Raul also nodded.

"It's a good plan. We're with you, señor."

2-8

The regiment conducted their underground trek for the next few days rather uneventfully, keeping a steady but leisurely pace. They were still licking their wounds from the ambush. Josik took the opportunity to become fully updated in the latest political affairs.

"So how did you end up having trouble with the Averitans?" he asked, finding himself following just behind the leader one day.

Deshawn was the only one with the knowledge and fortitude willing to answer. He let out a long sigh first.

"None of my people seem to have an answer for that. We're not really sure why it started, but it definitely wasn't by us. They just decided to surprise attack us one day—kidnap some of our people, beat our women, even mutilated some of the corpses after their former owners had been shot dead."

Josik turned his head toward Deshawn, his reaction one of disgust. He thought back to some of the torture techniques he learned about in pre-Authoritarian history class, and the strong emotions he had been encouraged to maintain toward them.

"Seeing those kinds of atrocities doesn't faze you?"

"No. In this world, you learn not to."

Josik had nothing to shoot back.

"Anyway," said Deshawn, recalling. "It took a few weeks of silence after the attack, but our village finally decided we had no choice. We started producing arms again and we went to war. That was probably six months ago. I was one of the first to sign up."

Juan Colella walked a few more paces before sharing a thought. "Señor, I'm surprised you didn't ask the Ispanians for help, especially since our attack happened only four months before yours did. Or if you had, my family never heard about it."

"Well, now we at least know that our friends the Ispanians suffer, too," Deshawn returned, settling a comforting hand around the old man's shoulder. "Maybe we can work together on changing something about that after this."

He turned to Josik for a moment with a smile. There were a few minutes of silence.

All of a sudden, Josik had another thought.

"Deshawn, I've noticed something. You seem different from most of the people I've met on this planet. Most don't think of the larger picture as you do, they focus on the problems of their own village and that's the end of it. It's logical, but it's limiting. But I can understand why your village would have reason to feel so resentful. I remember from what I've learned that your people were not well-treated by the other races in this land. So why do you go against this logic? Are you even aware of the history?"

Deshawn looked back with his answer.

"A bit. The dreams didn't reveal much on the actual details of the past, just how you've found yourself as an ambassador to them."

Josik looked away, still skeptical of the idea he was fulfilling some kind of calling. Deshawn didn't notice and continued talking.

"There are some photographs we have preserved from the days when we were enslaved, the beatings we endured and the poor living conditions to which we were confined. We were taught to look at those photos as a sign of continuing oppression by the albinos."

"How do you look at them?" Josik asked.

Deshawn looked back at his regiment marching behind him. He wasn't sure how much of his alternative views he was willing to let his men overhear.

"I look at it as a sign of where we've come, as the low point in our people's history. Sure, we're not in a great place right now either, but we still have our freedom. I imagine a day where we bring all the people together in this land, including the albinos, once this war is over. I imagine a society where we judge all people by their character, not their race."

Deshawn's language gave Josik flashbacks to his

understanding of the Civil Rights Movement. Some of the hairs on the back of his neck began to tingle with significance.

"Then let's take a first step towards that. Once this mission is over, I'll take you to the Ispanians to negotiate an alliance. Ours is an open and welcoming people, and will answer to a sense of duty. The village has been building its defenses over the last year as it is."

Deshawn stopped, Josik and the other men followed immediately. Juan and Raul also stopped, alert from their eavesdropping of the diplomacy taking place in front of them.

"I'd have to come back later with one of our official village elders. But yes, let's. Let's take that first step."

Josik smiled as he never had before. Deshawn turned to address his men, his hand firmly shaking Josik's.

"Men of the 99th! As representatives of the Ispanian and Rican people, we have an announcement—today begins a new alliance to band against the Averitans!"

As Deshawn had noticed, the men in the regiment had grown to accept Josik as one of their own. They looked at one other for a few seconds in silence—and then cheered and clapped loudly at this good news. Juan and Raul, looking around with some confusion, played along with their own modest applause.

2-9

Both the nighttime dream lessons and the daytime subterranean sojourn continued for Josik for the next few days, and the contrast in outcomes between the two events couldn't be starker. The prospective alliance that Josik struck catalyzed a strong sense of camaraderie with his black companions, as they enjoyed long, trivial conversations throughout the day that continued into their evening stoppages, cooking food and enjoying fellowship around a modest, artificial propane gas campfire.

Conversely, Josik's continuing exploits into the twenty-first century triggered feelings of anxiety and dread nearly every night. Even though Sam's health was improving, America's was not. Detecting his student's unease at all the bad news, Sam took him on a long walk along the beach one morning at dawn.

Sam let the sounds of the coastal Atlantic fill in for the first twenty minutes or so. The teacher explained it was a low tide day, so the two soon found themselves navigating around some pools. At one point, the older man squatted down and stuck his pointer finger around the edges of a bristled circular creature.

"Go ahead, try it yourself," Sam encouraged.

Josik did so, feeling the small feelers stick to his finger hairs.

"This is a sea anemone. Not sure if they still exist in your time. The stickiness you feel comes from a bunch of tiny barbs that are stinging you, but they don't release nearly enough venom to affect you."

Josik merely smiled, fascinated with this more unusual example of life. It was true—the biodiversity of his present was still only a fraction of Sam's, and so far he had come across very little animal life. Nothing apart from a few birds and squirrels.

"In a way, Josik, we are both much like this sea anemone. This little guy is facing a huge problem—his home, the ocean, has been getting much warmer over the decades. There's not much he can do about it, and his bad luck has him trapped here. We too, Josik, are the unlucky ones—washed ashore from a relentless, apathetic sea of misfortune. All we can do is hope for the tide to roll in and even then, the cycle could start all over again."

Josik thought about this for a little bit, maneuvered his mouth a bit in expression of this effort. Sam's outlook seemed overly pessimistic to him, and frankly a copout. But Josik reminded himself to tread carefully with his words, lest he upset the line of communication he was getting better at maintaining.

Sam read his mind. "That sounds like a bit of a copout, doesn't it?"

Josik reluctantly nodded his head.

"I didn't mean it to sound like that. Our roles in this world are obviously different. I'm still a citizen of this place, and you're just an observer. And I did play a larger role in trying to change the system. It's just that it didn't—"

Sam hesitated, gritted his teeth. A memory he was still trying to bury came back to mind.

"It didn't what?" Josik pressed.

Sam sighed. "It didn't work out."

"How so?"

Sam put his head down on one of his hands, trying to stop the flow. His eyes were beginning to water.

Still Josik insisted.

"Sam, this friend of mine, in the future, started teaching me how to face down the difficult past. And that's just to talk about it. Take your time by yourself to sort it out, of course, but don't use that to keep shutting out other people. I've been damaged—you've been damaged—we've both done damage to ourselves. Let's talk about it."

Sam crossed his arms.

"Alright, if you're so insistent. Then you start. What have you done that you regret? What happened to you that you're using as an excuse?"

"I was exiled from a dystopian society centuries

from now that systematically manipulates human psychology to maintain its regime. And then I planned to take my life and almost jumped off a cliff. And you?"

"I thought I was going to change the system for the better," Sam said, wringing his hands. "I was one of the first state legislators in New York to run as an independent, on a platform of establishing more centered, practical public policy. My independent colleagues and I rode a wave of popularity for our reform platform in the 2020s, brought about by the state's insolvency in implementing universal free public college tuition. By 2026, we took the state from the brink of financial disaster to a substantial surplus. So, I ran for the U.S. Senate based on that success that year and won."

"Wow!" said Josik, snapping to a standing position in excitement.

But Sam had no reaction. He simply stared back at the rising sun, his jaw clenched, while a tear ran down his eye.

Josik reset himself, conscious he was about to unearth the secret. Still he knew he needed to press on.

"So, what happened?"

Sam looked down for a moment, then returned to his previous position.

"I was married to someone at the time. She was staunchly, publicly Christian, and the secular liberals in the state had a field day with her. She didn't stand well to the attacks and death threats—and she died of a heart attack the week after the election. I resigned my office before my swearing-in."

There was silence between the two. Josik felt guilty for asking, and Sam was resisting the urge to say anything further, lest he sound resentful.

And then, the tide began to roll in.

2-10

By the next day, the regiment finally emerged from the covert depths of their underground infrastructure. It was around dawn, the sun was low, and the brisk late-March morning air met with a trace of crusted snow-ice on the ground. They began to climb a steep ridge, their presence obscured by coniferous and deciduous trees. Josik was told that there was a small Averitan military depot on the other side of the hill, complete with a fleet of jeeps, and that the company would have to part ways with him after they took care of the light military complement stationed there. A road curved from north to southeast through the depot, and the regiment had an army to rejoin. The two parties would be traveling in opposite directions.

After about a few hundred yards of this, Deshawn turned around and grabbed Josik by the shoulder, gesturing to him to stop and turn around. The group of men had been walking single file.

Deshawn pointed to a column of billowing smoke in the distance, to the south. A few taller, pillared buildings could also be distinguished, and the view of the whole town was framed to its east by the Blue

Wall.

"Guess what that is, Josik?" he asked.

The former prisoner didn't give it much thought.

"It's Appatown, isn't it?"

Josik mused at this realization for a moment. Despite his certain belief from last year that its society had consumed itself and warranted the wrath of its neighbors into oblivion, its structure still remained, and clearly for the stronger. Appatown had been underestimated, and the apathy of those around them gave them allowance to spread their ideology throughout the continent. Josik looked past the town at their latest concrete accomplishment, with the hand of their new Averitan Union: their impressive Blue Wall, which visibly stretched from north to south as far as the eye could see. So here were Josik and Averita's other enemies within its containment—doing so willingly with the goal of undermining it. Its construction had taken the other factions by surprise—Josik and his allies longed to tear it down to the surprise of its builders.

Deshawn, in the midst of Josik's thoughts, offered a reply.

"Yep," he said simply, unsurprised by his companion's ability to deduce. As much as he hated to admit it, Josik was a rather quick learner.

The men continued.

They engaged in one of their "small-talk"

conversations that Josik had learned to enjoy. They talked about cross-country skiing, whatever that was. He discovered that snow sports were the Ricans favorite pastime.

"Dude, I tried skating skis before we got deployed," one of the taller men explained. "I couldn't do it for more than an hour, I couldn't handle the glute workout. My ass was sore for a week."

"Emphasis on 'tried', man," said his comrade behind him.

"Alright, Dabrin, you lost your turn," the tall man announced. "What do you think, Kyrie? When are you gonna nut up for skating?"

"No way, man," shook the stout man named Kyrie. "Not now at least. I'm too fat to try that kind of thing."

Everyone laughed, including the Colella pair. Even Josik let out a modest chuckle, catching on to the humor. Laughter did not come naturally to him, as Authority discouraged it and comedy in all forms, save for historical political satires that would be broadcast during stories from the pre-Authoritarian, Capitalist-Exploitist Era. The government knew of laughter's scientific properties in bringing people together as a kind of common social currency, as they explained in their schools. But Josik was learning to not think of his Earth experience in an obsessively scientific Bohemish mindset. Without thinking about it too much, he was just laughing because it felt good.

Josik heard something in the air above him. There was a distant buzzing, growing louder. He looked up to see a jet drone, carrying a large payload.

"Guys!"

Everyone rushed towards the western slope of the ridge. They weren't in much of a mood to be incinerated.

Within several seconds, they had managed to settle down into what they thought was a comfortable distance, everyone crouching behind their own personal tree.

It appeared that the drone dropped its bomb, but nothing happened. No detonation.

"It's a test," Deshawn said, standing up with binoculars. "They're testing something new."

"How do you know that?" Josik asked.

The commander handed Josik his magnifying instrument. Looking to the drone, Josik saw it—A wire running from the aircraft down to the ground.

"You're right," reasoned Josik. "Whatever it is, they haven't figured out how to remote detonate it yet."

Deshawn modestly nodded his head, appreciating his well-educated friend's deductive capabilities. He motioned to everyone in the group.

"I say we move further away, just to be cautious. We don't know what kind of blast zone this thing has."

The men all nodded, about to stand up. They were all just a bit further down the slope than Deshawn and Josik.

As they walked away, the ground rumbled, and a terrible low bellowing filled the air. Josik and Deshawn were still standing, which made them vulnerable. They both turned around to look up the slope and saw it—the ground was collapsing on itself, sinking like quicksand as it spread. No big fiery explosion could be seen, just the soil and vegetation refining itself into tiny particles of dull brown dust, reverberating outward like a giant ripple of water.

The pair were helpless to avoid it. The sonic wave of the blast stopped short of them, but it stranded them both on the edge of a new cliff with a drop-off at least twenty feet tall. Deshawn slipped over on the slick ice-snow, but Josik was quick to catch him by the forearm. Josik couldn't hold on for long, as the snow had also worked against his favor.

"Josik, let go!" Deshawn cried. "Don't let me pull you in!"

Josik refused. "I won't leave you! Not after what you've done for me!"

Josik's chest was now over the edge. Not much time left.

Deshawn insisted. "Think of your destiny, Josik! Of Maria, of America! These things are your calling!"

Josik shook his head, confused. "What?"

"You have to trust me, Josik!" Deshawn cried. "If you love me, you'd trust me! I don't have time to explain!"

Josik breathed a deep, shuddering breath. His hip

was coming over the edge in another second.

"Josik—I'll be fine no matter what happens now," Deshawn said with lowered voice. "Trust me."

Yes, trust. It was a force Josik was coming around to accept.

He thought about this for only a second. With his thighs dangling over the edge and his eyes welling up, Josik let go.

***

The men managed to find a way to hoist Josik down as soon as they could find a way down, scarcely twenty minutes later. Deshawn was found easily, laying prone on his dust-caked front with bruises over most of his body. Josik rushed over once he reached Deshawn's level, taking care to gently turn him over.

Deshawn weakly coughed, a trickle of blood running down his right cheek, out his mouth, and from both his temples. His skull must have been fractured as well.

"Josik," he recalled.

Josik said nothing for a moment, reached down to grasp his arm, finding a way to comfort him. He was too late to save the freedom fighter.

"Josik, I . . . I . . ." Deshawn tried to form sentences, but the injury to his brain was too great.

After a few more seconds, he looked down at his uniform jacket. There was something in there? Josik thought.

Yes. Josik reached into each of the pockets. In one chest pocket, he found a compactly-folded map, which pointed the way to the Averitan capital—a place called Detroit.

"Other one too," Deshawn urged, interrupting Josik's examination of the map.

He reached into the other chest pocket as directed. He felt something small, hard, and metal.

He pulled out a pin with a symbol of something on it largely unfamiliar to him. It had a navy-blue field with tiny white dots in it. Taking up the rest of the three-quarters of the space were a set of alternating red and white stripes.

"America," Deshawn said, looking to the flag pin. "Save America."

He squeezed Josik's hand for emphasis.

"I will, Deshawn, and I'm sorry," Josik replied, sobbing. "I'm sorry I couldn't get to you earlier."

And then, Deshawn mustered the will to say one final thought.

"But you did, Josik. You got to me in a more important way. You . . . you . . ."

He was losing consciousness.

"Yes?" Josik asked with urgency.

"You taught me to love. Love my fellow man. Love all of them. Have to love . . ."

His eyes closed.

Love. That was Deshawn's last word.

***

The men joined Josik in another ten minutes to say their own goodbyes. Josik, with his strongest effort yet, performed his own silent prayer, hoping there was an omnipotent deity out there hearing him. Juan and Raul recited a quiet Our Father with him in Spanish. After many tears and wailing, a quick, impromptu funeral and burial was performed. They all resolved to remember the place as General Deshawn's Hill.

They arrived at the military depot around dusk. It had been abandoned; the Rican soldiers guessed in the wake of the bomb test being so close. Then Josik, Raul, and Juan parted ways with the Rican men, the former taking a jeep north to Detroit.

2-11

It was another early morning in the Complex, as they called it, starting at 0530 each day. A loud klaxon droned at this hour without fail, and the cell doors were opened within five minutes.

Prisoner I-62742 had learned to mentally insulate herself from the intended drudgery of the daily routine, clinging tight to prayer and her Christian faith, sometimes making a point to repeat a few Hail Marys even while standing. It was one of the few things that the guards didn't know she did, and she liked to keep it that way.

After a portion of the usual daily morning mash, the regular news broadcast was played on the giant cafeteria projector screen. It explained that negotiations between the Big-League Maga and the people known as the "Mini-Sodans" had grown tense over joining the latter into the larger Averitan nation, and that a procedural "cage match" between the leaders of the two peoples had been ordered. As the news anchor explained, the Maga declared his intention to make the "Mini-Sodans" "great again, greater than ever before." Then the broadcast cut to a shot of wrestling ring, the Big-League climbing in, clad in nothing but his hummus-colored hair, tattered plain-red tie, and a pair of spandex briefs. A few seconds later, a short, thin, pale man crawled meekly into an opposite corner, buried from head to toe in furs. Then a referee stepped in, a ridiculously oversized microphone in hand. He invited the Maga to speak into it.

"You're going down, Mr. Mini-Soda Man! You won't get in the way of our getting even-greaterness. What does that name even mean, that you're 'mini' and so tiny? Lemme tell ya, there's nothing tiny about our people when it comes to size, if ya know what I mean?"

He repeated for effect, spreading out his hands above his head for all to see. "If ya know what I mean!"

The crowd cheered raucously at Mr. Maga's words as they always had. They always loved a good innuendo of his.

After a few more minutes of staged banter, the match began. Two minutes into it, the Mini-Sodan was lifted above Mr. Maga, spun around a few times like a giant wooden plank, and then tossed out of the ring. It was determined that the Averitan people, once again, had won the debate.

The klaxon blared again and it was time for everyone to go to work.

The prisoner resumed her position from yesterday on the assembly line, screwing the wheels into place on the military jeeps. The task had to be done by hand, as the Averitans eschewed any labor-saving technology for their "job-killing" potential.

In her many hours having done this over the past several months, she'd occasionally notice herself in the chrome, would sometimes check that she had not become completely disheveled in appearance. Today was one of those days that brought some relief. While she was a bit more noticeably thinner, her brown face was still mostly smooth. Her hair was longer, a bit tangled, but was still black and retained its sheen underneath the red bandana she kept it guarded. With the blue jumpsuit she had to wear to the factory each day (except Sundays), the sum of her appearance was like a browner version of Rosie the Riveter.

The other people on the factory line were from a mix of racial backgrounds, but they all shared one thing in common. For one, they were all shackled together in small groupings of identical ethnic background. I-62742, for instance, was chained to her fellow villagers that were all abducted the same night. The other was that they were all imprisoned as either political opponents or prisoners of war. The government of the Big-League Maga had no patience for dissidents from its ultimate quest to bring the entire North American continent under one nationalist banner, whether they were internal or external.

Always supervising the workers from some distant, windowed room above were the Maga's party allies, all of them white and well-to-do. Some of their ancestors were the blue-collar type and complained about the loss of their manufacturing jobs. But once they gained the power to bring about the changes to stop this from happening, they found that they couldn't find any white workers to do them. They all wanted to be a part of the new ruling class. So, a bloated bureaucracy was established for these privileged citizens. All manual labor was left for designated enemies and the remaining socioeconomic underclasses.

All of this would have made for fascinating sociological study by Prisoner I-62742 if the brutal realities of her day to day existence weren't so pervasive. It was hard to ignore the constant cramped conditions, work drudgery, and sexual harassment of the guards.

Work concluded around 1700, leaving just enough time to pile into a group shower and prepare for dinner. It was Wednesday, however, which meant that a group of her fellow prisoners would skip the customary hygiene for a group Bible meditation. The whole culture of the Complex seemed bent on turning the different racial groups against one another, but the faith to which some of the individuals still clung acted against this, seemed to delay the inevitable.

On this day, the group reflected on a passage from Colossians, Chapter 4:

"Persevere in prayer, being watchful in it with thanksgiving; at the same time, pray for us, too, that God may open a door to us for the word, to speak of the mystery of Christ, for which I am in prison, that I may make it clear, as I must speak. Conduct yourselves wisely toward outsiders, making the most of the opportunity. Let your speech be gracious, seasoned with salt, so that you should respond to each one."

"That makes it pretty clear to me," started an aged woman named Claudia in the group. 1-62742 remembered that she came from the same village as her. "That we should be finding opportunities to mention our belief and show, through our actions and words, the joy and hope that this brings us even in a place as dark and miserable as this is."

A middle-aged, white balding man added another thought.

"I think another thing to remember is that we ought to count our blessings that we're at least in nothing like Paul's situation. We can still find these ways to remember our faith and share it with others while here, so just imagine what it took for him to maintain that all on its own. It's truly incredible and it makes you wonder what our excuses are."

Everyone in the group nodded, a few gave verbal affirmations, including I-62742.

But it still wouldn't hurt to pray for escaping this hellhole, she thought to herself.

The next day, Thursday, passed by without consequence. But Friday showed evidence that racial tensions had reached a snapping point. A brawl had reportedly broken out with scores of the Ispanian and Rican prisoners first thing in the morning, leading the two groups to segregate to different breakfast tables entirely. By the afternoon, the minority groups had all ganged up against the pale-skinned, black-haired Sino prisoners, who they resented for the status they enjoyed in pre-Averitan society. A full-out racial war broke out in the Complex on all sides, each group retreating to a different corner of the prison and factory. The supervisors stood watching behind their tinted glass, well-combed hair, and warm lattés. Their top priority was to edit the proper amount of footage of the violence to send to the news media that evening.

I-62742 had no stomach for the violence, crouched frozen underneath her cell's bunkbed as she witnessed the fighters fashion whatever bits of metal they could tear from the complex walls into clubs and shanks.

By nightfall, as the noise of the fighting quieted down from the lack of light, the prisoner was working frantically through the Rosary, praying that she would last the night.

Around her sixth decade of Hail Marys, an explosion was heard at the ground level. She crawled forward to witness the action, noticing a steady stream of bright purple sparks and smoke pouring into the air. The men and women fighting emptied the area in panic, not having seen anything like this before.

A dozen darkly clad figures in military gear stormed in, some headed up the stairs with rifles and flashlights. Three of them along with one of the prisoners broke off, walked down the corridor towards I-62742's cell. They wielded flashlights where a bayonet would normally be, searching slowly high and low. She focused on an Our Father as she reached one of the marker beads between the decades, wishing nothing more than to not be found now.

After what seemed like well over fifteen minutes,

these soldiers reached her cell. One of them didn't take much time, the man's body nearly flat to the ground as he exposed the prisoner's space. He saw the set of hazel-colored, retracted pupils stare back at him, meaning that he found what he was looking for.

He lowered his gun a bit, so his own brown eyes, still almost obscured by his black battle helmet, could be seen.

"Maria?" the soldier asked cautiously. The two with him crouched down, also looking into her gaze.

"Who are you?" she shot back.

The soldier did not respond either, instead removing his helmet to give away the identity of his hair, which was brown, long, and matted down with sweat.

"Who do you think I am?" Josik said, a relieved smile showing through.

Maria let her guard down, caught up in the sudden joy to be felt by the situation. She emerged from her measly sanctuary. She was saved, allowing herself to smile and get caught in Josik's gaze.

"Estás bien, señorita?" asked Juan Colella, humbly.

Maria had scarcely a moment to answer. Gunshots started not too far away.

"Let's go!" Josik commanded, slipping his helmet back on. Protected by the Colellas at their front and rear, the two scurried down the stairs and out the new small opening that led them out of the Complex.

2-12

The couple, once connected to the other liberators, were ushered into a nearby apartment. The other Ispanian prisoners, once found, were quickly sorted into other rooms. The tenement was filthy, like many in Detroit in this age, and stacked to the roof with family members of the Rican Resistance fighter who offered it. But for Maria, it was the safe, quiet space for which she had been longing for months. With a crude blanket handed to her, she fell into a much-needed sleep against Josik's lap.

But Josik could not rest, his body was fueled by the passion and love he remembered developing for the gentle creature now at his feet. He contemplatively stroked her jet-black hair, now flowing on the floor after having been liberated from the red handkerchief in which Maria kept it covered. With every subtle, loving pull of her hair, he seemed to pull out another memory of what they had shared nearly a year ago, and how it had led up to a common theme of unfinished business. It was a kiss he felt he owed to her, that he hoped she'd graciously accept. But it was also a future with her he longed to continue, for Josik felt he could never fully integrate himself into this new, true version of life without her by his side. And, being true to his Bohemx egalitarian impulses, he hoped that she felt a desire and a happiness to have him at her side too.

Still, Josik was reminded by himself—with each passing hour, in fact—that he could not hope to live out this dream—a dream with her, a real, natural family, and a meaningful living made in the midst of a tight-knit community—unless he made good on the rescue mission he undertook with the Colellas and the Resistance soldiers, followed with his own plan to sneak Maria back over the dreaded Blue Wall. He did his best with prayer to this end, even pulling Maria's rosary out of her pocket for help. Josik was still clueless on most Christian rituals such as the Rosary, but it at least helped him focus his thoughts.

The morning sun arrived with some good news as the packed apartment began to stir. The other Rican participants in the prison ambush all returned safely at that point, along with the prisoners they freed, which would add to their underground ranks. Resistance soldiers in Detroit joined the movement shortly after the formation of the Averitan Union, after learning that one of the new empire's first initiatives was the subjugation of their fellow blacks in declaring war on the Ricans.

The mother of the family prepared breakfast—a simple platter of hard biscuits and scrambled eggs. Josik, Raul, and Juan chatted with the other soldiers over the food, as they all packed around the counter for dining space. He retold his trials beyond the Blue Wall with the enlarged group, pausing at times

218

when the topic of General Deshawn was brought up. Maria, meanwhile, was not hungry—still unwell from the trauma of imprisonment. She sat wrapped in a blanket in a chair, staring thoughtfully out the room's one window.

"So, what happened to him? How did he die?" various men asked.

Josik reached into his breast pocket to feel for the flag pin before he answered.

"The Averitans used some kind of terrible new weapon on us," Josik responded. "A sonic bomb, one that shook the very ground beneath us."

He took the pin out of his pocket, made a fist around it.

"Most of us in the regiment were far enough away to not be affected by it. But Deshawn wasn't—."

Another pause. Josik bit his lip.

"Deshawn wasn't so lucky."

A silence fell around the counter. Everyone stopped eating.

Finally, Raul Colella spoke up.

"We'll do much worse to their damn albino leaders when we get our hands on them, I personally promise that! When they took my mother, they tore out my heart. ¡Mi propio corazón! When me and mi padre return to the Complex and finally find her, we will tear out theirs. We will carve it out of their chest and show it to them while it's still beating!"

A number of the black men shouted in agreement.

But Josik refused to entertain the talk of vengeance. He held his hands up, motioning for the men to listen.

"I came to know Deshawn enough to know that that's not what he would have wanted. He understood that your people had been oppressed for ages, and that the impulse for reprisal was only natural, but for his sake—please. By all means, fight the war, but don't do it out of hatred for these white people. I'm sure not all of them agree with what their faction is doing, just as I'm sure some of your people don't agree with the constant conflict."

"That's easy for you to say," said the muscular one known as Troy. "You look like one of them!"

Everyone raised their voices in agreement. Josik turned the pin through his fingers.

"Besides," Troy pressed on. "How do you know, as someone who was only with him for a few weeks, that that's what General Deshawn actually wanted?"

Josik thought for a moment, stared at the counter. At the moment, he had no answer.

Then he held up the pin.

"Deshawn gave this to me. I don't know what it's supposed to do, if anything, but he knew and I know what it means. It's about a great country that once sprawled across this entire continent, one that guaranteed freedom and justice to its people centuries ago through written law. And it brought people of all colors together, to debate the problems of the day through a peaceful process. Victory in this land once meant being a part of the group that helped the most amount of people, all through discussion and deliberation. The politics this system required was not free of conflict, but brought about its own thrill of challenge without all the bloodshed of outright military warfare."

"A way of winning without shooting each other?" Troy mused in response. "I find that fantasy hard to believe."

Josik wistfully threw his hands up. He couldn't explain much more.

"I don't know what else to tell you. You just have to believe me. It's the only way we could take the first step to make this fantasy a reality."

Juan, who stood next to Josik, nodded softly. He stayed silent, crying quietly. Josik turned to him, embracing the sad old man against his chest.

"I must forgive," whispered Juan between tears. "All these years I grew to hate these Averitans, and I must forgive. Where does it stop if we don't?"

Everyone else assumed that this was the end of the debate. They returned to breakfast. But this was interrupted by Maria rising from her chair, her eyebrows raised in a rare expression of horror.

"We need to get out of here, now!"

Raul pulled back the curtains to investigate. Machine gun turrets manned by soldiers in burnt-orange military garb could be seen across the street. Packs of C-4 were attached to the side of the building. Helicopters, armed to the teeth with Incinerates, were also close by. The Resistance fighters had made a terrible mistake.

Raul ran back to shield Maria, knocking her to the ground as the explosions tore out a giant, exposing hole in the building.

All the men, including Josik, got back on their feet to ringing in their ears, and made way for the stairs in the hallway. Josik and Juan individually slung Maria and Raul over each of their shoulders. Josik ran through the open apartment door. He looked back a moment—Raul and Juan suddenly weren't there, lost among the Rican soldiers knocked down again by gunfire.

Josik made it down to street, quickly finding his borrowed jeep. He looked up at the building. It was now engulfed in flames.

He started driving towards the city's freeway. It wouldn't be long before the Averitan soldiers would be in pursuit.

2-13

Josik, still with little experience driving, quickly found himself on one of the city's main avenues. A number of military vehicles were catching up to him, and a helicopter was overhead. They needed to get out of town. But how to throw off the Averitans's scent?

His speed exceeded 75 mph, the vehicle zigzagging left and right, in-and-out of the lanes. Maria sat still for a while, groping at the bottom of the seat for dear life.

An antiquated freeway on-ramp was ahead, so Josik swerved the car toward it to the right once they passed underneath the overpass. But it proved a risky move. He had turned into oncoming military traffic—unaware of the chase taking place, simply traveling, but still at grave hazard to Josik and his pursuers.

He found his way to the interstate's median, the predators behind him, struggling to adjust. One of the pursuing vehicles crashed head-on, creating a massive pile-up that expanded as its dark plume of smoke disappeared into the distance.

Ten minutes of this adventure passed, and the Averitan soldiers closed the gap. Maria saw them get their weapons ready to fire in the rearview mirror. She shot a look to Josik, hoping he could translate body language.

He nodded back in acknowledgement. His eyes had already spotted a nearby bridge that could provide them a new route through which to escape.

Josik drove past the off-ramp to the left. The highway curved right.

"Duck!" he told Maria.

A gap between vehicles opened up ahead. He hit the brakes to reduce the speed of the turn, but it wasn't enough to prevent such wicked drift as the jeep maneuvered its 180 degrees to the opposite direction. The soldiers opened fire, but only a few bullets hit their target. The glass shattered.

Maria sat herself back up in steps, using all portions of Josik's body for support. He turned the vehicle onto the off-ramp, thinking they had escaped the Averitans for now.

But he was sorely mistaken. As soon as they began the span of the bridge, a squad of cars could be spotted ahead. They had formed a barricade on the bridge.

Josik jerked his head back and forth between this view and Maria's, trying to talk and analyze simultaneously.

"We need to drive off the bridge!" he stated, shouting

over the sound of the lake's wind and the roar of the engine block.

"What?" she screamed "Are you crazy?"

"It's the only way left to go!" Josik pressed. There was no time for any of their usual discussion or debate on this matter.

Maria froze up again, only able to eke out a few words.

"Josik, I . . ."

"What?" he snapped, expecting further objection.

Maria shot a look at him.

"I love you."

Josik turned his whole face to Maria, searching for which emotion to feel. Finally, he settled on one with a few words.

He said it with his warmest smile yet.

"I love you, too."

The two pushed toward each other in a quick first kiss, as Josik's abdication of the wheel didn't leave them on the pavement for much longer. The vehicle drifted to the left, managing to break through the corroded steel at over 95 mph.

Josik and Maria found themselves lifted out of the car, barely managing to find the presence of mind to reach for each other's hands. Despite their collective terror at the risk to life and limb, the weightless sensation of falling underneath felt like a strong pleasure, especially with the act of doing it side by side.

They dropped into the steady river together feet first.

2-14

oth had the good fortune of knowing how to swim, and they found themselves on the shore opposite from the city in just a few minutes. They spent the next half hour trying to regain their physical state, coughing up water and embracing each other tightly for warmth. The water must not have been more than 10-15 degrees above freezing. Moreover, they had held their breath for a while underwater to minimize detection from the helicopters. The two could see the air units still hovering over the river, still searching the spot where the two had entered for signs.

At one point, even while they were still freezing, Josik broke away from Maria. He was looking towards the trees inland.

"Wh-what is it?" Maria asked, with quivering breath.

Josik held his finger up, showing off a surprisingly calm composure.

"I think we're being watched," he said. "I'll be right back."

Just like that, he ran off towards some bushes, his judgment clearly off.

After a moment, a pale woman, donning a wide-brimmed hat and heavy fur coat, appeared to Maria. Josik ran up right behind her, ready to pounce.

The pale woman curled her lip, taken aback by the lack of warmth. Yet she maintained a sense of buoyancy in response to his approach.

"Oh, hi there," she said, quite accented.

Josik looked her up and down, amused by the quirky, natural look to the woman's outfit. She might have laughed had he not been suspicious.

"Are you with the Averitans?" Josik interrogated.

"Oh, I don't know about the Averitans," the woman responded. "We love all our neighbors, but that Big-League Maga and his army have been a really big pain in the keister to us, eh?"

"Eh?" Josik mocked. "Are you asking me?"

"No," she answered. "No, uh, um, eh?"

Josik relaxed and stood straight, letting down his guard. He felt bad for making fun of the woman, and he didn't have a weapon with which to threaten this stranger anyway.

"Who are you?" Josik asked, resetting.

The fur-coated woman responded with a smile and removed her hat, revealing short, braided blonde hair.

"Captain Jane Smythe, at your service, sir," she said, bowing.

Captain Smythe turned to acknowledge Maria.

"And ma'am," she added.

Josik and Maria both grinned back, appreciating the pleasantries.

"Captain Smythe, me and my . . . girlfriend?" he broke off, looking over to the young woman referenced.

Maria smiled back. That was enough acknowledgment.

"Yes, girlfriend," Josik repeated with a wide, toothy smile. "She and I need a place to hide where the Averitans won't find us. They'll come for us if we don't move from here in the next few minutes. We're members of the Resistance, by the way."

Smythe snapped to action, unquestioning.

Just as a fleet of helicopters began to approach the shore, the Captain rushed the couple into a dense forest. Underneath the cozy darkness of the trees were several short log cabins, not more than eight feet tall. A whole village lived here, yet another isolated one that Josik had come across over these last several weeks. All of its inhabitants conveyed the same warmth and enthusiasm for interacting with people, unbending in their politeness with an overuse of their elongated "s-ORE-ys" and offerings for drink.

Josik learned that these people called themselves the Nucks, whose people once boasted a large and spread-out nation. They took a curious interest in the stories Josik and Maria offered when asked, and considered their foreignness a source of satisfaction. A few defectors from the Averitan side of the lake had joined them over the years, which is how they learned of the latest political and military developments. But they still preferred their comfortable, community-centered way of life, choosing to stay out of whatever widespread conflict had been brewing. They served as a refuge to those who wanted to get away from the war, but they were not ready to enter a conflict. Their fighting force, led by Smythe, numbered only a few dozen.

"With all due respect," Josik said to Captain Smythe, who was explaining all this over a hearty, lamp-light dinner of deer sausage and pickled vegetables. "Then why did you take us in?"

"At the end of the day," Smythe explained. "We're a refuge to others. It's been a tradition of our people for as long as we can remember. There's a tale our ancestors tell of this, and of how long ago we had a southern neighbor who shared our values. Two very big, powerful empires we once were."

"What does this tale say that happened?" Maria asked.

"The Tale of the Two Queens, as it goes, is something like this," Smythe started again, beverage mug in hand. "Two young daughters of a royal couple—an older one and a younger one—were groomed from birth to become their own rulers someday. Their parents had agreed to let them divide the kingdom, because they were both so fiercely independent. For their first several decades of rule, the two kingdoms worked side-by-side. They had some different ideas of how to run their lands, but they essentially valued the same things during this time: helping the poor, providing for the elderly, limiting their own power and respecting the powers given to other parts of their government, and welcoming foreigners. As the two queens got older, however, their way of running things began to differ more and more. The older queen started taxing the poor more and the rich less. She also started to turn away ships of foreigners, claiming that they were suddenly bad for the kingdom and that only the people living there currently were allowed to succeed. The older queen also found her kingdom much larger and much more powerful than the younger queen's because of wars the older one found herself in. But the older queen had at least used this power to the protection of her younger sister's kingdom."

Smythe paused for a gulp of her stout lager.

"Then what happened?" Josik asked.

Smythe wiped her mouth with a rough dishcloth.

"Well," she resumed, "the older queen and her kingdom became so powerful, spread out, and so negligent of the poor and working people that the peasants living there revolted and cut off the queen's head. Anarchy reigned. And without the protection of her older sister, the younger sister's kingdom fell prey to her enemies. What became of the younger sister's kingdom is what we say became left of our people."

Josik and Maria were both silent, looking down at their mugs. It was a sad tale, but it had turned some wheels in Josik's mind. Maria was nonverbally lamenting the plight of these people, and of this fractured land that she had been learning was in turmoil in ways she never had to face before in the tranquility of the Ispanian village. Josik meanwhile, was realizing an opportunity—to connect the pieces of Sam's history to the current age.

"I know its name," Josik declared, straight into Smythe's eyes. "What the kingdom of the older sister was. What promise it held."

Smythe raised her eyebrows, asking to hear more.

"America," Josik said. "It was called America."

2-15

The three did not speak much longer. The guests chose to retire after the physically exhausting turn of events that day. Smythe stayed up for much longer, however, turning over the revelation of this new history of America in her mind. From what she had heard, America sounded like a great, tragic legend, full of grand ideals of equality and opportunity, allowing all kinds of individuals to pursue bold visions to better themselves and the world around them. So why did it fall apart in the space (as he learned that night) of little over two generations, if the legend really was true? Josik didn't have a full answer for her, conveying that this was still a story that he had not been given the chance to read all the way through yet. He referred to his visions, the source of which was still beyond Josik, despite Maria's insistence that divine providence was involved. Still, Smythe remained skeptical, her faith weighed down by the fractured world that moved around her and her people.

Still, she began to wonder in the early morning—could the ideals of America in the past be used to unite the warring factions, in the name of a new, but revived cause? As per usual in these sublime, solitary moments of hers, she picked up her diary and began to write.

***

Josik and Maria slept together rather fitfully at first, the Ispanian lady fearful of the thought of being alone at night because it reminded her of her recent ordeal. Josik also thought back to the Colellas, whom he had just realized were now dead. How was he going to explain this to the Ispanian villagers?

As for achieving sleep, it also didn't help that the two were inexperienced with sharing such close quarters with another person, and found each other inadvertently trading elbows into one another's face. Still, when the two finally found a marginally comfortable position, Josik's mind was lifted away back to Sam's, where he was introduced to sound of rainfall.

He looked out his bedroom window. It was showering heavily outside.

Josik, as usual, maneuvered to the kitchen. He was spotted by a seated Sam, who was sporting a bathrobe and long, uncombed hair.

"Coffee?" he asked flatly, hands clasped around his own mug.

Josik nodded, surprised with Sam's uncharacteristically calm, lethargic movements.

Sam pointed to his machine, inviting his guest

to pour himself a mug. Once Josik was seated, a suspenseful silence settled over the room, save for the lowly ticking of the wall clock.

"How have you been?" asked Sam, at last.

Josik was surprised at the question. What exactly did that mean? He had never been asked this before.

"I'm sorry?"

"How have you been? I mean, how are things going for you? What, they don't ask these kinds of things in the future?"

"The future's a bit too violent to tolerate such pleasantries."

Sam smirked. "Probably good, anyway. Our pleasantries, luxuries, and rampant materialism are what's leading to the collapse of my society."

Josik thought back to his mandated libertine origins in Bohem, and took delight in the thought that maybe Authority's downfall was just around the corner.

Sam continued.

"Well, it sounds like this country is starting to lay the groundwork for that violent future you come from."

"Why do you say that?"

Sam rose from his chair, took a few steps over to his old transistor radio (one of the ones with dials and wood paneling). He switched it on to one of the FM channels:

"We're bringing you continuing coverage of this shocking story still in development. Methodist Hospital in California has just confirmed that President Parr passed away at 12:47 pm Pacific Daylight Time. She was the target of a terrorist bombing during a speaking event near the state's Capitol in Sacramento. The terror group, Antifa Liberation, has come out on social media taking credit for the attack, saying it was done on behalf of 'the people of California and of the proletarian masses being oppressed all around the country.'"

The radio was switched off. Josik looked down, his eyes wide. He understood the impact of this event.

"Why are you telling me about this?" he begged Sam.

Sam shrugged his shoulders, apparently numb to the emotional element of current events at this point.

"It's what you woke up to, Josik. It's your duty to know at this point. You're becoming an American, are you not?"

Josik nodded, a tear in his eye. He wondered if others had shed tears for this country before. Sam hadn't confessed this to Josik one way or the other, despite his obvious dedication to American history.

Josik sighed, his hands gently rubbing his face.

"I don't know what my purpose is yet. For earth's sake, I don't even know if I have one. Maybe it's making a difference for the Ispanians. Maybe it's something else. But I accept this duty. What else do I need to know?" the traveler said.

Sam started pacing around the room, his hand against his stubbly chin.

"There's not much more I can teach you at this point," the master of the house said. "What I mean, is that there's nothing much more I can teach you from lecturing you here. The two political parties split into four more than a decade ago. Terrorist groups aligned with the extremist elements of the left-right ideology are active in a manner not unlike banana republics like 1980s Colombia. The rest of the developed world is now feckless in its own divisions to face up the authoritarian countries reshaping the world order away from favoring constitutional democracy—not really away from democracy altogether, but towards the arbitrary whims of demagoguery and mob rule, if you'll remember those concepts from our Aristotle lesson. Many in this country now see the appeal, but the protected class chooses to ignore the simmering revolution squeezed in between their coastal, urban walls of power and influence. Dominated by the rich, they reinforce their socioeconomic bubbles in various ways across the political spectrum, depending on the neighborhood. For the liberal ones, they claim that unhappiness is simply a matter of economics and that prosperity is just around the corner of a new government program or handout without conditions, while similarly demanding a child's ability to change gender without question and demanding a women's ability to abort her child without question. For the conservative ones, they claim the rich guys have all the answers and insist we need to keep taxing them less and less, so they can use the extra cash to spread out their suburbs further away from black and poor people while driving circles in their SUVs around their McMansions."

Josik looked blankly back, visibly overwhelmed.

"I guess there are a few more things I can teach you," Sam said, smirking. "But with any academic class, there needs to be a practical portion of it, one where you can actually experience the concepts we've discussed. Starting tomorrow—or whenever you return here—we're going to go on a long field trip. We're going to travel to the spots where I've seen the dreaded pieces fall into place. Only then will you have seen what I have seen, learned as I have learned where this country failed. You may choose to use this knowledge however you see fit. Use it to make the future at least a little bit brighter from the one you've told me about. We'll be disguised. No one will recognize me and no one will know your true identity. Do you accept this?"

"Yes," Josik said without hesitation. "But can I ask you a question?"

"Yes, my friend."

"You told me your greatest heartbreak. And I'm so sorry it happened. That must have been so difficult to go through alone. I still don't know how we were connected, but I want to take the opportunity to help you. So, I feel I should ask... how did you end up from there to here?"

Sam looked away, his face managing a bittersweet smile.

"I'm not ready to tell you the full story. Not just yet, Josik. But I promise you, we'll have plenty of time together during this trip to talk about it. The story of Rachel and I... well, it's a long one with many different parts to it."

Josik nodded, a slight smile on his face. Sam rose, laid a hand on Josik shoulder.

"I'll be glad to have your companionship, Josik. I haven't felt such purpose in years, not since the day that voice told me to expect a visitor."

"A voice?" Josik wondered, looking up at Sam.

"Another story I'll need to tell you on the road," Sam replied. "But for now, take the time to rest and pack."

2-16

Josik and Maria couldn't be certain that they had caused the Averitans to be thrown off their scent for very long, so they set out to leave the Nucks two mornings later. They were going home to Ispania. The villagers were gracious, loaning a fully provisioned canoe and map.

The couple was preparing to put out into the lake at first light to minimize threat of detection. Josik had just barely launched their craft and lifted his remaining foot from the shore when Captain Smythe was spotted emerging from the trees, running toward them in a frenzy with raised hands.

The two both looked back. Smythe skidded to a stop just before the edge of the water, breathing heavily. Josik gazed back curiously.

"I forgot to tell you one last thing I meant to say last night," Smyth said, in between breaths, "when you were telling me about your friend's dream of his."

Josik thought back to the conversation, still fresh on his mind for the emotions it wrought. They had talked about Deshawn and his abrupt end, as well as the vision for the continent's future that he had passed on to Josik.

"I've been thinking about it since last night," Smythe continued. "And if you can find other factions that are willing to join in that union you've imagined, then you can count my people in."

Josik stood up straight, surprised at the thought just put into his head. The vision wasn't Josik's, it was Biwun's. Still, to make a new union a reality, a revived one at that?

Finally, he let a smile crack, Josik's eyes to the heavens. His brain was tingling with the thought. What seemed a vague reference at first had just given Josik a new cause, a new purpose. Still, he felt the need to tamp down his optimism. Him, a non-Earth native, a unifier of the downtrodden and oppressed factions? How could that happen?

"Well, I don't know about that happening anytime soon," Josik replied after a long silence. "But it sure does give me something to think about."

Josik reached out to shake Smythe's hand in appreciation, not realizing that he was too far away and throwing the boat off-balance in the process. Both Josik and Maria fell into the water, laughing hysterically.

The pair made their escape, paddling south to the Great Lake that opened up before them. The first three days were spent on the lake, except for the nights they spent sleeping on passing islands beneath the open sky. Spring, fortunately, had already begun, the temperature brisk but not freezing. The two slept well these nights, kept especially warm by each other.

They reached a large metropolitan city called Cleveland at the end of the third day, hiding out in its run-down, formerly bustling industrial sector for the night. These arrangements made for considerably less comfortable sleep, as Josik and Maria struggled to find sleep behind a pungent, rusted-out dumpster.

Over the next several days, they made their way up a river, continuing south. They didn't speak much during this entire time, choosing to simply enjoy each other's physical presence, as well as the natural beauty around them that they had never known existed in this vast, diverse land. Wildflowers could be seen in bloom, as well as the maples and oaks, green with spring growth. Birds tweeted around them during the day, while wayward rodents—not just mice, but ground squirrels and even the occasional ferret—were discovered inadvertently in the evening, when camp was setup on the shore for the night.

Finally, they reached the town called Akron, where a train would take them to the region formerly called Maryland. They hid out in the industrial slums for the night.

Throughout this whole time, Josik had not had any sleep time excursions to the past. That is, until he fell asleep that early evening.

2-17

Josik was with Sam again, but something seemed terribly wrong. The Bohemx was seated in the middle of the back row of a Toyota hatchback, his teacher in the driver's seat, but with darker brown hair and a smooth face. Josik thought he looked about twenty years younger. Seated to his right was a young, attractive, redheaded woman. She was fair skinned with wavy red hair, gentle, hazel eyes, and freckles on her cheeks. They were both wearing stylish flannels and dark-washed jeans, chatting playfully.

Sam shook his head.

"I can't believe you've never been to Folsom Lake," he said as a first verbal poke.

Josik tried to interject: "Hi guys!"

The girl just smiled back at Sam with eyebrows raised, preparing to retort.

"I guess I was just never much of a Sacramento gal. If I ever wanted to do anything even remotely interesting back in high school, I went to the Bay Area."

Sam responded with wide eyes in kind, over-exaggerating the offense. Josik waved his hand in front of Sam, trying to get his attention to no avail. He even tried jumping in the car while spreading his arms and legs in an exercise fashion, with no results other than a bumped head. No, in this version of the past, he realized, Josik held merely an observer status. The thought of this frustrated the traveler for a moment—this wasn't the kind of field trip he had in mind. Quickly he realized the futility of this mindset, and Josik prayed for patience for the things he was seeing now for whatever reason. Josik thought back to what older Sam had said the other day (or whichever day it was at this point)—the student realized that he was seeing and witnessing the same things that his teacher had seen and witnessed, in a manner of speaking. Once again, Josik was confused—but he accepted it.

"Wow . . ." Sam enunciated, preparing to raise a teasing finger in front of his good friend. "Listen here, friend. You were born and raised in Davis. Davis is definitely not the Bay Area, so you're a Sacramento native through and through. As such, you need to pay your homeland respect."

"Homeland?" she smirked. "Where do you think I live, the Gaza Strip?"

The two laughed for a brief moment.

Josik smiled for a moment at the feat of teasing, and thought to himself "oh, young love" sarcastically. He attempted to gather his bearings while Sam and his apparent girlfriend continued to prod one another.

Josik looked out the window. They were on a six-lane freeway, passing by a mix of small commercial businesses and walled-off residential developments. There were healthy green leafy trees everywhere, and green signs pointing to off ramps at least every few minutes.

The radio was playing public news broadcasting on a low volume, discernable by its repeat of headlines every half hour. The date and time were visible on the screen looking over the car's console:

03/21/2017 11:34am

Eventually, they took an off-ramp where many shopping places filled the space north of the freeway, while the southern part consisted of largely empty fields. After winding past the traffic-choked shopping regions, and proceeding through the stately suburban manors, they approached a trail. They parked, proceeded to step out to change into their hiking boots.

Josik followed behind as they crested what seemed like a man-made hill. His desire for romance tingled a bit after seeing them grasp hands, a small smile visible on both their faces.

They reached the top without incident, the vast, swelling brownish-blue reservoir below them. The sun burned warmly, and the oak trees were pollinating, setting the scene for a typical show of Northern California foothill spring pageantry. Sailors and boaters were seen skirting across the lake in the distance.

Josik noticed Sam pull a small, dark, flat object

out of his pocket. He noticed the young version of his teacher staring blankly at the flat rock, tapping his thumb every few seconds. After a minute or two, Sam shoved the object hurriedly back into his pocket. The young woman was looking at him this whole time, subtly tapping a finger on her thigh.

"Sorry," Sam said. "App crashed. Wasn't important anyway. Damn smartphones."

Smartphone. Josik told himself to remember that word.

"It's alright," the woman said, with a small grin. "How about this view though?"

"Wow!" Sam cried, looking with the woman over the scene at the lake. He turned towards the woman, motioning up and down with one of his hands. "Still not as beautiful as this view though."

Josik noticed the two share a bashful smile, the woman's face fully flushed.

"You know something?" Sam asked.

"What's that?" the young woman asked, eyebrows raised in interest.

Sam squeezed her hand. "I missed you."

The woman looked sideways at first, a coy smirk on her face. But her expression quickly grew into a beaming smile.

"I missed you too," she repeated back.

They leaned in to kiss each other a few times, a hand held on the other's hip.

They continued walking for some additional time, eventually stopping to set up underneath the shade of an oak tree. A picnic was laid out, with a small array of sandwiches and various crunchy sundries. Sam and his girlfriend sat crisscrossed, with knees folded in, as they squinted to look over the lake's steady boating scene.

Sam eventually broke the silence.

"You've hardly said anything about Barcelona," he declared.

"Oh, well," replied the young woman, easily embarrassed, "I've never been fond about talking too much about myself. It just always felt kind of selfish for whatever reason."

"Well, I'm asking, so you're not exactly doing it intentionally. Plus, you've already spent three months studying abroad there, I'm sure there's plenty of discoveries you've been dying to talk about."

The woman rolled her eyes sarcastically.

Sam leaned in toward her, over-exaggerated on fisted hands and knees. He had prepared another ridiculous facial expression.

"Tell me, Rachel," he said, with an unbelievable air of sultriness. "Tell me everything."

Rachel returned with her distinctive smirk and raised eyebrows, a halfway point between questioning the subject's sanity and being genuinely amused.

"Well, I thought my pictures on social media basically said it all. The plajta, the tapas, and the architecture all made for such a welcome break from this country. The part I didn't really capture were the political tensions I could sense growing underneath."

"You mean the independence movement."

Rachel nodded her head.

"Any insight in your political studies you could offer to that, comrade?"

"Well, you're in luck, because I'm taking a class in Western European politics this semester, as you may recall. A big theme they've been emphasizing throughout the course concerns resurgent divisions. That also gets into continuing ethnic and cultural differences in Europe, stuff that was overlooked in the face of the Cold War and whatnot."

Rachel interrupted, setting herself on her side while supporting her head with her arm.

"Am I getting another one of your lectures?" she asked, managing to keep a sarcastically straight face.

Josik rolled his eyes towards Sam, empathizing with Rachel.

"You're totally right, dear. You got me," he shrugged his shoulders.

He continued.

"After the collapse of the Soviet Union and the Iron Curtain, these differences created intra-national conflict again. Catalans versus Spanish, Flemish versus Walloons, just to name a few. Add onto that the mass migrations from the Middle East and Africa that have taken place over the last few years, then you start to understand Euro-skepticism and Brexit. European countries have historically been more ethnically homogenous than ours, and less experienced with long-distance immigration."

"So, what's our excuse?"

"A little bit of the same problem. The way I see it, lingering, implicit racism still held by some white people. But the more important problem has to be the gulf in political and economic well-being."

"The 1%?" Rachel asked gruffly. (Josik thought she sounded like a popular left-wing politician of the period.) "That's the problem, right? Just tax the hell out of 'em?"

Sam's closed mouth maneuvered a bit. He still had a hard time of politely showing his displeasure on political subjects on which the two disagreed.

"Alright," he said, arms crossed. "So, what do you think the problem is?"

Rachel sat upright, speaking as if she had waited a lifetime for this opportunity to answer.

"I think about the fact that so many students back in Berkeley seem so lost, so uncertain in everything. They can't figure out what they want out of life, let alone a career vocation, because they're so determined that they need to know what their passion is by the time they graduate. So, they either spend their college career doing things for themselves like throwing themselves into their studies, or they join organizations that only speak to their particular group—Queer-Straight Alliance, Flipinx, and the like. If they actually took the time to be part of something interested in the bigger picture, the broader community, then they could learn some useful selflessness."

"Sacrifice," Sam said, evoking religious language.

"You say it that way. There's a good quote I once heard in high school that I think describes the concept well: 'the real way to get happiness is to give happiness to other people.' "

"Hmph. So, which groups would you have students join?"

"Service clubs, so we can understand all the grunt work that's often required to keep a community together. Clubs with hobbies that aren't sports or tech-based, so the focus is on the team and not the competition or the gadgets. But I also think our generation of students needs to explore the value of religion and spirituality more than ever, because there's so much self-discipline and valuable time for reflection that comes with it."

Sam looked away, uncomfortable.

Rachel reached for his hand, but missed. She just ended up a bit closer to him.

"I know that religion isn't your cup of tea. It isn't something you grew up with, unlike me. But I know we're both open-minded enough to hear each other out. That's fair, right?"

Sam turned back to look at his girlfriend. He let the moments pass as he said nothing, simply taking in Rachel's appearance. Josik wondered what must have been going through his mind. Clearly, they hadn't seen each other in quite some time. Perhaps Sam just needed to remind himself what she looked like.

"Yes," he said, bringing his face to a thin, invisible barrier that he set less than an inch in front of hers. "That's fair."

"Good," Rachel said with a breathless smile.

She defied the barrier placed in front of her, and they began their first episode of passionate romance in over three months.

Josik looked on with curiosity, wondering if he should take notes for Maria's benefit.

2-18

Josik and Maria woke up to a thin brown haze that hung over the city, and spent a few minutes coughing and gagging. Josik's first instinct, upon catching his breath, was to put to practice his observations from the early twenty-first century.

He took Maria a bit by surprise with the first kiss, but her response to the passion with which he delivered it turned quickly positive. She reached for Josik's hair, while he returned the favor with his hands above her hips.

They would have continued were it not for Maria's realization of the toxic environment around them.

"Josik, Josik," she said, pushing him away, starting to cough again. "We have to go. It's not safe here."

Josik broke off in acknowledgement. He stuffed his sleeping bag in his sack and grabbed his leather backpack and satchel to go.

They slipped across Akron's industrial downtown, the area covered with block after block of polluted concrete. The streets were clogged with working-class throngs, shuffling dejectedly from factory to factory. These people were from backgrounds of all stripes— formerly Bohemx elites, second-class designated Ricans — but mostly, the crowd was taken up with poor, dirt-encrusted whites.

Once past the massive factory complexes, Josik and Maria waded through what they later referred to as the "swamp village." From this experience, they understood the housing of the typical Averitan working man that his society's propaganda purported to represent. The landscape of this zone was pocked with filthy puddles of water every few feet. The area not already taken up with wastewater was filled by tiny piles of cardboard not unlike the setup of a beaver's dam.

After a mile or two of this, they came to the set of train tracks of interest, littered with consumer-generated garbage. And after another few minutes of walking, they came across the town's train station. Almost an hour passed, as Josik and Maria waited hidden behind some trees. An eighteen-car train eventually arrived, the country's elite lining up to board in their pastel-colored attire. It was a shocking contrast to Josik and Maria's clothing, which consisted of grime-soaked, dark-colored sweaters and cargo pants.

They slipped into a cargo car just as the train began to pick up speed, finding themselves accompanied by five others. It was only the afternoon, but they were exhausted from the disgusting sights of the morning, so they fell asleep.

***

Maria woke up to the sensation of the train continuing along its steady pace to the southeast. It was certainly many hours later, because Josik could be seen sitting on the edge of the open car door, looking toward the sunset. In another corner of the space, two fellow strangers were playing a game of cards.

She approached Josik, her legs dangling over the edge next to his. She reached her arms around his neck and opposite shoulder, burying her head above his chest at an angle to see the sunset. Despite the dingy circumstances, she felt an overwhelming sense of peace in this scene, a welcome departure from the endless anxiety and stress back in Detroit. It wasn't comfortable, but the people and the nature around them here had found a way to coexist.

And it was a beautiful amber sky above them. Looking around where the sun was disappearing to the west, the great golden plains were illuminated below them.

"What're you thinking about?" asked Maria.

"It's quite a large land, isn't it?" Josik said. "I've been looking to the west for over an hour now and couldn't help but be struck by it. Whatever this land once was, it must have always been a beautiful one."

"Quite a romantic scene too, isn't it?" she replied with a playful eye.

Josik breathed a laugh. "I suppose I can't argue with that."

There was some more kissing, Maria leaning more

relaxed into his chest.

"Whoa," he said after a moment, pushing his novia's legs back from the edge.

Maria crawled back a bit, suddenly uncomfortable with the risk. Her caring boyfriend was the one who had put the idea in her head, after all.

Josik crawled back too, becoming more fluent in the art of matching body language.

The two returned to their embracing position. But Josik was not much at peace at this time, and started thinking out loud.

"Maria, there's something I should tell you."

"What is it, mi amor?"

"Smythe's pledge got me thinking again about these dreams I've been having."

"Like Father Biwun's? You think you have the gift of sueña?"

"I don't know. Maybe. There's something so much more powerful and vivid about these dreams though. It's like they're more than just dreams. They're more than just visions. They're like travels through time, reliving the past—all while I'm sleeping."

Maria was silent a moment, her expression tightened in thought. "Do they happen every night?"

"They were at one point. Months ago when I first met you. After you were taken, they stopped for a while. But they started up again at the beginning of Lent, and their reoccurrence hasn't followed any regular pattern since then."

"What do you see... or I guess, experience during these time travels?"

"There's a man named Sam. He tells me these stories about the past. About this place they called America. The same place Biwun told me about. But there's a lot of it I still don't understand. For earth's sake, I don't even know where I'm supposed to be most of the time when I'm with this man."

Maria's kept her head rested on Josik, her voice sounding tired.

"Josik, I couldn't tell you what these mysterious things mean. I'm human and limited just like you. But I'm here for you and I will pray for you to find the purpose in these things. I hope you won't be afraid to ask for God's help too."

"I will try," Josik said with a long face. He sighed.

"So, what happens next to everyone out there? I come in like some Messiah and save them all?"

Maria looked up at him, surprised by his stern tone.

"I'm not going to tell you that you're some hero, Josik. Your own mistakes are evidence of that."

Josik looked away, surprised that Maria would bring up the past.

"But you're a good person, Josik. And I believe that

because you have the right heart, because of your willingness to learn what you have from being among my people. You've turned away from the strange ideas that make so much of humanity unhappy. And it led you to rescue me from that hellhole, a debt I can never repay you."

Josik let out a restrained grin. How did she seem to know these things about him? Clearly, he had so much more to learn about love.

"It wasn't too hard for me to turn away from the Bohemx lifestyle," he said modestly, talking past the compliment on the rescue. "I never liked it to begin with."

"Well, there you go. I think you've found a home with me and my family, then."

"Maybe that's where I should keep my focus for now. Here and now, with my fellow Ispanians."

He laid himself down, with Maria resting on top.

"Just take comfort in the one place where I see some social harmony at work. Let the fighting on the outside take its course. After all, there are people like the friends I've made who must be the ones to make peace."

"Right," Maria affirmed.

"I mean, who am I at the moment? A student, still, of this life. I'm still learning. Not just what the past means, but how to love this woman I've been blessed with."

Maria looked hard at him a moment, pleasantly surprised at his use of spiritual language.

"Right," she said again, wrapping herself close against his chest.

"Right," he whispered softly in response.

2-19

That night, Josik found himself waking up to the backseat of the hatchback again, his prone head gazing sideways onto the young couple. Passing by all sides of the car was the setting of an evergreen forest, a fragrant pollen scent filling the air along with a bright sun.

Sam and Rachel, much to Josik's entertainment, were singing lyrics together along with music playing over the stereo:

> *"Cause when you're living in America*
>
> *At the end of the millennium*
>
> *We're living in America*
>
> *Where it's like The Twilight Zone.*
>
> *And when you're living in America*
>
> *At the end of the millennium*
>
> *You're what you own."*

They finished up after a few more minutes of their

belting, Josik let out some inaudible applause. The two started right into their self-critique, however, all smiles and laughs.

Rachel started off.

"You couldn't seem to make up your mind, where you supposed to be doing Mark or Roger?"

"Oh, I'm the one who's confusing," Sam replied, feigning outrage. "At least I wasn't making up a soprano part where one clearly doesn't exist."

"*Rent* is such a tricky musical to find the endurance to sing. It's like the 90-day 'muscle confusion' workout of musicals as far as singing goes."

Sam chuckled.

"Agreed."

Sam picked up an object from the car's center console, which Josik recognized as a smartphone. He started randomly tapping on the strange object with his thumb, his eyes darting between it and the road.

"Sam, you know I love you, right?" said Rachel, interjecting.

"Yes," Sam said automatically.

"Then don't do something hazardous to yourself like texting and driving," Rachel asserted.

Sam tossed the smartphone back in the center console.

"Sorry," he confessed. "Bad habit."

After another ten minutes of driving, the car passed through a town whose signs all around read "Georgetown." It was a homely rural community, with quaint restaurants and displays of mining equipment from eras past.

Sam drove through to a road that continued along a rising, winding route further into the mountains for about another twenty minutes or so. Josik started to feel carsick over this period, but the nausea reminded him of his need to orient himself to the date, as he looked to the console screen again:

5/25/2017 10:37am

Eventually they crossed over one of the area's many dams and pulled into a mostly empty parking lot. Sam and Rachel hopped out of the car and grabbed backpacks for hiking, Josik following their lead. All three walked along a narrow dirt path for well over an hour, outlining the shore of the reservoir that remained to their left. The elevation was a matter of constant up-and-down, but nothing too strenuous.

Finally, with their hunger getting the better of them, the couple stopped to consume some snacks on the rocky sand next to the lake. Josik sprawled out on a nearby granite rock, waiting for any insightful dialogue.

"Why do you keep looking that way?" Rachel asked, interrupting the sounds of mastication.

Sam was looking out to the east, to a barren hillside.

"I don't remember that being like that a few years

ago the last time I was here."

"Is that not normal?"

"No, it's not. The drought and wildfires over the years has taken a big toll on the trees and other vegetation at this altitude. It worries me."

"At least this year was plenty wet."

"Well, let's hope it stays that way."

Rachel looked down, realizing that the topic was an area of serious concern for Sam.

"I'm sorry, I didn't mean to dismiss you like that."

"Oh really? Because your party definitely means to."

Sam sighed after a silent moment, upset at himself.

"Sorry, I didn't mean it like that."

Rachel fretted a moment, exposing her dimples.

"Sam, I don't agree with that part of the Republican platform. Do I agree with some of their skepticism of the research that's thrown around so alarmingly by some scientists who are clearly influenced by a political agenda? Yes. Do I agree that we still have a moral obligation as a country to stop the clear and present damage of man-made climate change? Even more so."

"Try telling that to my parents. Every time I come home to their place, it seems like the fire-safety regulations are getting more and more burdensome. It's not their fault as individuals that stuff like the insurance rates keep going up, it's that living in rural California carries exponentially more risk from wildfire damage with each passing year. And it's clear where the source of the problem originates."

Rachel grasped his hand in a gesture of peacemaking.

Sam gave no reply, but simply sighed. He did not stir, clearly pensive.

"What's really on your mind, Sam?"

Sam's head popped back, moved sideways to stare intently back at Rachel.

"It's just . . . I've wondered a lot lately, what with all the depressing headlines, whether or not I should follow through with all this talk of public service and political ambition and changing the world I've gone on and on about over the years. I'm starting to think that that dark world of politics is just not for me. That I can never hope to change it without letting it change me in ways I could never forgive myself for. I mean, I'm just one person, right? Maybe I just need to keep my focus on the here and now, where it belongs. Not get so caught up in the horizon."

She patted the sand in front of her, gesturing for Sam to lay beside her. Once he did, she looked into his eyes, calmly stroking the back of his hair.

"Do what feels right, Sam, I believe your heart is in the right place and leads you to the right decisions. But that doesn't mean I'll never stop praying for God to help guide you to the right way, because we're only human at the end of the day. You're right, you shouldn't forget the small stuff, the day-to-day. But don't use that to pretend like you don't have a larger calling, a larger purpose, especially with the trouble our political system is in. You're destined to serve others with your talents, whether you like it or not. You can choose to dig your feet in about it and pretend like it's not there, or you can accept the sense of duty that comes with it. And that's what I've learned leads to true happiness."

Sam thought about these words for a moment, then leaned in close to her face, rather comically.

"You're not just making this stuff up, right?"

Rachel pushed out with both hands in response, half-amused and half-offended. Sam rolled back on the sand, over-exaggerating.

"I'm serious!" she teased.

But it was for Josik to tell if Sam was really taking her seriously in this moment. His infatuation was shining through again, revealed by a wide version of his smile.

They started packing up.

"I can't wait to see their house," Rachel said.

"What?" Sam asked.

"Their house. Your parents' house you were mentioning earlier."

"Damn right. Wait till you see the Hot Wheels collection in my bedroom. You ready for it?

Rachel looked away playfully, playing coy.

"Come on, there's no turning back now. Well, unless you count 'turning back' as heading down the hill to my dad's barbeque. You've never had the privilege of tasting my dad's smoked pulled pork, by the way. It's a labor of love—takes the whole day to cook."

Rachel did another playful rolling of eyes.

The trio walked back together, loaded up in the car just in time for Josik to fall asleep again.

2-20

Later that day, from where Josik awoke, he made away with Maria from the train at some point east of the Appalachians. They were relieved to have passed through the Blue Wall again, and the return to friendly territory it represented.

As planned with great assistance by Smythe, they had just enough provisions in their sacks for the final day of foot travel from the train tracks to the Ispanian village. They had no clear path to follow, just the map and compass in their possession that they had learned to use from Smythe (they realized they had so much to be grateful to her for on this leg of the journey).

Josik did not dream that night, as he woke up the next morning disappointed that he had to take a break from exploring the story of Sam's young love. It had given him a nice point of reference for the relationship Josik was developing with his own companion, after all.

The two finally arrived through the north side of the village that day, just after sundown. Maria was eager to be reunited with her family, so Josik let her run ahead to find their house. By the time Josik entered the front door, the whole place was stirring with joy, her parents and siblings jumping and hugging and kissing at the sight of her again.

Maria's mother, in gratefulness, kissed both of Josik's cheeks, shouting thanks to God and to Josik. Josik stayed silent, smiling and appreciating the spectacle he had helped to create, thinking to himself that the sight of bringing happiness back to these people was a reward he felt beyond measure.

Maria's mother heated up some pozole for Josik and Maria, once she saw that they were both weary from the day's travels. They both stayed up quite late, however, the parents eager to hear the details of their daughter's ordeal and her rescuer's journey.

Josik and Maria eventually went to sleep, but they resumed the story of their subcontinental tour at the parents' request in the morning. The parents encouraged Josik to make a report on his observations to the village elders that afternoon, especially regarding the death of the Colellas. He did so.

The reaction of the elders was one of anxiety and disturbance. It wasn't long before word slipped into the ears of the other villagers. The Ispanians were accustomed to being peaceful, not even interfering in a passive manner similar to that of the Nucks. But the upcoming June election for the next Village Guardian—an individual who governed the affairs of the village along with the Council of Elders—had brought up new questions of the growing Averitan threat, as the public heard stories of atrocities committed against the other villages. All the candidates agreed that a change of course against the Averitans would be necessary. One of the candidates called for intervention, but only with a great effort made towards establishing diplomatic relations. The most radical candidate, a man by the name of Miguel Afitna, advocated for a far more aggressive approach, arguing that the time for talk was long over. He seized on this latest news of the Colella tragedy, exploiting it as a call to arms.

Josik listened intently, curious about the implications. But he was committed to what he had said to Maria the other day—his focus needed to be on her and her family, as they were important to him more than ever.

So, he listened but pretended to take no interest, restraining his uneasiness and his instinct to worry about such affairs. For once on his time on planet Earth, he didn't want to have anything to do with anything political, and now he finally had the luxury to be able to pretend he wasn't affected by it.

The thought of ignoring a sense of duty still lingered at first, but was forgotten when he spent an afternoon resting in bed with Maria, as he desired. Maria apparently shared in his apathy on account of a lack of energy, spending most of the next several days in bed together.

They rather enjoyed themselves in this. Days and weeks passed by while the two relished in each other's recovery, spending most of the time in the family house or walking aimlessly around the city. They fell deeper in love, talking mostly of how much they loved each other and their hopes for the future, their passion heating up with the temperature of the late spring season. But they deliberately ignored conversations of current affairs, or anything about Josik's nighttime travels.

They kept hearing through Maria's parents of the same story of this Afitna, how much his popularity continued to grow and how much that worried them for whatever reason.

Finally, one Tuesday in June, Maria's father called the two out of the house to the village square.

"Josik, Maria," Manuel called, entering the bedroom they were in, "come join us in the square. You'll want to hear this."

Josik looked back with skepticism.

"This isn't about that silly election again, is it?"

"Silly?" the father replied, clearly angry. "Boy, let me show you what this 'silly' election means for the village. Get out here, inmediatamente."

The couple rushed out of the house, called to action by the unexpected reprimand. They saw a growing mob, cheering loudly, many of them carrying torches by the late spring's dim evening light.

As they approached, they saw a young, short, dark-haired man wearing a beret, posing to the crowd from a makeshift stage and intermittently shouting buzzwords like libertad and liberación to the masses. He began to speak.

"Amigos y amigas," he said. "Comrades. Tonight, we celebrate not just the victory of this movement, but of the solidarity of our people. ¡Viva la Ispania!"

People in the crowd shouted back.

"Comrades, again I speak. Tonight, we say to those others that said our message was too extreme, too radical. You all, the people, have demanded this. It is our turn to talk!"

There was cheering back in agreement.

"Our message to troublemakers—the message of Guardian Afitna, and of the Ispanian people, is this: you are not welcome around our lands anymore. Ispania will not stand by idly and allow our village to be raided and our women to be enslaved and raped any longer. Averita, you vile white scum of the earth, we will push you back and we will wipe you out wherever you go!"

For several moments, Afitna let the rhetoric sink into the crowd, stoking a sense of frenzied passion and hatred that was familiar to Josik.

"My God," Josik half-whispered in Maria's direction.

"What is it?" she begged.

"I've seen this before," he said while Afitna continued. "He's winning their hearts and cminds over just like the Maga did."

The people were quiet again, waiting on every word of their new leader, who with every bold new promise won their confidence over the steadiness and thoughtfulness of the past. Afitna had learned to equate these old values with spinelessness and indecisiveness, and now the Ispanian public had fully accepted the charge.

"As my first act as Village Guardian," Afitna bellowed. "We are immediately to war. Every able-bodied man aged eighteen to forty-five will be conscripted to participate in the greatest military force ever known to our people. We will act now. We will fight back. And God with us, we will bleach out the white scum! For the Colellas! For Ispania! ¡Viva la Ispania!"

Again, the better part of the village yelled in an uproar, overcome with the victory of their mob rule and the leader they had elevated to the head of it.

Josik and Maria, meanwhile, remained silent, not knowing their place to take.

END OF PART 2

PART III

NEW WORLD ORDER

PROLOGUE #3

An excerpt from Chapter 35 of Usami's The Decline and Fall of American Democracy:

If (and likely when) America and its democracy falls, it will be at the hands of an all-consuming crisis. The social, environmental, and international threats at play will push the system beyond its limits—a cascading series of events triggered by a single collective moment of panic.

The crisis will start at the hands of environmental, epidemiological, or fiscal catastrophe, whichever comes first. It could be triggered by another year of record-breaking storms that leaves the entire Eastern seaboard underwater and fires that completely and utterly char the Western states. It could be another downgrading of the nation's bond rating, sharply raising interest rates and triggering an exodus of debt investors. Uncle Sam, having formed an addictive overspending habit for the last several decades, would be forced to make sudden and austere cuts to social programs while the political will for new taxes faltered. Or it could be another global pandemic that exhausts the country's medical and economic resources yet again. I refer to this moment—whenever it happens—as the "Collapse."

Whatever the sequence of events, its passing now appears inevitable. Since 2000, the federal government has increased the national debt more than sevenfold to over $45 trillion at the time of this writing. Mass migrations have seen the movement of millions of people out of Utah, Nevada, Arizona, and California into the Pacific Northwest, Canada, and Alaska. There has settled in the collective psyche a sense that no end is in sight—that we have entered a tunnel with no light to be seen.

Here is how the fall of American democracy will come about: when the Collapse comes, the people will turn on the very notion of a democratic republic. Over the last several decades, public opinion has come to distrust nearly every government and political institution. It began with distrust of the executive branch with the Nixon administration. Public anger then spread to Congress, who had hacked its legislative processes to serve as a machine to the two-party system and the gridlock and dysfunction that came with it. Climate change, health care, education, immigration—the reader can take their pick. These very real national twenty-first century problems have been left unaddressed for nearly two generations now, a product of the parties' duopolistic control of Congress. Frustrated with this lack of legislative progress, without acknowledging the need for compromise in the American political system (and the bias of the modern political system towards special interests), the left and right battled between each other in state and federal courts. Through executive orders and other extralegal workarounds, they successfully amassed unprecedented power for the presidency as they traded control every four or eight years. Judges typically concerned with judicial independence and the rule of law—and not the political questions of the day—were then compelled to legislate from the bench. Judges are now widely viewed as political agents thanks to catalyzing events such as the 2018 Brett Kavanaugh Supreme Court hearings; thus, public trust had turned against the courts too. Mass media also lost public trust during this time, as accusations of blatant political bias and untruths abounded.

The two institutions left that hold the public's trust are state and local governments and the military. When the Collapse comes, I predict that state and local governments will also lose this trust as their ability to respond to natural or fiscal disaster will be woefully inadequate. Each state is simply too small-scale compared to the power and resources of the federal government. At this point, trust even in general concepts of representative democracy (e.g., agreeing in public opinion polls that free speech is fundamental to the operation of a free society, even if it does stir controversy) will evaporate. From here, the next stage of American society is less clear. Would the people turn to the military, expecting a coup? Would America's diverse society splinter apart into a form of tribal anarchy, each community existing as a country of its own? Would a new strongman come forward, promising a bold new way of life while mercilessly consolidating power for him or herself?

A final possibility would join America in the ranks of a new, rising, competing form of government that has taken hold in the minds of people everywhere in the twenty-first century. Popularized by China, political scientists have defined it as "practical authoritarianism." In reality, the system is simply an updated version of oppressive twentieth century communism. It puts in power a small class or party of individuals it designates as the sole authority; additionally, it preaches a kind of civic religion that enforces a rigid sense of collective identity. So, how does it avoid falling out of favor unlike how it did in the Soviet Union and Eastern Europe? Scarily, it may be a simple matter of economics. Communism in the style of Lenin, Stalin, and Mao regulated markets rather aggressively and crudely, expecting the people to be content with their deprivation of material goods. The old way of Communism expected collective identity without material well-being. In fact, such governments actively spread propaganda pretending that shortages of basic goods did not exist. "Practical authoritarianism" takes a shrewder approach in marrying the worst aspects of capitalist self-interest and authoritarian control together. It fulfills all the desires for material well-being in the twentieth century almost as well as the Western democracies. Practical authoritarianism couples collective identity and material well-being together, bucking the usual trade-off. In these new societies, volunteering, charity, altruism, and other forms of civic virtue are all but abolished. Life is reduced to mean nothing more than material things and what material value one produces for the state. Love for one's neighbor is extinguished and care for oneself is given the sole attention material capitalism so desired. It seems simple—reduce all concerns to the self and to the state.

This scenario—where the people of America submit themselves to the global scourge of authoritarian rule—is the one I fear most. Is the experiment of representative democracy, the Republic which America popularized around the globe over the last two and a half centuries, really at its end? As I have concluded, still no better alternative exists among all other available systems of government. There is incredible wisdom in spreading power as widely as possible, so long as the general public is both informed and empowered.

Despite these merits, revolution may be coming around the corner against democracy and republican government. Revolution has a nasty habit of allowing radical political minorities into power, and the result is too often massacre of the opposition and widespread chaos. How did we end up with this nightmare prospect in such a short period of time?

In the 1990s—only about a generation ago—the pundits talked of a peaceful, glorious "new world order" emerging, with free and open democracies as the way of the future. Are we in fact witnessing a different kind of new world order emerge, with superpowers China and Russia as its face? An opposing countermovement in defense of the democratic republic—of a free society that practices a government of laws and not merely of men nor women—is needed in this country. But the plan to bring together millions of Americans in this rescue mission remains at large. . .

3-1

It was an early start for Bohem's top officials. At no later than 0630, their shuttle departed the space station, bound for Earth. It was the first visit the new Authoritarian Consulate had made since the mandatory twenty-year rotation in leadership was initiated.

The three had agreed to make good on the last stage of Authority's Centenary Plan: a pledge to do everything in their power to extinguish every form of non-conformity in Bohemx society as they subjectively saw fit. They had already taken a first measure—banning all forms of body hair by imposing mandatory drug consumption. So now, the only way to distinguish any citizen of Bohem from one another was by slight differences in height and by body shape. But since most Bohemx rejected gender differences, individuals tried to hide their differences in curvature through medication and undergarment choice.

So there the Consulate sat, appearing nearly as clones of one another, lowly muttering to one another on occasion, as they coldly observed Earth, the sun, and the moon. It was only recently that the truth of Earth's current environmental status had been revealed to them, so they were not sure what to expect upon landing.

The shuttle and its entourage eased into the planet's atmosphere, the varied topography of the continent spreading out below. The coastlines were visibly worn miles above the planet, the result of the previous centuries' higher sea levels.

Within a few more minutes, the gentrified squalor of Averita's sprawling capital was in view. They flew over the new, gold-plated skyscrapers of the ruling class's downtown, aiming for a military installation on the outskirts.

The shuttle settled just past the barb-wired perimeter, taking care to steer clear of the soldiers doing exercises in their gaudy, orange-camo fatigues, all wearing berets. Awaiting the Bohemx delegation was the Big-League Maga's entourage, shepherded by its bombastic leader.

"Beautiful, beautiful," he muttered purposelessly, awkwardly yanking the arm of each Consul as they disembarked. He was also sporting an obnoxious orange beret like his soldiers, partially obscuring his vision.

He stretched out a big arm behind the three and flailed his other in the direction of the troops.

"Magnificent, aren't they?" the Maga declared. "Incredible. Big. Beautiful."

The Consulate pretended to pay attention. They

had become familiar with his vocabulary choice of the same five or six adjectives.

They decided to subtly roll their eyes and move things along. One of the Consuls had no patience for the staged shock and awe.

"That's enough, Maga. Let's talk."

The Big-League Maga shrank were he stood, his posture visibly withering without the usual verbal nutrients he expected would continually stroke his ego. The wide, smiling eyes switched to a scowl.

"Follow me," he muttered, turning and pointing to his left.

They entered a transparent glass chute that housed an elevator within, providing a panoramic view of the dilapidated metropolis. Below, the Consulate saw huddled masses at work on one of Averita's new infrastructure projects—a new rail line, to be exact. The workers mucked all day in the manmade swamp that filled the worksite—a channel concentrating a noxious soup of raw sewage and industrial waste. Prisoners were brought in daily from a local facility to continually replace those lost to disease. As was evident, a continually growing economy for the ruling classes was of utmost importance—all other concerns were secondary.

The escalator led the party to a massive ivory-colored tower, where they proceeded to its top floor. They sat in a boardroom, the table made of an impressive hickory oak.

"So why did you request an audience with me?" said the Maga, removing his hat to massage his mysterious hair. "We're winning, right?"

"That's true," another Consul spoke, with their usual dry tone. "Honestly, this alliance is probably the best decision we've ever made."

"We have more in common than you thought, right?" said the Big-League Maga, smiling again.

Everyone at the table released a light chuckle, everyone amused at themselves. Yes, their radical ideologies—steeped in principles such as the concentration of absolute power, fabricated history, and paranoia—made the leaders of Bohem and Averita a good match in the face of a potential third-force resistance that worried them both.

"And it's going really great, because we're winning, right? I'm winning! I mean, we've always been winning, but you know I'm winning like you can't believe. I took your small investment and made it grow, in no time, okay? And listen, my people, they love me now so much too. I mean, they've always loved me, I've let industries dump toxic waste in the street and they still don't care, and they still love me."

"Maga!" the third Consul, who had not spoken, shouted. Clearly, things were going well with their war, and their recommendation to Authority for providing its full support had been an advantageous one. But the closer relationship this required had begun to wear on the patience and sanity of the Consulate, as the man they were tasked with managing did so little of his homework but so much to take the credit, even when there was no motivating crowd around to keep on his side.

Maga made a pouting expression again.

"Tell me what you needed to see me for," he said, defeated.

"It's not what we need to tell you, per se," the third Consul uttered. "It's something we've been working on for a while that we need to show you. Come now, follow us."

The three floated away from the boardroom, rather coordinated. Maga stumbled out of his chair and caught up after them.

3-2

It was a brisk autumn day in the Rican village, miles away from the Averitans. On its outskirts were some abandoned older huts—a relic of the society's more primitive, less socially-cohesive days. They were obscured from the present-day village center by thickets of dense, twisted trees, shedding a colorful portfolio of leaves.

Yet a single warm light could be seen flickering from within one of these old, cozy huts, growing more visible as the dark night took over.

Within, there were four altogether—a married couple of Rican villagers (dressed in practical furs), and a young couple seated hip-to-hip—a blanket warming both their legs.

"I'm sorry to start this way, but I assume our secret lodging is still safe with you?" began the Ispanian, her somber brown eyes looking alert. "Are you sure I can't get you both something to drink? Tea? Coffee? Tequila?"

"Yes ma'am," said the Rican husband, removing his

thick fur parka. He was a man of few words. "And tea would be lovely."

"Thank you again for coming back," Josik asked as his companion left the room for a moment. "So, what latest news do you have for us?"

"It's nothing good, my friends," the wife said. "The war rages on. By now, we've seen the Ispanians march full-scale armies to battle. At first it seemed we might make an alliance with them. But a communique to our leader never came. They seem disgruntled and disorganized. They've swooped into our village at night, stealing food and other petty things."

"So, they are at war with you?" Maria asked as she reentered the room, greatly distressed at the thought of this development. She presented four full mugs on a tray, compelling a quick tea break.

"Our people doubt it," the husband asserted after taking a quiet gulp. "We think they are just desperate individuals, taking matters into their own hands."

Josik chimed in, grasping Maria's hand in a show of comfort.

"Let's bear in mind that Afitna is obsessed with maintaining his power," he concluded, using the political analysis skills learned from Sam. "Declaring war against your village would mean certain doom for both the Ispanians and the Ricans. It would be a threat to his regime brought on by his own foolishness. Surely someone has thought to reach out to him for a diplomatic solution? You are both at war with the Averitans whether you like it or not—why not form an alliance?"

The husband shrugged his shoulders.

"All I can conclude is that our people are being constantly injured and harassed, and we've just about had enough of it. We don't want to fight a war on two fronts, but we'll have no choice if this situation keeps up."

For a while, the two couples sat in pensive silence, Maria and Josik tensely rubbing their mugs. The prospect of a larger-scale conflict seemed unthinkable, since all four knew that it was a path to certain ruin to all the factions of the continent. Josik had learned that while the war had only gone on for about four months so far, about ten percent of both the Ispanian and Rican populations had already become casualties.

Maria and Josik looked at each other at some point during this silence. A sense of guilt began to rise as they remembered their choices over the last few months. They had escaped from the Ispanian village eight weeks ago to avoid the war, for their own safety. Maria's parents were concerned for her safety, and Josik wanted to avoid the draft. So they ran off together, continually finding comfort in one another. But as the events continued to swirl around them—and their curiosity for the news regarding them continued to build—so too did a sense of duty continue to build. A sense of duty commanded them both to quit their hermitage, pack their bags, and return to Ispania.

They could see tears welling up in each other's faces—then a knock was heard at the door. Josik rose, greeted the guest and welcomed him inside. The visitor was recognizable once he removed his outer furs. He was an Ispanian priest, made clear by his jet-black hair and Roman collar.

"Father José," said Maria quietly, crossing herself. The gesture was made not out of reverence, but of instinctive embarrassment. Neither she nor Josik had anticipated finding a way to explain their retreat to the wilderness to their village friends—at least not anytime soon.

"Wait," said the wife of the Rican couple. "Your village has priests too?"

Maria said nothing but motioned her hands in the father's direction. Her sarcastic expression was affirmation enough.

After a few minutes of warm chatter and some more hot tea passed around, Josik begged the obvious question.

"How the heck did you manage to find us?"

"Oh, you know," said Father José, a whimsical look on his face, "the Lord works in mysterious ways."

"Of course he does," Josik acknowledged, realizing how spiritually active he was becoming. "But He doesn't tell people where to walk. So, who told you where we were?"

"Well, I apologize," Father José returned with a sigh. "I don't blame you for wanting to run away from the horrors that come along with Afitna. You turned out to be completely right on that one."

The room fell solemnly silent.

Josik acknowledged that this retreat was the choice he and Maria had made, even if it was done so shakily.

"Then why aren't you with the villagers right now? Don't they need your words of comfort during a crisis like this?" he said with a sniffle.

The rest of the room remained silent, shocked at the challenging tone of this statement. Josik kept his gaze on the parish priest. But the holy man did not look shaken. Josik felt his heart soften, regretting what he had just said.

Yet, Father José expected Josik's resistance and was ready for the challenge.

"Why are you here, Josik?" Father José retorted.

Josik was taken aback, feeling defensive again. This guy, who randomly showed up at this doorstep from miles away, apparently had the gall to suggest his host was out of place.

"Why are you here, Father?" Josik returned.

Father José did not look back directly at Josik with his response.

"Theology is my strong suit, not shooting the breeze with the flock given to my care, so forgive my nervousness. But it wasn't hard for me to tell that you're set apart from the others who have come to us."

Josik wasn't the first refugee the Ispanian village had hosted, he had learned. Yet, this marginalized group became the target of the people's newfound populist ire, and they had been rounded up for internment. The event was, Josik recalled for the umpteenth time, the trigger for his retreat with his lover.

"So I've been told," Josik said, a flat expression on his face.

Father José, appearing to take some effort, looked at the foreigner square in the face.

"Josik, I only know your story because of what you have told me. And while I will not pretend that something has been revealed to me, I have prayed and reflected hard on all of this. Now I know for certain what you are called to do because now we know the evils into which our people fall without you there."

"Without me? What, to stop them? Stop them from what?"

"Their hatred and greed. First, they showed it to the Averitans, then it was the immigrants. Now it's becoming the other factions. And after that..."

Father José bit his lip and closed his eyes.

"The people will hate and envy each other. I can sense this. I see the same theme throughout Scripture and see it in human nature. The longer we imagine there is a pure human enemy out there, the more we begin to believe the enemy is growing more numerous, closing in on us. But it ignores the fact that the enemy has always been within all of us, the two wolves battling and clamoring for control. Soon it will be house against house, family against family. And I sense the other villages will all see this same social disease come to pass."

Josik looked at Maria, a long and sad contemplative look on his face. He had come to rely on her for advice on spiritual and moral matters, and had picked up on her body language after all these months with her. Maria's eyes were wide, pleading, urging.

Josik sighed loudly. He was not used to any kind of blind obedience, however slight.

"What must I do?" said Josik.

"Go back to them, Josik," the Father said, his face animated with spirit. "The Ispanians are your people now. Teach them again to love thy neighbor. Through this, they will do more than win in battle. For while God abhors war, only through it being fought now to its end can a peace be reached. They will bring about a great peace among all the villages—and with it, the Ispanians will be exalted among all other nations."

And in this moment, Josik no longer saw the decrees of a religious proselytizer, as he was accustomed for so long from his Bohemx days. He felt plainly a grace and power displayed before him. Josik the Ispanian was ready to take up the call.

Still he had one question for the holy man.

"What about Maria? Was it a mistake for us to have hidden here? Must we leave each other?"

"No, no, absolutely not," cried Father. "What is done is done. I didn't know what would happen with you until it had already happened. She has guided and helped you through all these trials that have come to you. And, Lord willing, you will be there alongside each other in the great trials to come."

Maria spoke up.

"So, I am to go with him?"

"Yes. But before you do, I must ask you something. For in these dark times, both your lives will be at peril."

Josik and Maria both looked up toward the priest, begging for the question.

"Maria," Father José started. "Are you prepared to marry this man and join together in the bond of holy matrimony?"

Maria's lip quivered a bit. She shot a look at Josik, then closed her eyes as if to think for a second. She spoke with a sniffle, tearing up.

"Josik, I've never been so happy giving out happiness to someone before. Your willingness to learn new things in this world inspires me. Plus, you're incredibly handsome. Te amo, mi amor. So yes. Absolutely, yes."

"Josik," said Father, turning now to him. "Are you prepared to do the same for this woman, with all the duties and responsibilities that come with that?"

Josik closed his eyes for a split second, remembering the woman who had taught him how to be truly human.

"Maria, mi amor, I've been truly connected to the world thanks to you. I've never felt so full of purpose. I'm ready to give you more of myself. So yes, I'll marry you if you'll have me. Te amo. It's the least I could do. I promise to stand by you all the days of my life."

Josik smiled widely to Maria. Maria returned the favor and smiled back.

And then Father turned back to the Rican couple.

"And do the two with us here tonight agree to be witnesses to the ceremony?"

The two Ricans looked briefly at each other.

"Absolutely," the wife said.

Father José reached into his knapsack, taking out a small velvet box. Inside, he revealed, were two simple copper rings.

And so, by the warm firelight, protected inside for the moment from the dark, wooded world outside, Josik and Maria became husband and wife.

3-3

The Ispanian couple slept well together that night, Josik fitting his front to Maria's back. Josik, in his pleasant slumber, woke up witnessing another couple again—Sam and Rachel. They were in a hotel suite, finishing dressing for the day ahead. Josik struggled to find a way to orient himself to the location and place in time. He looked outside—it was bright, a sky filled with puffy clouds, and a dense green forest below.

Josik looked back to the couple. They were wearing short sleeves, shorts, and applying sunscreen on each other, a sure sign of summertime. Finally, he walked over to a clock located in between the two beds in the room, and it displayed:

09:11am

Friday, 08/11/2017

Sam and Rachel finished readjusting their shirts and headed out the door, Josik sauntering behind. But the two stopped just outside the doorway, both visibly vacillating about the day's itinerary. Sam held his smartphone in his hand, using it to research options.

"I thought we were going to tour Monticello today," said Rachel, her expression mildly quizzical. "Along with having an unplanned debate of Thomas Jefferson's legacy in establishing ideals of human equality."

Sam smirked back.

"Darn," returned Rachel, sarcastically. "I just gave it away."

The two shared a playful kiss. Josik, the observer, marveled at their chemistry.

"What were you thinking about, sunshine?" Rachel asked, using her nickname for Sam.

"I've gotten a news alert on my phone," Sam explained, pointing to its digital screen. "There's a protest being held near the town center; details mention a monument to Robert E. Lee they have that's planned to be torn down."

"Hmm," she said, thinking aloud wistfully. "You mean to say that you agreed to travel all the way across the country with me to see my D.C. relatives, only to obsess with progressing intensity about Confederate history along the journey?"

Sam playfully stared down his companion.

"Not my choice to pay attention to it, sweetie. Apparently, some headline-grabbing group is making it relevant again."

"Alright," said Rachel, a quirky turn of her head in response. "But let's remember we need to be at the

University of Virginia campus by seven for dinner with my friend Lala."

Sam nodded in agreement casually. The two—with Josik keeping up behind—walked several blocks over to nearby Emancipation Park, with a sculpture of the Civil War figure still on display. A throng of a few hundred were assembled on the grass, holding colorful signs and flags. But at the time when Sam and Rachel were conversing in their usual banter, they could not recognize the hateful symbols in provocative display in front of them.

"Why did anyone think it was a good idea to celebrate these Confederate traitors to begin with? Shouldn't someone have said something before the statues went up?" Rachel asked.

Sam offered his analysis, the result of scrolling through Wikipedia and other Internet sources on the topic the night before. He always became curious in researching current events as they came up on social media.

"It's because they went up at a time at the height of Jim Crow laws, in the early part of the last century. Seems they wanted it as a symbol of entrenched resistance against losing the Civil War and slavery, and no one's really thought to bring that problem up again until recently."

"Curious," Rachel summarized.

Within a few hundred more yards, the picture of the crowd more clearly came into view. Gadsden flags, swastika banners, and other symbols of radical right-wing reactionaries could now be seen. A loud and dramatic man stood at a podium before all of them, shouting and pumping his fist with almost every word. The two stopped in their tracks. Sam clutched Rachel close to him. Josik wished he could have been comforted, too.

"What the hell is this?" Sam said.

Rachel said nothing in response, remaining shocked.

The pair immediately moved on to their next spot, Monticello, and took in Thomas Jefferson's complicated legacy as a proponent of human equality.

Sam and Rachel later discussed it on their drive to the University of Virginia campus, where they were going to meet up and dine with Lala, who Josik learned was a high school friend of Rachel's.

"I had no idea, that thing about Jefferson," started Sam.

"What thing?" Rachel asked.

"I remember growing up the detail about him originally wanting to ban slavery in the Declaration of Independence. But then learning about his views on black people being physically and intellectually inferior never connected. That is, until today."

Rachel looked sideways out the passenger-side window, confused for a second.

"Ohhh," she deduced. "You mean the belief he held about 'negro' people as many other well-to-do white landowners did at the time."

"Yep. This idea that black people, while being less able than whites, still deserved the same political freedoms? And then the idea that the slaves should be freed and then sent back to Africa to start their own democratic colony?"

"It's like an idea that the left today wouldn't acknowledge that could make sense given the scientific knowledge and beliefs at the time, isn't it?"

Sam's response to the subtle political jab was delayed, his free hand away from the steering wheel and thoughtfully rubbing his stubbly chin.

"In a way, I have to admit a certain practicality to that 'solution,' if you want to call it that. It's not that Jefferson believed that black culture was somehow poisonous to society, but that a distinctly different group of people couldn't integrate into a broader American society. If things had gone Jefferson's way, we not only would have avoided a Civil War, we would have avoided that kind of racial conflict altogether, in an ideal world."

"In an ideal world," Rachel emphasized.

Sam's face contorted, slightly discomforted by this conclusion, albeit logical.

"So perhaps we could have avoided a lot of unnecessary bloodshed, with the Jefferson 'solution.' But we never would have had the opportunity as a society to tolerate and accept different ethnic groups and eventually consider them part of the larger patchwork of the American story."

"Or the quilt of the American story," Rachel mused pointedly.

"You always had a flair for analogies," Sam said with a guffaw.

After a few more seconds of the lone drone of the car engine, Rachel laid out an open hand towards Sam.

"I think you're onto something," she said with a smile.

Sam gave a modest grin, with a wry chuckle that was barely audible.

He took her hand.

"God, I hope so. I'm happy we ended up with our diverse society instead of a homogenous one."

Rachel mused for a moment, a gentle smile on her face.

"Me too. I'm not a fan of how certain groups have used race and identity to their narrow advantage, but overall I still think the diversity is a worthy challenge for a society like ours."

"I think you're onto something," Sam said.

Rachel said nothing and simply laughed. Sam turned on the radio to signal the end of their discussion, and the two simply hummed along to pop music during the rest of the ride to the college campus.

The next several hours went by uneventfully from Josik's perspective. He was apparently incapable of eating or drinking anything in this environment, which led him to stare idly out the window while Sam, Rachel, and Lala chatted over dinner in a nearby diner. It was an unfortunately torturous affair, for two reasons. For one, Lala and Rachel seemed to speak over 90% of the time, catching up over every superfluous detail of each other's events in the last year. For another, the three active participants in this world were all feasting on gargantuan-sized, mouth-watering hamburgers. Josik began to wonder for what reason a cruel God would subject him to this scenario.

He hoped he would soon have an answer.

The party finally finished sometime after the late summer sunset, with Josik eager to rush ahead of them. They were to walk back Lala to her apartment, which meant taking a route through the University of Virginia campus. Under different circumstances, the three would have gone out somewhere; however, as Josik recalled, Sam and Rachel had an early start in their itinerary for the next morning.

What everyone expected to be a pleasant summer night walk through campus turned out to be anything but. A chorus of enraged chanting could be heard indistinctly from a few blocks away. Finally, they all turned a corner and witnessed the full scene.

Filling the lawn in front of the Rotunda, the campus's memorial to Thomas Jefferson and his complicated legacy, was a crowd of several hundred, armed with tiki torches. At its edges were protestors, who attempted to shout over the throng's cries of "you will not replace us" and "blood and soil."

"What the hell is this?" Rachel asked, looking to Sam for an answer.

Sam had none. He was visibly stunned.

Josik also was stunned. He thought back to Sam's lectures about America's unfortunate history with prejudice and bigotry. But he also bore in mind that—at least for most of the nation's history—it eventually found a way to confront and correct most of these injustices.

Still, Josik thought, wasn't this flagrant racism on display fifty years past its place in history?

Sam also thought the same.

Josik saw that the boundary between the militant racists and their adversaries broke down. Punches were thrown. The crowds stopped fighting with words on social media, Josik realized, and started fighting hand-to-hand.

Local police rushed in behind Sam, Rachel, Lala, and Josik, and the four fell to their knees in shock. Lala finally led the way out, running and shoving over the sea of combatants that had engulfed her and her friends.

Sam, Rachel, and Josik started rushing after her, knowing how fearful she was at this moment for her very life. Then suddenly, Sam realized that he was by himself in the mob. Josik saw him look back, and a sense of panic snapped into his eyes.

Rachel was sprawled on the hard-concrete

underneath all the people, holding tightly to her chest.

3-4

The Maga and Consulate were in an underground lab, about to observe the newest Bohemish weapon.

"You know, it's funny," the Maga mused, an index finger pointed. "I never realized that we made such a natural match."

Almost coordinated, all three of the Consuls rolled their eyes. Even when it was something sentimental, they couldn't stand what the Maga had to say. But at least now they took comfort in their new plan, one that would not tolerate his gross incompetence much longer. For an authoritarian populist, they observed, the Maga had failed to move past the crude, awkward governing style that his earlier historical counterparts practiced at the start of their rule. Perhaps the intentional ignorance and narcissism were genetic, kept in a ruling family over generations.

Regardless, after their many weeks on planet Earth (experiencing its underprepared foods, decayed cities, and stratified society), the Consulate concluded that despite the certain challenges, that Averita could be successfully assimilated into the next step—a fully

Authoritarian regime.

Below the leadership was a giant virtual glass box, immaculately transparent. Its area was massive—about twenty-five square miles. It had to be, since inside it was a perfectly modeled village, with over five-hundred residents who wandered its cobblestoned streets. It seemed to resemble all the traits of a miniature town of the European Renaissance, both in architecture and in layout. Homes and businesses were interspersed throughout with no evidence of centralized planning.

In terms of society and culture, the village resembled that of twentieth-century American society. Villagers were tight-knit and belonged to several community groups. Each various category of occupations had its own active trade group to share best practices and promote fellowship—welders, blacksmiths, and carpenters, for instance, had their own construction trade group. Dances and other performances took place every night to which the whole town was invited. Once a week, all the town's youth under eighteen years of age met to plan community service projects and interact directly with town leaders, with a focus on preserving and enjoying the local parks— a futuristic equivalent of the Scouts.

At the center was a classic village square, where traders bought and sold goods on tables and philosopher-types debated the problems of the day. Overlooking this square was a marble, domed temple—easily the tallest building in the town and open to worshippers during all hours of the day. Above and beyond the temple, the party of four observed this taking place below them, standing on a hovering platform with a transparent base.

One of the Consuls explained this experiment further.

"The test subjects were relocated from Bohem, as you may recall, nearly five years ago. They were inserted into this scenario with the memory of their past life completely wiped. We wanted to see if the conditions of the Old Society could be replicated."

The Maga looked blankly back, totally ignorant of sociological concepts, let alone any of the social sciences. He wanted to know how all this made him look like an even greater, more popular leader.

"So, what's the big deal?" with a strange underlining scooping motion with his hands. "Give me the bottom line."

The leader sighed in response, their patience running out.

"For once in your goddamn life, would you just learn something! Do you realize how insane you drive thinking people with your scatterbrained drivel?"

The Maga gasped quietly for a moment, clearly offended.

"I say the best things, okay?"

Another Consul interjected.

"Enough, Maga! Shut up and listen."

Maga said nothing more, wounded. He simply opened up another can of diet cola from his personal cooler—his fourth of the morning.

"Now," resumed the Consul. "Back to my highly technocratic explanation."

Maga quietly slurped a bit more sugarless soda.

"So, we let these hundreds of people form their own society however they collectively saw fit to do. All we did was build the town for them. The results could be described as troubling from our perspective. Recreating the Old Society was much easier than we expected—in fact, it seemed almost natural."

He continued, Maga having emptied his can already.

"Most of the test subjects immediately regressed to binary gender roles, with the exception of a few individuals. And this quickly resulted in the formation of the nuclear family—the building block of the Old Society. Everything else—the voluntary associations, the civic groups, the social clubs—quickly followed. It was a phenomenon not observed by our researchers for over four centuries, and thus, poorly understood."

"Until recently, we thought the study of the family was irrelevant. Bohemx society had successfully abolished it. Averitan society—your society—has come to realize its inconveniences. There can be only one loyalty to which all people must pledge for them to be perfected and made truly equal—they must be loyal only to us."

Maga nodded approvingly, unaware of how the

prophecy of one prominent piece of mid-twentieth century literature was to be fulfilled for his people, the ones he saw as his subjects. The Consulate, however, knew exactly what they were doing. The second of the Consuls held Orwell's 1984 novel in his hand. They stared at it a moment, reminding themselves of the object's service as a blueprint, a textbook on pragmatic totalitarianism. Of course, Bohemx society in its present form had evolved past this point—while fulfilling the goal of abolishing ties of family, friendships, and romances, technology was used to distract rather than surveil the people. There was no ignorant underclass majority in Bohem like in Orwell's novel—rather, the masses blindly embraced the tenets of Authority via the culture and technology set up for them, under the watchwords of perfect equality and the continuing reform of the old—that is, Old Society and its capitalist, exploitative ways.

Averita, however, was at a different point in the process, by the Consulate's assessment.

"Averita's pre-conditions for Bohemxiation are excellent," spoke the third Consul, bringing out a digital pad displaying numbers, graphs, maps, and charts. "Segregation of the high and low are sufficiently high."

They pulled up a map displaying the land around the Great Lakes region, pointing to the mitten-shaped peninsula.

"In most of the Union, levels of social capital continue to fall from already negligible levels. However, in this region and along most of the rusted-out cities, it remains abnormally high."

The Maga was suddenly following along, calmed by his nectar of artificial sweetener.

"Well, let's go Bohemx! I love it! I want complete control over my society—now!"

The Consulate all forced a grin, pretending to be amused. But in reality, they recognized he was acting like a toddler again.

"How do we get started?" demanded Maga.

The Consul hesitated, regaining their composure. Maga had already asked this question six months ago during an earlier meeting.

"We set up this experiment to find out how to perfect the process. In Bohem, despite it being our predecessors' first attempt, the conditions were much more amenable to de-socialization. Living aboard a cramped space station and distraction technology made it possible. Now we de-socialize all our non-Authority citizens at age eighteen via mandatory injection. This method, if successful, will replace the old one-by-one process."

"How well does your old process work?" interrupted Maga.

The Consul closed their eyes and sighed loudly again.

"It works quite flawlessly, Maga, with a 99.999% successful de-socialization rate. Yet very rarely, an individual will prove immune to the treatment. In this case, we will monitor them closely, assign them to Authoritarian work, or both. Most ended up becoming the exiles we sent to your predecessor to handle. For instance, subject J-65216 before he escaped."

Their colleague to their left perked up a bit, realizing the opportunity to put the Maga on the defensive. "Remind me how you ensured his termination?" they asked.

Maga raised his eyebrows, hesitating. "Our men and women in uniform did a great job, forcing him to jump off the old Ambassador Bridge into Lake Michigan, okay? He died on impact when he hit the lake."

"He . . ." the Consul muttered, disgusted.

The Maga smirked, pleased anytime he could draw others' ire to himself, even unintentional.

Then another Consul shouted, attempting to disarm Maga's attention-whoring.

"Enough of this! Back to the weapon. Now you will see how we've perfected societal deconstruction. Persons—," they declared, looking down to the ones in lab coats below. "Initiate the aerosol social solvent on my mark."

The bald scientists all ran to the stations around the contained town.

"Mark!" they shouted.

3-5

The Ispanian village was a very different-looking place. Its square, once a daily bustling marketplace for locals, was empty, boarded up. The local forges and other crafting workshops had been repurposed for the production of firearms—normally an amateur hobbyist's craft in this age. Finally, shifts of men patrolled the dirt streets in formation day and night. After months, the town had completely shifted into wartime mode.

Afitna's plans had not been without its setbacks. The Averitans began air attacks a few weeks ago, with varying success. Homes were mainly targeted, reducing them to crumbled piles of clay. This was much to the misfortune of those families—but it was much to the fortune of Afitna. With each family's livelihood that was destroyed, public anger and support for his war grew. They demanded of him quick, bold action, to Afitna's authoritarian delight. And yet, a part of the collective consciousness resisted this sense of trust, beginning to question if the growing costs were worth the sense of righteous struggle it provided.

It was just after sunrise one brisk fall morning,

when a squadron of armed men assembled. Afitna stood at the front of them, a bright-red beret on his head. He was just about to address them about the first offensive against the Averitans on which they were to embark. That is, until behind them strode Josik and Maria.

The soldiers looked back, noticing how the couple was decidedly out of place in this war zone. Josik started shaking with nervousness, his garb of a loose silk shirt and leggings confessing civilian status. Afitna looked down on them condescendingly, daring Josik to speak.

"Greetings," Josik said, managing a meek smile.

The soldiers stared back derisively, unmoving. In their eyes, he must have been a deserter or a holdout from the draft. Either way, they saw him as a traitor.

"And just who the hell are you?" Afitna responded.

He laughed along with the crowd of warriors, amused at his incredible ego.

Josik almost started, his first speech prepared, calling for peace and unity. But Maria recognized the danger in the situation, could read the faces of the audience about to turn on him.

"I am Josik, and . . ."

"You'll have to excuse my husband," Maria interrupted. "His mind has not been well for months. He suffers from delusions of grandeur."

Afitna grinned menacingly, recalling similar words

from his doctor. Josik, meanwhile, was trying to moderate a furious expression on his face, and held back saying the few Spanish curse words he knew out loud.

Then one of the soldiers in the group cried out.

"Ay! Isn't she the hija of Manuel Martez?"

"Sí," she answered. "And my father would be very angry if he were to hear that my husband, practically his own flesh and blood, was maltreated."

Afitna tightened his look on the couple, stumped.

"Alright, Josik. You get a pass this time. But keep him put away, Señorita . . . What is your last name now?"

"My husband took my last name. He doesn't have one."

Antifa led the soldiers in a hearty laugh.

"Well, well, Señorita Martez. We don't need the weak-minded roaming around the streets and damaging morale. After all—"

He paused dramatically, catching the soldiers' attention by making a raised fist.

"We have the white man to exterminate!"

The soldiers raised their guns with grunts in solidarity.

"But first," the dictator added. "We will make a side trip to our neighbors the Ricans. We will show them the might we have in building up our forces. And once we do, they will submit to our command."

To this news, many of the men were stunned. Few of them had ever even been to the Rican village, let alone thought of them as a potential enemy.

But they said nothing, offered no resistance. Afitna, it seemed to many of them, was still their only option, the only one who offered a defense to their homes and families. Who else but him would finally put a stop to the ambushes and air strikes? Why waste time with objections, like the priests had done? Following them was a sure way of having their only possessions looted, their homes and places of work defaced. The village church still bore the marks of this silencing, almost fully black on the inside.

Most of them said nothing and gestured nothing. Afitna led them on the march out of town.

As their footsteps faded away, Josik fretted. He said a little prayer for the Ricans, hoping he had heard the strongman wrong and that some kind of alliance between the two people would form on their own.

Maria urged him towards the family house. Josik followed.

3-6

Josik and Maria visited her parents that night and were relieved to see that her family was resilient. Like most of the villagers, they were affected by their society's last several months of lockdown, mainly in the way of smaller rations. But their spirits remained high, their demeanor alert.

Relieved at this, and exhausted in contemplating his next move, Josik turned in early that night.

He woke up again in Sam's hatchback. Outside were magnificent seaside cliff sides, with mansions built into the side of them. But the skies overhead were gray, the air felt cold. Additionally, much of the landscape had been blackened and turned to ash, as if they were in a war zone.

Josik could see Rachel in the passenger side seat again, looking around. It was a relief to see her apparently at ease, a contrast from last time's scare.

Josik needed his final bearings. He looked again at the car clock:

1/9/18 7:39am

So, what was the story here? Josik waited for quite a while in silence while he found out.

As Josik studied Rachel's facial features more, he noticed that she fretted quite a bit. Occasionally, Sam would look over to her and reach out his hand to hers, his expression also one of concern. Whatever was causing their anxiety, it must have been continuing for some time—Josik now noticed that Sam carried a few lines on his forehead.

"Remember," Rachel said at one point. "They said they don't know what it means. It might be epilepsy, it might be something else. I just have to stay away from super stressful situations."

"Yet, Rachel. Yet," Sam emphasized, his voice raised. "I just don't understand how you can be so nonchalant about getting these kinds of results back."

A couple's fight. This was new to Josik.

Sam moved his hand back to the steering wheel, his mood passively upset. He said nothing for a while, let out a tense sigh.

"Rachel, I've known you for what, two years now? I worry about you because I care about you. I'm doing my best to know these things about you. Please give me some credit."

Rachel bit her lip, as if she wanted to say something more.

There was silence again for a while. Rachel had her arms crossed.

It was her who broke the silence. She was crying, clearly scared. Sam also started crying, instinctively sympathetic.

"I'm worried too, Sam," she said with a sniffle. "And I know how much you care. We wouldn't have gotten this far in our relationship if I didn't think your motives were genuine. But you have to trust me that I'm taking ownership of my health."

Sam sighed again. "Yeah. Shitty luck." Rachel looked out at the blackened landscape for a few moments.

"Why do you worry about me so much, Sam?"

Sam didn't say anything for a moment, as he was making a lane change. Once it was comfortable, he shifted a hand from the steering wheel to her lap. She grasped it readily and brought it over her heart.

"Rachel, my dear Rachel," he whispered while choking back tears. "The bright jewel and sapphire of my life. When I think about how happy you make me, it makes me wonder about the kind of person I was before you. I don't want to imagine what I would be like if I went back to that. I don't want to imagine a life without you."

"Oh, Sam," she whimpered softly. "You don't want to lose me."

Sam sobbed. "Yeah. No, I don't."

Rachel hesitated a moment, biting her lip again. Then she inhaled, as if about to speak. Instead, she stopped herself, cleared her throat. She looked out the window another moment. Finally, she settled on these words:

"Then promise me this. When something dangerous to my heart condition like Charlottesville happens, tell me to get out of there, okay?"

"Yes, my love," Sam said. "I promise that."

Rachel gave Sam a kiss, and while resting her head on his shoulder said: "I love you, Sam Usami."

Sam took notice, and responded in kind.

"I love you, too, Rachel Wesley."

She fixed his hand to her side as she fell asleep on the headrest.

***

Rachel woke up roughly a half hour later. It was drizzling out. She peered out the window aimlessly for a few minutes, noticing a Highway 101 sign. Then they passed by a portable road alert sign on the shoulder.

"Hey, Sam?"

Sam was getting a bit drowsy himself, but perked up at the question.

"I love you too, Rachel," he said with a smile.

"No, not that, sorry," Rachel interrupted. "Did you see that last sign?"

"No, sorry, I didn't. What was it about?"

"It said Highway 101 is closed a mile ahead and that we need to turn around."

"Turn around? Not just take a detour?"

"Hold on. Let me use your phone to try to find out what's going on."

Rachel took Sam's smartphone and began tapping away on the screen. Sam kept driving.

Within the next minute, they spotted a barricade of Highway Patrol cars. The officers were motioning for the traffic to drive over the grassy median in a U-turn to the southbound lanes. Other cars making the turn were clogged together helter-skelter.

Sam, in his zippy hatchback, almost didn't brake in time, surprised by the stoppage.

"Sam, stop!" Rachel shouted.

He hit the brakes as they swerved onto the side of the 101, avoiding a hit to a sedan on its right bumper. Sam, Rachel, and Josik all jumped out to view the natural catastrophe up ahead.

Ahead, the highway had been swallowed up by earth. What was once part of California's idyllic coastal hillside was an ugly slurry of mud, torn trees, brown water, and woody remains.

"Sam, what is this?" Rachel begged.

Sam spoke with no doubts about where this started. With his obsession over the consequences of climate change, he had worried about the growing scale of disasters all around the world for years.

"The largest wildfire in state history made this happen," he said with gravity. "This isn't the last of it. This'll get worse. This is the new normal."

3-7

Back at Bohem's experimental town, society had almost completed its destabilization process. Maga and the Consulate stepped in to view it early that morning, admiring their work.

The town square laid empty, save for a few bloodied corpses. Every surviving person at this point in the process had retreated to their own corner, either somewhere in the streets or in any of the town's abandoned buildings. The trade unions, worship groups, Scout programs, even the families—all of these social bonds had been totally dissolved and destroyed. Each person was on his or her own for basic necessities—an animal-like, survival of the fittest scenario.

"Now," said one of the indistinguishable Consuls. "It's time to implement the final phase."

The Maga grinned widely. He did a terrible job of hiding his excitement.

The Consul motioned to the researchers, who with a few buttons and levers lowered giant digital screens all around the perimeter of the town.

Then another Consul, the one slighter taller than the rest, prepared for some exposition, his palm raised gracefully upwards.

"You see, Maga, what we will accomplish with this experiment is an endpoint all collectivist societies throughout the centuries failed to achieve. In simply enforcing lip service to the State, they failed to achieve one single loyalty at the disposal of all others. As long as other loyalties—distractions, rather—were allowed to be a part of human nature, then dissent would continue to breed, whether from family, religion, or ethnic group."

The Consul paused for a moment, taking a careful breath.

"From what we know we can now achieve, the first collectivists were cavemxn compared to our attempts to achieve uniformity. In the French Revolution, the leaders couldn't stay in power long enough to avoid chopping each other's heads off. Conformity wasn't truly tried in full force until the twentieth century, with the Nazis and Communists. Even then, their methods were crude and imperfect. No wonder neither group lasted to the end of the century.

"Democrats around the world assumed that this setback for collectivism would guarantee our place in the dustbin of history in the twenty-first century. As you can see now, we're well over seven hundred years from that date and we're not just alive, but thriving. As your capitalist pig ancestors would say, we have proven ourselves a profitable investment."

"An investment that will pay big dividends!" Maga added.

The Consulate smiled with satisfaction. They could see the Maga was satiated, leaving him caught off guard.

"The difference no democrat expected was technology. Based on initial revolutionary events, experts assumed the invention of social media and electronic political movements would lend its way to more transparency in governments, exposure to abuses of power, and generally giving voice to the voiceless.

"Ah, but how soon the experts always become comfortable in their bubbles of knowledge. They forgot how unstable the system has always been underneath its varnished, prosperous top layer. Each generation must be born again in the lessons of liberty for the experiment of democracy to survive. But after a while, they forgot to teach their children these things. They contracted that work to the 'experts.' Instead of teaching the next generation a sense of love of country, the experts taught to completely revise the nation's past. The present time was assumed to have the greatest potential for the best of times, if only the people on the 'wrong side' of history just got out of the way. Everyone forgot for a time about human nature, assuming the best of the future.

"Given these favorable conditions, our predecessors found an irresistible opportunity to use political technology to revive authoritarian conformity in non-democratic countries and fracture democratic unity in countries that preached freedom. We discovered a powerful contradiction in democratic politics to promote to our advantage—each voter demographic's tiny minority status. Once targeted, we had a volatile resource at our disposal. We began provoking divisions in race, class, gender, and political culture. The result was constant collective outrage and a constant divergence on solutions to problems ailing democratic societies—no one wanted to see beyond what mattered to their tiny group.

"Of course, now we have abolished all tiny group distinctions. But the technology remains, and flawed human nature causes our subjects to remain attached to such trinkets. So, with little scheming required on our part and all generations of collectivists, the digital screen and the consumerist spirit have proved our greatest allies. Now you will see this on full display."

The Consul motioned towards a glass entry door to the experiment.

"Maga, lead the way."

When the four entered on a plain rectangular hovercart, this same Consul was on display on screens all around the town. The townspeople, disheveled from the anarchy and chaos with which they had been infected, stood dumbly attentive. Not a single individual thought went through anyone's mind. With the quiet flicker of the screens, everyone had gone from savage animal to a collective hive mind.

Eventually, the visiting group made their way to the town square, the people around them still looking up at the screens. The Consul raised their voice to speak.

"People of Bohem," they boomed, their voice echoing throughout the town. "Your land and your people are ours now. This town is no more. We will see to your every need."

The third Consul, with help from one of the others, threw the Maga out of the cart and into the mindless crowd of people.

"Kill him, he is the enemy of the people! Exploiting capitalist pig!" they screamed.

He looked back, his face red with rage and his terrible hairstyle in disarray from the sudden shove.

"How dare you! The people won't stand for this! They'll see you're just fake rulers!"

"I'm sorry, Maga," the first Consul said over the screen. "As you would say, it's not personal—it's just business. You're fired."

The mob quickly overcame the Big-League Maga, who was physically out of shape. He was beaten down to gruesome, bloody pieces and was no more.

3-8

Josik woke up the next morning rather unrefreshed. All was safe in the Martez household, but he spent the morning in a state of restlessness, sensing his work was not complete.

It was yesterday's failed attempt to win the soldiers over to his side. How could he? Or rather, how could Maria? Perhaps he had been too hasty and simply chose the wrong moment.

But when would his next moment come? This was the question to which he desperately needed an answer, one for which he began to search desperately this new morning.

Josik spent a good portion of his morning pacing around the Martez living room, the children and parents being at school and work. It wasn't until late morning that Maria rose and questioned her husband's franticness.

She grabbed him by the shoulders, a form of gentle restraint. Realizing his over-exaggeration, he sat down on the family sofa, letting out a loud sigh.

"I saw more of the past last night, Maria," Josik confessed.

Since their escape into the woods, he had learned to be more open about his experiences living on Earth. His wife always listened readily, one of the things he loved most about her.

"And that makes you worried?" Maria asked.

"Very much so. I saw a natural disaster taking place, the result of human-made climate change. And I'm left wondering—why would a country that damaged itself like that apparently be worth reviving?"

Maria pondered a moment.

"Well, because all in all, it was probably a good thing. It seems like these people are trying to teach you the important lessons to be learned from it, and the mistakes to avoid."

"Yeah, that makes sense," Josik mused, taking this in.

Josik and Maria's eyes met, smiles lighting up between the two. He was reminded daily of the reasons he loved his wife, like her ability to help him make sense of this new world and his new experiences.

A sense of purpose rose up in him again, a feeling they could still accomplish some amazing things. Yesterday was a setback, but that wasn't Maria's fault. In fact, Josik could see now that she had acted in his best interests. Despite their differences, they were a team now.

Josik sighed. "Where do we start again, Maria?"

She had suspected that Josik's mind would turn back to the mission.

"The Ricans," she said, confidently. "We have a few friends we made there who will listen to what we have to say."

It was decided. They would stay at the Ispanian village one more night to pack their things, but they'd leave for the Rican village first thing in the morning.

That night, Josik and Maria gave the members of the Martez family their tenderest goodbyes. Maria's parents were afraid of what may happen next to them and the village, but they dared not try to leave. The Martez family was too well-respected for their flight to go unnoticed. Rather, the town's morale would collapse and the war would surely be lost. It would spell certain doom for their Ispanians, whom they loved.

But they took solace in the thought that their daughter and her loyal husband would be in a safer place. They made Josik tacos that night—his favorite meal.

Maria's mom also gave Josik a bright knitted rainbow-patterned shawl, a practical memento for the journey ahead.

Manuel Martez offered the final words on behalf of the family before everyone retired that night.

"I know you'll take care of her. When you come back,

take care of our people too."

"I will," Josik promised, holding back tears.

3-9

Normally, when Josik woke in his sleep these days, it was in a car from centuries ago. This time, it was different. For some reason, he was standing across a courtyard from Sam and Rachel, fascinated by the dark robes and caps they were wearing. Surrounding the two were their families, smiling and asking for the help of strangers to snap photos. They were just outside the university library. Josik noticed banners hung all around, celebrating 150 years of operation at the service of young Californian scholars. To the northwest, Josik stared up at a giant bell tower, which read that it was nearly noon. Josik was also impressed by the spreading view of the ocean bay to the west, and the suspension bridge that could be barely made out through the fog, most of which had burned off for the day.

Whatever was happening here—which Josik could only guess at—was surely a happy moment, making it irresistible for the observer to smile. But it only lasted another moment. The ocean bay and the college campus seemed to melt away, the family members dissolved and disappeared.

It was just Sam and Rachel again, sitting groggily next to each other on a plane. Josik was in the same row too, occupying the aisle seat.

So how was he supposed to tell what the date was here? He crossed his arms and let himself get mesmerized by the film being played on the small screen in front of him—one of the many superhero movies from that time in history.

After a while, Rachel muttered something.

"Sam?" she said, her eyes half open.

"Yes, sapphire?" Sam responded. Josik had mentally noted that this was Sam's favorite nickname for her.

Rachel shuffled around in her seat, not feeling at all bright nor cheery at the moment.

"I don't feel too good."

"Probably just motion sickness combined with the lack of sleep. Did you take some sleeping pills?"

"Not yet. Did you?"

"No," he said, making a face like he was getting away with something. "But I'll take mine now if you take yours."

"Deal," she said.

"Feel free to sleep on my lap if you'd like."

She did. They were both out within the next ten minutes.

Curious, Josik craned his neck over to see the date on Sam's watch.

07:13pm 07/11

Then he took in the couple, Rachel resting on her side and Sam sleeping upright with his mouth agape. Josik pleased himself with a quiet chuckle.

But just as he did, the scene changed again. The setting changed to Sam and Rachel squeezing themselves through a large crowd on a city street, many of the participants armed with picket signs.

"I didn't think Chequers would be this busy today," Rachel said.

"Wait," Sam realized, stopping in his tracks. "Trump's meeting the prime minister today. That's what all this is about."

"Can we get out of here, then? I'm not in the mood for politics right now."

Sam nodded. "That's one of the things I love about you, sweetie. We don't have to discuss solving the world's problems to get along. I have no problem adjusting the schedule."

As they turned around, a giant balloon representing a cartoon baby could be seen, carried as like in a Thanksgiving Day parade. It didn't take long for the two to realize it was a representation of the current American president.

"Ahh, well that's just mean," Rachel thought aloud. "I don't come to protest your leader when she comes to visit my country, and make obvious jokes about her like how she looks like Margaret Thatcher if she belonged in a nursing home."

"Oy!" a rainbow-haired protestor cried, whose gender was indiscernible. "She's not even my leader! Corbyn's the guy I listen to. Corbyn knows the right way, unlike your fat, racist Cheeto."

"You stupid Americans can't get anything right," another one shouted. "You're all just a bunch of racist, redneck pigs!"

The crowd around Josik, Sam, and Rachel started laughing. Josik felt himself tense up angrily, thinking back to the logic of his former Bohemx peers. He could imagine the self-righteous explanation from his ex-friend Meset: "When one is tolerant of historically marginalized cultures, one is immunized from intolerance towards peoples, histories, and cultures attributed to oppression. It's impossible to be intolerant of the intolerant."

The mob started making pig-snorting sounds, its members continuing to amuse themselves.

Sam got defensive, angry at Rachel but protective of her sensitive heart. He unproudly shoved through the raw energy of the young activists, whose message was fueled by digital technology and unrestrained from the institutions of old. Similar to their American counterparts—and caused by personal experience— these millennials had grown to hate the political, cultural, and economic status quo. Whether burdened by an uncertain future, sums of student debt, or by bad religion, they demanded more than just reform of the whole Western way of life—they demanded revolution.

As the couple stormed out of the crowd, Sam could be barely heard to mutter—not understanding the crass, fruitless kind of protest to which his generation had grown accustomed, supposedly in the name of driving political change.

"What the hell is this?" he said, dissenting.

3-10

Josik woke up to a cold, dank morning. The sun had just barely risen. His dream must have left him and stirred him before his normal waking time. Yesterday had mostly been spent struggling with land navigation; as Josik discovered, Maria had much more experience with a map and compass than he did, which he pretended to resent with jest.

They figured they were less than a day's journey from the Rican village. Winter was coming in just another six weeks, so nights were growing short. They could have risked trekking through the night with all the wildlife and other risks that that entailed. Instead, a safe bet was made, sleeping after a quick dinner of bread and lentil soup after sundown.

Josik looked around at the vantage point he saw from this ridge on which they settled. Nearly all of the maple trees were missing their cover, and the colors were not as impressive as they had been a few weeks ago. What did brighten his view was Maria, her round nose, ruddy cheeks, and open mouth peeking out from her mummy-shaped sleeping bag.

Josik chuckled generously.

"What?" Maria asked with a start, her face jumpstarting with a smile. "Is it me you're laughing at?"

"No," Josik said. "Just thought about a funny joke I made about Nucks the other day."

"What's that?" Maria said eagerly. "Tell me. Tell me everything."

Josik laughed, touched by her feigned obsession of him.

"What's a Nuck's favorite letter?"

"Let me guess. A?" she said, meaning the phrase "eh?" most often used as punctuation at the end of the tribe's sentences.

"No! None, cause Nucks are illiterate!"

Maria snorted rather inelegantly.

"Wow," she cried, her ebony hair now out of the bag. "That was terrible!"

"What's that your dad calls those? A dad joke?"

"No," Maria demanded, pretending to be taken aback. "You don't have the authority to call something a dad joke. If you wanted to make one, you should have asked my padre for permission before we left. That's how it works, you know."

"No, it doesn't." Josik pretended to be outraged.

"Yes, it does," Maria retorted, approaching his face. "Since I'm the Earth native here, I get to make the rules."

"Wow, I can't believe it," Josik said with an exaggerated shake of his head. "This is worse than that time we had that argument about those rabbits near the hut. You could have just let me provide and be a good hunter-gatherer for once."

"That doesn't give you license to brag about killing those poor things!"

Josik gave his shoulders a dispassionate shrug.

"We ate well that night, did we not?"

Maria reached her hand around the back of his neck, using him as an anchor point to draw her whole body nearer.

"Really, mi amor? Sometimes you just frustrate me—you frustrate every part of body and soul."

"I don't know what to tell you."

Maria leaned in his ear for a whisper.

"You mustn't tell me anything. I have some things you could do, though."

Josik looked to the heavens, thanking God again for his wife.

They had a late start to the morning.

They managed to find the Rican village in the late afternoon. It was hardly recognizable—there was hardly anything left of it. Averitan airstrikes of Incinerates had reduced all the buildings to piles of rubble, the village courtyard to a half-inch layer of ash.

Josik fell to his knees. He sorrowfully thought that he was too late, that these simple people had all been lost. He thought back to his experience with their soldiers, the time they navigated an underground system. The Ricans weren't naturally open to outsiders—very few of the factions were—but they were welcoming once they had gotten to know him.

But those people and that culture were gone, Josik thought and wept. He was certain that their extinction was yet another tragedy created in the war waged by Averita.

A holler came from behind Josik, and he looked. He couldn't believe it. Standing behind him was a Rican scout patrol, dressed sharply in fatigues and armed heavily with assault weapons and explosives. The soldiers raised their weapons. Josik and Maria raised their hands.

"State your purpose, trespasser," said a stout one towards the front of the group.

"I'm . . . I'm not a spy," Josik said hurriedly. "I come from the Ispanians. I'm a defector."

There was no response, neither verbal nor gestured.

"I ask for your protection and pledge myself to your cause. I have information I can offer."

The broadly shaped commander motioned towards the soldiers. They lowered their weapons.

"If you're fleeing the Ispanians, you have some real nerve trying to ask for protection here."

"I was friends with General Deshawn," Josik announced. Some gasps and murmurs went around.

The commander's expression softened, recognizing the significance of this relationship.

"Follow me," he said. "I will take you to our leader."

The soldiers revealed an underground entrance. Josik and Maria could both barely contain their relief as they focused on the audience at hand.

They were led to a broad, muscular woman, who, like many of the Ricans underground, was covered head to toe in dull titanium armor. Some of women, however, did not have the strength to fight, and focused themselves on tending to the Rican children. Josik couldn't help but take notice of the kids as he and Maria passed by, how they would fuss around with their meals and always find the energy to run around in circles. Even at the height of war, it was a comfort to think that things such as the nature of children remained unchanged.

The woman stood still as the Ispanian couple approached, appearing resolved.

"Who are you?" she asked simply.

"I am Josik. This is my wife, Maria. We are Ispanians."

The woman's frown tightened, restraining her biases against outsiders.

"And you knew Deshawn?"

"Yes, the general."

Silence dropped. Josik figured there was no easy way to build rapport between villages that had been in apparent on-and-off racial conflict as far back as present-day history could record. His initial strategy was to stick to simple facts.

Josik took out the flag pin from his jacket pocket, the one given to him over seven months ago.

"Deshawn also gave this to me," he said, holding up the small piece. "He knew about the discoveries I had been making, how our land was once so much more peaceful and so much more hopeful."

The woman's face relaxed. She was astounded by these words.

"That our land and all our people were once united as one?" she asked, as if repeating from memory.

"Yes," said Josik, nearly breathless from the drama of the moment. "We were once known as the United States of America. We can be united once again. I've come here because I've seen that vision."

The female warrior-leader turned away.

"I can't believe this. I won't believe this," she half-whispered.

"There's something you know," Josik stated.

"No," she refused, her eyes filling with tears. "I can't believe it. I can't believe that everything our people have suffered on this continent for over a thousand years can just be put aside by some crazy prophecy."

"It's not the first time you've heard of it, have you?" Josik said pointedly.

A growing crowd of Ricans looked on, eager for the truth. At long last, a missing part of their history had been revealed.

She paused. In that moment, she pleaded with God and herself for the wisdom to make the right snap decision. She could either give in to Josik's inquiries and risk appearing weak to her people, or refuse and remain confined away from the truth. The right choice was clear, and it was liberating.

"I was his wife!" she cried, stomping her foot towards Josik and Maria. "I am Wambui, and I was General Deshawn's wife! And there are things he told me about America, and I realize the time has come to reveal them.

"He would visit our home every few months when he had a leave from combat. In the last year before he... well, Deshawn would talk about these dreams he was having. He talked, as you said, of a long-lost land revealed to him, where these factions and wars did not exist. At first, I thought he was crazy, but I was taken by the idea. So, I told him to write down his thoughts to save for future generations. I thought it would at least save something, some plan to follow when they'd find some crazy way to finally build this utopia he described. For a while, I put my boo-boo's stories out of my mind. I wouldn't let him talk about them anymore, I thought he became too obsessed. I thought that was the end of it. One day in the early spring I went exploring with my usual escort. I snuck away from the rest of the group on a full-moon night. I was curious about things I had heard about the Follies across the wide river where we slept that night. I was taken in by the gigantic ruins. And I realized there had to have been some kind of history to this land after all. Perhaps Deshawn was right to speak of better times. So, in the piles of rubble I found just one thing worth keeping."

She pointed a shaky hand to the pin.

"It was that. So then I gave it to Deshawn the next time I saw him. He seemed very interested."

Wambui sniffled, still quite emotional.

"He had another dream that night, with a message so clear and direct it was unlike anything he had ever dreamed before. He told me the exact words he was told the next morning: 'The one who comes to the village with this flag is the one who can unite us.' How was I supposed to make sense of this? Was I supposed to assume that he was some savior of unity, since he already had it? I didn't know what to think."

She had to pause. Revisiting the moment of her husband's death was still not easy on her.

"And then he died. I thought the pin had been lost or buried with him, so that this little prophecy had no meaning anymore. Perhaps he had just misinterpreted. I didn't want to believe him, and now I have to live with that. I failed him. If I had, maybe things could have turned out . . . differently."

Wambui looked to Josik and Maria, then to her fellow Ricans. They felt sorry for her loss, as it was also their loss of their leader, and grateful for her courage at the same time. The people were moved, evidenced by how they stood silently still to wait for her next call. All showing of anger had been washed away.

"But now I see the words fulfilled," she said, tears running down her face. "I've prayed every day since he died that it would not be in vain. Now tell us your plan. Our people put our faith in these things I don't fully understand—but we believe them."

A trio of older Ricans in long, hooded robes approached Wambui, pulling her aside in whispering conversation. Josik and Maria looked on, sweating tensely as they speculated what was being discussed.

"Our Tribal Council is agreed," Wambui announced after several minutes. "We want to hear your plan to fight against the Averitans as a united front."

Josik cleared his throat to address the village. He could feel his shoulder instinctively square, as if his whole body was prepared and ready for this moment.

"It's not an easy plan and it will not happen overnight. But I came here because I believe our glorious cause will start here. We will unite all the villages against the Averitans, entering in our own union. I will go to each of the other factions to make this same case to

342

bring us all together. We will grow the union one-by-one, while using what we've discovered about the USA as a reminder of what we can accomplish together. This land, America, is one we all share. We are all Americans. If we're going to survive together, we must unite... or don't and die."

"Brother Josik and Sister Maria of Ispania," Wambui declared, rising powerfully. "Deshawn once said: 'United we stand, divided we fall.' Now I finally understand his words. If no one other Rican is objected, then let today mark the union of our two peoples!"

The whole village erupted in cheering, the only approval she needed.

3-11

Back inside the sleek ivory façade of Maga Tower, the center of Averita's power, two of the Consuls looked over Bohem's new subjects on Earth. From their top-floor balcony, the whole cross-section of the area's reformed society could be seen. In the immediate central part of town, the factories continued their mindless rhythm. Beyond that, in the slums, regiments of people were training for combat, starting with simple marching exercises.

But some parts of Averitan existence—and aspects of human nature, for that matter—had been changed. There was none of the usual casual chatter between the people. Their lives now consisted only of the work assigned to them by Authority, their individual identity erased by their permanently hairless bodies and gender-ambiguating jumpsuits.

The third Consul (it was impossible to distinguish which one it was at this point), who had been missing, entered the room.

"I bring good news," they said. "The city's oligarchs have surrendered their capital in exchange for being spared from social solvent. That covers the last portion of private property in the former union."

Another of them smiled, their glee spreading to the others.

"Ancestor Xi would have been proud of what we created here."

Then the three grasped each other with their right hands on each of their shoulders in a triangular formation, their secret sign of affection.

The third, who had not spoken yet, offered a correction to their fellow's statement.

"No. All the ancestors would have smiled on us right now. They never would have dreamed that this day was possible. Comrades, let us understand what we have done. We have created true equality for the people. True equality isn't just about economics—that was the unfortunate mistake of our ancestors. It's about equality of thought—all loyalties, devotions, and purposes in life are reduced to one."

Another spoke. "Let's have a toast to this moment."

They prepared three small glasses of what they called "gxn," or "synthetic spirits" by others who failed to see the apparently patriarchal connotations of the drink's older name.

The Consuls raised their glasses to the happiest moment of their rule.

"To bringing true equality to Earth, once and for all," one said.

And with a clink, they all took their shots.

Each of them let out a contented sigh. After about a minute, one of them asked a question, turning to the entrance.

"Good to see you've arrived, General Chris. Would you care to join us for a drink?"

The man slowly treaded into the dark, barely lit room. He wore a new uniform granted to him by Authority months earlier, a citizen's gray jumpsuit adorned with a syntho-leather black chest piece and shoulder pads with colorless stars on the top. In a show of conformity, his head was shaved, but he still appeared biologically male.

"I couldn't refuse, fellow comrades," Chris said with a hurried bow.

They took a moment to refill their gxn. Chris clinked his shot-glass with the three others in a silent toast, perfectly emotionless. He took the drink in one gulp, nonplused.

Finally, one of the Consuls struck up another question. "How was your shuttle ride, General?"

"Same as yours," replied Chris with a dull expression. "Perfectly calculated and uneventful."

The Consuls all let out a guffaw, detecting sarcasm.

"Quick-witted as usual, General," one of them said. "Besides having assembled your usual trove of quips, are you ready to make your journey to recover prisoner J-65216?"

"Who?" Chris asked, apparently confused.

"J-65216. The prisoner."

"Right, Josik. My apologies, Consuls, I'm so used to addressing prisoners by their chosen names."

"Well, better kick the habit," one of them quipped. "We'll be abolishing those pretty soon also."

"Right," Chris said. "I'll leave immediately once we're finished here. How is the new weapon?"

"Flawlessly effective. It's time we rolled it out on behalf of the People. Where is the nearest faction from here?"

Answered one of the Consuls: "To our south, several miles from here. The peaceful Sinos live in the forests there."

"Well, we'll be sure to change that," was said through a smile.

They clinked their glasses again, excluding Chris this time.

"To bring about peace on earth, we will begin today to make war!" one of them cried.

"I'll leave you, comrades," said Chris as he bowed to Authority one more time. Then he turned back and disappeared from the room.

3-12

In such cruel and unforgiving times, Ricans jumped on any opportunity to throw a party. Josik had some experience with nighttime festivities from being Ispanian—he was familiar with their love of tequila and vino. But parties with the Ricans, he discovered, were something else entirely.

In celebration of their new union, the underground town square was decorated with strings of lights and standing torches. They needed the lighting for playing music, courtesy of the town's guitar and drum experts.

Josik could see the people around them building with excitement as the day wasted away, signaled by the giant invisible skylight located at the center of their substitute square. Everyone changed into their colorful festive wear, notable by the loose-fitting dresses and shawls they wore.

The musicians picked up their instruments as soon as the lights of the night flashed on. A growing crowd gave a great cheer. Some inaugurated the event with shots of an amber-colored liquid.

"Hey!" shouted Wambui over the growing volume, rubbing up against Josik.

She pointed to a bottle she was holding of the stuff, her head oddly cocked.

"You want some?"

Josik was cautious and was about to decline, but Maria was curious.

"What is it?" she asked.

"Oh," Wambui said, with an overly generously hand motion. "It's called whiskey. Comes from a distant faction called the Bourbons. We trade with them for this beautiful nectar very rarely."

"Yeah, we'll take some! Right, Josik?"

Josik opened his mouth, about to object. But Wambui had already stumbled back to the bar table to grab some glasses.

An empty bottle later, the three were crouched over a table, yelling at each other about the intricacies of constitutional government over the sounds of soft rock in the background.

They were on the topic of an independent judiciary. Josik had introduced the concept to them.

"And why on earth would you let a small, unelected group of people have final say on how the law worked?" said Wambui, shaking her head.

"I'm not saying we give all that same power

back to a Supreme Court when we establish a new government," explained Josik. "I believe we should give Congress and/or the President the ability to take immediate action as a response to laws struck down as unconstitutional, so that the ball is put back in the court of elected people. The idea behind having a high court, still, is to provide a check and balance to the other two branches of government."

"Okay, you lost me, bombon," Maria said, giving her husband an unsteady poke. "Remind me what Congress is."

"The legislative branch. Like what we have in Ispania with its Council of Elders and in Rica with the Tribal Council. It's the part of the government that's elected to represent different parts of the country in making laws."

Wambui slowly waved her hands back and forth disapprovingly, teetering as she did.

"But if Congress represents the people, why hold the people down with this dumb Court? That doesn't sound like democracy..."

She flipped a hand at Josik's general direction, putting her sentence on pause.

"...that doesn't sound like democracy to me." She wagged a finger for unnecessary emphasis.

Josik shrugged his shoulders in response.

"Trust me. American history shows that it has a lot of benefits. Many people had some really basic civil rights given to them because of the Supreme Court."

The warrior woman could have pressed on, but was too drunk from the evening to concentrate.

"Let's have this discussion some other time!" she shouted, unable to stand up straight.

"Yes," said Josik, grasping her hand. "I'll look forward to it."

Josik and Maria danced away the rest of night along with the town, mostly absorbed in each other's eyes. As the night grew later, their hold on each other grew tighter.

Josik couldn't recall early the next morning when he had finally fallen asleep the night before, but he was happy to see it had been right next to Maria. It was still before sunlight when he realized this, so he gave a satisfied smile, settled his chin on her beautiful, sleek hair, and fell back to sleep.

3-13

Appearing to Josik in his slumber again was the couple from the past, ahead of him on a steep hiking trail. The two were decked out in brightly colored layered clothing, wide-brimmed hats, backpacks, and sunglasses. It could be seen ahead that they had a great mountain to climb.

For a few brief moments, they stopped for a break to catch a few breaths and a bite of food. It was Josik's golden opportunity to get his bearings on time and date. Relying on Sam's watch, he found this episode taking place at:

09:36am 9/21

They were presumably still in the year 2018, or so Josik gathered based on the nature of Sam and Rachel's conversations.

"So, you still haven't told me how your job hunt has been going," Sam said at one point during a food break. "I feel compelled as a millennial preaching from the commanding heights of the middle class to ask."

"Well," Rachel said, smirking at the tongue-in-cheek socioeconomic references. "I've had some great progress lately. I had an interview yesterday, actually."

"How'd it go?"

She gave a pause, her smile suddenly going flat for a moment.

"I'd rather talk about it some other time."

"That bad, huh?" Sam gave her his usual playful smile.

"Hey, I'm just counting my blessings that I got an interview as a sociology major," she retorted.

"Hey," said Sam, stopping to point a playful finger at her. "You're talking to a guy who studied political science, remember? I take offense."

Rachel stopped and gave him a pointless shove.

Sam gave her a stupid smirk back.

"I thank my lucky stars I met you in that SOC 1 class all those years ago," he said, leaning in for a kiss.

Then they started walking again.

***

After several hours, the geographic setting seemed to change even more—the trees had gone away completely, only to be replaced by small patches of snow. They were above the tree line now.

"How far up do you suppose we are?" Rachel asked,

a little short of breath.

Sam mused for a moment. He hadn't brought his GPS device on this trip.

"Probably about 13,000 feet. I'd rather not check my phone. I'm just enjoying the moment too much. But we're almost there."

Sam pointed ahead to a sign pointing to a rocky staircase. It read:

Mt. Whitney 1.9

Josik looked around at this strange, barren, twisted landscape of granite and basalt. With the lack of tree cover, he thought the imagery somewhat resembled the moon—that is, when he considered close-up pictures of the place he saw in his studies on Bohem. But unlike the moon, the views from this place were immaculate, untouched by human settlement. He also took notice of the gentle whisper of the mountain breeze.

"Just the way God left it," Josik said to himself.

After another two hours or so, the couple reached the peak, their gait slowing to a snail's pace. Josik was also exhausted, but suffered none of the same effects of exposure that came from standing on top of the world. Being a historical observer had many drawbacks, but plenty of fair kickbacks.

There were a few others there, even though it was past the peak time of the early afternoon. Josik saw Sam and Rachel have their picture snapped on top of the tallest rock—a great feat worth remembering, the student gathered.

Yet, Josik sensed a certain nervousness growing in Sam, the teacher's hands noticeably shaky.

Sam and Rachel had their late lunch of cheese and crackers as the other visitors left. Eventually, Rachel sidled next to her love, napping with her head on his shoulder as they both perched against a large granite boulder.

Sam, meanwhile, stayed awake, still nervous. At one point, he seemed to bow his head for no apparent reason, whispering quietly to himself.

Another twenty minutes or so passed and Rachel awoke. She gave her trademark four-inch distant gaze in Sam's eyes.

But her smile faltered, rather unusual. She sighed and turned her eyes downward.

Sam gave her a smiling response. "Hey, everything alright?"

Rachel looked out to the spreading view of the High Sierras again and smiled.

"Yes, I think so. Everything should be fine," she beamed, revealing her tiny dimples again.

"I'm happy to hear it," Sam responded. He felt awkward hearing the words come out of his mouth, realizing it wasn't something he normally said.

Then Sam began to rummage through his backpack.

"Rachel Mary Wesley, my light, my bright sapphire—I have a question for you. If I can just find it, that is," he said with an unnatural nervous laugh.

Sam kneeled on one knee and opened a small felt box. Rachel and Josik both had the same reaction—one of shock.

"Will you marry me?" he asked.

"Sam, I. . ." Rachel stuttered, an unnatural state for her. "I love you so much."

She started crying. Sam raised his eyebrows, unable to read the emotion.

"I. . . I can't."

"What?" Sam returned immediately, surprised. "Why not?"

"Sam," Rachel said, in between loud sobs. "I was going to tell you. The interview I had, it's . . . it's for a job in . . . in New York. They want me to come out and work for them in New York."

Sam gave a loud sigh. It was the only way he could calm himself down in the moment.

"Are you going take it?" he asked.

Rachel sobbed a few more times.

"I . . . I don't know yet. I don't know anything about my life yet. I'm so sorry, but I know I can't be ready for this, for marriage."

Sam said nothing more and held Rachel tightly in

his arms. Josik watched closely, heard the whispering mountain breeze pick up. At first, it merely drowned out the sounds of Rachel's sorrow. But as he continued to watch the pair's embrace, the scene quickly blew away and dissolved into nothingness.

3-14

Josik, Maria, Wambui, and the Ricans had been on the trail for several weeks now, doing their best to avoid detection. They traveled on a route unfamiliar to Josik—though to him, just trekking through these mountains again caused a brief flashback to his past trauma. When he found himself in these moments, Josik would say a little prayer to himself, asking God to help him carry on. At his low points on some of these days, it was just enough.

Indeed, the faith of everyone in the party was just barely enough to lead them onward. Since leaving their underground sanctuary, they were low on food, supplies, and morale. But that was a hardship all were willing to accept for their new cause. It was either this option—to seek out and unite with the Sinos—or the fighters could wait to be starved out, alone. It was the only way they could win not just the battle, but the war. This glorious cause was everything left to them and the 600 or so left back home.

Finally, they came down to the other side of the mountains just as the first snow had begun to fall, continuing northwest. Josik, Wambui, and others gave thanks to God that no one in the party of over 1,000 had been lost. Mass was said by the army's chaplain almost daily—a safeguard against what many feared was the inevitable.

Eventually, they came to what they called the Ohio River, and proceeded to follow it for days. At one point—trusting century-old maps—they crossed over it on a rickety concrete bridge. The Ricans were surprised not to have seen Averitan soldiers marching to battle by this point, since the military posts that they passed sat nearly silent.

Still, they kept up their guard. Everyone in the army had been converted into a soldier—men, women, even the adolescents.

One day, they were walking through the flat wooded region known formerly as Indiana. They saw their first sign of enemy movement since starting their march, a gigantic bomber plane. It passed over them going to the southeast, then turned around to where it had originated.

At this point, they had finally reached the Sino village. Josik was impressed with its layout—for its quaint look, much attention was clearly given to the town's architecture, in contrast to the simple mud houses of the Ispanians and the crude wooden structures of the Ricans. The town's church at the center was probably the tallest tower he had ever seen from any of the factions—well, with the exception of the Averitans.

But there was no one to be seen walking about in

the middle of this sunny, brisk December day. The snow looked like it had not been walked on for days.

The army men and women all looked around to each other. Where were the people? They decided it would be best to search the houses.

Josik motioned for two soldiers to follow him into a mini mansion across the street from the church. Inside it was dim—the town's lamps had been unlit.

Throughout their search for people, they passed through various partitions of multi-color curtains—a substitute for doors, it would seem. The soldiers, including Josik, kept getting distracted at various points by the ornate furniture they were passing by. Some of the details of the dressers and tables they stooped over to notice were obviously crafted by hand—artifacts that must have been passed through this homeowner's family for hundreds of years' worth of generations.

"Hello? Is anybody in here?" Josik shouted for the umpteenth time.

Josik heard a low growl toward the back door. Finally, some kind of answer.

Josik yelled for his companions. They pointed their flashlights at a short man hunched over on the ground, busy devouring a long piece of flesh. The man's eyes were bloodshot, his graying hair ripped out in places. His simple robe and skirt had been torn through in many places and stained with blood.

The man spoke no words and gave no response to

his visitors' discovery. He just kept eating. One of the soldiers leaned in closer to look.

"Oh my God," he half-whispered, crossing himself. "It's an arm."

Everyone in the group gave a groan. Despite this, one of the women was brave enough to look closer.

"It belong to a woman, by the looks of it. Maybe his wife's? Marriage troubles?"

But the others were too shocked to give a laugh. They were starting to step back.

"What happened to this man?" another asked. "If we can even call him that anymore?"

"Well, he doesn't even seem to care that we're here," Josik observed. "It's possible it's some form of rabies."

"No," said one of the women, who had some medical expertise. "Rabies doesn't devolve someone into a cannibalistic animal."

One of the younger men in the group interjected. "Listen, can we just get the hell out of here and do the diagnosis later?"

It was a good point, everyone affirmed nonverbally. They all rushed out to the village square, where the rest of the army had also finished. Chatter quickly filled the area as each soldier recounted to one another the horrors each of them had discovered.

Josik, meanwhile, ran over to Maria's search group. Seated on the ground was one of the Sinos—a young man with long black hair and pale skin.

"A survivor," Josik thought out loud.

Maria was kneeled over next to the man, trying to calm him down. She turned back to acknowledge Josik for a minute and went back to work.

"Listen friend, it's okay," Maria spoke calmly, grasping his hand. "We're here to help you. Now tell us what happened so we can help."

The man's eyes darted to her, both bloodshot. He remained hunched over, as if he had forgotten how to walk upright.

"There were planes," he said. "And they dropped this strange red mist on us. We thought we were fine at first. But then everyone changed. Including me."

He suddenly leaped upright towards Maria, attempting to claw at her face. Josik acted instantaneously and shoved him back.

Josik gestured for a group of soldiers to restrain the man, looking visibly disturbed.

A group of galloping horses and riders arrived, seeing the troubled expressions of army. All of the cavalry were dressed like their leader, who was at the front in her military garb of long brown boots, gray leather gloves, wide-brimmed hat, slender brown pants, and red double-breasted jacket. Her pants and jacket closely fit to her figure, yet modestly covered all her features, save her unblemished fair-skinned face.

She dismounted and took off her hat, revealing her

braided blonde hair.

"Captain Smythe," declared Josik, approaching the leader of the Nucks with an outstretched hand. "Seeing you is a very welcome surprise during these events."

Smythe's eyes widened, shocked that Josik seemed to read her mind.

"We are blessed that me and my people are not the only ones who have noticed a change," she said. "Is this village also preparing for battle?"

"We don't know," Josik fretted. "It's not ours. These Ricans abandoned their village with almost nothing left."

"Then where are the Sinos?"

Josik pointed to the lone survivor, who was screaming and howling under the ropes being used to restrain him.

Smythe sat on the edge of the well in the village square's center, absorbing her shock.

"My God," she said, steadily removing her gloves. "The Averitans must have done this—whatever in the devil's unholy name that they've done. Their war technology grows more sophisticated every day. A week ago, they finally located our humble village with a drone spy—it zipped over us at a speed so fast we only realized it when we started hearing the drone of their cargo planes minutes later. We left immediately, grabbing everything we could. The first people I thought to find were the Sinos. We were even going to submit our people under them in exchange for joining our forces together."

"But wait, where are the children?" Josik inquired, learning to show concern for the well-being of families like the one he hoped to start someday.

"There's a system of tunnels built by the Rican resistance fighters that followed the length of the bridge going underneath the lake," Smythe replied, wringing her hands nervously. "We had never used it before until last week. We sent a few parents to guide all the children to beg for shelter with the fighters. I can only hope and pray that they all found a safe place to go."

Her eyes began to water. Josik faced himself in front of her, comforting her with a hug.

"We too are all disturbed and desperate in these dark, dark times," then Josik admitted. "But I see now that we have cause for hope."

"Hope?" Smythe repeated, her thoughts and speech patterns turning back to basic survival mode. She allowed her trickle of tears to continue undistracted. "My people's children might be killed, and you say there's hope?"

Josik looked across the square to Wambui, motioned for her to come over.

"Yes," he said gently, turning back. "I believe and pray with all my heart that there is cause for hope."

He continued. Josik was about to make an introduction, one he hoped would advance the cause.

"Captain Smythe, this is Wambui, of the Ricans. Do you remember the legends of the country called America?"

3-15

Josik entered his dream and felt that he had immediately hit a wall of sadness, judging by the scene set before him. There was a light drizzle of rain, the overcast layer of clouds flat and low above. He looked around the blocks of city streets that stretched in all directions, most of the buildings obnoxiously tacked on with neon signs. As he looked up, he could see a pyramid-topped skyscraper, the tallest in sight. It was night out, so the homeless were huddled in blankets and covers of cardboard on the side streets, attempting to sleep over the sound of nearby protestors. They were also trying to sleep over the sound of loud music coming from one of the buildings directly across the street.

Josik sighed calmly as he watched, and heard the occasional car cut through the light rain, thinking of nothing else. Then one of the cars—a sleek, black sedan, pulled over in front of the loud building. Out of the car stood Sam, as well as another man his age who was slightly taller. They were laughing as they walked toward the place, being friendly. Josik caught up to them, noticing that the protestors had stopped and harassed them. The protestors were filthy—the result of chronically unwashed hair and wearing nothing but burlap sacks.

"What is that jacket made of?" a young man with a bird's nest for hair demanded.

"Leather," the man next to Sam said confidently. "And no, you can't buy it."

A loud gasp went around the group.

"You killed our sacred cow brother for that?" spoke a wrinkled, skinny old woman with white hair. "Gaia will not spare you from the coming Green wrath. Not one capitalist will be safe after your rape of our planet has finally been stopped. They will send the People after you."

She pointed her picket sign accusingly at him, as if to condemn. Then two city police officers entered the scene, gently threatening the Gaia worshippers with handcuffs. The crowd started moving down the streets instead of resisting.

"You're lucky we're pacifists!" the woman shouted.

After thanking the officers and letting them return to their beat, Sam and the man entered the club.

"Shit, some of those People's Party activists are downright crazy," the man commented as they walked in. "At least their candidates have ideas worth voting for. Sure beats those dipshit Republicans."

It was barely lit inside, which made identifying the faces of the barely clad women patrolling the front area that much more impossible. Josik saw Sam turn to his friend, a look of nervousness on his face.

"I still don't know about this, Sean," he said. "Everyone who's ever talked to me about this kind of thing has always told me it's just a waste of money."

His brother pointed up a finger as preemptive emphasis.

"That may be true, but we can worry about all that later. When I see my brother's been feeling down for too long, I can spare no expense."

Sam's brother handed him a roll of dollar bills.

At that moment a smiling, very young blonde women sidled up next to Sam. Sam involuntarily recoiled.

"I'm trying to hold your hand, asshole!" she shouted over the loud music. Then she trotted away with a flip of her long, wavy hair.

Sam still looked nervous.

"You sure about this?" he questioned.

"Anything for you, brother," the tall one said, comforting the back of his shoulders. "C'mon, they have great hot wings here."

Sam took the opportunity to catch up with his brother after they both got their respective baskets of fried goods.

"You ever hear of Gearshifters International?" Sam asked.

"I think I might remember them. They gave me some certificate for being student of the year or something back during elementary school one year. Haven't heard of them since though."

"Oh," said Sam aimlessly, while dipping his wing in ranch sauce. "I've been thinking a lot lately about getting more involved in the community, so I've started visiting their meetings. I joined them over the summer."

"Oh," his brother said. "That's cool. So, what do you do?"

"Well, so far, I've just seen how they meet for breakfast every Wednesday morning. They also have guest speakers that talk about something going on in the community or local government. Somewhere in there they do all these service projects on the weekend."

"Yeesh," his brother concluded.

"Excuse me?" Sam asked.

His brother looked directly back, a bit surprised he had to explain himself. He took a sip of his drink, a plain mojito.

"That sounds like a lot of time to commit. Wouldn't you rather spend that free time when you're not working—oh, I don't know—not doing more work?"

"Well, I don't think of it as work. It's helping other people. It makes me happier than what I do at my job."

His brother nodded blandly and wiped his fingers on a napkin.

Sam let some awkward silence pass.

"So, how's Lynn?" he asked, wondering about his brother's girlfriend.

"Oh," he responded, staring down at his glass. "She and I broke up."

"What? Why?" Sam said, shocked by the unexpected news. "You two always seemed happy when you were around each other."

"Yeah, it was fun," he responded, returning immediately to his hot wing. "But she took this job in LA, and I wasn't about to uproot everything I have here in the Bay Area to go be with her. All that sacrifice for just one person? No thanks."

Sam looked down, upset again for the moment.

His brother put down his food, giving an impatient sigh.

"Listen, bro, you really need to move on. It's been what—over two years now? It makes no sense to take a chance on someone like her. You can't seriously think it would make sense to transplant everything across the country to New York to be with her? How would you even know that she's the one?"

Sam put a grin on his face.

"How do you know that 'the one' even exists?" he said.

His brother grinned back, approvingly.

"There ya go. Let's have some fun tonight!"

They clinked their mojito glasses together.

Sam's brother handed him some more $20 bills, and they stayed by each other as they approached the nearly naked women, transitioning from one lap dance to the next. His brother was right—it was fun, between the easy pleasure and the thick buzz from the alcohol.

Everything was fine in Sam's mind until he approached one redheaded woman. She was tall for his taste, but she reminded him of someone else under the dark lights.

Sam felt a pit in his stomach. He saw Rachel in her.

His brother interrupted his panic for a moment.

"Heeey," he said, slurring his words. "We're going to the back room. You—"

He stumbled on the words for a second, the loud music not helpful.

"You wanna bring your girl too?"

And at that moment, Sam looked at "his" girl. He remembered the trust he had, the joy he once felt, and the lessons he had been learning. He was just beginning to understand what it truly meant to be a part of a community and to help others. He had Rachel to thank for that.

And then Sam also remembered the commitment he had once been ready to make. A commitment that logically meant he would love Rachel no matter what. Even, he said to himself at this moment, if there were thousands of miles between him and her. Sam asked himself seriously for a moment if this was just the alcohol talking. He thought about it and decided with unexpected conviction.

"No," Sam said defensively to the girl. "I'm sorry. I don't wanna be with you."

"Sam, Sam, Sam, Sam," his brother repeated, grasping Sam's shoulder. "There's no commitment. It doesn't mean anything to be with her. It's just tonight."

Sam jerked away, upset.

"No. I don't want that. I want the right thing for me, not the easy thing. I want to do great things for people, and I want someone who wants that too."

"Hey bro," his brother responded, not even standing up straight. "Just do this tonight. Nobody needs to know about it."

"No," Sam said, tears in his eyes now. "No, thank you. I need to go find her."

His brother pulled away from the stripper next to him, reaching out.

"Where are you going?"

Sam looked back, a smile on his face and tears in his eyes. He grabbed the smartphone from his pocket, opened an air travel app.

"Enjoy your night, brother. Tell mom I'm going away for a while."

3-16

Josik woke the next morning and suddenly the victory of the previous day sank in. Now the Nucks had joined the new American cause, joining them with the Ricans. This meant another long journey was ahead of the growing army—they were going to beg for the help of another key faction: the Ispanians.

A week or so passed, and everyone in the group slept little and ate little. Josik sensed that everyone was marching scared, worried that whatever terrible attack that had been unleashed on the Sinos was lurking just around the corner.

During this time, their one Sino patient was kept largely under restraint. Maria took the opportunity to psychoanalyze him, noting with each passing day that his antisocial symptoms were subsiding. Unlike at first, he started cooperating with those trying to feed and clothe him. By the time their blitz of a march was almost over, he was striking up conversations. Maria recommended his restraints be taken off. The Sino man, whose name she learned to be Ming, was grateful.

Maria gathered only vague and disturbing details of the Averitan attack from Ming's perspective. He described again the unexpected dumping of red mist by plane—within hours, it became hard to communicate with his family and others around him. After another few days, it felt as if Ming's human self—along with his personality, his memories—had been locked away in a dark corner of his mind. In its place, a greedy, selfish, animal version of himself was unleashed, and his instincts became solitary and survivalist, like that of a wolf or a mountain lion.

But even in his animal state, Ming was fearful. So, he hid himself in a closet under a musty blanket so no one would see or smell him. It turned out to be a smart instinct, because the other villagers had all mangled each other by the time he came out. Within another few hours, the Ricans had arrived and saved him from his changed state.

Maria conveyed this information to Josik, with little success. He was too focused on working with Wambui and Captain Smythe on contingencies, should their first strategy to convince Afitna and the Ispanians with last-ditch diplomacy fail. But perhaps Maria's frustration was worth it, as the plans were laid out one night and the men and women were amped for battle.

That cold night, as the soldiers were still stirring, Josik and Maria talked, while lying awake on their cot.

"Josik," Maria asked. "What happens at the end of all this?"

He sighed. "I don't know yet. I've been praying for some guidance."

Maria gave a little grin. "Well that's always a good place to start."

Josik reached over and gave her a kiss on the cheek. He sighed.

"I just hope it's enough. I'm still waiting to see what my dreams are supposed to say. But how am I supposed to put my faith in something so uncertain, with no clear instructions?"

"Well, it could mean one of two things, I think. One is that God has put faith in you to figure out the solution all on your own. Or you just haven't uncovered things that he's laid out for you to discover."

"What if it's both?"

Maria said nothing, just softly nodded her head.

Then her voice dropped to a whisper.

"Josik?" she asked.

"What is it, Maria?" Josik said.

"Do you think Mama and Papa are still alive?"

She turned her head around to him, waiting for an answer.

"Yes," Josik said with confidence. "I'm almost sure of it. If they managed to raise up a daughter with such grit and toughness, I'm sure they've found a way to survive."

376

Maria turned back, giving a sigh. She wasn't too reassured.

Well, Josik told himself. *At least I did my best, as any good husband would do.*

***

The morning finally came after a long night of fitful sleep. The soldiers took no time to cook, as the command was to eat light and move light with trail food. It was another twelve miles to the Ispanian village, after all.

A short prayer was said by the army chaplain just before sunrise. Then the march began.

Wambui and Josik marched in front, the Rican foot soldiers following behind in their camo wear. When they arrived in the Ispanian village, it was hardly beyond recognition. It reminded the two commanders of the Rican village, albeit at an early stage of siege. Air-dropped Incinerates had clearly been at work, as a number of burned out and felled trees scattered the area

Josik looked around at this spot for a moment, realizing he had seen this place before. But it was beyond recognition. It was the once bustling town square, now filled with craters and tree debris, instead of people and colorful shops.

Not far ahead was a perimeter of soldiers, armed with assault rifles and donning berets. They coldly held up Wambui and Josik. Self-proclaimed General Afitna, now wearing a uniform decorated in star pins and medals, approached them from the other side of the men.

"Oh," Afitna said at a glance. "It's the traitor. Where is your wayward wife? Have you abandoned her for this broad?"

The men standing guard gave a brown-nosing laugh.

Josik was not amused nor intimidated. Wambui maintained her same expression—an unblinking stare of raw, unfiltered fury.

"Afitna," he projected. "Our soldiers march here today in the name of the new American alliance. We come here today to ask you and the Ispanian people for your support and to join forces together. United we stand, divided we fall. What do you say?"

He stretched his hand out in between the barricade of soldiers.

However, it was quickly knocked away.

"You realize the cruel and wicked enemy that we're dealing with? I had a squadron of spies sent to Appatown to sabotage their factories. They were caught and drawn and quartered. Drawn and quartered! Do you know how many centuries ago that method was last used?"

Josik didn't even know what the term was, although he did think he may have seen it mentioned in one of his Bohemx textbooks on Capitalist history.

Afitna continued. "And then, in further retaliation, they began these savage bombings. So, don't tell me to fight this war your way, so we can ask these sub-humans to unite together. No way. Either submit to me, or prepare to be beaten into submission."

Wambui and Josik both tightened their faces, nonverbally recognizing that this meant some of their followers were about to make the ultimate sacrifice. They ran back to their lines while Afitna stood his ground, knowing that the Ispanians soldiers were about to make the next move.

Josik gave a shout to the ranks, saying "on my mark!"

Afitna, meanwhile, ran his men into position.

"Open fire!" the general screamed.

The men hesitated for a moment, all giving him a look.

"What, you want my guards to go take care of your families? I said open fire!"

Hearing these words, Josik gave the command.

"Change formation!"

Others throughout the Rican army repeated the command, and the lines all spaced out with aisles facing the Ispanian soldiers. The Ispanians were perplexed by this, and held their fire again.

Afitna was livid. He started single-handedly strangling men, spouting Spanish curse words.

Josik heard the sound of horseback, turning to see

the Nucks charge through the aisles of soldiers. As they passed their fellow Americans, they grasped their specialty weapon—a lightweight polymer rifle with extended bayonet. It was suitable for these kinds of charges, whether it required stabbing or slashing.

Afitna had terrified his men into taking their first shots, right onto the coming cavalry. A handful of horses and riders went down. But it was not enough to hold their line.

The Nucks smashed through and scores of foot soldiers were swept off their feet. The lines of American soldiers charged forward with a battle cry. The battle for Ispania had begun.

***

The soldiers had been instructed that there was only one objective of the battle: take Afitna, whether dead or alive. Once the Ispanians were without their leader, it was expected the Ispanians would surrender or the Nuck-Rican alliance would be in a position to sue for a truce.

In the flash of a few minutes, the simple clay streets of Ispania were filled with the sounds of gunfire and shouting soldiers. Afitna directed his men to retreat, attempting to hide in the village back alleys and from rooftops. But they were badly outnumbered and were being quickly flushed out. The Nucks speeding around also made any attempt of theirs to form into ranks practically impossible.

Josik and Maria brought a small number of the army's experienced fighters with them on a hunt for

Afitna. They barged into each building, flipping over every table and opening every cupboard in search of him.

In one of the alleys, Josik suddenly stopped running as he gave out a loud cry. He had tripped. One of the soldiers gave the obstacle Josik encountered a quick inspection.

"Marble," the middle-aged man in camo fatigues observed. "It's beautifully sculpted."

The group was taken in by the beauty of the moment, absorbed in the microwave-sized piece of rock. Then one of them was shot from behind, snapping them back into action. The sniper came from behind a well, obviously a lone gunman.

Josik, Maria, and the others looked back, taking shots all at once. Running away after the shots was Afitna, given away by all his flashy medals. Josik and Maria were the first to run ahead to catch up to him. They could see where he was going—down a familiar alley where some of the most respected elder members of the village lived.

"No!" exclaimed Maria. She flashed a look at Josik, realizing Afitna's sinister new plan.

"Quick," Josik said with a thought. "We need to get to your parents first."

They turned a corner, reaching the familiar adobe brick house. Josik kicked down the door in a moment of frantic heroism.

He and Maria were ready to search the rooms to find Señor and Señorita Martez. But they were too late. Standing in the living room with a machete to both of Maria's parents was Afitna, with his arm hooked around both their necks. Both the Martezes looked weak, unable to fight back. Afitna had done the unexpected. He had kicked in the kitchen window, which explained why one of his pant legs was soaked with blood.

Josik decidedly pointed his rifle at Afitna's chest.

"Let them go, Afitna."

Afitna raised his eyebrows to such a degree only a madman would.

"Or else what? You'll let her parents die too?"

There was a moment of silent standoff.

Finally, Josik spoke.

"Let's make a deal, Afitna."

Afitna's response was oddly instant. "Fine. But let's discuss it outside. I won't catch you shooting me without the people knowing the truth about it."

Josik looked to Maria for consent. She nodded frantically.

They all went outside the house. It looked like the ammo had run out, because the soldiers had been reduced to fighting hand-to-hand in the streets. Josik strapped his rifle around his chest, but kept a hand around the holster of his sidearm pistol. He and Maria kept less than two strides from the hostages. Then, Afitna gave the command.

"Cease fire," he said.

Silence fell among those who were within eyeshot. They stopped their fighting.

Afitna lowered his machete, still viciously grasping around the Martez couple's necks, depriving them of oxygen.

"Stranger," he said, speaking to Josik. "You may have taken my power, you may have taken my town, but you will never take away my glory."

He faced his soldiers one last time. Josik panicked, realizing this was not a man ready to make a deal. This was man willing to blow up everything for his cause.

"Death to the white scum!"

Josik shot Afitna right in the neck, but not soon enough. On his way down, the general cut through the throats of both of the Martezes.

Josik blacked out from the shock. When he came back after a few minutes, he saw the three bodies on the ground. Maria was also there, weeping over her parents.

3-17

When Josik finally slept again, he was brought to an eerily familiar place. He was standing, facing a tall obelisk, and immediately behind him was a large rectangular marble building. It looked like the Follies that Biwun had shown him, but from an earlier age.

It was sunny, but cold out, with flat ugly stratus clouds filling the sky. Patches of snow could be seen on the ground. The trees around the area were still bald.

That's when Josik remembered that the spot on which he was standing was at the center of Washington, DC—the American capital he learned about over a year ago. He took a moment to simply look around, taking in the glory of this notorious city. After all his textbook lessons, Josik was finally seeing the center of America at its heyday—or at least, shortly after its heyday.

Josik noticed Sam sitting on the steps of the building behind him—the one he remembered to be the Lincoln Memorial. Josik saw the young man wearing blue jeans, brown shoes, a relaxed white dress shirt, black tie, and a green insulated jacket. Trash in the form of streamers, water bottles, cardstock, and poster board was littered annoyingly around the area's crusted piles of shallow snow—the result of another day's noisy protests and counter-protests between warring radical activists. Meanwhile, Sam seemed to be pensive, or somber. Josik walked toward him to get a closer look.

Sam held a small tobacco tin in one hand, blackened from heat exposure, and a black oblong satchel in the other. He started checking his watch incessantly, looking left and right. Every few minutes he quickly checked the smartphone in his pocket, only to put it back with a sigh, his breath showing each time. He must have been waiting for someone.

And it was at this moment that Sam looked and stood up. Someone was approaching. It was her. It was Rachel.

She was wearing an overcoat and plaid scarf with a navy-blue skirt, suit jacket, dress shirt, and thin golden necklace underneath, somewhat slim fitting but meant to communicate official business. She did not smile immediately, distracted by her own thoughts.

"Sorry I'm late. My event was surrounded by a group of Libertarian protestors. More like anarchists. The violence escalated to the point that riot police had to be called."

"My God," Sam said. "Are you okay? You look okay. It's crazy to see the Republican Party finally splintering apart like this."

Rachel chuckled, revealing her breath in the chilled

air.

"I know the growing chaos all too well living in this town. The new People's Party is even worse. They've been burning any car in sight that isn't 'green' enough since the inauguration. But it seems like each of the parties has its own young, radical contingent now—except for the old farts and corporate interests left in the Democrats."

"Well," Sam mused, "At least it's not as bad as the amoral companies funding the whole Libertarian operation."

"All the more reason to stay independent," Rachel said with a fretted grin.

"Amen to that," Sam said with a nervous guffaw. "Democracy's getting awfully exhausting these days."

Rachel normally would have laughed, but her anxiety in the situation only allowed her a modest grin.

They stared awkwardly at each other for a second, taking in their respective changed features. Sam had grown out a chinstrap, along with a few inches of hair, some strands of which could be seen gray from close up. Rachel's hairstyle was shorter and neater, regularly straightened to look professional.

"You have some time to talk?" Sam said after a moment.

She nodded and said, "Yes, definitely. Just don't take too long, it's awfully cold out."

Sam motioned his hand to the steps.

"Um, have a seat."

They did not embrace. Rather, they both shuffled awkwardly.

Sam was going to start again, but Rachel beat him to it.

"Well, thank you for taking the time out of your trip to see me. You seem well. Are you well?"

Sam grinned and laughed breathlessly and nervously. "Yeah, well, I'm alright. I was just going to thank you for taking the time out of your busy business trip to see me. Remind me of the big event you're at this week that you mentioned? Something about getting to rub elbows with the Secretary of Commerce?"

Rachel offered him a laugh. An honest and modest laugh.

"Yeah, well he's not exactly the most wanted man in Washington. It's an event at the White House and various other government buildings celebrating the National Endowment for the Arts. Basically, the program that makes my job possible."

"Hmm," said Sam warmly, smiling. "That sounds like a bit of an adventure."

"Yeah," Rachel responded, reminded how she appreciated Sam's generous compliments. "Yes, it is."

Rachel noticed a pin on Sam's lapel, pointing to it.

"What's that?" she asked, not recognizing the tiny bronze colored gear.

"Oh, this?" Sam said, felling a little embarrassed. "I took your advice about getting involved in the community. So, I joined my local Gearshifters club. Last fall I led a book drive for a new library geared towards low income kids in South Sacramento."

Sam saw Rachel react to this news with one of the widest smiles he had ever seen.

"What?" Sam said, pretending not to smile back.

But Rachel just kept staring and smiling, unafraid to show him praise. Josik smiled too. It seemed to him that the ice had broken.

"I'm proud of you," she said, gently squeezing his arm. "Doesn't it feel good to serve?"

They both realized this had gone a little too far, and froze back up a bit.

The pair mumbled over each other for a minute, both unsure what to say. Finally, Rachel grasped the little burned-out metal box with her hands.

"What happened to this?" she asked.

Sam bit his lip, realizing this was not his first time explaining it.

"It's what kept me from visiting you sooner."

"I thought that was about your soulless job that you finally quit."

Sam's face contorted a bit more. Having no job prospects at present was not a pleasant thought either.

"These ashes are what's left of my parents' house. They were two of the victims of the fires in December that happened in Northern California."

Rachel's face contorted.

"Oh Sam, I feel terrible. I hadn't even thought to ask about it. I had seen the videos on social media, but I just didn't absorb the story's full details. The fires went through Georgetown?"

Sam looked down.

"Yes, it didn't even stop there. I'd show you the pictures on my phone, but I just can't bear to look at them again. It went all the way down to the bottom of the Divide before it was contained, thank God for the American River."

Rachel closed her eyes.

"I can't imagine the shock you must be feeling. And I wasn't there to stand by you through any of that."

"There's more," Sam said, tears dripping down his face. "My parents . . . they're reported missing. They still haven't been found."

"Oh," Rachel whispered. "Sam, that's . . . all that grief is beyond words."

She refused to hold back any longer. She gave him a tight embrace, never expecting to let go. Sam managed to calm down quickly, realizing that after three months had passed since the disaster, he had finally started to feel peace. Seeing Rachel again gave him that extra aid to heal.

They held each other so long and so strongly that Josik imagined they forgot to think about how long they had been standing there. Josik witnessed Sam and Rachel in a state so peaceful and so soothing that all three had all but forgotten the tragedies of America and its cathartic twenty-first century. At this moment, Josik noticed that the city also changed in its appearance. The dank cold that sunk over Washington like the dirty business of politics was transformed into the air of a crisp, electrifying evening. The sight of the turbid, silt-choked Reflecting Pool was now the sound of waves gently lapped by the evening breeze. And the sights of the city? Their pure edifices seemed to gleam with new life, as their evening lights promised that a new and brighter day was coming.

At the end of it, the sun was gone and the night began. And in that moment, they kissed.

They caught each other's gaze for a moment, then kissed again, their arms wrapped around more tightly. Rachel suddenly popped down and away, Sam looking on in a moment of shock.

She reemerged in his view holding the contents of Sam's elongated case, a glossy wooden guitar. She held the pick in her left hand, about to strum a chord.

"You've been practicing?" Sam said with a wonderful smile and twinkling eye.

"I learned the basics from the very best," winked

Rachel subtly. "This song talks about how much I missed you."

The pair sat on Lincoln's memorial steps as Josik looked on. Rachel sang and strummed:

"The other night dear, as I lay sleeping,

I dreamed I held you in my arms

But when I awoke, dear, I was mistaken

So I hung my head and I cried.

You are my sunshine, my only sunshine

You make me happy when skies are gray.

You'll never know, dear, how much I love you

Please don't take my sunshine away."

Sam looked back tenderly at Rachel, singing the words with her in unplanned harmony. Then he took her hands in his, a fresh trickle of tears beginning.

"Rachel," he said. "I'm a better man now. I don't want to help myself anymore, and you taught me to believe that. There's not much left for me back in California. I didn't see a future in my career, so I'm looking to start anew. It took me months just to ask for time off in my last job to come see you, so I finally quit. Living in California may be nice— and having all my things there was nice too—but none of that is going to matter when I finally finish my time here on this planet. It doesn't really matter where you live— what matters are the people you share your life with wherever you go."

"Sam," Rachel said softly, "you've learned so much."

"Rachel, I want, with God's help, to change this world of ours together. Even if I only get the chance to help just a few. Will you give me another chance?"

Rachel paused to give an answer.

"Do you still have that ring?"

Sam looked ambushed by the question. But yes, he did, in his jacket pocket. He pulled it out.

"I wasn't expecting this, but I did come prepared just in case."

Rachel giggled. Then she spoke.

"Before you start wondering, let me confess something to you. Not a day has gone by that I haven't thought about how I pushed you away. Somehow, I thought it would be best that we would both move on and learn to live without each other since I didn't know what I wanted yet. But the more I tried looking for someone else, the more I realized that I was just making comparisons. I realized I was looking for the exact same thing we had had all along. So, when I agreed to see you here tonight, I prayed that I could tell if this was the right thing after all. And . . . it is, Sam. It's all come back to me. I can't explain my love for you, Sam, and I don't ever want to know why. I couldn't stop how it started and I can't stop it being here now."

With these words, Rachel's hands felt weak and she

began to cry, her smile still on her face. She managed to work in sentences in between her sniffles.

"Sam, sunshine, if you'd allow it, I'd like to finally take you up on your proposal."

Sam just stood there a moment, his mouth open stupidly like a fish.

"Sam," Rachel said. "Will you marry me?

He leaned his head in, his nose pressed against hers. In the same motion, with his eyes closed meditatively, he placed the ring on her finger.

"Well, I guess I'd have to say yes."

The two chuckled a moment, then came in close again to give each other a tight, embracing kiss.

And Josik continued to look on the two throughout the rest of their magical evening, as he too saw hope and promise in the lights of Washington's city sights.

3-18

The next day was the funeral for Maria's parents, as well as all the fighters that had died in the previous day's battle. The entire town turned out in solemn support. The town pastor presided over the ceremony, and everyone, including Josik, dressed in black.

After the ceremony, Father José approached Josik, grimacing under a large load covered by a red cloth in his hand. Josik removed the cloth, revealing the sizeable piece of marble he recognized he had tripped over the previous day. It appeared smoother, a beautifully crafted half-dome with a pointed top.

"Where did you find this?" asked Josik.

The parish priest simply handed him the heavy package, staring intently but saying nothing.

"He's gone mute," explained Mother Sofia, the town pastor. She stepped a little closer to the two of them, making her short brown hair, round face, white Roman collar and black flowing robes more apparent. "He's been like this ever since you returned and the battle began. He noticed when you tripped on that marble piece. I suggest you take it."

Josik accepted the strange gift with inexplicable calmness.

"Will he be all right?" he asked.

"Nobody knows yet," Mother said. "The doctors say the shock of the battle gave him a mental block on his speech. For now, keep him in your prayers and return to your calling."

Josik thought that Mother Sofia had a practical way at looking at the world through spiritual lenses.

***

Something sudden and somber and powerful changed in the minds of the Ispanians that day. They needed only to look around at the devastation of their town and the members of families everywhere who were no longer there. The aggressive military tactics were the wrong choice. Their leader, too, was the wrong choice.

It was natural, then, that they looked to Josik for leadership, just as the orphaned Martez children looked to Josik as a father. He and Maria carried the Martez name. The Ispanians would have let them do whatever the couple wanted.

The Council of Elders temporarily appointed Josik as Guardian of the Ispanians and commander-in-chief of its armed forces. His first act insisted on the joining of forces with those of the Ricans and the Nucks. The

Council granted him this move conditionally—on the promise that the Ispanians would get to host any resulting assembly to establish a new inter-factional government. Josik agreed to broker this condition; within days, the three tribes had their new coalition.

Before sundown, upon the advice of his field commanders, he gave the order to perform a reconnaissance mission of the surrounding wooded hilltops. They reported back after nightfall.

Command headquarters were established at the town armory—a rather plain building with firearms and swords stacked all around the room. At the center they made space for a table, covered in hand-drawn maps and electric lanterns.

"General Wambui," Josik said, pointing to a section of the map. "Anything to report?"

"Pine Forest Hill is quiet, sir," she said, rather calmly. "We've seen no watercraft on the bay or signs of forces at the Follies to the east."

"Captain Smythe?" asked Josik, moving along.

"Sir," she said, massaging her hat. "We can't confirm we've seen any military movement. But we did manage to capture a picture of this."

She passed a small 3 by 5-inch photo across the table. It was a picture of a mostly cloudy sky, but a large rocket craft could be made out in the center of it. Josik seemed surprised, not knowing what it meant.

"It's some kind of shuttlecraft, Commander. It kept

ascending into space after we took the picture. Sir, none of the factions have even the remote ability for space travel, at least that we know of. Our people explored the possibility, but concluded it would be way too costly a project to take on ourselves."

But Josik had reached his own conclusion.

"I recognize that spaceship. It's not from any of the factions."

"Sir?" said Smythe, her eyes raised.

Josik pounded his fist firmly on the table. "Damn it! They're coming for me."

Smythe and Wambui looked at each in shock, then looked at the commander-in-chief. He was looking past them, pointing his handgun at a visitor who had just entered the room.

"Captain Chris," declared Josik. "Were you banished from Bohem too? After double crossing enough innocent people it looks like the universe has caught up to you."

Chris, the former captain and servant to Authority, stepped out of the dark shadow of the doorway and into the lantern light used to fill the room. Time had changed his features and clothing choice. His face was filled with red-gray whiskers, his body clothed in a plain brown fabric poncho. He also looked like he had added ten to twenty pounds of mass, making him broader in the shoulders and waist. Despite his radically different appearance, one feature remained unchanged by which Josik instantly recognized him:

those eyes that could be manipulated to produce any emotion.

"It was General Chris up until now. There will be time to explain later, God willing," responded Chris. "The ship spying on you. It's a Bohemx shuttle. They know you're here. There's no way the Averitans could have made that technology. The Bohemx gave it to them. The Bohemx are behind the mist attack on the Sinos. In fact, they're behind the entire war."

"Because of me," muttered Josik. "It's because they're after me, aren't they?"

Chris paused a moment before he answered. "They see you as a very real threat."

Smythe and Wambui looked at each other, anxious.

"I need to find my wife," Josik said, walking up from the table and out of the armory.

"Where are you going?" Smythe asked, angrily.

"Order the troops to stand by!" he yelled back, leaving.

Wambui and Smythe looked at each other and at Chris for a moment, judging their commander with apprehension. But still they stuck to their duty and went out to give the order.

3-19

Josik hunted for Maria in a frenzy, stumbling over his words to describe the discovery. As he walked briskly down the path to the Martez house, he heard footsteps behind him. He turned around, still walking. It was Chris, walking with lantern-light.

"Stay away from me!" Josik shouted. "I could have you arrested, you know."

"Josik, I know you must be angry at me. I don't blame you," Chris declared with a shortness in his breath. "Give me a chance to explain what happened."

"You damn well know what happened. You betrayed me, basically condemned me to death. Give me one good reason I should believe anything you have to say."

Chris stopped to catch his breath as Josik huffed along.

"Because Biwun knew too!" the ex-general projected.

Josik stopped, turned around.

"Biwun? How do you . . . Biwun knew what?" he asked.

"I knew him too, Josik, on Bohem," Chris cried, walking towards the leader.

He paused, stopped with just a few feet apart in front of Josik. Chris took another couple of breaths and then continued over the sound of crickets. Josik stood alert, listening.

"Years ago, I first met him in a prisoner cell like yours. I tried to manipulate him as I did with you later. At first, I was successful in getting him to share his true feelings about life on Bohem—just as I was with you. But he read right into my soul. Biwun felt the conflict within me, and before I knew it, I told him everything. I was renouncing everything my empty life had ever stood for. He spoke of these vivid dreams he was having, with details that sounded exactly the same to my own I was having at the time. Both of our actions in the dreams were limited, obscuring any meaning to them. So how to solve this? Together, in secret, we developed dreambugs—genetically altered microorganisms. We had only enough time together to produce just one culture that would go unnoticed by Authority. And you know who I decided to inoculate with the dreambugs?"

"Me?" cried Josik, incredulous. "Why me?"

"Biwun told me to watch you. He told me that he had been told in a dream that we should watch you. I didn't want to believe him at the time. I thought his preaching about his faith in a God was illogical. But

400

that was my Bohemx propaganda speaking, Josik. He was right. Biwun was right."

"You realized he was right when I told you about my dreams," Josik said.

"That's exactly right, Josik. Once Biwun was sentenced into exile, I prayed for a sign. I didn't know what to do. He never told me what to do next. He was my only hope to make any sense of purpose out of this world. I can't say I had ever done that before."

Josik took a step back. "You did something crazy," he said. "You used me as a lab rat."

"You could say I did that, Josik," said Chris. "But in that moment, all I could think was how I put my faith into something I didn't really understand."

Josik continued to walk away, flustered.

"I have to find my wife," he said dismissively.

***

Josik found Maria and expressed everything he had just seen and heard in a panic. But she insisted Josik's cooler side prevail.

Maria held him tight, pressing as much possible of her body against his. And she half-whispered these words.

"Mi amor, God must want you to do this. We stand at such a crucial moment for this new alliance. Think of what Deshawn was told about you, what Biwun was told about you. The moment we make a stand, we will be united. And this new country, if God wills it, will take form. You must be the one to do this, with others at your side."

Josik nodded, tears filled his eyes.

He said nothing more that night, too tired and emotionally exhausted to say anything else. Tomorrow would be a new day to talk with Smythe and Wambui about military strategy. The two had been working with Maria day and night on a defense against the mist attacks, for which they worried was imminent.

Maria went back to work with them, promising she would join Josik in bed at some point that night. Josik lay awake during his time alone, worried about what would come next. An endless string of scenarios played out in his mind. They all came back to the same question: what would it take to unite the people into the new country he was being called to form? Josik thought back to what Sam had told him about the dreambugs: was the cause all based on a deception, a scientific experiment?

Josik prayed God would give him an answer in the midst of his sleeplessness. But Josik couldn't hear anything, and tossed around in his bed in frustration.

Finally, Maria cozied up to him after several hours. They didn't talk, but were comforted by each other's warmth. Josik figured this was enough of an answer— he was blessed with an incredible wife who had led him to the stuff of life. Faith, family, and community had led him and these people through these trials and tragedies.

God, Josik prayed in his mind. *I hope—no, I plead with you—that this will be enough to weather the coming storm.* Perhaps, these warm feelings were the truth he needed. Perhaps it was time he stopped thinking about it and just felt it.

He cried quiet tears. Then, as sleep so strangely works, Josik slipped into it.

***

Josik was in a place in the past that could be recognized as a twenty-first century hospital. However, the student had no knowledge of this fact, mesmerized by the long corridor in which he was standing. Josik spotted Sam seated in a chair in a middle section of this.

As Josik approached Sam, he could tell that some years must have passed. Some crow's feet had settled in around Sam's eyes, as well as visible gray hairs around his ears. Additionally, he was wearing a crisp navy-blue suit and solid-color tie. He also bore a pin on his lapel, resembling the seal of the state of New York.

He seemed tired. Josik looked out a nearby window, where it was dark out, except for a half-moon.

A nurse in scrubs emerged from one of the patient rooms.

"She's stable enough to see you now, Senator-elect," she said with seriousness.

Sam and Josik walked in. It was just them except

for one other on the bed.

Rachel, who was there in her hospital gown, also looked a bit older and quite a bit paler. Still she held a weak smile when her husband came in, happy for some good news she had just heard.

"So, the Secretary of State says it's official now," Rachel spoke, sounding throaty. "I think this calls for some celebration."

Sam flashed a smile and a breathless laugh, finding it to be hard to be happy. It wasn't the first time this week he had felt this emotional conflict. After all, he had done better in the election than polls expected, by about two points, beating out the incumbent Democrat by less than 5,000 votes. The Libertarian and People's Party candidates in the primary also hadn't been the "spoilers" analysts had expected. Under that scenario, the second finalist spot would have been handed to the Republican candidate during the top-two primary earlier in the year.

"It comes at a cost, I've learned," Sam started speaking in a flurry. "They've had to post National Guard troops all around the perimeter. The Libertarian and People's protestors joined forces, and now they won't leave. How did they even know I was here? And how do I convince them to give it up, wasting everyone's time and attention when we could get to solving the country's problems? They complain the election system was rigged against their candidates. I understand their frustration, but I know that problem better than anyone else in this campaign and now know it's still a lot better than the one we had before."

Sam finished by sighing loudly.

"I'm sorry," he continued, sitting down hurriedly on Rachel's bed. "It's just another thing no person in my position should have to worry about. I don't know how any person is going to figure out how to manage all these deeply divided factions. It's broken, incredibly broken. And our biggest problems—the debt, immigration, jobs and education, climate change—still aren't fixed yet."

Rachel responded by tightening her face, her courage apparently stronger than Sam's in this moment.

"But you're one step closer to finally fixing them, Sam," she said. "Show them what the first member of the Independent Senate caucus can do for the country. Don't just be the one to find compromise between the two crazy sides, insist on the common-sense reforms that many of the states have already pioneered in the last decade. Make Congress debate with you on ranked-choice voting, or public financing, or the dozens of other ideas that are out there now on building a better democracy. The only way the public is going to trust the system again is if you help build a better system worth trusting. You can be the first elected official who has delivered real, positive, long-term change for the public good in decades."

Rachel let her head fall back and closed her eyes with a quiet sigh.

"Okay. All my free political consulting has made me tired again."

The two laughed a little, smiling.

Sam tightened around her hand. After a while sitting in quiet, their smiles left, turning to tears.

Sam cleared his throat, working up the courage to say what he needed to say next.

"Rachel, my light, my bright sapphire. There's no danger now, but they say there's a real risk you could go into cardiac arrest again from the long QT syndrome if you carry this baby to term. I have to ask . . . and I wonder too about this world our child would have to grow up in . . ."

Long QT syndrome? Josik digested this bit of news quickly, figuring that somewhere in the last few years that this was the source of Rachel's heart problems.

She objected already, cutting him off.

"No, no," Rachel said with an unusual confidence that had continued from her earlier pep talk. "I couldn't do it."

"But Rachel, this isn't about you! Think about what this child would have to do. What I—"

Sam stopped, realizing what he was going to say would have been selfish. He couldn't help the thought. He wasn't raised to be too terribly selfless.

Rachel sighed, not angry but somber.

"What you would do without me, right?"

He nodded, feeling guilty for admitting it.

Sam rested his hand on her belly, reminding

himself to think of the child. Rachel kept making a point of that over and over in the last eight and a half months. They hadn't planned on preparing for a child at the same time as a Senate election. Rachel simply saw it as God's will. Sam, meanwhile, had grown to accept the responsibilities of approaching fatherhood. Along with his friends in Gearshifters, his marriage was one of the few things that allowed Sam to keep life in order during the non-stop years he had since his engagement to Rachel in DC. It had started with his success in being elected to the New York House of Representatives. Since finding himself rocketed to a rising star in the Democracy Reform Movement, he couldn't resist the thrilling fray of running for higher office. Sam had come to see it as his calling. And all along the way, his incredible wife always managed to remain calm in the worst of situations, to help him see the best in people when Sam was ready to push them away. Sam loved that most of all about Rachel. It also helped that she generously offered her strategic insight in ways none of his campaign staffers could.

As Sam was lost in his reflection, Rachel asked him a question.

"You want this child, don't you Sam?"

Sam took a quiet breath to return to the moment and said, "Yes, I do. I just want to give him a world worth living in."

Rachel looked down for a moment.

"And there are others like you who want to fix things in this country and save that future world. Isn't that worth passing along to this child? Isn't that worth the risk?"

"But what if the government collapses? What if democracy and the rule of law becomes despised around the world? What then? Won't all these things I do for our child be in vain?"

"No," Rachel said steadily. "Because maybe the idea of American democracy making the world a better place was never about politics or power. I mean, that was never its purpose in the first place. Maybe we weren't ever supposed to wait for the 'right' policy or person to come riding along and to solve all our problems. Maybe we missed a part that says the whole reason for these rights and freedoms we've been given is to empower us, as citizens, to see the problems right in front of us and to take action before anyone else has to do that. Maybe that fact is supposed to remind us that we all have a stake in this world we've created over generations."

"Like all the community work I've done in Gearshifters," Sam whispered in reply.

Rachel looked back with a weak gaze, becoming tired again. "Yes, maybe that's exactly it. You'll have to find out for me as the expert though. I don't have the energy right now to do the research."

"I'd have to look back on some of my old philosophy readers from college. But I'll read them over again and report back to you with my findings."

"I expect a five-page essay, nothing less," Rachel grinned.

At that moment, a soft buzzing came from Sam's pocket. Sam read the phone for several minutes, his face motionless.

"News reports say that a group of ranchers, businessmen, and state public officials began a new governmental organization today called the Heartland Congress. Their first resolution calls on the federal government to auction off parcels of Yellowstone to the people. The pieces are moving into place."

Rachel looked back with a sad expression, taking deep breaths. She seemed too tired to make a response.

Sam looked at his phone a final moment, then at the window. With a deft jerk, he slid the window open and tossed out the dark, flat object as far out and as far away as he could.

After closing the window back up, Sam reached down and gave Rachel a soft kiss. She closed her eyes, appearing to fall asleep.

"I don't know all the answers yet to help save this country," he smiled and whispered. "But I do know what it means to have community, thanks to you. It's about real, human connection—a gift from God. You taught me that."

Sam allowed more silence to settle into the room— he couldn't think of anything else to say. He didn't want to leave her even a moment, and he couldn't fully explain to himself why. Did he think he could transfer some of his life force to her, even if it meant losing the drive and confidence that had led him to his political victories? Was it fully explained by some simple chemical process going on in his head? Or was it simply the connection Sam felt to her, the memories they had created together? He was struggling with a battle in his mind again, tempted to give everything up and let the voices of fear dictate his choices. He felt stupid for not being able to tell them to just shut up.

Josik fully connected with Sam in this latest skirmish and was astounded. He could see how Sam, like him, had suffered with these choices since he was a teenager. Josik felt in Sam the same senses of fear and dread and guilt as he remembered feeling almost every day on Bohem. His mind flashed back to the old memories of over-analysis and the useless chains of logic happening inside.

Josik sensed from this connection that Sam was being urged in his mind to make a bad choice. He grimaced as the fear and dread continued to rise.

But suddenly the feelings ebbed away, like a soft wave. Sam turned back his focus to his rock, the sunshine he had come to always find in the dark. It was as if Josik could feel Sam being lifted, giving a quiet thanks to God he would rarely admit.

Sam found his refuge again in the love of his life.

"I love you," he said to Rachel.

In response, her eyes opened. She touched him and looked at him with her soft hand, using her gestures to offer comfort since she didn't have the energy to convey it in words anymore.

"I love you with all my heart," she said with a short

breath.

Sam kissed her on the forehead. She managed to give another one of her smiles —another ray of light she had found in the darkness.

"I really need to rest," Rachel whispered.

Sam left her to rest. He prayed, despite the torturous logic taunting him, that sleep would be enough to heal her, since he was not able to enjoy any of it at this moment.

Josik changed his focus for a second to look at the clock again. At first, he thought the room was spinning and that he would pass out at any moment. Then he simply realized the hours were flashing by and the people were moving in a blur around him. When the speed turned back to normal, it was the late afternoon. Dark clouds had rolled in, dumping an ugly mix of rain and ice outside.

Rachel and Sam were still there, along with a team of nurses. Rachel was moaning and groaning, Sam braced next to her. She was in the throes of childbirth.

And then at this moment, with one final noisy bellow from the mother, a baby emerged in the arms of one of the nurses. After some cleaning up, the baby was placed into Rachel's arms. Sam leaned in close, looking at the baby, smiling with a finger outstretched. Then he looked at Rachel. His face and heart sank.

She struggled to smile. She was struggling to breathe, her eyes fluttering. Then they went closed and her neck went slack.

Her heart monitors went on alert. A stunned Sam was shoved to the back of the room by a team of nurses, leaving another nurse to pull the baby away from Rachel.

They resorted to paddles, some final attempts at revival. A few moments later, there was a single sound left —the sound of flatline.

The nurses ushered Sam away in a frenzy, trying to hand him the baby and offering their condolences. Sam refused.

"No," Sam yelled, pushing back with his arms. "No! I don't want him. I can't."

He was getting dizzy, lightheaded. Sam began to stumble down the hall.

He turned back again to the nurses to answer their calls.

"I can't be here right now. I can't deal with all this right now. I'm not safe from myself. I need . . ."

Josik could hear the other voices in the room go silent. He saw the darkness closing in around Sam again. His friend was sinking, quickly.

"I need to go away right now," Sam said with one more look back.

Josik could hear Sam's ragged breathing too. The clock, too, also grew in volume, ticking faster. Ticking louder. Ticking even faster.

Sam panicked. He ran down the corridor, abandoning

the nurses, the room, and the child. So, Josik ran and followed him. At one point they turned a corner.

The ticking stopped. Josik stopped in his tracks and looked around.

The hospital was completely gone, replaced by the beach and the house where Josik and Sam first had met. A gray-haired man with a bushy black-speckled beard was in front of Josik, facing the sandy cliffs. It was cloudy and overcast.

Josik trudged towards the much older man, forgetting how difficult it was trudging through sand. The man kept his gaze forward. As Josik approached, he could hear these words being softly sung:

"In all my dreams, dear, you seem to leave me

When I awake my poor heart pains

So when you come back and make me happy

I'll forgive you dear, I'll take all the blame.

You were my sunshine, my only sunshine

You made me happy when skies were gray.

Do you know, God, how much I love her?

Why did you take my sunshine away?"

Josik turned to look into the older man's face and recognized an aged Sam, his forehead and area around his eyes crinkled by decades of sunny weather.

But still Sam kept looking at the cliffs as tears ran

across his cheeks, saying nothing after completing his song.

Josik looked at the cliffs, too.

"You know, I once almost took my life up there too. But then a light blinded me. A friend pulled me back from the brink."

"A saving grace," Sam spoke as the growing ocean breeze dried his moistened crow's feet. "How did you know I almost did it too?"

"A lucky guess. Or maybe divine revelation. It's hard to tell between the two most times."

Sam chuckled.

"For me, the saving grace was a voice. I thought I could hear her, Rachel, comforting me. And then I thought that everything would be alright."

"And it wasn't?"

Sam turned back and faced his house.

"I thought it would be. And now I finally remember what happened. I moved away to here and had this house built to stay away from it all. But still I found myself curious how the end of it all would go down, so I started listening to the radio. Can you believe how shocked I was that my worst fears for the future of American politics and Western democracy had been realized? Like so many political elites before me, I failed the people who voted me into power. I wasn't brave enough to help fix the system once Rachel was gone. I failed the idea of the Republic. I failed democracy. I couldn't live with myself to stand idle with what I had done—I needed to do something, even if it was futile. I knew I had wasted my opportunity to do a lot of good. But I became so trapped in my guilt that I could never leave this spot. So instead, I wrote my book, my life's work—my offer of atonement. I hoped that someone someday would read it. And now I see that at least that hope has become real."

Josik asked, "Do you remember anything else?"

"I remember . . . there was a storm, a hurricane. I was poorly prepared. Then a wave came up and I . . . I was here again. I've been here ever since."

"You died?"

Sam dropped down to his knees, feeling the sand. He looked back to the cliff, tears filling his eyes again. The sun was also beginning to peek out of the clouds.

"Yes, I died. And when I did, I thought I was going to join her, Josik. But I didn't. I've been reliving the years I spent here in my normal life, over and over again. Every time I'd start over my exile, I'd forget everything that was going to happen again. But not anymore, Josik. I sinned in abandoning my duties many years ago, but you've made me realize it's time to make my true penance. Josik—you've opened my eyes to what's happened. I started praying again every day when you first arrived, hoping that you were the answer to my confusion. That's why I despaired that time you disappeared for so long."

Josik knelt with Sam, reaching for his hands.

"But Sam, you've done so much good by teaching me what you know. I've learned so much from you. Sam, thanks to you, the future is about to make a new America, one that has finally learned from the lessons of the past. Your work is about to begin a new era in the history of the world."

"So tell me why I'm still here!" Sam cried bitterly. "Tell me how to break free from the cycle!"

Josik looked around, searching Sam's feelings to which he was still connected.

"Sam," Josik started, "didn't you say that you remember everything you've repeated from your first time here when you started your current time here? But this time was different. This time is the first and only time you've ever seen me."

Sam had a revelation.

"It's been different this time," Sam said. "It's all been different this time! Thank God, thank God, Josik! You've broken the cycle! You've set me free!"

Sam held his friend tightly, an embrace that lasted for countless moments. After a while, Josik spoke.

"This country still needs your help, Sam. It demands your talent, however long it will last in this century. It may be your way to make your final amends and find Rachel."

Sam tightened his face, looking to the ocean with his moistened, wrinkled eyes.

"'Give me liberty or give me death.' There are

millions of people who've come before me and taken that risk—isn't that an idea worth fighting for?"

Josik again embraced his friend, his teacher, for whatever he was about to do. The student felt that more words were not enough to express the sorrow felt for Sam. The two cried together, quietly, for the country that they loved. It was more than America's lofty ideals that had come to mind. The intense moment was about the people they knew and loved. It was those people who were a part of the rich and emotional story of America. The fact that there were others who were willing to sacrifice their lives to make those people's lives possible escaped both Sam and Josik's logical understanding. They were both moved by the thought they weren't just some human animals born in one of the lucky American centuries. They had become, for whatever reason, a part of the American family. It escaped a simple, logical, self-interested Darwinian explanation of the world that they both might have otherwise taken.

Finally, they let go.

Sam said, "History has been changed by this. The question is how. I have to think about what I must do next."

Josik replied, "Don't think too hard. If there's anything I've learned, it's that after a while we're called to do what feels right."

3-20

Josik woke up after a few hours. He said a quick prayer, feeling both nervous and undaunted. He rose from his knees and dressed in his new military fatigues. He held a private meeting between Smythe, Wambui, and Maria that morning at headquarters, ignoring Chris waiting outside. Their discussion: the latest findings from the Sino survivor of the red mist attack.

As Maria reported, Ming had now made a full recovery.

"We were able to estimate his oxytocin levels from before we found him, which had been virtually zero. The chemical in this mist seems targeted at neutralizing it."

"Why is this significant?" Josik asked.

"Oxytocin brings about feelings of love and sexual attraction."

Josik looked away for a moment, a little embarrassed. Maria pretended not to notice and continued.

"But it also goes much deeper in facilitating all kinds of social bonds, not just romantic partners. It's a chemical that brings about true happiness and fulfillment."

"So how do we shield it from these chemicals?" Wambui said, asking the obvious.

"I don't know. I can't even imagine how we would create some kind of immunization against it. Our only hope, I think, would be to create a huge surge of oxytocin that would overwhelm the concentrations of this other agent in the air."

"How do we do that?" asked Wambui.

Maria didn't say anything but sat, thinking. She didn't have an answer.

Chris ran in.

"Commander-Guardian Josik, sir. Sentries from the hill have reported in. They've spotted two unidentified glider planes coming our way. ETA is fifteen minutes."

All four in the room panicked, leaping from their seats. "This is it! This is it!" Josik yelled, forgetting his residual feelings towards Chris.

***

"Well, let's not talk about it, let's do something! We'll all be eating each other tomorrow for breakfast if we don't!" Smythe yelled.

"Wait, wait, hear me out," Maria interrupted. "I think I know what to do. It may not work but it's our best hope."

"Do it!" Josik bellowed.

"What do you need?" Wambui said.

"We need everyone together in the town square, now. I mean everyone."

"Deal," Josik said as he rushed out the door.

***

The whole Ispanian village and its hodgepodge of visiting factions—where the catch-all term "American" was beginning to catch on—turned out in minutes, encouraged by the word of attack. Panic did not spread into the crowd, although some of the town elders were worried they would be trampled because of their slow and steady gait.

A stack of wooden boxes were set up in the middle for Maria to climb. She stood before the crowd, numbering nearly ten thousand.

"Brothers and sisters of this great land," she cried. "The attack that is coming will attempt to dump a vicious red-colored chemical mist on us. It will attack your mind, and you may be tempted to break away from the group or start attacking the people around you. You must resist. The only way to stop the chemical from working is by overwhelming it. We must come together, brothers and sisters. Think and pray for our common humanity. Think deeply during this moment of the ties that bring us together. Think of our faith, our family, and God who loves us and smiles when

He sees us together. Let those bonds we know now connect us all together."

The people were so moved by these words that they all fell silent. They all locked in arms around one another. Some began praying by themselves, others repeated common prayers in unison with each other. Once Maria jumped down and joined next to Josik in the crowd, the people moved in closer to each other, to the point that everyone was pressed up against one another on all sides. Somehow, without much instruction, the people had figured out what to do.

Josik finally noticed he was standing next to Chris this whole time, now arm in arm. They looked straight at each other, saying nothing. Josik let a feeling of the moment wash over him: forgiveness. Without a word, Josik raised a smile to the man who imprisoned him. Chris smiled back, grateful that they had made amends.

Josik and Maria and Chris and Smythe and Wambui felt a warmth and belonging as they never felt before. They looked around to the smiling faces around them in the crowd and saw and felt that it was very, very good. And the people also felt that it was very, very good.

At one point, they all looked up. And instead of seeing a menacing veil of red coming down as they expected, they saw something else. Instead, it felt like a gentle and impassioned shower drizzling down on them, intensifying the feelings of love and fellowship.

The main five and everyone in the crowd shed a

tear. It was a joyful tear—a tear for those who had sacrificed their lives to make this moment possible. The people felt a connection to them, though they were gone. But now they were all together. Past and present Americans and all lovers of a free and better world were all together. Though different and many, now they were one.

At this moment, Father José cried out, his tongue loosened:

"¡Gracias a Dios! Give thanks to God!"

3-21

Josik woke up in the beach house once more, leaping out of bed. He saw the sun just beginning to rise outside the bedroom window into the clouds gathering overhead. He ran to the kitchen, expecting to find Sam there. There was no one. Josik checked all the other rooms of the house and the outside. Everything was clean and organized but still no one. Josik checked the kitchen again, turning on the radio for clues. The station Sam normally had turned on for news radio was silent. Finally, Josik looked around the walls of the nook again. He grabbed a sticky note placed on the bare blue-colored wall. There was no calendar or wall clock to be seen. The note read:

"Gone to DC. -Sam"

***

After spending the better part of the morning navigating the surrounding woods, Josik came to the side of a concrete road. It was overcast and cold, the sun seemingly absent. He started walking north. Over an hour later, a caravan of cars approached him from behind, all SUVs with chipped and rusted paint. They stopped. An older, white, heavyset man emerged from the driver side of the front car, wearing a hat and pin on a dirty red sweater. Josik recognized the small metal trinket as the Gearshifters logo.

"Looking for a ride?" the man asked.

"Are you headed to DC?" Josik asked with the faintest of smiles.

***

The caravan continued driving for the next hour or so, regularly dodging potholes on their chosen route. Billboards on the side of the road looked totally unused, covered in indecipherable graffiti. Eventually, they turned onto a freeway exit taking them to the water's edge. The group of people, nearly a dozen in total, unloaded from their cars and brought with them large backpacks.

"In case we're here longer than expected," the older man explained. "It's good to be prepared. Kai, would you let the base camp know that we're just about to cross the Potomac?"

A short, spectacled, very young Asian man nodded and spoke into the hand-held piece connected to a transistor radio device kept in his satchel. Then the group loaded into a large motorboat and began to cross the river, passing by the remains of a large concrete arch bridge to their north.

The group docked within twenty minutes near a large rectangular marble building. Within a few minutes, they had crested the hill approaching the building. Josik could see the statue of Lincoln behind him, the Reflecting Pool in front of him. He was at the spot again that he knew would one day become the Follies.

Kai led the way forward, appearing nervous. Josik and the others followed along as they passed through lines of thick canvas tents camped on the sides of the walkways. They eventually passed over another poorly maintained road and reached the base of the Washington Monument. As they approached a large tent at the base of the obelisk, a middle-aged man emerged. It was Sam, with gray hair and well-trimmed beard. He wore a maroon corduroy button-down shirt, American flag pattern tie, and slim-fitting slacks.

"Here at last!" Sam said with a warm smile that Josik was unaccustomed to. "I'm glad you arrived safely, my friends. How was the drive from Colchester?"

"Bumpy as always," said the large-bellied man. "But we found a new friend on the side of the road who would like to join us. What is your name, by the way?"

"I'm Josik," the former student said while returning Sam's smile. "An old friend of Sam's."

Sam laughed a moment, clapping Josik with a hug. "Of course!" he proclaimed. Sam went down the line of the group, learning each of their names and greeting them all with a hug. Eventually, he reached the very young Asian man.

"What's your name, son?"

"I'm . . . I'm Kai," he said hesitantly. "Your son."

Sam stared at the young man for moments in disbelief, examining his features.

A blonde-haired man in a suit approached and interrupted Sam, tapping him on the shoulder.

"Sam," he said. "It's time."

"God willing," Sam said, looking towards Kai and Josik. He also slipped on a blue blazer, with an American flag pin on the lapel. "We will have time to talk about this later. But for now, we have a movement to march forward!"

***

Sam led Josik and Kai toward the front of the crowd that the teacher commanded: thousands of people gathered and walking forward together in DC. Josik found himself constantly looking back at the size of the throng in unbreaking amazement. Many held American flags above their heads. Their volume grew with each step, as individuals led the others in patriotic songs and chants.

Josik soon spotted a barricade up ahead as they approached what he recognized as the U.S. Capitol building. Several armored soldiers lined its perimeter, all armed with rifles. Sam stopped. The crowd followed.

A soldier standing above the others on the steps of the Capitol spoke into the bullhorn, warning: "Halt. Move no further. Trespassing will violate the will of the People."

Sam held Kai's and Josik's hands for a moment,

moving the hundreds others to do the same to one another. Then he let go, grasped a stack of papers from a knapsack he had been carrying. He also put a bullhorn he had strapped around him in front of his mouth as he spoke, the papers raised defiantly above his head:

"We are members and leaders of America's people. We represent not only America's greatest tradition, but its heart and soul: its community spirit. We are educators, service club members, clergy, business owners, public servants, youth organizers, and community leaders from all fifty states. On our sacred honor, we come to present an application on behalf of the states to Congress calling for a convention for proposing amendments to the United States Constitution."

The commanding soldier responded: "Congress has come under the protection of the People's Collective. For the safety of its members, visitors from the public are now prohibited."

"On whose authority?" Sam questioned.

"The People's authority."

"So basically, the Eurasian Communist Party, now that the Capitol has been mortgaged to them along with a number of the West Coast cities," Sam said bitterly. "We can't accept that. Please let us through so we may petition our members of Congress."

The soldier repeated, "Congress has come under the protection of the People's Collective."

"Right," Sam said sneering, "the People. And where are the members of Congress right now?"

"Out of town. They are currently out of session."

"Then we will wait here until they return," Sam stated with an adamant smile.

Sam began to sit as well as the other marchers, but stood back up with hands raised as they heard guns cocking. The weapons were pointed at the crowd.

The commanding soldier said, "Leave now. Your defiance is a violation of the will of the People."

Sam had dropped his bullhorn by now. He looked around at the crowd. The mood on their faces was anger, disgust at the authority forced upon them. This, he could tell, was not freedom. Sam closed his eyes for a moment, softly said a quick prayer few could hear.

Then Sam responded, yelling at the top of his voice. "With love, we are the will of the People. Whether the people realize it now or in a time to come."

The soldier commanded, "Open fire."

***

The crowd reeled; people ran away screaming in all directions. Josik and Kai ran for the nearest cover as the bodies fell around them. After what felt like a long time that only really lasted a few minutes, they found the courage to return for Sam's body. They were surprised to see that the soldiers had lost interest in the massacre, returning to their normal mode as the two men dragged a badly bleeding Sam away from the

Capitol. They laid him down on his back out of the view of his attackers, elevating his feet in an attempt to prevent shock.

"My son," Sam said weakly, his face pale as the mix of snow and ice that was beginning to fall and darkness gathered in the sky. "I'm so so very terribly sorry, I've forgotten already. What is your name?"

"I'm Kai, father," the young man said, giving Sam a strong hug. "I'm so thankful to finally meet you."

His father gave a breathless chuckle.

"I just wish it was under better circumstances. Maybe somewhere like a coffee shop, you know?"

Kai started crying, touched by the unexpected and lighthearted humor.

"It's no use, Josik," Sam said as blood began to fill his mouth. "Stay close to me. I have some things to say to you both."

First Sam turned to Kai.

"You see this pin?" Sam said, pointing to the American flag pin on his lapel that was now surrounded by several holes flowing with blood. "Take it."

Kai did so with fidgety hands.

Josik reached into his pocket to find the place where his own flag pin normally was. But it was gone. Where had it gone?

"My son, that flag pin belonged to your grandfather.

It was the first thing he bought when he moved to this country from Japan. If you remember anything about him, it's that he loved his country. I loved it too. It's one of the few items that survived when my family's home burned down many years ago. It's yours now."

Tears were running in a steady trickle down Kai's face.

"Thank you, father."

"Son, I'm sorry I left you as a baby. There's no way around that fact. As you know, your mother died just when you were born. I panicked and left and never should have. This man next to you here finally helped me to see that. Can you forgive me?"

"Yes, father," Kai replied with more tears.

"I can tell you have so much of your mother in you," Sam said with a brave look in his eyes, looking into his sons'. "Ask for God's help always, and do your best to bring others together again. With America gone, people need a refuge. Take care of these people, just as you take care of that flag pin. Do your part to ensure democracy will survive somewhere, so that people will know where to find it when they are ready for this country again."

"I will, father," Kai promised, holding his father's hand to his heart.

And finally, Sam turned to Josik, giving him a smile. Josik was tightly holding his other hand. The teacher was shaking now, both from the cold and the great loss of blood.

"Josik, my friend, you must know what to do now. Build us a better America we would have been proud to live in. Remember those we forgot—the poor, the immigrant, the drug-addicted, and the lost and the lonely. Help them build something new from the old. Something that gives them hope and meaning. Rebuild everything else we once had and even better things will follow.

"And Josik?" Sam asked.

"Yes?"

"Pray for me, both of you. Pray for all these things."

Sam's voice shook with fear for this moment. Then he searched past Josik and Kai, motioning his head weakly to a nearby field.

"Look," he said.

The two turned, looking to the field that used to boast the manicured lawns surrounding the Washington Monument. It took them a moment to realize something miraculous had taken place. Despite the continuing winter, Sam revealed a reason for hope. Replacing the unruly grass was a beautiful field of lilies, just beginning to bud and bloom.

When they turned back to Sam, they realized he had taken his last breath. Josik and Kai stayed there kneeling, looking on. As the snow came down faster, they felt frozen for a moment in time.

3-22

It was a new day and a new morning for the American forces. Last night had been full of celebration, a sense of triumph at last. The people felt they could win. They believed now that it was their destiny.

Although they had turned a corner, Josik and the other commanders recognized that the war was only now just beginning. So, they gathered the army the next morning to begin their next march. Their objective was to liberate the other villages under the thumb of Bohemx rule, or at least whatever would be left of them. The commanders weren't sure about the spread of social solvent's use. At the very least, they saw it as their duty to find out.

Before they left, a small band of strangers approached Josik. They all wore dark flowing robes and their leader wore a knapsack.

"May we join you?" the fair-skinned man with freckles and brown hair said.

"Who are you?" Josik asked with a quizzical expression.

"We are the inhabitants of the Follies. The Legas. We're not known for aggressive tendencies. We have spent the last several hundred years guarding some of humanity's most precious documents. Each generation of our people have been charged to wait for the day the American world order would return. So, we came here as soon as we heard the news relayed to our local priest."

Josik turned to Mother Sofia. "Does the Church have some secret communication system I should know about?" he said, raising his eyebrows.

Mother Sofia shushed him with a quivering hand, explaining: "I'll brief you later."

He turned back to the Legan leader. "No one's ever heard of a village established at the Follies. It's widely acknowledged as a no-man's-land. I've seen them with my own eyes. Were you in hiding this whole time?"

"No," said the robed man. "Our lifestyle is not quite that different from yours here. I have never heard of the Follies, but we have lived at our ancestral lands we call the Mall for over seven hundred years. Perhaps you simply did not have time to notice us during your visit?"

"No, that still doesn't make sense," Josik mused, his hand thoughtfully rubbing his chin. "A mystery, to be sure."

"Huh. Regardless of all that, we bring glad tidings. Please accept these gifts from our archives. We think you will find them useful. There is much more history we can offer about them."

The youthful man handed Josik a stack of aged parchment sheets from his knapsack. As Josik flipped through them, he recognized them as the Constitution and the Declaration of Independence.

"I think we'll find a use for these," Josik said with a smile.

***

By late morning, the American forces had scaled up the well-traveled path and reached the top of Pine Forest Hill. The view from there was the clearest Josik and anyone else could remember in recent memory. Josik, Wambui, Chris, Smythe, and Maria all looked at one another and out towards the spreading view. They could see other ridges ahead, some of their tops and trees decorated with the first dustings of winter snow. They looked to the east and could see the muddy flatlands. Beyond that was the shining sea.

And the five looked back at the men and women following behind them and could see that they too were inspired by the unexpected vista. Josik prayed that it would be enough to bear them on for the trials and sacrifices ahead. For the people saw that this was their country—a wide, diverse, great land full of new possibilities and second chances. Its people—the first new Americans—came from every walk of life the generous land offered.

Yet somehow, they came together. They were united. The old things of the past centuries had passed away; now they were making things new.

In the middle of this, Josik thought he could feel

Sam's presence. He knew the older man wasn't there, at least not in this world. Josik's lessons with his teacher were now over—a blood test by Chris that morning revealed that his dreambugs were gone.

Josik experienced a new sensation. He could sense Sam's joy from the world beyond, where his teacher was together with Rachel and Kai. As Josik prayed, he thought he could hear them singing of their gratefulness to him sometimes. In these moments he thought he heard Biwun also, who said that many blessings were on Josik and all those working together with him.

Suddenly, Josik felt a small object in his pocket. He removed it with slow anticipation. His American flag pin had returned. Josik knew work on the new nation had just begun.

Epilogue

"Mama, can we go inside?" groaned little Alejandra, wearing a Scout uniform. Since she turned five, she seemed determined to have a mind of her own, always questioning. Maria wondered if she would follow in her father's footsteps in national politics someday.

"No, silly niñita," said her mother. "Papa and the others are still working in there. They'll come out and announce any minute now. Be patient."

Alejandra looked back at her mother with a blank face, then plopped herself on the ground sitting. Her mother believed that she oddly enjoyed getting her blue uniform skort a bit dirty.

They were looking at the simple marble building called the Gobiernita—literally translated to "little government building." Mostly taken from blocks of the old Capitol building and other American monuments, it was meant to resemble its predecessor—albeit for a much smaller legislature. At present, it only had walls, a window on the back side, a second story with balcony, and a smooth half dome of white marble on top. Maria remembered for a moment that the dome topper was the same one gifted to Josik by Father José. The Gobiernita had flooring, unlike most Ispanian buildings, but was not meant to hold more than about a hundred people.

Ispania, like the other villages, had nearly doubled in size in the last few years to over 50,000 inhabitants. The sudden growth in families was thanks to the American nation's newfound unity—mainly the result of population rebound from the devastation of war, but also the result of new trading opportunities that had richly increased the overall food supply.

Just as a larger crowd was beginning to assemble, the 54 delegates emerged and emptied into the Gobiernita's second-floor balcony. The individuals represented the 27 factions committed to joining the new country, encouraged by the news of its army's successes. There were representatives from the Ispanians, Nucks, and Ricans, of course. But there were also ones from new factions ready to come together, including the Jabi, Sinos, Rus, and others. Despite their different histories and their different skin tones, the appeal to a better way of life for all was universally irresistible. All told, the new country would number about 1.8 million people, spread across the areas once known as Virginia, Maryland, West Virginia, and the Industrial Midwest. Representatives from faraway lands were also visiting the growing Ispanian city to keep an eye on the negotiations and to report back to the fantastically large villages where they originated, including Boston and New York City. After all, they welcomed the news that villages throughout the continent were being liberated daily from Averitan rule, as the antidote to their social solvent was being set up—however slowly—everywhere.

It was a joyous crowd gathered just outside, for a festival had been thrown in the village for the occasion. Ispanians sang and danced alongside their visitors, including a number of Averitan defectors (dressed in their celebratory denim jacket and jeans attire) from the now-crumbled Blue Wall. A new fusion style of music the Ispanians called cambio—a combination of the widely diverse cultural backgrounds—was played by a large band gathered in the streets. It roughly combined the deep bass beats from hip hop, violins and brass instruments from classical music, guitars crafted and played by local Ispanians, and the vocal arrangements of a four-part harmony chorus. (Maria quietly hoped the music of this motley combination would improve and evolve in the years to come.) Vendors of all kinds were selling their wares—not just widely varying styles of foods, but also clothing and even American flag pins.

As the doors opened from the Gobiernita's upstairs, Josik emerged at the front. He was dressed in formal Ispanian attire—a choice of multicolored robes with a plain linen shirt underneath. He looked out at the crowd, which had numbered into the thousands. They greeted him with cheers and waved small American flags—their design included a fourteenth stripe colored purple and twenty-seven stars set against a blue field in the upper left-hand corner. Josik soon realized he had forgotten one important part of his outfit, revealed by the pieces worn by many gathered there. So, he took the familiar American flag pin from his pocket and secured it on the part of his poncho just over his collarbone. The leader took a moment to reflect on his special clothing, remembering their origins from the generous Martezes.

Josik accepted with solemn reflection that he held in his hands the document the people had anticipated for more than three months. The work was not easy, with many difficult compromises and late-night deals made over hard liquor. But like the results of the First Constitutional Convention, he knew it was a start. He looked over the crowd, reflecting a moment on the sacrifice of patriots that the purple stripe on the new American flag represented. He looked to his daughter, hoping the new government he helped shape would be good enough to pass onto her and to generations to come. Then, as he read the first words on the pages of paper in his hands, the people felt summoned and fell completely silent:

"We the people of the United States, in order to reform a more perfect Union, reestablish justice, safeguard domestic tranquility, rebuild the common defense, guarantee the general welfare, and discover the blessings of liberty for ourselves and our posterity, do once again ordain and reestablish this new Constitution for the United States of America."

They, the people, erupted at the good news in cheers and fresh flag-waving. The band took up their instruments and began playing a new verse to an old American hymn—the people joining them in singing the words to their new national anthem:

"O beautiful for ages past

New World Order

Whose history now resumes

Freedom returns like coming spring

A lily flow'r in bloom!

America! America! May God watch o'er thy shores!

We ask thy care, through love and prayer

For now and evermore!"

THE END

ACKNOWLEDGMENTS

The individuals, groups, and movements to which I am grateful are meaningful and they are many. First, I'm grateful to my dad Robin and my mom Katherine. They are the first and wisest teachers I have ever known. I also thank my lucky stars for my eight siblings, who have never failed to be my first sounding board for the jumble of ideas I've had throughout life (some of which eventually made its way into this book). It is necessary to recognize them all, in age order: Jessica, Rebecca, Benjamin, Jonathan, Anna Claire, Nathaniel, Jennifer, and Christina.

Thank you also to the Boy Scouts of America, whose opportunities it has afforded me are too many to count (and before you ask, yes, I am an Eagle Scout). A special shout-out must be offered to my Cubmaster Dave, who offered me and my dad the opportunity to start on the Scouting journey when I was just seven years old. I can't even imagine how my life would have turned out differently if it wasn't for all the excitement and adventure he taught me to expect from Scouting. I also thank Camp Winton for the best four summers of my life I spent working there "for a future much brighter," next to "the shining clear water." I owe a tremendous debt to the best Scout camp in the nation for teaching me the true spirit of service and for leading me to the Scouting profession.

Speaking of Scouting, I must also thank the volunteers and professionals surrounding me that make one of America's—nay, the world's—most important youth movements possible. Thank you for teaching me lessons about the career that I never even knew I needed to know. It's also led me to new friends I'm thankful to have in the greater Sacramento and El Dorado county communities—including those servant leaders I now know in Rotary (for whom the concept of "Gearshifters International" in this book is parodied). Many thanks are also given to the teachers and leaders I've known in the Catholic Church, as well as the lifelong friends I made in the UC Davis Christian dance group known as Agape—I couldn't have grown in my faith and spiritual life without you. The joy and hope presented in Ispanian culture reflects the unconditional love you show for others.

Next, I give my thanks to the folks working on the front lines of the Democracy Reform Movement. I hope and pray that the day comes—however long it may take—when we may realize ourselves as a major force in American politics. Special thanks to Kevin Harville for having been my partner-in-crime for the cause when we volunteered together in Sacramento—I'm grateful we can eat, drink, travel, debate, and act together as we long to make the world a better place. America needs folks from all walks of life like you that put country over party.

Acknowledgments

A major shout-out also goes to my girlfriend, Marie Weider. Thank you for generously giving your time and talent to this book's cover illustration—not to mention being buddies together in our quest for the good life.

And finally—the college professors at Folsom Lake College and UC Davis: I have to thank you for your knowledge that provided the logos behind this book. I count many of you as mentors—whether you meant it or not, your work inspired me. Those folks who I can think to mention (seems like I have too many to remember all at once) include Professors Reese and Repetto from Folsom Lake College for instructing me during my formative years in political science during community college. Thanks also to Professor Oliver for inspiring me to become a confident writer in our two semesters together. Next, my appreciation for my mentors at UC Davis: first, Professor Boydstun for the two quarters I got to spend under your tutelage—I always relished an opportunity to answer one of your questions when called on. I also find myself looking back to your lectures on policy subsystems quite a bit these days—indeed, with an eye towards developing strategies to bring about successful policy reforms I believe we so desperately need. Additional thanks to Professor Hosek and Professor Jones whose instruction provided this book's commentary on America's historic problems with economic disparity and race relations, respectively. And how could I forget Professors Wilson and Peri, my faculty advisors for my economics honors thesis? I count myself extraordinarily lucky to have studied my self-dubbed topic of age-based wage inequality under your wing. (Look it up, I'm sure it'll catch on as an academic concept one of these days. You can find my published results in UC Davis's 2017 *Explorations* journal.)

I'll close this book's message and these thoughts of gratitude with a quote from one of my favorite, albeit quirky, professors (that I hope to see on a t-shirt someday): "Do well by others and please use your turn signals in the common interest."

Appendix A

"To put it very bluntly, democracy is about the love *of people."*

–E.E. Schattschneider

The Four Principles of "Consensus Culture"

In a divided, rancorous age, reforming policy is not enough to build a "more perfect union" in our diverse society. We must seek to reform ourselves through a new kind of shared culture. Indeed, "politics is [in many cases] downstream of culture." (Perhaps it may be more accurate to say that politics and culture exist in a very active feedback loop—regardless, this still makes culture important to reform.) Many are already unwitting adherents to this culture by exhibiting the following traits: listening to others, following the facts, and finding common ground. The following four principles I list here are the framework for a new "consensus culture" that I propose—let it be a strategy for good-hearted people to come together on a shared goal, whether in the workplace, in politics, in volunteering, or even in a household. While new in its definition, these four principles originate from many of America's highest ideals: those shared by its Founding Fathers, those from codes of youth-service organizations and service clubs, and even those from many of the country's religious and spiritual traditions. Here then is the list of those four principles:

1. Act Together: We can be collective in action without being uniform in thought.

2. Pursue Truth: We can pursue truth in our decisions while accounting for as many different, reasonable perspectives as possible.

3. Positive Change: We can make needed, positive change while respecting our past and our traditions.

4. Love of Country: We invite all to aspire for "a more perfect union" and the common good together, united by our love of America.

Appendix B: Further Reading

A large part of this book's knowledge stands, to borrow the 12th century saying, on the shoulders of giants. (Another significant chunk comes from experience, selections from political science textbooks and readers, online blogs, full-length speeches, TED talks, documentaries, newspaper editorials, and more, but I won't go into those details here.) The following is a list of those books and authors to whom their ideas and elements are alluded in *The Last American* in homage:

- *The Republic* by Plato (c. 380 BC)

- *Politics* by Aristotle (c. 350 BC)

- *The City of God* by St. Augustine of Hippo (426 AD)

- *Summa Theologica* by St. Thomas Aquinas (1485)

- *Democracy in America* by Alexis de Tocqueville (1840)

- *Up from Slavery* by Booker T. Washington (1901)

- *The German Ideology* by Karl Marx and Friedrich Engels (1932)

- *Brave New World* by Aldous Huxley (1932)

- *1984* by George Orwell (1949)

- *The Human Condition* by Hannah Arendt (1958)

- *The Semisovereign People: A Realist's View of Democracy in America* by E.E. Schattschneider (1960)

- *Bowling Alone: The Collapse and Revival of American Community* by Robert D. Putnam (2000)

- *Who Are We? The Challenges to America's National Identity* by Samuel P. Huntington (2004)

- *Polarized America: The Dance of Ideology and Unequal Riches* by Nolan McCarty, Keith T. Poole, and Howard Rosenthal (2006)

- *The Race Between Education and Technology* by Claudia Goldin and Lawrence F. Katz (2007)

- *The Hunger Games* by Suzanne Collins (2008)

- *2030: The Real Story of What Happens to America* by Albert Brooks (2011)

- *Coming Apart: The State of White America, 1960-2010* by Charles Murray (2012)

- *Capital in the Twenty-First Century* by Thomas

Piketty (2013)

- *The Centrist Manifesto* by Charles Wheelan (2013)

- *Common Cents* by Paul C. Haughey (2016)

- *Our Towns: A 100,000 Mile Journey Into the Heart of America* by James Fallows & Deborah Fallows (2018)

- *How Democracy Ends* by David Runciman (2018)

www.ingramcontent.com/pod-product-compliance
Lightning Source LLC
Chambersburg PA
CBHW031048110726
47900CB00003B/857